A Change of Reign

Realm of the Unimages

Alex Maister

This is a work of fiction. Names and characters are the product of the author's imagination and any resemblance to actual persons, living or dead, is entirely coincidental.

This book's dedicated to my wife and daughter

Only the purest will rule in
these fair lands. It shall be
sworn and abided by each
unicorn alike.

*–Extract from the historical
records of the Circle*

Chapter 1

Thirteen Weeks and One Day Ago

"I'm on a roller coaster! Whooooooooooooooooooooooaaa!" Princess Sallina exclaimed as she hurtled through a tunnel towards an unknown, distant destination. She was quite scared, but at the same time, she knew there was really nothing to be scared of. This was magic, and magic was something that she was comfortable with. After all, she was a unicorn.

Professor Tinzy had talked about this rather oddly shaped, snakelike object that went up very slowly and then came down so incredibly fast, but she had never seen one before now. They didn't have anything remotely like this in the unicorn city of Starpoint, where she came from. They didn't even have funfairs in Starpoint.

"Whooooooooooooooooooooooaaaaa!" she cried out again—only this time, she was enjoying the thrill of the ride, despite the anticipatory fear that accompanied it.

The whole experience almost made her forget why she was there in the first place.

She slowed down for a bit as she went up to some unknown higher point, and then whoooooooooooooooossssshhhh, she hurtled back down the magic tunnel once more at full throttle, screaming at the top of her lungs.

Boy, this is fun, but also scary, she thought.

This was no ordinary roller coaster ride, oh no! Something incredibly strange was transforming her physical state as she careened through the tunnel. She was not feeling like herself at all; she was overwhelmed by dizziness, as if a terrible illness was taking hold of her entire body and contorting and reshaping it in all kinds of strange ways. Oh yes, something very peculiar was happening and the Professor had never mentioned anything like this!

One moment she could see a black hoof, and then it was gone, replaced by those five peculiar things called *toes* that were sticking out from where her hoof had once been. Then another hoof turned itself into some oddly shaped things called *fingers*. Oh, my goodness! What had become of her black, delicately decorated, front unicorn legs that she had relied upon to walk about in her world? Of course, she was accustomed to sitting down and using her front hooves, with their fingernail-like extendable protrusions, just like human beings used their hands, so therefore it wasn't altogether an unusual experience, but... fingers, what oddities those were!

Now, as she slowed down once again, climbing, there appeared a bright smattering of stars around her, and she rose higher and higher in the magic tunnel, heading toward a mysterious zenith. Her every nerve and muscle could sense that something strange was about to happen as she anticipated a terrifying, sudden drop—a feeling of acceleration that would force her stomach and brain to occupy more or less the exact same physical space. It was a very strange sensation, and not one she wanted to experience too often.

But still...oh, the exhilaration! It was incredible.

This time, she didn't just drop; she kept on rising, up and up and up, as if there was going to be no end to her climb, as if she was going to spend the rest of her waking life just climbing, climbing, climbing toward some unknown, infinitely high point that couldn't ever be reached.

She came to an abrupt halt.

There was no movement at all. Suspended and fixed and transfixed, she was momentarily frozen in time and space.

Am I safe here? she wondered.

But the feeling lasted for only a few fleeting seconds as she continued to take in the awesomeness of her magic tunnel ride and noticed the many bright rainbow colours glittering all around her, with a myriad of stars shining somewhere in the distance beyond. What a spectacle to behold! She gave in to a momentary, false sense of serenity and happiness...

Then, suddenly, the tunnel turned pitch black, as if someone had turned off the house lights. And

then...

Whoooooooooooooosssssssssssssssshhhhhhhhh!

She felt like she had been transformed into a lightning bolt, striking down from the heavens to someplace far below.

But this time the descent felt different. This time it was straight down, a vertical drop, as if she was plunging into a bottomless pit, falling like a stone down into some strange void of emptiness, and nothing could break her fall until she impacted the hard ground.

She cried out loudly, for she was truly afraid this time. Her hoof kept switching to a hand, then back to a hoof, the transformations becoming more intense and frequent.

Her face felt odd. There was a sudden flutter of hair that passed in front of her eyes, but this wasn't the hair that she was used to—her long jet-black mane, which normally ran along her back—this was entirely different. It was the same colour, but it was much longer and finer than her normal body hair, and there was an abundance of it, plus it appeared more delicate and brittle, like it could drop off at any moment. This certainly wasn't the hair she had been used to all her life, whilst living inside the skin of a young-lady unicorn.

She screamed as she kept plunging, faster and faster, down, down, down, as above her the distant night sky began to disappear in a blur, and below there was absolutely nothing. Incredibly, the absolutely-nothing was met with more nothing the further she fell, falling faster, faster, faster, plummeting towards somewhere unknown.

She screamed even more loudly, but there was nobody to hear her. There was nobody around anywhere, she was all alone here with nothing around her at all, just this dark void that expanded out in all directions into what appeared like infinity…and, of course, this strange, bottomless pit.

Dropping like a stone, she felt like her fall lasted for hours, but in real time it was just a few seconds. She felt little wind resistance, only a mild breeze that whooshed around her, and that made the free-fall just a tiny bit less scary.

Then everything changed all at once.

Below her in the void was some light.

Her drop was slowing rapidly as an intense gust pushed upward from beneath her feet as if to help break her fall, acting as a brake. Her arms and legs cavorted about as the air twisted her around like a spinning top.

She glanced down below once again to see what was lying beneath her feet, and she swore she could make out a bunch of trees in the distance. The darkness all around her was disappearing as a crescent moon glowed above her head, far away. It looked a lot like the moon Professor Tinzy kept talking about from his previous journeys. She'd never seen such a gigantic object hanging in the sky, but she had heard a few strange stories of entire worlds that floated out somewhere in the great beyond.

She looked down once more, and then, PLOOSH! She shut her eyes tight.

She landed with the softest of thuds on a cushion of moist green leaves. Then she opened her eyes momentarily. The light all around was a lovely midnight blue, and she knew it was night where she was. Trees surrounded her everywhere, and thousands of leaves, maybe even millions, lay scattered all about her. Another batch of leaves fell on top of her as she sank into the soft undergrowth. The leaves nearly covered her entire body, effectively concealing her in this lush green canopy of the forest.

Then there was nothing. Her eyes closed, and she graciously succumbed to peace as her fear and exhilaration gave way to sleep while she lay there alone in the forest.

Little did she know that she was about to face the greatest challenge of her young life. When she returned home from her journey to a faraway land, she would be able to either condemn her own kind… or to help liberate them from a meticulously cultivated threat now spreading in the hearts and minds of those who would unleash their hidden desire to enslave their own kind.

Princess Sallina had hardly any idea how dangerous those she once trusted could be. How the darkest of thoughts often took on an existence of their own, as they found fertile ground to root in those who were easily susceptible to the allure of false lies and promises. These lies and promises were often delivered with the utmost conviction.

Chapter 2

Eight weeks and three days before Princess Sallina's epic rollercoaster ride through the stars, another important event had taken place on Starpoint.

That was the day the wisest unicorn heads of the kingdom chose to gather for a secret council session of Unimages to discuss the future of their lands, as well as an impending threat that could destroy their planet and all who lived there.

The meeting had convened at the Royal Castle of Starpoint, situated right in the centre of the kingdom. Technically, Starpoint was the only proper city of the unicorns, with all other unicorns living together harmoniously in the many villages dotting the land, as they had done for many centuries. But as happens so often in places that have enjoyed continued peace and a carefree co-existence, things were all about to drastically change—and not in a good way.

The great meeting room of the castle wasn't at that point used all that often. Even though it was the most important meeting room in the entire royal domain, it wasn't even a quarter of the size of the official grand meeting room, where almost all of the royal functions were held, and it wasn't even in a nicer part of the castle. It was in fact located in one of the smaller castle turrets, and there were numerous steep and uneven steps that one had to ascend in order to get up there, which put most unicorns off ever using it. It had, over the years, become a dusty and largely unoccupied space that in all truthfulness served little practical purpose for the ordinary citizens and nobles of Starpoint.

But centuries ago, there had been stories—by now, long forgotten—of what had occurred within these ancient walls of Starpoint, and how a much darker world had risen from seemingly nowhere to dramatically alter the lives of all unicorns in the city and beyond. Stories had been passed on relating how it had taken nearly an entire century to find the courage and means to bring peace and tranquillity back to this land and its living creatures, particularly these magnificent unicorns, who had for a long while forgotten their truest and kindest ways.

Considering that the room had no fewer than three hundred eighty-four steps leading to it, its main occupants were small rats and spiders who built their nests and cobwebs there, going about their business pretty much uninterrupted. But what better place was there to hold an important and secret meeting than in a room most unicorns avoided?

Of course, there was also the fact that not even one of the great Unimages was under one hundred years of age. This may sound like a lot of years, but in human terms they were equivalent to only about thirty-five years old or so. In fact, a hundred is hardly an age at all when one considers a unicorn is able to live for over three hundred years, especially if they take very good care of themselves. (Just for the record, the oldest unicorn ever reached the ripe old age of three hundred and sixty-one years before passing away.)

Back to the secret meeting.

Sitting around the giant, horseshoe-shaped conference table were all the illustrious Unimages (at least, all those who could be bothered to ascend the three hundred eighty-four steps). Standing at the podium in front of them was the equally illustrious and distinguished Professor Tinzy, who in Starpoint was also known as the great Unimage Tinzy.

Professor Tinzy loved teaching more than anything else and was also one of the main faculty members of Starpoint School, a seat of learning for only the most gifted unicorn children in all Starpoint. There were, of course, several schools in Starpoint, to support a population of more than three hundred and thirty-two thousand unicorns and their many offspring, but Starpoint High School—or Starhigh, as it was sometimes called—was the most famous academic institution of them all. It was also the school whereby tradition the children of the royal family were always educated, Princess Sallina being one of them.

She happened to be a famous and popular student in Professor Tinzy's class, and she always looked forward to his informative and often lively lectures. The grey-bearded and always-distinguished Professor Tinzy taught several subjects at Starhigh School, but Sallina's all-time favourite class was history because he had a way of making stories of the past feel so exciting and real, as if those events from distant times had only just happened yesterday.

However, on this occasion, Professor Tinzy was addressing no ordinary class, but a meeting held in the presence of no less than her majesty Queen Noony of Starpoint herself…who also happened to be Princess Sallina's strict and resourceful mother.

"Ahem." Professor Tinzy cleared his throat, his grey hoof supporting his chin as he stood on his powerful hind legs at the podium and adjusted them for the best standing position. He studied the Unimages seated before him and then Queen Noony, who sat at the apex of the table.

The Mages were of all different shapes, sizes, and colours. Unicorns in their diversity had become completely integrated centuries ago, and their varied looks and colours were sources of appreciation and marvel, rather than reasons to segment and segregate. One of the unwritten laws of Starpoint was that all unicorns were created equal (although truth be told, there were a few who felt they were significantly more equal than others, as you will find out).

Professor Tinzy cleared his throat once more and then blurted out, "This terrible meteor is unfortunately heading directly for us, and we simply cannot stop it!" He had considered a gentler, more gradual introduction but never quite worked out how to make the bad news sound less alarming than it was. He pointed towards the centre of the room as the Queen and Unimages looked at each other with bemusement.

A three-dimensional image instantly appeared in the centre, depicting a strange object that appeared to be hurtling through space. In the not-so-far-off distance was what looked like their planet (known as the Universe because the unicorns believed only their planet existed and the rest was like window dressing in the billions of bodies of outer space) and capital—Starpoint. The image showed the object hurtling along its trajectory directly toward their homes, and it looked like the projectile was most likely going to crash somewhere near the city of Starpoint itself.

As the Unimages and Queen Noony studied the moving images with terror and wonder, they could see that Starpoint would soon be engulfed by gigantic flames, and then their wonderful world would crack apart, burn up, and disappear into a smoulder of dark ashes.

There was a stunned silence in the room as the terrifying images slowly faded away to nothing and the hologram slowly vanished.

Now, while the room remains stunned, would be a very good time to introduce you to the main members of the Starpoint Council. And where better to begin than with Her Royal Highness Queen Noony?

Queen Noony was the presiding queen of Starpoint and had been for almost seventy-nine years. The Queen was a very elegant-looking unicorn, adorned with several layers of fancy clothing that befitted someone of such an exalted position, and she wore a small but impressive crown that rested firmly on top of her venerable and weathered head.

This was an ornamental crown that she wore when attending official meetings, not the royal crown that stood permanently on display in the castle library behind a magically fortified, protective glass cover for all citizens to see. She hated wearing the official crown and avoided doing so as much as possible, as it was far too heavy to be in any way comfortable when resting upon her head. Fortunately, it was used only for the rarest of ceremonial occasions—which thankfully didn't come along very often. She rarely had to climb these stairs with the crown resting upon her head.

A truly imposing figure she was, with her lush black curls that ran along her thick and equally magnificent black mane, and her bright-blue oval eyes, along with an almost golden patch of hair that stuck out on the top of her head like a mohawk and helped give her that extra-special presence befitting one of such royal ancestry. She had originally come from royal stock dating back to the very origin of the unicorns themselves, a time when only those considered to be the purest and lightest complexions could rule for many centuries.

The so-called purest blood had since been diluted by the so-many different herds of unicorns who had over the years intermixed, many having acquired gradually darker complexions, so that now being of light-skinned royal stock was something of a rarity, and certainly not something that bore any significance, unless of course one was the Queen. Sallina's father had been a proud darker-skinned unicorn whose long lineage had its origins in the remote rural lands at the edge of the kingdom, so Sallina had a darker complexion than her mother—one that some purists who harkened back to the past would feel didn't suit her as a member of the royal succession.

Those who were mostly pure or made themselves that way understood the importance of image and perception in society, and many of them aided the fairness of their hides with powerful magical spells. Lightness was such a close companion to brightness, and if you were light and bright in both your body and soul, you were destined to go much further than the others whom you once stood beside, and you got to secure your place in the upper echelons of modern unicorn society. Fortunately, during the years of the Queen's reign, this obsession had become less of an issue and the attention towards attaining such physical purity had greatly diminished in importance.

To return to our meeting, Queen Noony stared impassively at Professor Tinzy, allowing herself time to process his exclamation further.

As for the council members around the table on either side of Queen Noony, there were:

Firstly, the worldly and wizened Unimage Lommunar. He was thought to be around two-hundred twenty-nine years old, but nobody knew his exact age because he didn't wish to reveal to anyone how ancient he really was; keeping one's age a secret was one of the unwritten roles of the civilized unicorn society. Lommunar scarcely raised an eyebrow at the news of their impending doom.

Then there was Unimage Snimminz. He was precisely one-hundred twenty-four years of age. He coughed spasmodically as he lifted a hoof to his chin and tried very hard not to reveal his concerns about the very real and disturbing danger they were in.

Unimage Callindra sat next to Snimminz. She was well over two hundred fifty years old and one of the oldest unicorns in the room. Indeed, she was the second oldest Unimage in Starpoint, and more than likely to take over from Unimage Lommunar. Her face remained totally blank, devoid of any emotion.

Unimage Callindra was one of the few Unimages of purer stock left in Starpoint who operated in high council, but even she had faced a degree of genetic dilution in her family lineage. Her face as well as her body was incredibly pale, and her hair, which was bright gold in her younger days, had turned grey. Few really saw her as she was because she had learned early on to change her level of fairness with the aid of powerful magic.

Unimage Paterline. A unicorn of around one hundred eighty years of age, he scarcely raised his eyebrow. He was by far the darkest unicorn in the room—even his eyes were as black as coal. But he was truly admired and considered to be one of the wisest unicorns in the land.

Closer to Professor Tinzy, sitting to his right, was Unimage Konstanty. He was around one hundred thirty-two or one hundred thirty-three (he had lost precise count as age wasn't that much of a concern to him). Unimage Konstanty was the youngest-ever Unimage to have joined the Unimage Council, but he was so incredibly talented and smart that he first joined when he was scarcely even a hundred years of age. Unimage Konstanty was rumored to be of purer stock, although as is the case with many such rumors, more-educated Starpointers were quite quick to point out that there would most likely have been at least some level of dilution along the way. Right now, he was grinning without much concern at all about this potentially seismic event set to take place, but it was pretty hard to tell how he really felt about anything, as he often had a kind of clownish and mischievous look about him that concealed his true emotions and less-innocent and more-malevolent innermost thoughts.

It wasn't any of the Unimages who broke the silence; it was Queen Noony. She briefly cleared her throat before speaking with gentle but firm authority.

"So, what happens when this thing eventually hits us in our homes?"

Professor Tinzy's eyes scanned the room. "Oh, nothing actually, my Queen."

Queen Noony beamed, and her muscles relaxed just a little. "Oh, thank goodness. You had us worried for a moment. I was starting to feel unibumps all over my back."

She slumped back into her royal chair as a wave of relief swept over her.

"Because nothing will be able to survive this monumental event," Professor Tinzy muttered, almost not wanting to speak the words out loud.

"What—what was that?" Queen Noony asked with a renewed sense of alarm. "Speak up, Professor, I couldn't quite make out what you said."

Professor Tinzy blurted out, more loudly this time round, "Ehmmm… nothing can survive this meteor! We will all simply perish; every single one of us will be taken and cease to exist almost instantaneously. In fact, everything will disappear around us. Our lives will no longer exist in Starpoint or beyond. In fact, pretty much all life as we know it will simply not happen. So, when I say, 'Nothing will happen,' I mean… after this meteor hits, there will be nothing *to* happen. Ever."

"Wait a moment." Queen Noony raised a hoof in sudden defiance. "Are you telling me that everything will simply die because of this darned meteor heading our way?"

"Yes, that's precisely what I'm telling you, my Queen."

That almost seemed like an insult levelled directly towards the Queen, but everyone in the room knew that Professor Tinzy had a way of using words a little more recklessly and flippantly than most others, and he didn't mean anything underhanded or out of turn by being incredibly direct and to the point.

"Oh no, this has almost certainly ruined my dinner tonight and will most likely affect my sleep for the rest of this week," Unimage Paterline mumbled under his breath, shaking his head with dissatisfaction.

"What did you say, Unimage Paterline?" asked Queen Noony.

"Oh, noth—nothing, I was just saying something to myself. It's already forgotten."

Queen Noony stood up sternly on her hind legs and stretched her long and almost chubby equine body to its full height. The other Unimages were taken aback by her size and rotundity as she addressed them more formally than she had before. She was, after all, no ordinary unicorn in her magnitude; she was in fact a good third larger than most of those present, and quite round due to her intense love for all kinds of food—in fact, anything that was tasty and, especially, sweet. She was the Queen, and nobody ever dared tell her that she was more than a little bit plump for even her large and majestic size.

"I simply don't understand your point. Are you telling me, Professor Tinzy, that our world is soon about to come to an end?"

"Yes, I'm afraid that's exactly what I'm telling you…unless…"

"Unless what? Speak up, for goodness' sake…I'm sure we're all keen to hear!"

"Well, I'm not sure, my Queen, but there may be a possibility that we can avert a terrible catastrophe, but it's more than a bit uncertain and more than a bit unclear as to how it can be accomplished," Professor Tinzy replied meekly.

"There'd better be a really good solution to this predicament!" Queen Noony exclaimed loudly. "If we are about to face such imminent doom, someone had better come up with a solid working plan on how we can avert such a meteoric disaster from ever happening."

"That's very good advice, my Queen," Unimage Konstanty spoke up for the first time. "Meteoric it appears to be, in all senses of the word, and for my liking all a bit too fantastic and incredible. This is bordering on an epic fantasy; it is something that has most likely been designed to entertain us, and to divert our thoughts from more pressing matters that are at hoof. I suggest we shouldn't try to pretend to be so clever or funny, making up such silly monstrosities as a formidable meteor when no such entity is likely to exist. It sounds like a literal flight of fancy."

"I wasn't trying to be clever or funny or fancy about this, Unimage Konstanty," Queen Noony retorted sharply. "We're talking about what could be the end of our world—we are being warned of a doomsday that may soon be upon us all. This is not something to trivialize with your light-hearted humor, even if under normal circumstances it might be construed as being funny."

"To answer your question, my Queen, yes, we are working on a plan of sorts," Professor Tinzy said. "All hope is not yet lost."

"'Of sorts.'" Unimage Paterline guffawed. "Seems a bit vague for such a grievous situation, wouldn't you say, my good Unimage?"

"You see, my Queen," the Professor continued, ignoring him, "everyone present already knows that all the magic in Starpoint runs on this wonderful stuff we call Pinny, and we used to have lots of it in storage in the past. But what they don't all know is that our Pinny supply has been running dangerously down for the past few decades, and fresh supplies have virtually ceased to come through."

"I thought our Pinny supply was perfectly fine, Unimage Tinzy. This is the first I've heard of it," Queen Noony snapped, then realized she might have overdone it a bit.

"Well, it's not so fine, my Queen," Unimage Snimminz countered. "We've already shut down two of our Alicorns due to limitations in our Pinny supply, and the three remaining ones are currently running at half power at best due to a lack of sufficient Pinny. We were going to bring this matter up with our Council before, but until now it wasn't so much of a concern, as we could run on even just one Alicorn for a few years if needs must and it were under normal circumstances."

Snimminz pointed the small, craggy white stick he was holding firmly in his hoof. A blue beam shot out and created a holographic image of Starpoint in the middle of the horseshoe table where the image of the meteor had been.

The city of Starpoint was called *Starpoint* because it was shaped like a shiny star. At the end of each of its brightly illuminated points, which were especially noticeable at night, stood a mighty Alicorn citadel that helped to radiate powerful magical energy for all the city's inhabitants to use. Each Alicorn citadel was shaped much like the unicorn's horn from which the powerful magical energy of Pinny radiated.

Pinny was an almost-invisible magical essence that had abundantly covered the whole of Starpoint. It worked in much the same way as humans understand radio waves, transmitting power and providing all unicorns with the ability to access their intrinsic magic and manipulate it at will, depending on their skill. Pinny, long ago known as Painubti in its original form, had always been a bit of a mysterious substance, although it was known to power almost all the magic in all the lands.

But over the centuries, the supply of Pinny had begun to dwindle, and the unicorns had gathered together a few centuries earlier to create the great city of Starpoint and its five gigantic Alicorns to power all their magic in a more confined space with what remained of their Pinny supply, which helped to ration its usage.

"Even if we have only our three remaining Alicorns to radiate Pinny, our Alicorns ought to be sufficient to protect us from this horrible object, oughtn't they?" Queen Noony queried.

"I'm afraid it will not do," said Professor Tinzy matter-of-factly.

It was just at this moment that everyone sensed something else was taking place just beyond the chamber. It had been heavily raining all day long, and now as the evening approached, the weather outside had intensified with the onset of a bright and fierce lightning storm, which was joined by a fierce downpour of rain. A sudden flash of light shot out beyond the chamber, closely followed by the sound of not-too-distant thunder.

Queen Noony looked for a few moments as though she was frozen in thought. Whether it was deep thought or some sense of trepidation that temporarily arrested the functioning of her muscles and nervous system, nobody quite knew. But she had a habit of becoming very still, and many believed that this was when she was at her very best, as she carefully mulled over any given situation and sought to find some kind of resolution to a particular dilemma.

Then Queen Noony opened her mouth as an idea started to materialize in her mind. "What if we can get all five of our Alicorns working again to thwart this danger somehow?"

"Then it might be possible to deflect the meteor away from Starpoint, or perhaps we can even halt it completely in its tracks," replied the Professor.

The collective sigh of relief was quite audible.

"I think we're taking this matter far too seriously," Unimage Konstanty piped up. "Depletion of our magical resources, the dwindling supply of Pinny in Starpoint, an end-of-the-world threat… isn't this all going a bit too far? Am I the only one who thinks that all this is all utter bunkum, sheer nonsense? Professor Tinzy is well known for his more-than-occasional absentmindedness, and I think he may have completely lost his entire brain somewhere, perhaps left it behind on one of his recent journeys."

The others were too cautious to react, and nobody quite knew who was going to speak next. Then sudden laughter erupted from somewhere in the chamber.

It was Unimage Callindra, who had broken into a chortling fit. Everyone else soon followed, though they laughed less confidently and more than a little nervously…except for Queen Noony and Professor Tinzy, who were both shocked. They stood there in utter amazement, failing to see what was so terribly amusing.

"I'm afraid that denial won't make such a threat disappear. The prophecies of the scroll of Tinzin have never been wrong before, and they even warned us of such an event posing an existential threat, that was set to take place around this time period!" Professor Tinzy exclaimed above the roar of laughter still filling the chamber.

His forceful declaration brought the echoing fits of laughter to an abrupt halt. The forced merriment was replaced by a wave of murmurs that echoed around the room as the Unimages whispered to each other.

Queen Noony stood there silently, waiting for some kind of sign that she should move the conversation on as she pondered the gravity of this threat, which she believed was all too real. Even though Unimage Konstanty had dismissed this situation as being no more than a figment of Unimage Tinzy's overactive imagination, she knew a lot better than to trivialize something as potentially dangerous as this. Unicorns were known to be somewhat cautious creatures by nature, but they broke the mould with Konstanty, who was unusual in his ability to trivialize almost everything he came across and take things in his stride in the most relaxed and uninterested manner possible.

"What time frame do we have for this meteor to destroy us?" Queen Noony asked the Professor.

Professor Tinzy didn't respond straightaway. He calculated silently in his head for a few moments before he spoke.

"It's hard to say exactly, your Majesty. I cannot provide you with a very clear timetable. I reckon sometime under a year; it could even be a bit longer, maybe," the Professor replied. "Sixteen months on the outside."

This got a few more off-the-cuff remarks muttered between the Unimages, this time less cautiously, as if it didn't matter that much if they were overheard.

"So, now it appears we need to have copious amounts of luck as well," Unimage Paterline remarked cursorily.

"Well, the bottom line is," Professor Tinzy insisted, "that we cannot ignore the fact we desperately need to replenish our stocks of Pinny in the near future. There is no mistake; we must go out and find more!"

"So where do we go to do that?" Unimage Paterline challenged Professor Tinzy.

The room fell silent.

"We have been discreetly sending out search parties for some years now. We've been travelling across the many lands, without success thus far. However, it's not all bad news. I did come across some potential Pinny in one of my recent travels. It's just that—" he paused.

Sudden gasps of excitement filled the chamber. Unimage Konstanty squinted to focus on what the professor was about to reveal.

"As everyone here is fully aware, I do occasionally use magic to travel to far-off, new places. I have travelled to one such place that may have some Pinny, and it's possible that I can travel out there again and acquire some for us."

Queen Noony sat back down slowly and began to smile, all her nervousness starting to disappear.

"Well then, my dear Unimage Tinzy. Looks like you have given yourself the most vital and pressing task of our times. I hereby command you to depart immediately and go find us some more Pinny from this faraway land, wherever it may be. We will then hopefully be able to power up all our Alicorns once again, returning them to their full capacity, and then we will find a way of using our powerful magic to successfully halt this terrible meteor and its menace."

All the Unimages, apart from Konstanty, sat back in their chairs and relaxed just a little.

"Your Majesty, I will of course do my very utmost," the Professor promised, and then made a low bow. "This journey will not be without its peril, but I will find a way to overcome any obstacles. Please don't ask me where this place is, as I simply cannot tell you. I must keep this strange land a closely guarded secret, for reasons I cannot yet explain to you all. But should I somehow fail, I will ensure that the vital details are made known to you, and then you too can work out a way to solve the puzzle of this very great predicament."

This left the Unimages feeling somewhat baffled and wondering what all this secrecy was about, and why Unimage Tinzy was so keen to go it alone on this mission for which he had volunteered. Fortunately, this was Unimage Professor Tinzy standing at the podium, and as it was known that he often didn't make much sense when he spoke, they simply went along with the oddness of it for now.

Queen Noony struck her front hooves together as she applauded this new moment in Starpoint's history.

The others did precisely the same, apart from Unimage Konstanty. He sat there brooding silently, refusing to join in on the excitement of the moment. His gaze burrowed deep into the eyes of Professor Tinzy, as if staring at him directly would somehow reveal the secret location of this abundant supply of Pinny.

"If there is any Pinny out there, it's going to be mine and I will use it in the best way that I can and by any means I can muster," Konstanty kept repeating privately to himself.

There was a darkness that had found a home in Konstanty's heart and soul, and it slowly and relentlessly ate away at all that was once good in him. Often, those beset by the evilest of desires start off with the noblest of intentions. The hardest life lesson of all is that every one of us is susceptible, as these wicked thoughts and ideas early on find a way to disguise their true intentions in the very things we cherish, such as our freedoms and individual ways. Once allowed a voice inside our thoughts, they twist the truth and change how we see the world.

It is often far too late by the time those who have been taken realise they've been duped, and their once-noble intentions have been perverted. Even worse, once one does come to this realisation, it's extremely difficult to change paths, as doing so means accepting having been fooled not just once, not twice, but so many times. One truly wonders how many terrible outcomes could have been averted in the course of history if only those who turned out to be perpetrators of evil and corruption could have accepted their failures early on and acknowledged the simple truths that we all share.

Chapter 3

The thirteen-year-old girl who was really a unicorn stood outside the gates of Doberry School, staring at the school's entrance… with her human eyes!

Everything felt so strange!

So much had happened since she'd learned about the secret council meeting of Unimages and the extent of the mission Professor Tinzy was then about to go on. Sallina was special to him as she was the future heir to the throne, so he knew he could confide in her. He had trusted Sallina with the mission details, on the condition that she kept them to herself and revealed them to the council only if he didn't return after a month's absence.

More than five weeks had passed, with no word from the Professor. It had worried the princess, so much so that she decided to travel to this place referred to as "Earth" to find out what was going on. Before leaving, she had passed the information to her close friend Numi, instructing them to pass it on to the Unimages should she fail to return. Her friend, of course, thought she was completely mad, but Sallina felt she just had to go.

There had been a whole process in those weeks since she'd arrived, in which she had to learn where she was and understand enough to be able to attend school, and where her newly acquired mother helped her to find her way… but that is something we can look back on at another time, as our story now shifts to the secondary school where Sallina is going to make a remarkable discovery.

Clearly, she hadn't bargained for having to join an educational establishment in such an unfamiliar world. However, being transformed into a human! With light-brown, tanned skin! And here she was now, about to attend school somewhere she couldn't have even dreamt of not so long ago!

She wasn't going because she needed the schooling, but because her foster mother had said there was a professor teaching in this particular school who sounded a lot like the 'man' (actually a unicorn) for whom Sallina was searching.

Taking a deep breath, Sallina started toward the front entrance, surrounded by other children all dressed in the same school uniform—a bright-crimson blazer with a matching, slightly darker-crimson skirt, black leggings, and black shoes. So far, she had no books, only a notebook, which she carried in a small shoulder bag.

As she passed by a couple of giggling girls of a similar age, she noticed a boy in the distance watching her carefully. She observed him discreetly for a few moments but didn't recognize him. He appeared to be a similar age as she was when she appeared on Earth... which made her feel so very young, because as a unicorn she was already nearing the important milestone of fifty years—a significant time, as it was the unicorn equivalent of reaching early adulthood.

Sallina entered the school and made her way toward her first class. She wasn't exactly sure where it was, but she had received some directions from her foster mother, who had printed them out for her, and she had memorized them.

After a few turns in the corridor, she found herself arriving at a classroom, which was already filling with students of about her apparent human age.

Sallina walked into the room and found a seat, where she sat herself down.

"I'm Becky," murmured a red-headed girl with a collection of freckles.

"I'm Sallina. It's very nice to meet you."

Becky grinned, then exclaimed, "Shall we be friends? It'll be fun."

"Of course! We certainly shall."

Becky shifted over to sit next to Sallina as their teacher arrived. Sallina quickly turned her attention to him. Was this her Professor Tinzy? The man walked in the shuffling manner that was akin to Professor Tinzy's trademark gait. Professor Tinzy always looked like he had been distracted by an important random thought that needed to be answered instantly in a sudden explosion of what seemed like incoherent muttering... it *was* incoherent to others, that is, for the Professor would often smile to himself after each mutter as if pleased with the answer he had just given to himself.

The professor made his way to the blackboard and started to write his name on it. Sallina watched, riveted.

"Well, then. I am Professor Brian Walters," he said assertively as a few students filtered in, taking their seats. "And I am privileged to be here teaching this class. In just a few moments, I'm going to be calling out your names. If I state your name, raise your hand."

Professor Walters rummaged through his briefcase and produced a small notebook that contained the students' names. As he leafed through the notebook, he suddenly had an urge to sneeze. "Achoo!" He sneezed loudly… then again.

How very odd, he thought to himself.

He normally didn't sneeze in his classroom or at school. And this wasn't like a sneeze he would get as a precursor to a cold; this one was entirely different. He had suffered from such sneezes for his entire life, and he knew exactly what things or creatures would most likely bring them on. His sneezes were usually directly associated with the presence of animals— usually wild animals, as opposed to a domestic cat or dog. He glanced around the room, but he couldn't see any wild animals about, only children, and being in the presence of children didn't usually make him sneeze.

"Hmm," he muttered to himself. "How curious."

Glancing back at his notebook, he called out the first name. "Tara Smith…are we here, Miss Smith?" A hand slowly went up in the back of the classroom.

"Miss Lindon…is there a Miss Lindon about?"

Princess Sallina raised her hand. Becky gave her a friendly smile as Professor Walters nodded, then…

"Achoo!" Once again, he let out a loud, fierce sneeze, startling a few children in the front of the class. "I'm so sorry. Now where were we?"

Princess Sallina looked around the room. This wasn't at all what she was expecting. If anything, this was likely going to be far too boring, and the other students were nothing like the schoolchildren she would normally mix with back home on Starpoint. Also, once the Professor had opened his mouth and spoken, she suspected he wasn't the professor for whom she had been searching.

"Okay," said the professor after reading all the names, "today we are going to talk about…"

As the professor continued, Sallina quickly realised that this was not even a smidgeon of Professor Tinzy standing before her, dully pontificating, and she began to wonder what in the world she was doing in such a strange and humdrum place. It was clear that there was no inkling of magic in a classroom like this; there were no dreams being woven to create something beautiful and striking out of thin air, only a steady deluge of facts and information about how these creatures called human beings lived on this rather grey planet called Earth.

How very dull and tedious this world seemed, and how very uninteresting this class was to these poor children, who had to endure it no matter what. The human children had so little idea of what was going on around them beyond the narrowest streams of information being channelled into their tiny minds, and clearly, they had little interest in absorbing what appeared to be irrelevant and useless knowledge. They were already looking bored to death, and no doubt they would traverse an entire existence with no appreciation of all the marvels and wonders taking place around them, and the incredible power of magic that surrounded all who were alive.

For the first time, she began to appreciate how crucial magic was to everything she knew and cared for in the world, and she began to comprehend the actual worth of those precious, hard-earned kernels of wisdom she had acquired on properly using and controlling magic. It was only the kindest and wisest of professors who were able to guide her down this path, and now she was starting to realise that such precious knowledge and wisdom could be the difference between life and death for all her kind.

She couldn't help but start watching the clock instead of Professor Walters as the lesson dragged on with painful slowness. Lunch could not come quickly enough, but after what seemed a unicorn eternity (which is a very, very long time!), the lunch bell finally rang, and it was like music to her ears.

In the cafeteria, Sallina found herself standing in a slow-moving line, sliding a tray along a rack behind a queue of other students. In the front of the line, she saw that peculiar boy again, though now he looked strangely familiar. She had a nagging feeling she knew him from somewhere, but she could not quite place him.

Then it dawned on her. Perhaps he looked familiar because he was in fact a unicorn child from Starpoint! But how could that be? She just as quickly dismissed this from her mind. She knew of nobody besides the Professor and herself who had ever made this long trip to this strange world.

Suddenly, Princess Sallina started to feel giddy and disoriented. The boy she thought she knew but couldn't name crossed the cafeteria holding a tray of food, glancing over toward her every so often with what appeared more than idle curiosity. Then Sallina lost her footing, went limp, and slipped backwards into a stranger directly behind her.

Rudy was a couple of years older than she, and he was wearing a slightly mean, annoyed expression. He wasn't pleased when Sallina collided into him.

"Eh, watch it there, you fool. What are you doing, bumping into me?" he blurted unkindly. "Are you looking for a fight? If you are, I'll give you one."

Sallina regained her footing and turned to him. "I'm very sorry, this was entirely my mistake. I meant no harm."

After gathering her balance and regaining her senses, she approached the checkout. She noticed the paltry selection of food on her tray – a solitary apple, a small bottle of water, and a little tub of strawberry yogurt that claimed to be low in fat. The cashier gave her a disinterested look and scanned her school ID badge. She was heading away to find a table when she noticed an older man standing across the room, chatting with a student accompanying him.

She was immediately entranced by him, so much so she almost bumped straight into another girl holding a tray, who deftly swerved around her in the last second and threw her a quick glance of annoyance before carrying on to her table.

Sallina's heart began to race. This older man appeared normal in size but was a lot older than the other professors she had seen so far in the school. He had a patchy grey goatee and long grey hair, tied into a ponytail. He had a sharp, craggy nose upon which rested a pair of silver glasses, and he was wearing a dark-grey waistcoat that matched his facial hair perfectly.

This is him! she thought. *For sure! This is exactly how Professor Tinzy would look if he were a human being!*

She was absolutely certain of it.

She fixed her gaze on the professor and waited for him to finish his conversation with the student. As he turned away and headed out of the cafeteria, Sallina followed him. She hurried across the room and bolted through the doors, not noticing the sign clearly stating no food was permitted to be taken out of the cafeteria.

The door swung open as she pushed her way through it, but before she could get her bearings and work out which way the ponytailed professor had gone, she walked straight into Professor Walters, who was hurrying along the same corridor.

CLANG!

The inevitable collision made her lose her grip on the tray, which fell and landed with a loud clatter as it hit the hard concrete floor. Her yogurt, the apple, and the bottle of water bounced off the tray on impact.

She looked down in dismay and then up at a rather annoyed Professor Walters, while over his shoulder she could see the man who looked like Professor Tinzy disappearing down the corridor, out of sight.

"I'm so very sorry, this was entirely my fault," Sallina said apologetically. She looked down again, and Professor Walters let out a sudden sneeze whilst holding onto his nose.

"Let me help you," he said as she bent down to retrieve her scattered morsels. "You know, Sallina—that's your name, isn't it? —lunch needs to be consumed in the cafeter—"

He looked back up toward her with her bottle of water and apple in hand to find she was already gone.

He glanced down the corridor, then turned again as the boy that Sallina had been watching earlier picked up the strawberry yogurt and held it out. Professor Walters let out another sudden sneeze, hastily covering his nose with his hand.

The boy—whose name was Szymon—lifted the tray and put the tub of yogurt on it. The professor took the tray without hesitating and put the drink and apple back as well.

As Sallina raced away—finding it a weird experience to run on just two legs!—she glanced back to see Szymon, along with Professor Walters, disappearing behind her. What an odd-looking boy, she thought. His eyes were emerald-green, he had fair hair that sat like a mop on top of his head, and his skin was so very light coloured, it almost hurt her eyes.

"She must have been in an awful hurry," Szymon said, and he too rushed off in Sallina's direction.

"Wait a sec, now—now hold on!" Professor Walters stammered as he stood there with Princess Sallina's tray in his hands.

Princess Sallina made her way down the corridor, took a right turn, and was about to take another turn when she caught sight of the man, taking a drink at a water fountain. She eagerly jogged right up to him, not considering how unusual her actions might appear if he didn't recognize her at once and wasn't in fact the unicorn she was seeking.

"Sir… Professor… hey!" Sallina called as she came to a halt right behind him.

The man looked up, swallowed the water he had in his mouth, and said, "Yes, who are you?" The words were accompanied by a mild gurgle.

"Professor, oh my gosh, I can't believe that it's really you. It is, isn't it? You're him!" Princess Sallina blurted as he watched her curiously through his silver-rimmed spectacles.

"Excuse me a moment young lady, do we know each other? I don't recall having ever come across you before."

Sallina immediately turned as she sensed someone else approaching. It was Szymon, running up to them.

"Professor Walters is looking for you, Sallina. He has your tray of food!" Szymon stammered.

"Sorry, what?" Sallina looked confusedly at Szymon. "I don't know you."

"Looks like it's a double case of mistaken identity," the professor remarked glibly. "You'd both better go on, then—it's virtually time for your class."

With that, the man she thought was Professor Tinzy wandered off without even as much as an indication of passing curiosity about such a strange encounter.

This really bothered Sallina, as she had tried so hard to get the professor's attention. She glanced back at Szymon, and her expression hardened.

"Excuse me, who in the world are you? You've been getting in my way!"

"You . know Professor Walters? I think he's extremely allergic to us... magical creatures. Haven't you noticed?" Szymon remarked meaningfully.

Sallina eyed Szymon carefully, her expression still stern. Then she realised the full meaning of what Szymon had just said to her.

"Now wait a second. Who are you calling magical creatures? Do we—"

Szymon smiled wryly. He mimicked with his hand the shape of a unicorn's horn and waited.

"Oh my! So, you're another one from Starpoint, too? It can't be."

She was suddenly quite excited about the prospect of meeting another unicorn from Starpoint here on this distant and peculiar world. It had been some time since she had encountered another unicorn—since her arrival on Earth, in fact. In all those weeks, she had become used to being almost a human herself, but you can't really get used to what you are not. How could you? It's little wonder she felt mostly alone, and vulnerable too, in so many ways. The surprising and reassuring presence of what seemed to be another unicorn in human form brought her some welcome relief.

"You're Princess Sallina," Szymon exclaimed, almost proudly. "if I recall correctly..."

"Yes, I am!"

"You're... a not-so-often-seen young royal busybody who keeps getting into trouble and causing mischief," Szymon added unceremoniously. "We always follow your mishaps with the greatest of interest and laugh about them."

"Hey, that's not fair," Sallina retorted. "Who are you calling a busybody and a mischief maker? There's nothing wrong with getting things done, and I've achieved a whole lot of things in my young years that I'm proud of. Who are you to speak of me in such a way? You can be punished for such disrespectful behaviour to one of royal lineage."

"I'm very sorry, my Princess. I didn't mean anything. But we both find ourselves in unusual circumstances where our customary graces seem out of place. Let me introduce myself. I'm Junior Unimage Szymon, hailing all the way from our home of Starpoint, and I am humbly at your royal service."

With this, he offered her a low bow of respect. It brought a warm smile to Princess Sallina's face, although not too much, as she was used to being respected and bowed to by even junior mages like Szymon, who was almost a child. She still had half a mind to give this fake-human Szymon a proper dressing down, but she too was out of her usual comfort zone, and being so removed from her normal way of life meant she had to adjust to the situation she found herself presently in.

"I wouldn't bother approaching that human-looking creature," said Szymon, raising his head. "The good Professor won't be able to recognise you no matter what you say to him. He won't be able to recognize anyone from Starpoint. He thinks he is perfectly human, like everyone else here, and has forgotten who he really is. He is suffering from amnesia."

This troubled Princess Sallina. "So, it is definitely him. I wasn't one hundred percent sure until just now. That's some consolation, at least."

"As far as I know, my Princess. I'm pretty certain that it's Professor Tinzy… or rather, Unimage Tinzy. My father too sits upon the magic council, so I have seen our illustrious Professor in his natural unicorn form a few times back home."

That wasn't exactly what Princess Sallina wanted to hear. "That's good to know. But I am deeply troubled that he doesn't remember who he is. This is a really unfortunate situation. No wonder we haven't heard from him in some time now. How's he to get back home if he doesn't remember who he really is? He has important business here, and not knowing who he is will make it a lot harder for him to do what he has been tasked with. How will he be able to do anything at all?"

"That is a very good question, your Highness. I was thinking precisely the same thing."

"So, who is your father?" Sallina enquired.

"My father is Unimage Konstanty, the youngest-ever Unimage on the magic council. I'm sure you must have heard of him before. Everybody knows him."

"Oh gosh, of course I have! He's second only to the great Unimage Lommunar. I nearly forgot. Well, well, so, you're Unimage Konstanty's son. That at least explains how you had the means to come here, as I thought I was the only one apart from the good Professor. I am pleased to make your acquaintance, Szymon. It's nice to come across someone who's also from back home and knows what it feels like to have four hooves, and a horn sticking out of one's head!"

"Likewise, your Majesty. I'm extremely pleased to meet you, Princess Sallina. It is an honour to be in your presence."

"Oh, don't get so formal, Szymon, we're in the wrong place for that. The question for us, then, is what's to be done with poor Professor Tinzy? I urgently must speak to him. It is of the utmost important—a matter of life and death."

"You can certainly speak to him, my Princess, but you do need to be realistic about what that may accomplish. I fear Professor Tinzy will have absolutely no memory of the unicorn you are or the unicorn he in fact is, or should I say *was*. He may even consider us both completely crazy, to suggest that all three of us are unicorns from a faraway place. As far as he is concerned, he is an ordinary human."

Chapter 4

Despite Szymon's well-founded concerns that she wasn't likely to get anywhere in her attempt to recover the Professor's memories, Sallina insisted she had to at least try to reach the inner unicorn that existed somewhere inside him.

"You know, Princess, such a feat won't work without the aid of pretty powerful magic, which happens to not function here, as we are stuck on this boring human planet where magic doesn't even exist," Szymon remarked as they stood outside the Professor's office.

Sallina stared at the nameplate on the door—Professor T. Tinkerman.

"See that?"

Szymon gazed at it quizzically and shrugged.

"Tinkerman. Tinzy. They're similar, no? That must be a sign he is in touch with his inner unicorn self, don't you think?"

"Hmmm, maybe. It could just be you making it up," said Szymon.

"I think I heard something," muttered Princess Sallina. She knocked as softly as she could on the Professor's door. There was no immediate response. She knocked a little bit harder. Still no reply. Sallina knocked again, this time a little more forcefully, even though the resulting soreness of her knuckles made her wince.

"Wait a moment… who's there?" came a muffled reply from within.

Sallina waited by the door with eager anticipation. However, this evaporated immediately when Professor Tinzy opened the door and gave them his renowned bothered-and-somewhat-distant-look, which hinted at more-than-mild annoyance over their uninvited and unwelcome intrusion into his busy worktime.

"Can't you see I'm rather preoccupied? So who are you? And begone."

"Professor!" Sallina said gaily.

"Yes. Hurry, please—I really must not be detained from my most valuable work any longer than is necessary. Is this visit of any importance?"

Princess Sallina simply couldn't control herself anymore. She burst out in excitement, "Professor Tinzy! OMG, oh my gosh. I can't believe it's really you! Can't you see it's me? SALLINA!"

Princess Sallina thought that such jubilation could perhaps jog the Professor's memories and trigger a belated recognition, and perhaps he would come to realize who was standing right before him. After all, she had been one of his most admiring students for a long time, and she felt that her mere presence in front of him would help to trigger those memories that had somehow been lost or buried deep inside his mind.

Professor Tinzy scratched the short goatee on his chin ever so slightly and pondered.

"Hmm. I'm afraid I can't see that 'it's you,' as I cannot recall ever seeing you before, and certainly not in my class. Stop wasting my time, both of you."

Sallina really couldn't help herself. She rushed toward the Professor and embraced him fondly, just as a daughter would embrace her father after a very long absence.

"Good heavens!" said Professor Tinzy, startled by her abrupt display of unfounded familiarity, and he pulled away, more than a trifle embarrassed and made uncomfortable by the unwelcome intrusion into his personal space. "I'm *certain* I've not come across either of you before. What exactly is it you want from me?"

"May we please come in and explain ourselves more clearly to you, sir?" Szymon interjected quickly, perceiving the awkwardness of the situation.

Unrelenting, Sallina continued her advances toward the Professor, who reacted by retreating into his small chamber. This inadvertently allowed Szymon and Sallina entry into his private study, which was the last thing he wanted.

"You're Professor Tinzy! For goodness' sake! We're all from Starpoint! You, me, and Szymon. Why don't you *recognize* us?" Sallina blurted out in frustration.

"Excuse me here, young lady. I'm Professor Tony Tinkerman. T. Tinkerman, it says so on my door. I am not this strange fellow 'Professor Tinzy' you are speaking about. This is clearly a case of grossly mistaken identity."

Sallina continued to blabber. "We have to talk to you, Professor. It's about your secret mission. How can you not remember something that's so important?"

Realizing Sallina was speaking in a high-pitched, excited voice that could travel some distance and be overheard, Szymon hurriedly closed the door.

"Your Majesty," he whispered, "I think you're scaring the Professor with information he cannot even begin to comprehend. Calm down. We need to be serene."

Sallina suddenly came to her senses, took a deep breath, and stepped away from the Professor, who himself took a deep breath in relief.

"My apologies, Professor—I didn't expect a sudden outpouring of emotion. We are all living in such difficult times. It's hard sometimes to maintain control of how I feel."

An uneasy air surrounded them as Princess Sallina and Szymon gazed at the Professor's ridiculously messy desk, which brimmed with stacks of files and papers scattered about, along with several empty mugs of days-old coffee and a small white ornamental teapot and teacup lying to one side, both having been used until the last drop of tea had been consumed.

"Please, Professor, sit down and we will try to explain things to you," Szymon gently pleaded. "We would greatly appreciate it if you could hear us out for just a few minutes."

Not quite knowing how to react to these two lunatics standing before him, the Professor moved back to his comfy chair and small square cushion and sat himself down. He looked at them quizzically as they came closer.

"Does this have something to do with your school grades? I've really no control over these things. I merely mark them, but it is not my duty or my right to review these marks in light of any extenuating circumstances that may arise. You will have to speak to the principal about any such matters—there are rules that need to be strictly observed. Or should I say, your parents' ought to do this, as you are both minors and not in a position to raise such concerns by yourselves. This has absolutely nothing to do with me."

"It has nothing to do with our grades, Professor," Princess Sallina said.

She proceeded to illustrate in a calm and collected manner how she had travelled through a magic portal to come to Earth looking for him, and she told him what in fact had happened some weeks earlier when she embarked on this extraordinary journey. She also reminded him about the magic-council meeting and what he had told her of its proceedings, and the extreme urgency of the situation and the impending threat posed by the giant meteor that was on its way to destroy the whole of Starpoint and everyone and everything in it.

Professor Tinzy sat there, listening intently, without saying a word. When Sallina came to the end of her account, the Professor took a deep breath and, like a fisherman about to dive into the sea without the aid of an oxygen mask, held it as long as he could. A full twenty-three minutes had flown past, and there had been a lot to take in.

Sallina and Szymon studied the Professor's face eagerly, hoping that at least a flicker of memory would reveal itself and he would be able to recognize them. But no, there was nothing of the kind. It looked more like the holding of his breath was turning his face, particularly his cheeks, bright red.

"Okay, let's see if I understand this properly. I'm some kind of uni-corn," he said, very slowly. They both nodded in eager anticipation.

"I come from a place called Star-world."

"Starpoint," Sallina quickly corrected him. "It's called Starpoint."

"You're also both magi-cal unicorns." He appeared baffled by this preposterous assertion. Sallina and Szymon glanced quickly at each other. This didn't look good; it didn't seem like he believed anything they were telling him.

Professor Tinzy studied them carefully. Even though his body had barely moved, his eyes now looked wild and alive— after all, there was so much history they had witnessed that no amount of amnesia could have taken those memories away. Surely?

"I came here to find pai—what was it called again?"

"Painubti. 'Pinny' is the more common name," Sallina replied.

"Yes, Pinny, and this thing helps us all to drive—what was it again?"

"The Alicorns—they power all the magic in Starpoint. Without our blessed Alicorns, the Pinny couldn't spread out and power our magic. It's how everything works where we're from," Princess Sallina patiently explained, hoping that the discussion would trigger some deeply buried memories for the Professor and help them to rise to the surface again. She looked toward Szymon, feeling increasingly concerned.

"I'm on a very important mission to stop something very bad from happening… particularly this meteor that is threatening to damage your world. Is that right?"

Princess Sallina and Szymon exchanged puzzled glances.

"Yes, that's exactly right, Professor. You still sound unsure about all this, but I assure you she is telling you the truth," Szymon chimed in.

"Please try to remember, Professor. It's so important you do," Princess Sallina pleaded softly. She reached out and touched his hand to reassure him, but he immediately recoiled. "So much is at stake, and all our lives are in terrible danger."

"Wait a moment," he muttered.

Professor Tinzy picked up his teacup and studied it carefully. Then he held it up to his mouth and pretended to slurp the last remnants of the tea that weren't even there. They could hear the loud slurping sounds as he pretended to suck in and savour the last vestiges of his now-lukewarm drink. Both Sallina and Szymon stood there, paralyzed and frustrated at the same time.

A reaction duly came. It started with a brief gurgling sound that built up into a chortle and then escalated into full-blown laughter at the completely idiotic story he had been told. He laughed out loud. He even banged on his desk with his open hand in amusement, sending a number of papers flying and almost spilling what was left in his nearby mug.

Sallina and Szymon looked on aghast, mouths open, unsure about what more they could do to convince him of who he really was. Could they have somehow been mistaken? Maybe this wasn't Professor Tinzy after all, but someone who strikingly resembled the great Unimage. They would have settled for a few memories, but so far, they had received nothing from him whatsoever.

Princess Sallina tried to break into a fake smile to defuse the ridiculous situation, and the creases of her mouth slowly widened as Szymon stood there and watched her expression transform with all the power she could summon from inside herself. It almost looked like she was about to erupt like some gigantic volcano ready to spew its red-hot lava high into the sky.

But then something completely unexpected happened. Professor Tinzy stopped laughing out loud; in fact, he simply froze up and went very still, like a statue. They noticed the sudden transformation, and Princess Sallina quickly grabbed hold of his arm to check whether he was still alive.

"Professor, are you alright? What's happening? Can you hear me?"

The Professor's face turned from white to pink, then to red across both his cheeks. For a few painful, lingering seconds, it was as if time itself had stopped... until a sudden, sharp exhalation of breath whooshed from his mouth, and he started to breathe again as normal.

"I have to say, you two should enrol in Miss Hendricks' creative writing program. You would do incredibly well, you'll earn top marks."

The Professor smiled and gave them a meek, helpless look that was out of place on the great Unimage Tinzy but was perhaps better suited to his alias of Professor Tony Tinkerman.

Szymon was by now exasperated.

"Everything she just told you is the Horn's honest truth; I personally attest to that." He looked desperately for some signs that Professor Tinzy had accepted their story.

"Young man... uni-corn, hah. Whatever it is you think you are. I am certain that I will need to report this disturbing incident to the principal. Youngsters do have the occasional flights of fancy, I grant you that, but this one, it takes the biscuit."

Professor Tinzy picked up the last biscuit on a small plate that lay by the teapot and munched it with a big chomping bite, ingesting it fully.

"I must implore you to leave my office, as I grow weary of this foolhardy game you are both playing at my expense." He got to his feet, eyeing them suspiciously. "I have a lot of important work to do, and this is a huge waste of my precious time."

"But—" Sallina began.

"No, please leave me alone. Now! Before I lose my temper and do something I will no doubt regret."

The Professor motioned for them to go at once, gesturing a quick retreat to the door.

Princess Sallina turned to Szymon, who shook his head in defeat. She finally realized that whatever was wrong with Professor Tinzy, there wasn't going to be an ordinary way to remedy it. He had truly forgotten who he once was. All his greatness, and his admiration for her as his star pupil...they didn't exist. She meant nothing to him nor to anyone she knew.

Sallina turned away, head bowed, and moved dejectedly with Szymon to the door. As soon as they had stepped outside, the door closed abruptly behind them.

"I think it went reasonably well under the circumstances," Szymon slurred quickly, trying to inject a spin of optimism into their failed attempt to communicate with the Professor.

Sallina slowly raised her head, forlorn.

"How can you possibly tell me that, Szymon? This has been an utter disaster. With Professor Tinzy unable to remember who he is, we're all doomed. Surely you must know what's at stake here, even as a junior Unimage."

Feeling lower than she had ever felt in her life (which was pretty low, as she had never felt so low before), she slouched off down the corridor. Szymon hesitated, then followed her, though he wasn't as concerned.

What neither of them realized at the time was that as soon as Professor Tinzy had shut the door, he suffered another debilitating attack. His face once again grew incredibly pale as his cheeks reddened, and he froze up like an ancient statue. Professor Tinzy found himself standing still by the door, unable to animate himself to move or even twitch a muscle, although inside he was gasping for air to fill his empty lungs. Then, a momentary sharp intake of oxygen allowed him once again to breathe, and he slowly hobbled over to the table, where he tried to pick up his phone.

As he lifted the phone receiver and held it to his ear, he accidentally dropped it as his fingers froze once again, and he stumbled and fell back into his seat. Clinging to the arm rests for dear life, barely able to move, he tried in vain to retrieve the phone receiver but gave up and concentrated on taking a few more deep breaths of air as he tried to keep himself alive. There was something terribly wrong with him; he was an extremely ill human, and he knew right then that he should see his doctor straightaway.

Then he realised, even a doctor wouldn't be able to help him, and he had to be taken to the nearest hospital for immediate attention and treatment, or who knew what might happen. And in the darkest recesses of his mind, he felt there was something lurking that was important and that he had to do, and while he didn't know what this thing was, he couldn't let go of it. No, it was truly so important, a matter of life and death; but no matter how hard he tried, he couldn't figure out what it was.

Professor Tinzy had no idea why he was feeling so unwell. This was not the first time that one of these attacks had happened; only now, they were occurring more regularly. Every time, he would feel like he was on the verge of dying, yet at the same time he knew he wasn't, and somehow his breath and then his movement would return. It was a very peculiar feeling, but who knew if any of these attacks could end up being his last, and that he might never breathe or move again?

To add insult to injury, he also had these two strange students—one claiming absurdly that she was a unicorn princess—both bothering him when he was in such a fragile state of existence. He could not make any sense of it. Giving up on his attempts to find reason, he looked over at the papers he still needed to grade and let out a quiet moan. All he had to do was to reach out to that phone and call for help. He had to focus and find that last reserve of energy to cry out for someone to

come to his aid, or he would never forgive himself for not
having worked out what he was brought here to do. Something
that he simply couldn't recall.

Chapter 5

About an hour later, Princess Sallina had made her way back to her home on the edge of Doberry. She entered the small, cozy cottage, which was tucked away down a narrow pathway and partially obscured by trees.

"Is that you, my dear?" she heard Margaret call out as she made her way down the corridor.

"Yes, it's only me." Sallina entered the kitchen to find Margaret busily preparing supper.

Margaret was a short, skinny woman, and in fact she and Sallina were almost the same height. Margaret was in her late sixties in human years, and from what Sallina could glean, she had led a colourful life. Margaret had once been married and had a child of her own, but in her late twenties, she had suffered a nervous breakdown. When she returned to her family some years later, she found that she had lost them. Her husband had remarried, and her own child was disinterested in her.

This had troubled Margaret deeply, but there was nothing she could do, because in those days she hadn't the fortitude to fight for those things she cared about the most.

"Hello, my dear. Where have you been?"

"Oh, here and there. I had to meet up with someone after school, and then I was chatting with this boy for a while."

"Oh, chatting with a boy. Who is he? Anyone I know?"

"No, someone I met recently. He's nobody, just a friendly boy I came across. Nobody important."

Princess Sallina did not know why she was openly lying to Margaret, who had been nothing but kind to her since their paths crossed so unexpectedly in the leaf-strewn forest.

Margaret had been enjoying a leisurely amble through the woods with the aid of her walking stick, carefree and at peace with the world, enjoying the fresh air and the wide-open space, when she suddenly came to an abrupt stop. Something wasn't right.

Ahead of her lay a pile of leaves near some bushes, forming an unnatural mound. She took a few careful strides forward and looked down. She was just about to poke her walking stick at the pile of leaves when she detected what looked like fingers sticking out from the bundle. Even more alarmingly, the fingers seemed to be stirring. Then she heard a cough coming from within.

She stood there, completely startled, as a face appeared and a girl sat up, the leaves falling away by her side. Wiping a few remnants of leaf from her face, she stared at Margaret blankly, her dusty, tanned face still partially covered with mud and moss. She wriggled some more, and her bare feet appeared. She seemed surprised, which struck Margaret as odd.

From Margaret's viewpoint, the only truly odd thing about the girl she'd found was that she seemed not to be wearing any clothes! Margaret's first reaction was to take off her jacket and pass it to her. The girl got unsteadily to her feet and put the jacket on as she kept her eyes locked with the older woman's.

Margaret hadn't been exactly sure what to say. If anything, the girl looked like she was in a mild state of shock. But there was something so warm and inviting in those pretty eyes looking at her that she felt any potential fear and uncertainty simply evaporate.

"Eh, are you alright, my dear?"

The girl—who was of course Princess Sallina—cleared her throat with a sharp, raspy cough. "Help me, please… Ehm. Can you tell me where I am?"

As Sallina spoke, Margaret noticed a beautiful silver necklace lying close by the girl's feet. Princess Sallina noticed only the sun shining through the trees and took a few cautious steps towards it, as if there was some magic in its bright radiance. As she did, she passed right by her necklace. Margaret stooped to retrieve it with her walking stick. She turned towards Sallina, holding it, but Sallina continued walking toward the bright sunlight, completely unaware of what Margaret had found.

Then Sallina began running towards the bright sun, its rays of light flickering as she kept looking upward. She extended her arms above her head, as if trying to reach out and catch the sun there in the bright sky. Somewhat bemused by her exuberance,

Margaret quickly pocketed the necklace and hurried after the young woman.

"Wait, don't leave. Do you know where you're heading, my dear?"

There was no response as Margaret tried her best to catch up, but she was no match for the youthful exuberance of the Princess.

Margaret spoke urgently. "Stop, let me help you. I can help you find yourself; I know you are feeling confused, and you must be scared."

Sallina stopped and turned towards Margaret. "I'm not confused. I'm feeling amazing."

"Tell me, do you know who you are?" Margaret asked her.

"I think I'm lost," Sallina replied. "I do not remember coming to this incredible place, but I do so much like being here in the forest. I have always liked being in the forest since I was very little. It must be my favourite place in the entire world. I don't know how I know this, but I do."

"Oh, this is comforting to know. Well, you are safe here with me, dear girl. And I will help you if I can. You are welcome to come back home with me. You can rest and clean yourself up. Would you like to do that?"

"Home," Sallina muttered. "Yes, it would be good to go back home and make myself clean. I think I'm a bit of a mess."

Margaret stepped up closer to Sallina and opened her arms. She hugged Sallina, who just stood there, not sure how to react. Slowly, Princess Sallina's arms circled Margaret and hugged her back, and somehow, this was a very comforting experience for both her and the friendly older lady.

At her house, Margaret gently tended to Sallina, giving her food and trying to find out how she had ended up lost in the forest. Initially, Princess Sallina didn't know what to say, so she said nothing.

That was okay with Margaret, for she had been used to regular emotional and physical drama in her past. Having gone through so many things herself, she had at one point been a mental health worker at an institute where extremely ill people were given constant care. Often, patients were both mentally and physically unwell and needed 24/7 support. She was now retired, having given so much of herself in all her years of service, and she instinctively knew when not to probe too much into the lives of emotionally fragile people. She presumed Sallina had suffered some kind of traumatic experience that might have led to her partial state of amnesia.

Margaret, being a white human, also realized that looking after a dark-skinned child might draw some unwanted attention, but she had decided the moment she saw Sallina that this was not going to become an issue in helping out the poor thing.

So, gradually over a couple of weeks, they formed a close bond, and increasingly the difference in colour between Margaret and Sallina no longer existed in Margaret's mind. All she saw was the daughter she never had. Finally, there was a child in the world that she could help to look after and take good care of.

Margaret had managed to get Sallina enrolled at Doberry School after having a private word with a good friend of hers who worked in a senior administrative capacity there. She had managed to get Sallina enlisted for the new term without being asked too many questions, having explained to her friend that it was of utmost importance that not too much about Sallina's previous life be disclosed due to her difficult and unpleasant past. Margaret was fortunate that her administrative friend had been an orphan and was incredibly sympathetic to the difficult situation, given that she was putting herself at great risk by enrolling Sallina with what she knew to be false records.

Margaret knew that in the longer term, the day would most likely come where the awkward questions would be asked and she herself would be forced to confront the reality of Sallina's mysterious and unknown origin, but she felt for the time being, it was probably best to let Sallina work things out in her own good time.

"A word of caution to you if I may, my dear. If you walk around looking terribly lost and confused, then some people will start to wonder whether you belong here. And as for chatting with the boys… well, I can't stop you from doing this, as it's a perfectly natural thing for growing-up girls to do, but you mustn't trust anyone who you meet, at least not until you get to know them a lot better. This always takes time, from my experience in such matters. Who knows what this young man seeks from you?"

"Oh, I have a pretty good idea of what he seeks from me," Princess Sallina said. "We share similar things, you know, in terms of our unusual identities, and I believe he seeks a kindred companionship."

This piqued Margaret's interest. "Oh, really? That's rather astute of you to say. Then tell me, how will he find this companionship with you? I thought you couldn't remember much about where you came from or your past life."

"Yes, I don't remember much," she lied. "But you know, Margaret, sometimes one can get a distinct feeling that one already knows a person well from somewhere, even if one doesn't yet know much about them. It's like there's this mystical bond that was meant to be, and all that needed to happen was for us to cross paths and enter into each other's lives."

"I know precisely what you mean," Margaret found herself murmuring, a sincere smile forming on her face as she fondly caressed Sallina's hair. "It was the same when I first saw you. You were the daughter I never had, and I knew intuitively that I had to look after you and find some way to protect you from whatever it was out there that brought you to me in such a vulnerable state."

"Thank you so very much, Margaret. I really don't know what I'd have done without you there helping me when I needed to find myself a friend. In fact, you are so much more than a friend to me; I feel you are family."

They hugged each other tightly, just like a mother and daughter, although in reality they were human and royal unicorn! But this didn't matter. They were both aware of how natural this mysterious bond seemed, as if it was meant to be all along, and grateful.

The flood of memories from the forest soon vanished from Margaret's mind as she held Sallina tightly in her arms. She was so incredibly fortunate to have found her, Margaret thought, and how terrible it would be to have to one day let her go. Who indeed was this lovely girl she had befriended and taken in as one of her own? And what was her unfortunate story? She dared not let her mind wander too far, as in her heart, she still hoped that she would never, ever need to one day find out about Sallina's mysterious past.

"Margaret," Sallina suddenly blurted. "Did I have something important on me when you found me in the forest that day?"

Margaret took a short step back and eyed the young lady with concern as well as curiosity. She wondered what had triggered the question. Had some part of Sallina's memory returned? Or was it just a short recollection of her time in the forest, with little understanding of who she was and what she had been before? Was it something to do with her meeting this boy earlier on in the day that had triggered it? Perhaps the meeting had sparked her memory and she was now looking for something important to her, an item she couldn't yet place as she did not mention it by name.

Margaret remembered holding the silver necklace in her hand.

"Oh, yes," she found herself telling Princess Sallina, almost without thinking. "I had nearly forgotten all about it. There was indeed something I found lying by you in the forest that day."

Margaret left the room, returning moments later. She opened her palm to reveal a silver necklace with an ornate star encrusted with shiny little objects that may have been diamonds. She had of course assumed that these diamonds were fake. Little did she know that they were real, or the true value of the necklace in her hand.

She handed the necklace to Sallina. Sallina studied it intently, engrossed by what she saw. She knew what it was and how important it was to her, but she couldn't let Margaret know anything about it. In fact, she couldn't let Margaret know an awful lot of things, including who and what she really was. Sallina was certain that Margaret wouldn't be able to comprehend how different she was from anyone else.

"Thank you, Margaret," she said. "For looking after this for me. You don't know how much it means to me. It's of great importance and immeasurable value."

Margaret gave her a small smile, one that showed she cared about how Sallina felt about her necklace, despite harbouring concerns about the potential consequences of what this object might trigger in the young lady's mind. Margaret couldn't hide from the fact that she was afraid of Sallina's concealed memories and what secrets were yet to be revealed. She couldn't help but feel these were dark and mysterious memories that would somehow drive her foster daughter away from her and her cottage, and back to wherever it was she had come from.

Margaret really didn't like feeling that way, as ultimately, she wanted only what was best for Sallina, but she was afraid that one day she would lose this young lady for whom she already had a very deep and precious love and a maternal urge to keep as her own.

With this thought, there arose the sadness that comes from losing something so valuable in one's life. She let the sad thought go, as she knew that no good would come from hanging on to a desire for something she could never truly possess. This wasn't just something she alone felt, as she was wise enough to know that every parent who has ever brought up a child had to face this bitter truth at some point. Like so many harmful things in life, the only solution was to let go and move on. Sallina was only a borrowed treasure who had appeared from nowhere and, for a while at least, lit up her life.

Chapter 6

The next day, Princess Sallina stood outside Doberry School. Everything around her seemed to be different. It wasn't the rain falling onto her adolescent face, which she steadfastly ignored, or the looming dark clouds hovering above, which looked intent on unleashing their fury at any moment. Nor was it the constant swarming of human students scurrying about frantically like ants with their silly umbrellas and hats, trying to avoid getting soaked on this typical rainy English day.

She recalled how Margaret had told her that a wise man once asked, 'Why do humans try so hard to avoid a few drops of rain coming down from the sky and then go home and jump into the bath?' Sallina had given this puzzle some careful thought, and the only answer she could find was that humans appeared to care more for their clothes than they did for themselves, but somehow it didn't make any sense, or did it?

The difference between today and yesterday was the feeling of reassurance Sellina experienced as she subconsciously clasped the valuable necklace in her pocket. The necklace was a deep connection with her past and who she really was, and it reminded her of her vital purpose and why she was there: to seek out Professor Tinzy and, with his help, obtain the precious Pinny that their people back on Starpoint so desperately needed.

It was a daunting challenge, but with the necklace now back in her possession, she felt more confident that this royal mission could have a chance of succeeding.

She was reflecting on the perilous situation all unicorns were in, when she saw him— Szymon—in his school uniform, casually walking towards the school entrance, with no hat or umbrella to shield him from the rain.

"Szymon!" she shouted, hoping he would hear her through the pounding rain. "Szymon, wait for me!"

He turned slowly to face her as she rushed toward him, and together, they stood to the side to let the other rain-drenched students through. Both of them were getting soaked by the falling raindrops, but neither was too bothered by this.

"Hello, Prin—I mean, Sallina. You okay?"

"Oh, yes, I'm good, thank you." She beamed. "I've found it. I had it. And I've got it on me."

Szymon looked at her, befuddled.

"What do you mean, 'it'?" He had no idea what in the world she was talking about.

She pulled out the Starpoint necklace from her pocket and held it out to him. The star pendant glowed with a bluish light. Szymon's eyes lit up; he was instantly mesmerized.

"This is my magic! With this, I can make magic work here. With this, we can perhaps get the Professor to remember who he really is."

Szymon was momentarily dumbstruck. He had heard about this fabled necklace and its supposed super-magical powers but had never seen it. In fact, *most* Starpointers had never seen it. Many even pooh-poohed its existence as nothing but a myth. But here it was, right in front of his eyes. It was real!

He then noticed the blueish glow was generating a few inquisitive looks from some of the passing students.

"You'd better put it away," he mumbled. "I must go now. We can talk about it later."

He turned and hurried off to class, leaving Sallina standing alone in the pouring rain staring after him, somewhat bemused by his offhand attitude toward the necklace.

*****

By afternoon break, the rain had stopped, and the sun was starting to peek through. Sallina was once again standing by herself when she caught sight of Szymon across the concourse and shyly waved to him. He locked his eyes onto hers momentarily, then he turned and silently hurried away. Confused, she decided to follow.

Szymon was jogging alongside the school field when he took a sudden right turn and headed towards the entrance to the art block. Sallina continued to pursue him. She entered the building. Inside, she looked for him down the corridor but couldn't see him anywhere. In fact, the corridor was completely empty. A few seconds later, two boys of similar age walked past, but they were preoccupied with their own discussions and took no notice of her.

Sallina checked a few of the classrooms, but the doors were locked. There was no sign of Szymon anywhere. What was he up to, she wondered? She really couldn't understand why he was avoiding her.

The shrill clang of the school bell made Sallina jump, and she quickly headed off to her next class.

Szymon's odd behaviour occupied Sallina's mind until the end of the school day. As the school emptied out, she looked around for Szymon again, desperate now to continue their earlier conversation about the necklace and how she could potentially use her magic to help Professor Tinzy perhaps remember who he really was. But just like at break time, Szymon was nowhere to be seen.

Then she had a strange hunch.

She at last found him at the bike-storage area. But she was too late; he was already off and pedalling.

Sallina sighed deeply and set off in pursuit.

She covered the distance quickly, exiting the main school gate and continuing to run as Szymon sped away, oblivious to being followed. He took a sharp left at the end of the road and Sallina gave chase as fast as her two legs could carry her.

Suddenly, something prompted Szymon to glance over his shoulder. Luckily, Sallina was alert enough to take evasive action, jumping quickly behind a parked Luton white van.

Moments later, Sallina poked her head out from the side of the van, but Szymon was gone. Breaking her cover, she ran down the street and turned sharply to the right at an intersection…just in time to see Szymon in the distance. Head down, Sallina sprinted as fast as she could…

BEEEEEEPPPP!

Sallina sprang back, stopping in her tracks as an oncoming car screeched to a momentary halt, the driver glowering at her before continuing on her way. Heart pounding, Sallina took a deep breath and set off once more in pursuit of Szymon.

At the end of the road, Sallina turned to find herself in a quiet residential cul-de-sac. Not far away, she noticed Syzmon's bike set on its side by the front of a semi-detached house surrounded by hedges. With no one looking, Sallina ducked through onto the path and, crouching down, she approached the house cautiously. Her heart beating nervously, Sallina popped up and peered tentatively through the front window. The room beyond was dark. There didn't seem to be anyone inside.

Szymon, meanwhile, upon entering the house, had headed straight for the living room, ignoring the small, furry dog that was yapping around his feet. At one corner of the living room, a large, circular object sat concealed under a thick purple blanket. Szymon lifted the blanket to reveal a black, crystal orb resting on a small pedestal.

With all his might, he lifted the orb off the pedestal by a few centimetres and moved it towards the middle of the room. Then he disappeared and reappeared with a bucketful of water. He muttered to himself while spreading the water around the orb in a circle, forming a puddle on the room's wooden floor. The small dog started running around the orb in a circle. Annoyed now, Szymon shooed him away.

Szymon once again left the room. When he returned, he closed the curtains at front and back.

Outside, Sallina was moving silently along the side of the house to see where it took her. She turned the corner to find a wrought-iron gate with a lock on it. She moaned to herself as she realized she couldn't go any further, but she wasn't one to surrender easily. She pulled the star necklace from her pocket and held it in her hand. She fixed her eyes on the necklace, focusing her mind. Within seconds, the necklace began to glow. It was as if she was unleashing powerful energy into it.

"Please, this must work," she muttered to herself.

She gently rubbed the star and started to hum to herself her magical words, "Help me oh shiny star, set a lock free for me, and conjure me oh shiny star, a magical key."

The necklace continued to glow and emit its peculiar bluish light.

"Come on, you must work for me! You've never let me down before." She shook the necklace, hoping that this might add something to the incantation, but absolutely nothing happened.

Once again, she repeated the words. "Help me oh shiny star, set a lock free for me, and conjure me, oh shiny star, a magic key."

The necklace continued to glow, the blue light growing even stronger. Yet it seemed that nothing much was happening, and her attempt to summon her magic was a failure. Sallina bowed her head in despair, a tear forming in the corner of her eye. The tear fell and landed on the pendant and was immediately absorbed by the radiant blue light. Suddenly, the blue light shot out towards the lock on the gate, and the lock turned itself as if it was doing it of its own volition. A moment later, the lock opened.

Sallina cried out in excitement, then put her hand over her mouth, hoping her yelp had gone unheard. She waited a moment and then put the necklace back in her pocket, happy her presence had not been detected. She carefully pushed open the gate. It didn't squeak. She stepped through and edged around to the back of the house.

Chapter 7

Princess Sallina came across a small, well-manicured garden, along with a small patio area near the back windows and rear door.

She headed to the back window and peered in. The curtains were drawn, but she could see through a narrow gap into what was apparently the living room. There she saw Szymon circling the orb and waving his hands strangely up and down. What was he doing, she wondered? Especially as he was purposely treading in the puddles of water that lay around the orb and the nearby bucket.

As she watched, the orb began to glow and turn from black to a bright yellow. Something was clearly happening to the orb, and she realized that her pendant wasn't the only item that was showing it could activate magic on this strange planet called Earth.

To make what she was witnessing even more compelling, she saw a head begin to appear on the top of the orb—it looked like it was pushing itself out from within. It slowly rose as if it was trapped and desperately wanted to free itself from the orb's confines. As the head pushed itself higher by a few centimetres at a time, the orb also seemed to react—it lifted off the ground, the water around it evaporating into steam.

After almost a minute of this to-ing and fro-ing, the head straining to the left and then right, the orb had risen to almost at the same height as Szymon's face. Then, for some strange reason, the face circled around the orb in a mechanical motion as if it was looking all around the room, and Sallina recognized exactly who it was—Unimage Konstanty! She had seen him a couple of times before.

He turned his head completely around as he looked towards the back of the room, and for a moment she was terribly afraid he had spotted her. But it seemed as though he hadn't. Sallina breathed a sigh of relief and continued to spy through the window and watch as the face of Szymon's dad continued to swivel around slowly until he was back to facing Szymon once again. They were now talking to each other, and she really wished she could hear what they were saying.

She took her necklace out of her pocket and held it in her palm. Once again it began to glow. She gripped the necklace and muttered some words that would be incomprehensible to anyone else. She then put her ear against the window to try and listen in on their conversation.

The necklace once again emitted its strange blue light, and this time the light travelled in almost a split second directly towards her ear. Her ear started to glow blue… and then something even odder happened. She found that her ear was expanding outwards, stretching right onto the glass of the window. It then managed to attach itself to the glass and became part of it.

She didn't know how to explain what had happened, but somehow, she was now connected to the glass window, and, more importantly, she was also able to clearly hear the conversation taking place between Szymon and his father.

"You've bothered me again at a very inconvenient time. What is it? Be quick," Konstanty demanded.

"Sorry, Father, but I have some important news. You know how yesterday I told you that the Princess is here in Doberry? Well, she also has the Starpoint pendant with her. She carries it around her neck."

This apparently took Unimage Konstanty by surprise… as well as Princess Sallina, who was listening outside the window. She wasn't at all pleased, and now listened even more intently for what else might be occurring behind her back.

"Really… that's incredibly odd, for her to be in possession of such a valuable item," Unimage Konstanty declared. "I didn't even know it had been found by anyone, let alone a girl. The last I heard, it had been lost and nobody knew where it was. It is a far too valuable an object to be left with such a…young, dim-witted girl. I know she's royal, but really. Are you sure it was the necklace? Are you absolutely certain?"

"I swear it. She has it here in Doberry; I saw it with my own two eyes. And she says it can help her cast her magic, despite the absence of widespread magical enablement anywhere in this land. She can cast spells."

"But that's impossible. How can she cast her magic?" Unimage Konstanty questioned. "Except for the minimal magic allowing us to communicate, you have been unable to activate any magic in that forsaken place."

He went on, "We know magic on Earth is almost completely blocked, for reasons that I am unable to understand. I suspect it has something to do with the absence of Alicorns to provide enablement, or Pinny. After all, without Pinny and the Alicorns, we too are unable to cast spells anywhere on our world, so perhaps the same principles apply on this place called Earth."

"She claims her magic works by using the natural power of the pendant, Father. Isn't that one of its qualities? That it has the means to cast magic without the aid of Pinny for enablement, and that it is one of only a handful of items that are truly magical by their own nature and can work entirely of their own accord?"

"This really can't be—that would make it incredibly unique. I thought that all inherently magical items had been destroyed or lost several centuries ago, or they were confiscated after the Great War and in almost all cases are beyond reach. They were either hidden or destroyed so that no unicorn could ever use them again to cause a war or bring about any kind of conflict that could be made much worse through magic. Some postulated that the Starpoint necklace might have the ability to cast magic almost anywhere without the aid of Pinny, but nobody in the Council believed this notion. We grew accustomed to believing it was a myth, invented to create an aura of mystery and inspire curiosity when we told these tales to our children. Besides, it has always been a rule of the land that all magic requires enablement."

Szymon didn't know how to respond to his father's rambling thoughts and history lesson as he listened attentively.

"But what if she's right about this pendant? What if she can make her magic work without the assistance of Pinny? It could be incredibly useful to us, don't you think so, Father? For our cause."

Unimage Konstanty was stunned. His son, Szymon, had had an idea! He couldn't quite believe it. He pondered his son's suggestion. Yes, useful the pendant could be, that was certainly true enough. But also, acquiring it would be so incredibly risky. And it wasn't necessarily a good thing if Szymon's tale was indeed true, as someone highly knowledgeable in magic possessing the pendant and able to use magic in that strange land was certain to prove a worthy adversary—not someone for his son to befriend or with whom to search for Pinny.

With such a powerful device in existence—and in Doberry, of all places! —Professor Tinzy and Princess Sallina might find some way to uncover the Pinny and take it back home, where they would be heralded as the true heroes of Starpoint... and not Konstanty, which was his primary intent. The Professor and the Princess... he could see it now, them being lauded everywhere they went for years and years as Starpoint's greatest saviours!

And then where would he be? Where would the cause be? He would be a hapless nobody, with no place back in the Circle, his desire to one day be its greatest leader crushed forever.

On the other hand, thought Unimage Konstanty, *it's a pendant, an object. It doesn't owe its loyalty or allegiance to anyone and can be used by whoever has the means to wield it and understand how it functions. Isn't it simply a case of finding a way to get hold of it for one's own personal needs? Isn't there no better option than to ally it to their greatest of all causes, and make it part of the solution?*

Then the truest words of his precious Circle invaded his waking thoughts.

Only the purest will rule in these fair lands. It shall be sworn and abided by each unicorn alike.

These words were not just a set of ideas—they defined the path he had chosen, the cause he now unquestionably served.

Konstanty's eyes narrowed as a plot began to form in his mind.

He had his son there on that distant world. His son could do his bidding and could find a way to relieve the Princess of her precious pendant so it could be put to a far worthier use: serving him and those who had sworn him allegiance in achieving their goals and ambitions.

"Well, I've thought about it," Unimage Konstanty said calmly. "And I suggest you work closely with the Princess to help Professor Tinzy remember who he really is."

This delighted Szymon, not the least because he was more than a little bit fond of the Princess and had felt odd and uncomfortable when forced to avoid her. His instinct was to spend more time with her, and to earn her trust and friendship.

"I will, sir," Szymon said dutifully. "Does that mean you will let me borrow the remembrance scroll?"

At this point, Sallina was getting quite worked up over what she was hearing. She tried to move herself a bit further along the side of the large window to gain a slightly better view, but much to her surprise, she quickly discovered that her ear was firmly glued onto the glass! Even worse, she managed to accidentally step on a tennis ball and almost lost her footing, but with her ear being so well stuck to the window, she was prevented from tumbling to the ground. However, being held up by one's ear whilst losing one's balance proved to be incredibly painful!

OWWWW, OW, OWWWWWWW, Sallina said to herself, wincing, as she pushed desperately against the glass with her hands, straightening herself up hurriedly to stop her ear from being torn away from the side of her head.

As she settled back into eavesdropping on the conversation between Szymon and his father, she realized she was still the subject of discussion.

Unimage Konstanty looked like he'd been pondering the previous conversation.

"One thing still troubles me greatly about this," he said. "The Princess may find a way to place her consciousness in your head when she attempts to uncover some of those hidden memories of Professor Tinzy's. As you'll need to be in her presence to cast the memory spell using my scroll, your proximity to her and Professor Tinzy when she uses the scroll could accidentally leave you open to her enchantments as well. If she has this window of opportunity to peek into your mind, I do really worry what she may find inside there, as she must not at any time be aware of our intentions and the true purpose of our presence here in Doberry."

"What is she going to find inside my head that is of any real use to her?" asked Szymon.

"Try not to think too deeply about this, my boy. I know how much thinking about things can trouble your thoughts. Let me try and help you deal with it; I'm sure I can figure out a way to turn this to our advantage. But I do worry that she can discover how you and I are collaborating and scheming to recover the Pinny, and how we have been following our Professor Tinzy to see where this quest takes him so that we can take over the mission and come back as the saviours."

Sallina felt her face going red with rage as she carefully listened to these two conspirators colluding right before her eyes. What was worse, she had been inadvertently colluding with them, too! She didn't like what she had been hearing one bit.

And now it became clear why Szymon had been trying so hard to avoid her. Revealing the pendant to him had gotten him flustered. He didn't know what to do and had been awaiting further instructions from his father before engaging in conversation with her.

But one further thing bothered her. How had they found out what the Professor was up to in the first place, and how had both managed to get ahead of her in coming over to Doberry?

There were things here that she couldn't begin to comprehend, and what she had already just found out was frightening enough in itself. What means did Szymon's father have to allow someone like his son to travel to this land? As far as she knew, there existed only the one gateway, and it was a secret that only she and Professor Tinzy knew.

"Of course, there is most likely a logical explanation for this," Sallina muttered to herself.

She began mulling it over. It was entirely possible that Professor Tinzy was not the only person who was aware of the secret of the magic tunnel. Plus, Szymon had been in Doberry for at least some weeks before her, as he seemed to have settled in quite well and knew his way around the place. In fact, she began to wonder whether Szymon or someone else had been here before, and how it was even possible for Szymon to have such a house. So whoever knew about the tunnel and this land had found out about the Professor and his trip to Doberry even before she did.

As she reflected, she realized that something else bothered her about all this. What was she missing?

Why had both Szymon and she managed to avoid losing their memories, when Professor Tinzy had lost track of his past? Did it mean that Unimage Konstanty's memories could also be scrambled if he travelled to Doberry? Perhaps being an adult was the key. She had heard Professor Tinzy mention that going to Earth was a lot safer for children than it was for adults, but she had not quite understood the true meaning of this until now.

Unlike the Unimages, Szymon and she were both still young, and somehow their memories had remained intact following their travel to Doberry, whereas poor Professor Tinzy had completely forgotten who he was. Frequent travelling to Doberry must be hazardous for adults, so what was the use of an adult travelling here if they could not remember their intentions or who they truly were?

"I have it!" Unimage Konstanty blurted exuberantly. "I know how you can protect yourself when this spell is cast! All you need to do is eat carrots, which are similar to a vegetable we often use at home—"

His son gawped, wide-eyed. "Wh-what...? Why? I don't understand why carrots are good for protecting myself from a memory-recovery spell..."

"—when Sallina enables the remembrance scroll. If you do so, she won't be able to read your mind! It's not so much to make the spell effective as that carrots just happen to possess certain properties that protect one's mind from being accessed when the spell is activated."

"What?" said Szymon, again. "Carrots. You must be joking! You know I really hate carrots. But I'm not casting the spell, so why should she be able to access my thoughts?"

"Okay, let's get this straight. I'm not asking you whether you like them or not. They are meant mainly for your personal protection... and you must do exactly as I tell you! When a remembrance spell is cast, those close by are vulnerable to having their minds read, and that's just the way it is," Konstanty said sternly.

"Must I do this terrible thing, Father? I really don't like them."

"Yes, it is your duty to follow my instructions. For goodness' sake, they're just a vegetable. And they're good for you!"

His father's words were no encouragement at all. Szymon absolutely loathed the orangey things. Just thinking about them made him retch! Now his own father was instructing him to eat them. YUCK! It wasn't that he was physically allergic to them or that he could become sick from ingesting revolting, raw carrots, he just detested their taste.

"It's either you eat some carrots… or I will not give you the remembrance scroll to pass on to the Princess so you can fulfil your task."

Realizing his outburst had been maybe a tad too harsh, Unimage Konstanty tried to adopt a softer demeanour.

"Besides, my son. We have no other option," he said in his best impersonation of fatherliness.

Szymon pondered the predicament. There seemed to be no way out. He would most likely have to chew those blasted, horrible-tasting carrots, or he would not be able to face Sallina and join up with her to help Professor Tinzy remember who he really was.

"Father, I was thinking. Why must I be there when this spell is cast? Can I not simply give her the remembrance scroll and let her get on with it?"

"NO!" Konstanty barked, infuriated. "Are you such a dim-witted fool, boy? You are charged with the ability to read the remembrance scroll, and this requires your personal presence. I cannot charge her with it as she is not here for me to equip her with the means, is she? We don't want her to know that we are talking to each other, nor anything about our current plans. I'm still hoping that the last remaining bit of Pinny will give me the means to charge you with the scroll, given the sheer distance over which the spell has to be cast, through a long and winding tunnel that goes through who-knows-where to get to you over there.

"Once you are properly charged, you will be the only person holding onto the magic, and all Princess Sallina will do is enable the spell with her magical pendant. She may have the means to find the door, but YOU are the one who can open it. She will see nothing that you won't see first, and nothing she can do will be without YOUR control. This is about who is really in charge. Do you understand now?"

Szymon nodded meekly, as he knew his father was right.

It was at this precise moment that Sallina heard the annoying sound of yapping.

The door to the living room had been opened, and Szymon's dog bounded into the room, circling the orb and barking away like crazy. Konstanty stared at the irksome four-legged pet and Szymon could see his father was clearly unhappy with the animal's interference as the dog kept going around in circles, yapping away like crazy.

What Sallina didn't know was that Szymon's dog had in fact previously been an apprentice of Unimage Konstanty called Yiparthur, who the Unimage had managed to transform into a dog after the younger man had taken so many trips that he'd forgotten who he was. In doing so, Konstanty had in fact saved 'Yippy' from the terrible fate of being lost in this world, and he'd instructed Szymon to keep the dog permanently at the house.

Previously, in the periods when nobody was around, Yippy had managed to survive on his own, as he had still retained some human abilities that had been transposed from his even-wiser unicorn self. As time went by, though, Yippy lost pretty much all knowledge of his unicorn self—or even of his period of being a human—and reverted to being just a dog.

But, on occasion, Yippy briefly recalled his former self, and it was in moments like this that he'd run around wildly and bark away, as this was his way of attempting to warn the world that something very dangerous and wrong was about to happen. But Yippy didn't know exactly what it was that was wrong, or who he was. He just ran around in circles and barked like mad.

"Shut your stupid dog up! I thought the little beast had been securely caged outside. I can't stand dealing with these domestic pets!"

Konstanty had long since forgotten who Yippy once was, as he was so preoccupied with the many important things taking place or about to take place. Something as trivial as a former apprentice whom he had chosen to treat in such a derisory manner scarcely even entered his waking thoughts.

"Umm, the door was closed, Father. Somehow, he managed to open it. Yippy, be quiet or Father will be very angry with you—which, trust me, you do not want him to be."

They both watched as the dog made his way towards the curtains, heading toward Princess Sallina. Konstanty's head swivelled round to see where the dog was off to. Yippy was now barking wildly at the curtain.

Sallina panicked. The dog clearly knew that someone was there. She grabbed hold of her necklace and started to mutter her incantation as quickly as she could. Her ear was still stuck rigidly to the glass, and she needed to invoke the magic spell to set herself free from it. She whispered, fearing Szymon and his father might hear. There was something about Unimage Konstanty that terrified her, and she was worried about what he would do if she was discovered snooping on their private conversation.

She could see Szymon approaching the curtain, his feet visible beneath it on the other side of the glass patio door. Yippy was still barking furiously.

The blue from the necklace shot off a narrow beam to her ear, and for a few moments her ear glowed bright blue.

Her heart racing, she gasped as she saw Szymon's hand grab the side of the curtain. But just in the moment that he drew back the curtain, Sallina managed to break free from the glass windowpane.

Szymon pulled back the curtains to find nobody there. Yippy, he thought, had been barking at nothing more than the empty garden at night.

"There's no one about, Yippy. Look for yourself, you silly dog. Father is going to be very cross with you."

Yippy sighed and looked up at his master, wagging his tail. He certainly knew that someone had just been there. In fact, Yippy could smell Sallina's presence as her scent lingered on, so he continued to bark and wag his tail.

Szymon had no time for such foolish games. He returned to the orb, where his father was waiting. The orb was fading fast, and he immediately became worried he might not be able to finish his conversation with his father, though Konstanty was trying hard to maintain the connection.

The orb began to glow brightly once again, and this time he saw an object sticking out of the orb, heading in his direction. Szymon cautiously reached for it as he realized this was the scroll. It was bright yellow as well but faded once he pulled it out of the orb.

"Now that I've given it to you," bellowed Konstanty, "be very careful with my valuable scroll because I will want it back! And don't forget to munch on those carrots constantly when she casts her spell!"

Konstanty's face began to fade again, his rasping voice becoming muffled and distant. A few moments later, his image had virtually disappeared, and the radiance of the scroll was all but gone.

Szymon now held onto the scroll and watched as the orb twisted itself around and sought to re-join the pedestal. Once the orb was back on the pedestal, the glow completely disappeared, and the sphere sat there just as it had before.

Chapter 8

Terrified by what she had just witnessed, Princess Sallina ran from the house as quickly and silently as she could, not daring to look back, then sprinted down the road. Only when she had got to the end of the street, panting heavily, did she peer round the corner to see if Szymon was following. To her great relief, the son of Unimage Konstanty was nowhere to be seen. She had managed to flee from the window and the pesky Yippy just in time!

Leaning against the wall, Sallina gathered her composure and calmed her breathing, reflecting on what she had overheard. This reflection soon turned to resentment. It was evident her new friend at Doberry School was no friend at all and was in fact a spy who had been sent by his father to snoop on her and Professor Tinzy, to satisfy their own yearning to secure the sacred Pinny and bring it back to their homeland!

She would never be able to trust Szymon with anything ever again, as clearly, he came across as weak-minded and completely beholden to his father and his ambitious desires. What exactly those were, of course, she didn't know the details of, but Unimage Konstanty was strong and determined, and he seemed to be after the Pinny more for his own gain than for the good of the herd.

Then she started to think a little more carefully. What did Szymon and his father really want with the Pinny? Did Unimage Konstanty already have plans for Szymon to somehow get hold of the Pinny and bring it to Starpoint and then pass it on to his father?

Surely, none of this mattered, as right now who would get the credit was trivial. All that mattered was that they could find a way to get hold of enough Pinny to power the Alicorns and generate sufficient magic to stop the giant meteor from destroying their planet. In the face of such a calamity, what did it matter who stood at the front of the line in trying to save the day? Why would anyone be so determined to seek status and credit at any cost when faced with such a terrible situation?

Staying alive ought to be a strong enough motivation for fixing the terrible mess they were in, even for those who were so self-centred that they didn't think much about the wellbeing of others around them.

Or was there another, hidden reason? Did the great Unimage Konstanty not care at all about the threat his home world faced?

A strange thought crept into her mind, and she was surprised that it had even found some way to exist, as it was a dark thought and not the usual kind of thought she would have.

What if there really was no meteor? What if it had all been made up for some other intention that was not yet apparent? No, that couldn't be it. If someone had made it up, surely, they would have been found out.

But, what if it was all a façade—an invention, a hoax, a fictitious threat made up to scare all the wise Unimages and the Council of elders? All created by Konstanty so that he could search for Pinny, hoping the Professor would lead him to its source? Had Konstanty somehow orchestrated the whole thing, using dark magic to fool everyone—including the Professor—into believing this made-up threat? Was Unimage Konstanty following a hunch that this threat could motivate the Professor to take terrible risks to seek out a source of Pinny?

It was such a crazy idea, but what if this was true? If there existed no real threat, then neither she nor Professor Tinzy needed to be in Doberry. There was enough Pinny back home to keep Starpoint ticking for some time, and someone else could eventually figure out a way to obtain some more as supplies dwindled further.

And what was going to happen to poor old Professor Tinzy? It looked like everyone wanted to get hold of some Pinny except for him, because he had unfortunately forgotten who he really was. Oh! What was she to do? The more she wondered about it, the greater her confusion and anxiety grew. She calmed herself down, and then she thought about it another way.

She remembered the Professor once telling her not to let doubt creep into her mind. All dangers could be easily dismissed by those who actively deny them, for whatever reasons they may have. Perhaps they too are afraid deep down, and rather than acknowledge the danger facing them, they pretend it doesn't exist until it's too late to do something useful about it. There are also times when a truly powerful external threat doesn't suit those seeking to alter the ways of others to satisfy their own wants and needs, as they prefer to make up their own fictitious dangers that can blind the weak from discovering the truth. These fictitious dangers are ones they feel they can more easily control and manipulate to suit their own purposes.

If the Professor believed that the meteor was real, she too believed it, because she trusted him above everyone else in the world.

"Hey!" came a voice from nearby. "Are you okay?"

Sallina froze, fearing it might be Szymon—or even Unimage Konstanty—or who knew who! Then she bolted without looking to see who had called out to her,

Margaret's words resounding in her head:

Never trust anyone you don't really know.

Sprinting now as fast as she could, she could feel herself transforming into her original being. One moment she was human. The next, she was a proud, royal unicorn galloping along at full and terrific speed on four legs. Of course, it was all a trick of her imagination… or was it? She felt terribly confused and so afraid… yet everything seemed so real, as if she were both human and unicorn at the same time!

The road ahead looked empty for the present, and she was truly grateful that nobody could see her running about if she was transforming from one form into another as some kind of wild, misshapen beast.

"Who am I really?" she found herself asking as she ran. "Am I a human or am I a unicorn? I don't know what I truly am anymore."

After a few minutes of intense thought, she decided to keep her views focused on what she directly knew to be real. She had to believe that the meteor was in fact genuine, and that Professor Tinzy knew the difference between a genuine calamity about to befall their citizens and some illusory magic that had been cast to mislead him and so many others.

In the long history of unicorns, ignoring a big problem had almost always led to may more problems springing up all around, and not facing something that was so dangerous was the worst thing one could do. Professor Tinzy was highly proficient and extremely knowledgeable in the ways of magic, and even Unimage Konstanty would find it exceedingly difficult to fool him. This dark thought that had just emerged within her must have been driven by her fear more than any kind of logic. Thus, Sallina decided to seek refuge in her intellect and trust in the Professor and not get carried away by strange and sinister possibilities.

There was also the matter of the prophecy of the scroll of Tinzin. The scroll had never been wrong before, and the prophecy had been examined not by just Professor Tinzy, but by most of the other Unimages when it had been reviewed in the great Unimage Library, which was accessible only to a chosen few. She didn't know much about the prophecy, but she did know the Professor had once mentioned a threat that would endanger all unicorns, and it would come from the stars. This threat was no doubt the oncoming approach of the meteor. Still, could they all have been fooled?

No, stop it, she thought. *Let these doubts go away. Cast them aside. Get on with the task I have been sent here to accomplish.*

For now, she simply had to find some way to help poor Professor Tinzy regain his true identity, and with the Professor's help, find a way to get hold of some precious Pinny and bring it back safely to Starpoint. Only now their mission had become more complicated and challenging, because hot on their heels were Szymon and his scheming father, seeking, in who knew what ways, to interfere with their plans.

But Princess Sallina had never been any kind of quitter, and she knew that Professor Tinzy still desperately needed her help. And after all, she did have one advantage—the Starpoint necklace. And Szymon had the remembrance scroll. Despite how she felt about Szymon and his father, she knew that for now at least she had to find a way to work with Szymon so they could, as a first step, free Professor Tinzy's memories and help him recollect that he was a great and venerable unicorn.

Calmer now, Princess Sallina continued on her way. A lone car drove past her, and to whoever it was behind the wheel, she appeared to be nothing more than a young lady who was making her way home from school. Nothing unusual, nothing at all. But to anyone who knew what was going on, the young woman was anything but what she appeared, and on her shoulders lay the burden of protecting all those in the home, so far away, that she loved.

Chapter 9

The next day Princess Sallina was back in Professor Walters' classroom, listening to a math lecture. Walters appeared quite excited about his chosen topic, going on about the important mathematical properties of triangles.

"Note that we classify triangles according to the lengths of their sides." Then he sneezed. "Excuse me. An equilateral triangle is a regular polygon… AKKKISHHOOO!" Another explosive, unexpected sneeze. "Excuse me."

Professor Walters headed over to his jacket and pulled out a white hanky.

Sitting by the window—her recently selected favourite spot—Sallina looked out, as she often did in all her classes, and was surprised to see an excited Szymon standing nearby, waving at her. She didn't bother to react but looked back only to see Professor Walters sneeze once again.

She knew she had to wait until recess before she could go out and talk to Szymon. Part of her didn't even want to see him again, but another part of her was glad that he was there. Something about Szymon continued to attract her, but she scarcely gave this matter further thought, because he had proven himself to be a menace to both her and Professor Tinzy's future wellbeing. She wasn't going to trust him even for one second, she reminded herself. He was certainly not her friend.

Patiently, she bided her time while the end of the class approached, and when it did finally arrive, she didn't display signs she was in any hurry to get out. As she casually walked out the door, Szymon, who stood just past the entrance, grabbed her by the shoulder.

"I have to tell you something important. Come here."

Szymon looked worked up. Sallina glanced around at the last few students departing the classroom, since she didn't want Szymon to think he had her undivided attention.

"What is it? Last time I saw you, you purposely ignored me."

"Oh, did I?" said Szymon, taken aback. "I didn't mean to, maybe I didn't notice you at the time. I swear, I would never purposely ignore you. I've got something to tell you, it's hugely important. A terrible thing has happened, and you need to know!"

"What? What terrible thing? You're making me feel worried now." Princess Sallina had no idea what Szymon was about to tell her, so she decided to pay greater attention to what was agitating him.

"It's Professor Tinzy. This morning an ambulance arrived, and it took him away to the hospital."

This unexpected news greatly alarmed Sallina.

"Oh my gosh, no. I hope he's okay. Please tell me that he's alright."

"I don't really know his condition, but I don't think it was life threatening or anything dangerous, but you never know. I also have some good news to share with you."

"Tell me some good news, please," she almost pleaded, trying hard to lift her spirits, which were sinking fast.

Szymon had now managed to get her worked up, so she was eager to hear what he had to say that was positive, as Professor Tinzy being seriously ill was the last thing she wanted to hear.

"The remembrance scroll—I happen to have it available. Do you know what this means for us?"

"You want me to, uh, magically deploy the scroll on Professor Tinzy to see whether he can remember who he is. *Was!*"

"Yes, that's it!" Szymon replied, somewhat surprised as he tried to figure out how she managed to stay one step ahead of him in their conversations. It was as if she knew exactly what was going on in his mind. "The Professor is in a lot of trouble; his memory loss must be affecting his health as well. We have to find a way to help him remember."

"And why is it that you want me to do this now?" Sallina said, trying to play it cool. "Is it because I'm the only other person—well, let's say 'person'—who can help you?"

"Yes, exactly. Well, I cannot cast any magic myself—I don't have the enabler you have dangling around your neck, and my powers don't seem to work here anyway. I'm unable to make any kind of magic work, in fact, but I think you can. What I can do is give you the means to cast your magic so that Professor Tinzy remembers who he really is."

Her plan was working. Szymon was offering her his help. It meant Sallina didn't have to try and persuade him, thankfully. But at that very moment, all she could think about was the irritating and upsetting sight of Szymon discussing with his father their plan to deceive her for their own ends. It still made her feel bitter and disappointed, and she had to fight hard not to show it.

"I'm not sure I can do what you ask of me," Sallina said, suddenly feeling uncertain about what to do. "I'm not confident I can work a spell with another Unimage's device. It's going to be difficult, and it may simply not work."

This took Szymon by surprise, and he took a small step back. "What's happened to you? Don't you realize your necklace affords you incredible powers? You are the only one who has the means to cast your magic as if you're doing this in Starpoint. It's a rare gift that only you have!"

Without even realizing it herself, she nervously started to fidget with her necklace. "I'm feeling kind of thirsty right now. I'd like to take a break."

She was about to turn and head away when she suddenly stopped in her tracks. She held the necklace in her hand, and she felt very alone and helpless. How could she even consider abandoning the Professor at this point? No matter what she felt about Szymon, Unimage Konstanty, and the devious schemes she had good reason to believe that they were up to, she still had to do anything she could to help Professor Tinzy recall who he was.

She sighed and turned to face Szymon.

"Alright, it's worth a try, I suppose," she admitted meekly, letting her gaze catch Szymon's unpleasant stare, which was directed towards her.

"'You suppose.' You suppose... Oh, that's real nice of you, Princess. What's gotten into you?"

Szymon couldn't figure out her sudden change in behaviour and her reluctance to take charge of an incredible opportunity that could help the Professor regain his lost memories. He was completely flummoxed to learn that she was less than willing to attempt to help Professor Tinzy out.

The only possible explanation was that she was afraid, and that deep down this princess was quite a timid person who was a lot less impressive in real life than he'd heard. After all, he didn't really know her all that well, and it was possible that Princess Sallina wasn't the royal unicorn that he thought she was.

She could in fact be nothing more than a coward, he reflected, one who possessed too little confidence in her own abilities. He started to wonder why the Starpoint pendant was being wasted on her. Clearly, she wasn't worthy of such immense power, which could otherwise been put to good use. The pendant should instead have been in the hands of a proper Unimage, someone who could do something constructive with it, rather than clinging around the neck of a frightened young girl.

"I'll need to practice this a little," Sallina said. "I haven't tried out my magic properly in this place, and before I attempt anything as powerful as a remembrance spell, I'd best first practice it on a few simpler things. Don't you think?"

Szymon realized that he must find a way to boost Sallina's self-esteem, which she was clearly lacking in abundance, because without her and that powerful pendant able and willing, he and his father were severely limited in their use of magic in this strange land.

"You shouldn't ever be afraid to use your magic. After school, why don't you come with me? I will show you the scroll and then we can figure this thing out."

It was at that moment they found themselves in the presence of Professor Walters, who had observed them talking to each other just outside his class. He had decided to approach them, and he eyed the young man from head to toe. Before he could say a single word, he sneezed. Luckily his hanky was still in his hand, and he managed to cover up his nose just in time when it blew off.

"Bless you," Szymon blurted out.

"Th-thank you. Look, you two, I want to know what's going on between you. You're acting more than a little suspicious to me."

Szymon was confused. "I don't understand. There's nothing going on between us. We were just talking to each other about something personal."

"I mean… I want you to explain to me what you are doing loitering about outside my classroom. I noticed you earlier—you were distracting my students first by the window and then by hanging around near the doorway during my class. Have you nothing better to do with yourself than to provide an unwelcome distraction?"

Szymon was at a loss for words.

"I suppose you thought I wouldn't notice, but let me tell you, nothing much escapes my attention. I see pretty much everything."

Szymon exchanged puzzled glances with Princess Sallina. Then Professor Walters let out another uncontrollable sneeze. His inability to control his sneezing was starting to annoy Walters, and he couldn't hide it.

"Sir, I can explain," Szymon said hurriedly, trying to get a few words in before Walters sneezed again.

Professor Walters stared directly into Szymon's eyes, as if he were trying to peer deep into his soul. This unnerved Szymon, who tried his best to pretend not to be.

"Go on then, explain away," Walters challenged him.

"Well, it's like this, sir. Today. Eh. Today is Prin—I mean Sallina's—birthday. So, I was asking her how she felt about being older, and what she was planning on doing for her birthday."

"Sorry," Professor Walters replied. "It's her birthday? I didn't know."

Sallina picked up on the clever deception straight away. "Szymon wanted to wish me a happy birthday because he knew that I was all alone. He was waiting for me so he could— give me a present."

She stopped abruptly, feeling as though she had already over-stretched the lie and it was in jeopardy of falling apart.

"Oh, really, I see," Professor Walters retorted, unconvinced. "So, it's Miss Sallina's birthday. Well then, I'll have to make an exception on this occasion. You'd best be gone from here. I don't want you both continuing to loiter about outside my class. I've got some things to be getting on with."

Professor Walters turned, then stopped. "What was the present you were going to give her? You must have it on you, boy."

Szymon looked worried for a moment; he didn't know what to say or do.

Princess Sallina stepped in to alleviate the tension of the situation.

"He's going to show it to me, but it's rather big. You know."

Professor Walters looked surprised. "Big? How so? Are you trying to be funny?"

Szymon then realised what she was alluding to. "Well, sir, if I told her what my present was, it wouldn't be much of a surprise, would it? But it's too big for me to have sitting in my pocket or holding in my hand, so I will be taking her to see it. I'll give you a riddle: it goes round and round and does it twice wherever it goes."

Professor Walters was about to sneeze again, and he decided he had enough of attempting to figure out what was really going on between these two students. Although he was a naturally curious human, he did realise that there was a limit to how intrusive he should be in investigating the affairs of his students. He turned around and started to walk away.

They both nodded appreciatively and hurried off, leaving Professor Walters on his own to disappear down the corridor. He let out another loud, uncontrollable sneeze into his hanky.

"Goodness, I don't know what's got into me lately!" he muttered to himself as he returned to his classroom.

Chapter 10

Later that day, immediately after school, Sallina was watching Szymon as he entered the combination code on the chain with which he'd secured his bike.

Szymon's bike was ordinary, nothing fancy, with faded blue and yellow colours. This was less sophisticated of a machine than Sallina would expect for a young practicing Unimage—she couldn't tell whether it even had any gears. Though she had never been close to a bicycle before, it looked like a rudimentary device.

Szymon climbed onto his bike and smiled at her. "Hop on the back if you like," he chimed cheerfully.

"Where? I don't see another seat," Sallina replied.

"Oh, my house isn't far. You can sit on the seat, and I'll stand and pedal. It's quite a natural thing for humans to do."

"I'm not sure that's such a good idea," Sallina said, grimacing.

"I know it's not ideal, but it's the only form of transportation I have."

"Well, it's not really my thing to be so close to someone I barely know," she retorted. "Besides, I doubt I can get on it safely and keep my balance once it gets going."

"You can always sit on my lap, if that would be more comfortable?" Szymon offered kindly.

"Definitely not! But thank you for your generous offer. I prefer to walk instead, as it's not that far, right? Just a few roads down towards the left."

She realized as she gave him directions that she wasn't meant to know exactly where he lived, and she immediately regretted opening her mouth. Szymon looked a bit puzzled by her last remark, but he didn't question her on it.

"Please yourself. You're the one who will have to walk alongside me."

"Walking is supposed to be really good for you. I may only have my two legs right now, but I can manage very well with them, almost as well as I could with four," she said.

Szymon lurched forward on his bike as he took off, and she followed him on the pavement. She tried her best to keep up.

Szymon was about a hundred yards ahead of her when he decided to pull over and wait for Sallina to catch up with him. Clearly her two legs were not able to keep up with him on his bike, which was in fact fitted with a change of gears that he put to good use. She approached him as he stood there idly, resting on the seat of his bike, one foot on the ground to keep himself upright.

"Don't expect me to keep on chasing you if you're going to ride so fast and not think of me. I suggest you ride that thing a bit slower," Sallina suggested.

"If I ride any slower, I'm likely to topple over! You're only following me on foot because you don't wish to ride on the bike with me—it's your choice."

Sallina wished to snap back at him, but she thought the better of it and didn't respond to his rebuttal. She was surprised when he climbed off his bike.

"I have another idea. Why don't you ride the bike instead, and I'll walk? I'm a pretty good runner, and I reckon I can keep up with you, but I'll have to give you directions first."

Sallina looked at his bike as he offered it to her, firmly gripping the handlebar to keep it upright. She took a small step closer toward it, somewhat uncertain.

"So, what do I do with it?" she asked.

"It's super easy, Sallina. First, you need to get onto it, and then you turn those pedals around in a circular motion with your feet, which makes the chain move, and that propels the bike," Szymon explained. "It's quite rudimentary."

She carefully examined the pedals and the chain and then looked back at him, even more confused.

"Never mind. This was a bad idea!" Szymon was about to get back on when she touched his arm rather forcefully, taking him by surprise.

"No, wait a second, I'm sure I can manage this on my own." Sallina didn't wish to be defeated by this human contraption. "It does looks like a lot of fun. I shall give it a try."

She took hold of the bike as Szymon let go and climbed onto it, sitting herself down as comfortably as she could on the narrow saddle.

"I've just thought of a perfect solution to make this experience work." Sallina clasped her necklace. "You'll like this," she said, smirking. "'Spin and turn, whiz along. Two wheels will do the job just fine, now come along.'"

As she spoke her incantation, a pale-blue light emanated from her Starpoint necklace and lit up her entire hand. The light shot out from the necklace and immediately covered both wheels of the bike. Szymon looked on, mouth open in amazement.

The wheels of the bike started to turn of their own volition, and the bike began to propel itself forward. It quickly gathered speed, and soon the Princess was whizzing along down the street at a lightning pace.

"Hey! Wait for me!" Szymon broke into a sprint to try to catch up, Sallina having taken off a lot faster than he had ever achieved when using his feet.

"Wait for me, Sallina!" he shouted again, as Sallina took a left and disappeared. With great effort, Szymon tried to push himself even faster to catch up with her. Sallina was ignoring his distant pleas, clearly enjoying the thrill of riding his bike.

As Sallina continued to careen down the road, a young mother who had just parked her car took her son out of the vehicle and relocated him in a pushchair. The sandy-haired five-year-old looked up and bellowed, "Mummy, look! I want. Can I have that?"

The boy pointed at the bike. Fortunately for Szymon and the Princess, the mother was too focused on putting the straps on the pushchair to pay any attention to the bicycle that suddenly shot past them at an unnatural speed, followed by a young man panting away whilst he tried his level best just to keep up. The little boy waved to Szymon as he shot past him. Szymon grinned back sheepishly, still struggling to keep up with Sallina on his bike.

Sallina realized that she was not far now from Szymon's house, so she slowed down while she rubbed her necklace. The thought crossed her mind once again that she wasn't meant to know where Szymon's house was situated, so it was best for him to catch up with her and give her the final set of directions. This way she could hopefully avoid arousing any further suspicion.

The bike came to a near-stop and remained perfectly upright without the need for any additional support as Sallina climbed off and turned her attention to Szymon, who was still a fair distance off. A light-blue glow around the wheels was proof enough that the spell was still working its magic and helping to keep the bike from toppling over sideways.

"What were you do-doing?" Szymon stammered, clearly out of breath. "You could have got-gotten yourself lost or had an accident… I haven't had the chance to tell you where I live."

"Oh, I'm sorry," she replied. "Did I make a wrong turn?"

Szymon shook his head. "No, you're still on the right path, but we soon need to turn left again further ahead. We're almost there—it's not far."

Szymon was starting to regain his breath. Sallina smiled, pleased that she'd gotten away with fooling him into believing she had no idea where he lived.

But maybe she hadn't been as successful in fooling him as she thought, as he suddenly said, "Although, you were extraordinarily lucky in your guessing. You could have easily made a few wrong turns along the way, but you didn't. How did you manage to take the right turn several times without any idea of where you were going?"

"Oh," said Sallina, having to think quickly. "I… don't know! Guess I was just a little lucky, that's all." She shrugged. "I have a good sense of direction. Always have."

Szymon looked doubtful. Sallina did her best to avert her gaze as she fiddled with the bike handle.

"We turn left over there, and then it's a few houses along on the right-hand side of the road," Szymon said, pointing the way.

"Ah. Good. Very well, then!" Sallina exclaimed. "Here, please take it, I don't want to get back on the bike. You can have it. After all, it's your bike." She rubbed her necklace lightly and the bike started to fall onto its side. Luckily, Szymon managed to grab hold of it in the nick of time, and he climbed back on and started off as Sallina trailed a short distance behind him, making little attempt to keep up.

Szymon took the left turn and arrived at his house. Sallina appeared moments later and joined him as he waited by the entrance to the driveway. Now it was her turn to be out of breath.

"Come on… this way, Princess," Szymon blurted.

Sallina's ear tingled for a moment as she recalled the very close encounter with the patio door and how she had almost been discovered by his overzealous dog!

She didn't realize, once they got there, that he had let go of the bike after he had climbed off. The bike was simply standing upright by itself, its two wheels seeming to be perfectly balanced. Sallina wondered how this was possible, then realised it was because she had been absent-mindedly fidgeting with her pendant again, and the magical blue light had drifted onto the bike as it dissipated.

Szymon was quite amused to see this, but rather than reach out for his bike, he simply left it alone. His mind was on other things.

At that moment, something made Sallina look up. Across the road, she saw a man in his late fifties looking directly at them, seemingly taking an interest in the unusual sight of an upright bike that appeared to be defying the laws of gravity!

Szymon, fortunately, had already noticed, and he quickly grabbed the handlebar to pretend he was holding the bike upright. He then proceeded to ignore the man, who continued his walk along the pavement, shaking his head in quiet disbelief.

"You need to be much more careful when you use your magic!" Szymon admonished Sallina, royal though she was and not accustomed to being criticised by one of her subjects. "You cannot practice it so openly—people are always watching us!"

Sallina saw the man disappearing down the road. "A few minutes ago, you were positively encouraging me to ride your bike, and now you're giving me a hard time because I took you up on your offer and did what I felt I had to do," she pointed out to him.

"Well, a few minutes ago, we were not being stared at by some stranger. Also, that boy in a pushchair, he noticed how fast you were riding your bike. It looked unnatural. You're going to get us into trouble."

"What boy?"

"Well, there you go. You see, you didn't even notice him. That's how risky it could be when you use your magic in public."

"And why is it 'unnatural'? Because I'm a girl? Are you implying that girls are not good at riding bikes fast? Or performing feats of magic?"

"Don't be so silly. It's only because you're using your magic that I'm bothered. Humans simply don't use magic in this place. They're not familiar with how it works or seeing it in action. What you did may seem very unnatural to them if you are not holding onto the handlebars or moving the pedals to justify the bicycle being upright. Do you not see? To us, magic is a perfectly normal thing, but it scares humans out of their wits. There are some who can ride their bicycles skilfully and make it look magical, but I would say your way of doing it makes it obvious that magic is being used."

"Oh," Sallina muttered a little sheepishly before going on the attack once again, "But, riding a bike is perfectly natural to them, isn't it? I think riding a bike is a highly unnatural thing, and as I found out, it's really strange… So, this your house then?" she added, quickly changing the subject.

Szymon calmed down and took a breath. "Come on in. You're my guest today." He lowered his bike sideways, and the blue light disappeared.

They headed to the front door, and Sallina suddenly felt dizzy and extremely weak. Szymon grabbed hold of her arm to support her.

"Careful. Are you alright? You look like you're about to faint and fall to the ground."

She took a step away from him and steadied herself by re-focusing on her surroundings.

"Don't worry about me. I'm fine. I was just overcome by a sudden dizziness. I don't know why that happened—it's not something I have felt in this place before. Not like this, least ways. It might be because it's so hard to use my magic properly. I must have strained myself. I don't know."

"Yes, it could be due to using your magic, that could be it."

"Oh, the feeling has already gone now," she said, and smiled. "I'm fine."

He nodded and they entered the house.

Chapter 11

As they entered the hallway through the front door, Yippy came running out and started barking at Sallina. Sallina was convinced Yippy recognized her from yesterday, but luckily dogs weren't able to talk, and her secret remained safe for now.

"Oh, he's so cute," she said. "What a lovely dog you have. So delightful."

"GGGRRRRR..."

Yippy was now growling at Sallina. *Will he ever let up?* she wondered as the pesky canine showed her his 'I mean business' fangs.

Please shut up, she thought to herself. *Please just leave me alone.*

Obviously, he would not. In fact, it was clear that Yippy had every intention of revealing who she was, and he would not stop barking his head off.

Szymon guided Sallina to the living room, and then he went straight to the covered-up orb. He carefully removed the cover and swivelled the orb to face the centre of the room, as he had before. It took him a great deal of effort, and Sallina was tempted to help out, but Yippy kept on barking right by her feet, eying her suspiciously at the same time. So she stood very still and just watched him bark at her.

While she waited, Sallina noticed what appeared to be a scroll sticking partially out of the cupboard. She slowly made her way over to it, keeping a watchful eye on Yippy, who followed her every step of the way and kept barking. She was about to slide the item out, when Szymon, having repositioned the orb, approached her in haste.

"Not yet, Princess," he said. "First, we need to prepare. You will need to bear with me for a few minutes. Is Yippy still bothering you?"

Sallina looked down at Yippy, who growled back at her for the umpteenth time.

"Oh, don't worry, he's harmless. I do like dogs," she said, not entirely convinced that she meant what she said.

Szymon returned to the centre of the room. Lying nearby was a bucket half-filled with water. He picked up the heavy bucket and poured the water in a circle around the orb. Sallina remembered this step from before and knew he was preparing for Unimage Konstanty to appear.

"Hopefully this will do us for now. I prefer it to be a short call," he said, grinning sheepishly. "I always end up getting scolded for something or other." He started to chant something that she couldn't quite make out.

"I thought one couldn't do magic in Doberry?" she asked.

"Oh," he said, interrupting his chanting for a moment. "I'm not doing magic; I'm just preparing a connection for my father to enact *his* magic. Look at this as a long-distance direct call. I'm setting up the line by allowing my father to make the connection, and he is the one dialling in and making the long-distance call."

"So, you cannot by yourself initiate the call and contact him directly here?"

"No, unfortunately I cannot, but once I make the enchantment, he can sense when the line is available. It's as good in some ways as me trying to call him, if you know what I'm saying. If he fails to get in touch with me, it usually means he is preoccupied with something important or he's not in a talking mood."

"Ah," said Sallina, as Szymon started chanting again. Several small flames erupted from the top of the orb, and after a few moments, a familiar head started to appear from inside. As the flames subsided, the head slowly rose and lifted out of the orb into the air above it, just as it had done yesterday when Sallina watched the conversation taking place.

As the head rose higher, so did the orb. It was now hovering almost an inch above the ground, levitating. She didn't recall the flames from yesterday; this seemed to be a new addition to the proceedings, or perhaps she had missed that bit and joined them further into their direct-dial conversation.

"Why was it burning like that a few moments ago?"

"I think it's something to do with making the initial connection," Szymon muttered, then continued to chant while trying to ignore her presence.

After the orb had risen another inch or so higher, she could make out Unimage Konstanty's unicorn face in its full form, staring at both her and Szymon. No neck or torso was visible—it was as if the call allowed only the face to appear.

"Oh, hello. Who do we have here with us today?" Konstanty said, pretending to be pleasantly surprised. But it came out sounding a bit garbled, as if there were some issues with the quality of the present connection.

Sallina was starting to feel more than a little uncomfortable about being in the presence of the high-level Unimage. Konstanty was staring directly at her, and there was something rather disconcerting about the way his eyes seemed to peer straight into her very soul, as if they were trying to bore their way deep inside her mind and read her waking thoughts. She felt a sense of intrusion into her personal space, and she didn't like having the feeling one bit.

"Unimage… I—I'm Princess Sallina," she managed to murmur.

"Yes, of course you, are my dear. I recognized Your Young Majesty straight away, although in your present human form, you do look somewhat different. So does my young Szymon, of course, standing next to you. Both of you look different."

"Father," interrupted Szymon, "we're both ready to work on the spell. I'm not sure how long this connection will last."

"Oh, yes. Good mention… Do you have the necessary items we discussed?"

"Yes, I do," said Szymon, chuffed with himself. "One second… I've kept them in the fridge. I'll go fetch them." Szymon shot off like a spring, leaving Yippy still looking up at Sallina and growling directly at her. Konstanty noticed the irksome dog.

"Why doesn't he get rid of that little mongrel as well whilst he's at it?! We don't want any further distractions from such a tiny beast with no useful purpose," Konstanty said to his son.

Szymon, as he headed off, gestured to Yippy to follow him. Yippy didn't want to budge, so Szymon came back and grabbed hold of his collar and nudged him along, leaving Yippy standing on his hind legs, looking back towards Sallina and Konstanty and growling.

"You have to forgive him," Konstanty continued muttering, not happy to let an uncomfortable silence linger during his son's temporary absence. "My son has always been a bit absent-minded—that's my boy," he remarked, attempting to make light conversation while they both waited for Szymon to return. "I'm not sure if it's because of the enormous distance and being stuck in such an odd place—what's it called, Doberry? —or maybe it's him being his usual clumsy self."

Sallina managed to break out a smile. She wasn't sure that she ought to comment on anything, as she felt uncomfortable in Unimage Konstanty's presence. Although deep down she did find his opinions on his son disturbing, especially the way Unimage Konstanty was willing to poke fun at his son's regular absent-mindedness. She knew, of course, that as Szymon's father, he was wrong to do such an inconsiderate thing, but perhaps it was Szymon's slight inattentiveness that helped her get away with having known the precise route to his house, and it might also have saved her from being noticed yesterday outside the patio door. Clearly Yippy had been a lot more alert than his two-legged master, and she wouldn't get away with fooling this dog.

She realised it was Szymon's absent-mindedness that she liked a lot about him, and that she would most likely be less taken by him if he was as sharp and observant and as ruthless as his father. She considered his so-called weaknesses to be a blessing in disguise.

Szymon returned to the room a few moments later with a transparent plastic bag packed with fresh carrots. He quickly tore it open and took one out, which he stuffed directly into his mouth. He hesitated for a moment before he began to chew and slowly ingest the vegetable, since he detested the taste of carrots. But eat them he must, he knew that. It was his father's express wish for him to consume carrots when casting the remembrance spell, and Szymon dared not to disobey him.

"Did you wash those carrots properly before you started to chew on them?" Sallina piped up, watching his unhappy consumption with mild bemusement. "They are meant to be cleaned."

Szymon suddenly stopped chewing and looked at her and then at this father.

"Oh, no, I don't like to clean them. I prefer to eat them raw with some dirt still on them, and straight from the bag. I'm more of the organic, natural type," he mumbled with his mouth full, continuing to chew.

"What she meant to say was that as a human—oh, never mind. What does it matter anyway what you eat in this place? A little dirt, or whatever one finds on these carrots, is the least of our concerns right now. Let's carry on," his father said.

Then, to her surprise, Sallina saw two arms appear from *inside* the orb! They looked strange, as if they were detached from any kind of body. The effect was ghostly.

Konstanty slowly lifted his left arm and produced a wand that stuck out from the orb, and he started waving it about in the living room with an increasing amount of energy. Szymon was about to reach for the wand when Konstanty shook his head to signal that this was not his to take. Szymon duly pulled back, knowing better than to challenge the Unimage.

Another uncomfortable silence ensued, with Konstanty and Szymon both looking at Sallina. This spurred Sallina to react in some way.

"I want to confess... I'm truly honoured to be in such esteemed magical company with someone so skilled as yourself, Unimage Konstanty," she murmured with as much sincerity she could muster.

What she would have much rather said was along the lines of, *Even though you're helping Szymon and myself with crafting this spell, I do not trust you for even one second. There's something I personally dislike about you, especially the way you mistreat your son.*

Szymon kept chomping away at the carrot stuffed in his mouth as Konstanty continued to enact the enchantment. Konstanty was mumbling something Sallina was unable to properly make out, and his eyes also seemed to have slipped down from staring at hers to keeping closer watch on the precious pendant that was barely visible beneath her blouse. The necklace began to emit a bright blue light, and Konstanty was completely transfixed by its glow.

"Sallina, I mean Princess, you must also recite the enchantment from the scroll," Konstanty instructed her. "Szymon… pass her the scroll now so she can read from it."

Szymon shot over to the cupboard while holding onto the remaining carrots in the bag and returned with the paper scroll, which he handed over to Sallina.

"You're using my magic to cast your spell," she said out loud as she looked at the light emanating from her pendant. "I don't really see the point of doing this right now, as Professor Tinzy is not here with us," she added, opening the scroll and looking at the writing on it.

"Oh, don't worry, Princess," Konstanty replied. "Consider this to be a first dry run to determine whether we can cast the spell using our combined powers and gifts… and my son's able help, of course. We have to determine whether we can successfully enact a spell in Dowhatsit—where is it, Doberry? —you know, as there's no point in us performing the incantation in the presence of your Professor Tinzy if we can't properly release the magic. The paper scroll has been handwritten by my son, but eventually it will be replaced by the actual one that I will present to you if, and only if, we are successful today in bringing our talents together to cast this spell."

She silently nodded, then fully unrolled the scroll and looked closely at the writing inscribed on the parchment. She began to vocalize the enchantment to herself and then began to raise her voice. As she spoke, the blue light from her necklace cast itself directly onto the paper scroll, which then itself began to glow a bright blue. She knew that she had to continue to read the words on the scroll in order for the magic spell to be activated.

She continued, "For all those memories both great and small, for those who had once forgotten themselves for who they truly are, I enchant them again, to help them find a way to recall their past to their present."

As she uttered these magical words, the door to the living room was nudged open by a few inches, and Yippy managed to charge into the room again, just like the day before!

Sensing something important and potentially harmful was taking place, Yippy ran a few circles around the room and barked his tiny head off. But it was too late to stop the enchantment now, and Sallina continued her spell casting as Konstanty also focused his mind on the delicate task at hand. The scroll began to glow much more brightly.

A yellow flash of light from Konstanty's magical wand covered the paper scroll and lit it with a bright-yellow incandescence that suppressed the blue glow from the pendant.

As Szymon found himself involuntarily drawn to the paper scroll, blue and yellow lights erupted and shot directly towards him. Fortunately, he had his fresh carrot in his mouth, which he had kept on monotonously chewing. The light immediately dissipated around him as it encountered the carrot, as if there was a magical aura protecting him from being invaded by the oncoming energy.

Instead, the light dropped down around his feet in a sudden, intense burst of energy and enveloped a running and barking Yippy... who suddenly stopped yapping and stood extremely still and confused. Yippy turned his head towards the orb slowly and laboriously, and to all three of them in the room it seemed as if he had been taken over by some sinister power that he had absorbed into his very being and didn't know how to shrug off. His dog eyes were mesmerised by the orb. In this trancelike state, his eyes began to cloud over.

"Well, it looks like it is working," Konstanty said, smirking. "Yippy has been reminded of his earlier puppy self, which I don't suppose he was expecting when the magic invaded his soul! Imagine, such a flood of distant memories filtering back into his waking consciousness! No doubt it is proving to be a rude shock to the mongrel's tiny conscious mind. By a sheer fluke, he appears to also have proven himself useful as a suitable test subject upon which to enact this carefully crafted spell. This is fortunate for us."

Sallina stared down at poor Yippy, who remained transfixed as he cast his gaze upon the orb, watching the blue and yellow lights fade and disappear around his body as the spell took complete hold of him. Then Yippy let out a short yelp and he took off, out of the living room. One can only wonder if he had some kind of frightful recollection of his past memories, with no indications of these returning.

"He has clearly had enough—it was too much for him," said Konstanty. "He must have recalled a few unpleasant memories from his younger days that he'd prefer to have left buried in his past."

Sallina was surprised as she held on to the glowing paper scroll in her hands, which still exuded energy. The luminescence of the illusory scroll sticking out of the orb began to fade as its magic transfused the paper scroll lying nearby.

"Now, my dear, you possess the true power of the scroll in the item you hold in your hands, and it is ready to be used properly on its intended subject," Konstanty announced determinedly, gazing at Sallina.

"Does this mean it works?" asked the Princess.

"Oh, yes, everything seems to be just fine," Konstanty replied.

Szymon stood there almost paralyzed, not knowing what to say or do other than to keep on chewing away at the carrot as he had been instructed by his father. He had already consumed two carrots from the bag, and he had just inserted the third one into his mouth and begun to chew it.

The magic that had a few moments ago consumed Yippy wasn't used up yet, as the paper scroll still glowed... and then the blue and yellow light shot off back toward Konstanty. His face suddenly lit up inside the orb.

Konstanty's eyes started turning bright red. Angry red flames shot out from his unicorn eyes and struck the illusory scroll that was sticking out of the orb, which then lit up and tore itself up into myriad tiny pieces as the flames engulfed it. The tiny pieces all drifted towards the paper scroll and Sallina had to close her eyes so she wouldn't be forced to let go of the scroll still in her hand.

She saw something terrible, but it was not out there—it was somehow flickering inside her mind.

A dark and foreboding vision crossed her waking thoughts, and it came from neither Yippy nor Szymon. She could only conclude that she was catching a brief glimpse into the depths of Konstanty's mind and managing to access his inner workings that he was not able to shield from her.

She saw Konstanty, alone, as he stood atop a tall mound, now in his full unicorn form, his eyes blood red. They appeared to be on fire as he looked up at the bright night sky, which was also ominous and engulfed by flames. A fiery object was hurtling towards the hill, a gigantic object that had come from somewhere in outer space to destroy their world.

Was this a glimpse of the ominous meteor that was set to threaten all life and devastate everything on Starpoint?

The meteor-like object was on fire, and it seemed to be expanding in size as it came ever closer to the mound and to Konstanty. Konstanty stood defiantly and stared up at it without flinching, but she could tell that fear was starting to engulf him. Even the mighty Unimage sought to cower and run away as the object grew bigger in size and stature and came closer to him.

Konstanty lowered his head, his still-defiant gaze averted from the oncoming object. The object collided with a faraway hill, and everything erupted in flames all around Konstanty and everywhere Sallina could see.

Then suddenly the vision was no more… not just that of the meteor, but the whole dark and foreboding revelation that had unfolded in her mind. Sallina opened her eyes. The paper scroll was still there safely in her hands. Szymon had continued to munch away on another carrot, and the orb was back in its original state.

Konstanty was no longer present—his image had somehow vanished. Szymon was looking somewhat surprised as he studied the orb. Whatever had just happened was now over. He stopped chewing and spat out what was left of a carrot, then looked at her apologetically.

"The call's finished. Looks like the line was cut," he muttered to Sallina.

"Did you see the place as well?" Sallina asked him as it replayed in her mind.

Szymon remained silent for a moment. He didn't want to answer.

"Yes… I think I saw what you saw. This is brilliant news, yes? We can help the Professor to remember."

Sallina was aghast. "How can you say that if you saw what I saw?"

"What?" said a baffled Szymon. "The magic worked. Now we can perform it on the Professor, so that he can remember who he is," he continued with a growing sense of excitement.

That was when Sallina realized Szymon had not in fact seen what she had. An alternative notion was that he might have seen the same thing, but it didn't bother him at all. This thought immediately concerned her, and therefore she quickly dismissed it from her mind. Szymon didn't choose his father, and he never picked the path that he was traveling on. Even if he was involved in something that would turn out to be insidious, she strongly believed that he was sincere and meant her no personal harm. He was genuinely trying to help her bring Professor Tinzy back to his former self, and there seemed nothing underhand or malicious about his actions. If anything, he came across as being more naïve than anything else and filled with good intentions.

"Yes, of course, we must next try it out on the Professor," Sallina said, punching the air with fake triumph.

"Exactly!" Szymon exclaimed, with his own punch to the air.

But there was one thing that puzzled the Princess. Why had this silly boy constantly chewed on dirty carrots throughout the casting of the spell? Did he have some desperate urge to consume raw and unclean carrots when magic was being prepared? She decided she would follow this up with him another time.

One good thing, she thought to herself, was that at least she now possessed the means to help Professor Tinzy remember his former identity, assuming he was okay after his trip to the hospital earlier in the day. She looked at the scroll that she held in her hand, and she knew this was the exact tool required to help her access Professor Tinzy's blocked memories.

She also noticed that Yippy was not running around anymore like before, so she headed away from the room and made her way towards the entrance hall where she had last seen him. Yippy was on his small cushion in the hallway, curled up and fast asleep.

Poor Yippy, she thought.

For him, it appeared, the preparation of this spell had been a bit too much to chew off. The test, however, was a success, and about this she was pleased.

What she didn't think about—and probably should have contemplated further—was that Unimage Konstanty had witnessed first-hand how Sallina had been able to deploy her powerful magic in Doberry. Sallina was suddenly vitally important to Konstanty's future plans. She had been wise to sense the presence of some unknown danger in Szymon's house, but little did she know how much actual danger she was now in.

As soon as the connection to Doberry had been severed, Unimage Konstanty, who was alone in his study in his private home in Starpoint, began to contemplate how he could use what he had just witnessed to his best advantage. One single over-arching thought quickly began to preoccupy him. In the privacy of his own home, the words jumped right out of his mouth and filled the otherwise normally silent room, "I must have that pendant; it will be mine!"

Chapter 12

It was difficult to describe the sinking feeling Princess Sallina experienced the next day when she approached Professor Tinzy's office door with Szymon by her side. She had the scroll securely tucked away in a small duffel bag, along with Szymon's bag of carrots. The batch of carrots had been Szymon's idea, and she decided not to question it.

But there on the door, beneath the professor's nameplate – a hastily written note was stuck down with sticky tape:

"Due to an unforeseen illness, I'm unavailable until further notice."

"Oh, no," Szymon muttered. "They must have kept him at the hospital overnight."

"We better go there now!" Sallina said urgently.

"After school—we still have classes to attend," said Szymon.

"Yes, you're right. We can't draw undue attention to ourselves. If we were both missing from class, it might raise a lot of eyebrows! But I shall be frantic with worry all day now, wondering how well the Professor is. Or not."

"Me too," said Szymon, mournfully.

* * *

Three hours later, Princess Sallina ran to the bicycle rack, where Szymon was busy unlocking his bike. School was over and she couldn't wait to get to the Professor and find out if he was all right.

During their time apart, Szymon had managed to find out where the hospital was, which pleased Sallina. He also told her that he had overheard two members of staff talking about the Professor and that his condition was not thought to be too serious.

"Well, let's get going!" Sallina said eagerly.

"Do you want the bike?" Szymon offered, a little hesitantly.

"Umm… no. I think after yesterday I shall take your advice and avoid using such contraptions ever again!"

"Fair enough," Szymon said, climbing on and getting set. "Let's go!"

Thirty minutes later, Sallina and Szymon arrived at the hospital. Szymon parked his bike at a public bike rack and the two nervously stepped toward the entrance.

Inside, Szymon paused.

"Let me do the talking here," he said to Sallina, trying to keep his voice down. "We don't want anyone examining what we have on us. If they find the scroll, we'll have to provide a much more detailed explanation as to why we decided to come here to visit the Professor."

"Okay."

At the hospital reception desk, Szymon cautiously approached the busy receptionist, but she couldn't tend to his enquiry as she was tied up on the phone. Szymon stood patiently whilst she spoke to someone on the phone.

The receptionist looked tired and a little stressed from attending to her essential duties, but she managed to break into the occasional smile as she spoke to the caller.

"I'm very sorry I cannot help you. If you keep trying the number I just gave you, they may be able to assist you in this matter. Yes, that's right. Thank you, good luck, bye bye."

The receptionist replaced the phone in its docking port and turned her attention to Szymon.

"Hello, young man. How can I help?"

Szymon explained to her they were both students from Doberry School and that they were there to check on Professor Tinkerton because they cared about his wellbeing.

The kindly receptionist appeared to go along with it and didn't ask any awkward questions. Sallina was standing close to Szymon, and she wasn't too pleased with participating in this deceit, but she forced herself to remain quiet.

The receptionist gave them a set of directions to the ward where Professor Tinzy was recuperating, and both Szymon and Sallina smiled and waved goodbye to her as they headed off down the corridor. She had even given them each a visitor badge, and Szymon was pleased with himself, grinning to Sallina as they strolled along.

As they made their way further down the corridor, Sallina threw Szymon a somewhat icy glance.

"I know," he murmured, as if he could easily read her mind. "But if I didn't make it sound really important and express how much we wanted to wish him well, we wouldn't have been able to get in to see him at all. Maybe I ought to have told her we have a magic scroll inside your bag, and that the Professor is in fact a wise magical unicorn who we are in the process of rescuing, and the fate of Starpoint hangs in the balance."

Sallina gave Szymon a withering look but chose not to respond with any words.

After getting lost and taking the wrong turn now and again, Sallina and Szymon eventually found themselves in the correct ward. They were a little perturbed to discover how busy it was all over the hospital. Every bed was occupied. But one thing was in their favour: it looked as if Professor Tinzy might be in one of the three beds that had drab grey curtains drawn around them. Sallina deduced this after quickly scanning the ward and the faces of the patients.

"Come on then, I think he's in here," she whispered.

Sallina took several purposeful steps forward, and she came to a stop at the first curtained bed. Slowly, she parted the curtains. An old man she thought to be in his seventies gave her a friendly wink as he looked up from his worn copy of *The Hobbit*. For a split second, she wondered what this book was all about, as it appeared to be rather thick and had an attractive cover, and he seemed to be fully engrossed in it.

Sallina politely smiled back before letting go of the curtain, and she moved on to the next curtained bed. Peeking through a narrow gap in the curtains, Sallina could see the bed was unoccupied. However, it had been recently disturbed, so somebody was probably using it—they just weren't there at this precise moment in time. Could this be where Professor Tinzy had been resting moments ago, or did it belong to someone else?

She waited a few seconds, and then she decided to check out the third bed, but Szymon had beaten her to it. He slid open the curtain a little, peered into the secluded area, and waved her over. As she approached, he smiled.

"Found him! Looks like he's napping."

They slipped behind the curtain and found themselves staring down at a peacefully asleep Professor Tinzy. Without hesitation, Sallina gently nudged the Professor's shoulder.

"Professor! It's me! Sallina."

The Professor didn't stir. Szymon gave him a gentle nudge as well, albeit a little more forcefully.

"Professor, we're here to see you."

"Huh?" moaned the Professor as he was rudely woken from his slumber. "Oh no! Not the two of you again!" He put his hands to his eyes in dismay. "Why are you following me everywhere I go? What do you want from me?"

Sallina was already unpacking her duffle bag. She quickly pulled out the paper scroll and unrolled it, then placed it on Professor Tinzy's body.

"Hey! What have you got there?" he asked. "What's that for?"

"It's for you, Professor. Please give us a few moments and it will all become clearer. Then you'll remember everything, hopefully."

Szymon immediately readied himself for the incantation and reached for the carrots, which he had pulled out of the bag.

"Those for me as well?" the Professor asked. "Carrots?"

"Oh, no, they're for me," Szymon responded as he stuffed a raw carrot into his mouth. "They help with the spell. I'm not overly fond of them, but I'm told I need to eat them."

"Wh-what spell?"

The Professor began to look increasingly petrified as Sallina removed the Starpoint necklace and pendant from around her neck and held it in her hand. The pendant started to glow as she gently rubbed it with her fingers.

Suddenly, Szymon turned around in alarm as he heard footsteps approaching and saw a shadow forming beneath the curtain's hem.

"Sallina, someone's coming. Quick, we'd better hide!" Szymon stammered in a loud whisper. He grabbed hold of the Princess, the duffle bag, and the scroll and pushed her toward the curtains by the window. "Go behind the curtain and keep perfectly still! Quickly!"

Sallina and Szymon took a curtain each and had just managed to hide behind them when a woman opened the curtains surrounding the Professor's bed. Holding their breath, they waited as the nurse picked up a clipboard that lay at the end of the bed and checked through the notes on a piece of paper.

"So, how are we doing today, Professor?" she asked Professor Tinzy whilst he watched her with a dumbfounded, irritated expression.

"Oh, I'm feeling better… but you know, I'm not alone here." The Professor gestured with a little nod of his head toward the window curtains, but the nurse didn't notice as she was far too busy looking at a form she had in her hand stuck on the clipboard.

"No, you're not alone, Professor, as you know—and we all know—that the Lord will always be here with you in our times of trouble," she replied reassuringly, smiling warmly as she replaced the clipboard. "Unless of course you mean your neighbours… Although, looking at you, I think you're a man of God. You should carry on resting; you're looking far better than you were yesterday. I dare say you're firmly on the mend."

She appeared to be in a bit of a hurry, because as soon as she put down the clipboard, she turned around and disappeared beyond the curtains.

"But—" was about all Professor Tinzy could muster before she was gone.

A split second later, Sallina and Szymon suddenly reappeared close by the bed. This gave the Professor a bit of a fright, and he was about to scream out loud to alert others to their unwanted presence, when Sallina covered his mouth with her open hand.

"Now now, Professor, please, you'll get us all into trouble," she said gently as Szymon took a chomp out of his carrot. Sallina cast a quick, disconcerted glance his way.

The Professor looked with displeasure at these unwelcome, highly persistent intruders who were grinning foolishly at him.

"Can't you two leave me alone? I'm not feeling all too well, you realize?" He let out a few spasmodic coughs and brought his hand to his mouth. "I need to get some rest; I suppose you heard what the nurse just told me. I may be on the mend, but I'm still feeling weak and tired. She thinks God is likely to be here with me, and that's always a bad sign. It means I could… you know."

Ignoring him, Sallina held onto the pendant once again as Szymon placed the scroll across Professor Tinzy's chest. The Professor sighed deeply.

"Very well, get on with it, if you must," he said sourly, shutting his eyes and concluding these two bothersome students would be gone a lot quicker if he played along rather than kick up a fuss. "If I let you do what you've come to do, then perhaps I can get back to having some rest."

Princess Sallina wasted no time. She clasped the pendant, which soon began to glow and emit its bluish light directly onto the scroll.

But this time, the blue light was accompanied by a yellow light; the preparation by Unimage Konstanty was clearly working its enchantment, and the spell looked like it was taking effect. Szymon swiftly took another big bite from his carrot as Sallina spoke the words.

"For all those memories both great and small, for those who had once forgotten themselves for who they truly are, I enchant them again, to help them find a way to recall."

There was a sudden bright flash of white light that emanated directly from the scroll itself, as if a flash photograph had been taken in a studio.

A couple of the patients and visitors on the other side of the Professor's curtained bed noticed the light emanating from within but thought little of it. Although photography tended to be frowned upon in hospital wards, it didn't stop patients, family members, and their friends from taking pictures of their loved ones, so this flash of light was really nothing out of the ordinary.

Back behind the curtains, Professor Tinzy appeared increasingly lost and confused. His eyes had clouded over, and they seemed to be completely out of focus, and his vision had started to become blurred.

Unnoticed by anyone there—including Sallina and Szymon—a faint blotch of blue magic was stuck on the scroll, and there it remained, out of sight and out of mind to all present.

Much to his amazement, when the vision-fog disappeared, Professor Tinzy saw an image rising above the scroll, right by his feet. It was a tiny image of a unicorn, glancing around the space as if it was surprised to be there. After a few moments, this creature set its eyes squarely on the Professor. At first, he had trouble recognizing the creature, but that was only because he had forgotten pretty much everything about his previous life. But as the veil to his past lifted a bit, he started to remember that she was someone important and held in high regard.

"Mother!" Princess Sallina exclaimed, as she looked down at the tiny unicorn standing on top of the scroll above Professor Tinzy's tucked-in legs. "Is that really you?"

Queen Noony turned around to look at her daughter and smiled.

"Yes, of course it is. I heard your summoning and here I am, just in time and on cue. The scroll seems to have wanted to call me to speak to the Professor and help him remember something. Professor Tinzy, I hope you are aware that you need to proceed with the utmost haste on this urgent mission! There's no time to waste."

Behind her and slightly above her equine head, a miniature holographic meteor manifested as it hurtled through space. Queen Noony despondently looked up at this vision and then spoke hurriedly.

"Several smaller space objects fell near Starpoint yesterday and created a bunch of horrible craters in the ground as well as setting off nasty forest fires. Citizens are becoming terribly concerned that something far worse is heading their way."

She looked up at the tiny meteor gravitating above her head, and she trembled as it hurled itself across space.

"My daughter Sallina has come here to help you, Professor, along with her newfound friend, Szymon. You will require support. And although I was never asked whether she ought to be embarking on this perilous mission and head off to this far-flung land, it looks like she may be able to provide a critical level of support at such a perilous time."

Then she suddenly began neighing like an Earth horse, and it was a ridiculous sound that splintered into sudden bursts of laughter. "I'm sorry, but you look so strange, I can barely recognise you. What has this place done to you? Your faces. My gosh. They're so comical."

Professor Tinzy was mesmerized by this odd vision lying on top of his legs. He wasn't sure whether he was dreaming it all… or perhaps it was just the medication they had been administering to him, and this was merely some kind of strange hallucination as a side effect.

"Are you someone I know?" he asked Queen Noony, retaining a sense of calm that surprised everyone. "Because you look familiar."

"Of course I am, you buffoon. I'm your Queen. Don't you recognize me? Have you lost your mind?" she rebutted curtly.

For a moment, the Professor was confused, as his memories were failing him… and then it all came back in a flood that felt like a sudden rush to his brain.

"Oh, gosh! Oh, no! I'm so very sorry for not recognizing you… your Majesty," came his timid reply. "I do remember a little bit about you, but it's not much – not yet at least. You're especially important—" and then he froze up as his head throbbed with other peculiar thoughts that were flooding back into his mind.

A strange word struggled to come out of his parched lips, and it managed to break itself free after wrestling to get out of his mouth and enter into the open world between him and his companions where it could be audible…

"Unicorn!" he gasped, the word that described him and the others present. "Your Majesty, I am merely your humble unicorn servant who has been led astray," he quipped. He tried to sit himself up in the bed but could barely move.

There was the slightest hint of a smile on Sallina's face as she realized that Tinzy was starting to remember who he really was. Szymon wasn't so sure how well the spell was working; something about the way the Professor was behaving bothered him.

The Professor spoke up, now more coherently than he had a few moments ago, "I'm very sorry, your Majesty... I must be an old and absent-minded fool. I had taken leave of my senses."

"Shh, right now you're inside a hospital ward, so it's best to keep your voice down," Szymon quickly told him. "We don't want anyone looking in."

"A ward, a medical ward... oh, yes, I'm currently in a hospital. I've not been too well lately! In fact, I've been out of touch with things for some days or weeks, and hardly able to remember much. I feel as if I've turned into someone else," he muttered.

"It's all right, Professor—you've been suffering from a bout of amnesia," Sallina said.

"Amnesia... oh dear, that's really not a good situation to find oneself in!" Professor Tinzy exclaimed in shock as he tried to sit up and lean forward a little, but he couldn't really move as he was still too weak, and it looked like he was stuck to his bed. "This is so unfortunate, but not entirely unexpected. Still, not quite the same when it happens to you."

"You must find us the Pinny, Professor, before it's too late and all of us are doomed. If you fail, I fear there will be no home for you to come back to." Queen Noony openly shared her angst and for a moment set aside her regal demeanour, and then she began to fade. "You mustn't abandon us, Professor, as we desperately need you to rescue us from that nasty, horrible object that is coming down on us to end it all."

She began to vanish as the glow of the scroll started to fade. A few seconds later nothing was left to see as the meteor, the Queen, and any hint of their presence had disappeared into the ether.

"She's gone!" Sallina cried as she grabbed the scroll, and it was unfortunately a lot louder than she had intended. The Professor tried to move his legs to get out of bed, but he found it exceedingly difficult to do anything with his body in this present state.

"Shh, quiet down. The spell looks like it worked, but it's over now," Szymon chimed in, his mouth still partially stuffed with a carrot.

He held in his hand the remainder of the carrot he was chewing… and then he had a powerful urge to spit it out, which he did, and it landed on top of Professor Tinzy's legs. This alarmed the Professor, who wriggled both his legs.

"Oh, no. I'm so sorry, Professor. I hate carrots. Forgive me," he pleaded apologetically as he tried to remove the mess and stuff it into his pocket. "I hate them so much."

"Then… why were you eating these things and making a mess?" Sallina couldn't help but ask him.

Szymon had to think quickly. "Well, because my father… told me I had to, and by doing so I could help you with casting your spell to successfully enact the scroll."

Sallina scowled at him. "How in the world can a bunch of miserable carrots help anyone support a remembrance-enchantment scroll? These two things are completely unrelated. You clearly know next to nothing about magic."

"Oh, yes, I do! You couldn't have done this without my help," Szymon said, more than a little stung by the accusation.

Professor Tinzy watched as the two of them wrestled verbally. He wasn't particularly amused by their banter, and he felt an oncoming headache taking effect.

"Please. When you're both finished with your debating, how about someone help me get out of this cramped bed? I need to go to the toilet urgently; it seems like it has been some time since I last made a visit."

The two young, humanised unicorns were surprised by the Professor's brusque request, but they quickly put aside their differences for the moment to help the Professor make an urgent visit to the nearby gents'… assuming they could find where it was in or around the ward.

Chapter 13

"So," said Sallina. "We've found the Professor and used the magic to help him remember who he really is. The big question is—"

"How do we get him out of here?" Szymon interjected.

"That's precisely right."

Escorting the Professor to the lavatory had been relatively simple, as it happened, for the facilities were located within the ward. But escorting him out of the building was not going to be as easy to pull off.

Szymon started brainstorming. "If only we could magically transform ourselves into nurses or doctors, like we transformed ourselves from unicorns, to—"

"That's it!" Sallina chirped excitedly. "We'll find a way to disguise ourselves! Come on."

"Where to…?" Szymon said, fearing that wherever it was, it was going to be somewhere they ought not to be. "I'm lost in here. This place is so huge and has endless corridors. Now we need to find an empty room and figure out how we can disguise ourselves."

He was right.

"I spotted a room down the corridor while we waited for the Professor outside the toilets. It's got just what we need!" Sallina said gleefully. "But we shall have to be very careful."

"Oh heavens, that's a problem. We're so out of our depth here," Szymon groaned.

When they eventually got to a storeroom just outside the ward, the door was still partially open.

"See?" Sallina said, looking toward the door. From where they were standing, they had a clear view of crates labelled 'Staff uniforms'.

"Excellent," said Szymon. "Be careful, though."

"ME?! Why me?"

"It was your idea. So far, your ideas have made things awkward."

Sallina let out a despairing sigh and walked over to the shelves that had piles of new uniforms. Without hesitation, she grabbed two sets and passed one to Szymon.

"Let's get changed and then go back to the Professor."

Szymon looked at her and saw that she was already taking off her outer garments. He immediately turned around and started doing the same.

"What if it doesn't fit me?" he complained.

"Make do with what you got. We can't wait around all day."

Szymon acknowledge the urgency of the situation and continued to change. Once they'd dressed, they turned around and faced each other.

"Everything's too big on us," Szymon remarked.

"It'll have to do. Fold the sleeves and roll up the trousers."

Szymon watched Sallina adjust her disguise and copied her.

"What do we do with our clothes?" he asked.

She extended her hand to him and then stuffed their clothes into her duffel bag.

Once they were ready, Sallina walked right out as though without a care, turned left, and just kept on going down the corridor and back to the ward.

The sight left Szymon speechless. In fact, he was in awe. "Wow," he said to himself.

Back with the Professor, Sallina and Szymon drew the curtains round and nudged the Professor, who appeared to have drifted off to sleep again.

Sallina and Szymon each took hold of the Professor by his arms, while he clung to them tightly with his arms draped around their shoulders. Somewhat awkwardly, they managed to get the Professor out of his bed. They helped him across the length of the hospital ward step by step, although the Professor did lose his footing a few times, as he was still very weak and could barely walk.

A couple of the patients watched with idle curiosity as the trio passed them by, their interest slightly piqued by the sight of the two unusually short and rather young-looking staff nurses. However, once again, none of the patients thought anything was particularly wrong with the present situation, mainly because most of them were pretty well-medicated and weakened from their illnesses.

Luckily, the ward at that time was not attended by any proper nurses—Sallina and Szymon had chosen their moment to perfection.

And luck was still on their side when they exited the ward into the corridor, for there, as if waiting for them specially, was an empty wheelchair.

"Eureka!" Szymon exclaimed. "Our lives are about to become a whole lot better."

As soon as Professor Tinzy was sitting in the comfort of the chair, he let out a sigh of relief. But he wasn't the only one relieved to have found a much easier way to travel, as both Szymon and Sallina had struggled to carry the Professor across the ward, and they were starting to doubt they could continue for much longer.

"Good choice. There's no way we could have made it out of here with me on my feet. I'm far too heavy for you two to keep helping me walk step by step down these corridors," Professor Tinzy mumbled. "I don't know why I'm still so weak and unable to do things like I used to. What has happened to me?"

Szymon attempted to reassure him. "Don't worry, Professor. We can push you out in the comfort of this wheelchair, and you'll be home shortly. You're just tired, that's all."

"Oh, that would be rather nice, dear boy, I thank you for your kindness. By the way, do I know you? I remember her well, of course—how can I ever forget such a lovely face? But you, I don't recall us ever meeting before, yet you look strangely familiar."

Professor Tinzy smiled at Sallina and turned his face as much as he could towards the young man who was behind him pushing the wheelchair. He craned his neck as best as he could to take a better look, but it was awkward to turn around whilst sitting back in the wheelchair.

"I do have one concern, though. Aren't you two a bit too young to be working in a hospital?"

Sallina cast a worried glance at Szymon, who shrugged.

"Don't worry about anything, Professor. We'll get you out of here if it's the last thing we do. Szymon and I are here to rescue you. Szymon's a close friend of mine... he's here to help us."

Szymon nodded to Princess Sallina to indicate his confirmation.

"That's reassuring to hear. You know, for a moment, I could have sworn that this young man looked familiar, and not in such a pleasant way. Must be my weary eyes playing tricks on me. I probably conjured up a partial memory that has done nothing but confuse me further."

Szymon and Sallina exchanged puzzled glances once again, but Szymon could not resist enquiring further.

"Why do I look familiar, sir?" Szymon asked, keeping his voice low as two much-older nurses passed by with quizzical expressions. Sallina and Szymon instinctively bowed their heads, averting their gaze from the staff as they desperately sought the way out of the building.

"Well, you look rather like this Unimage I knew back where I come from. My memory's all a bit boggled right now, but you do look familiar to me."

Szymon was about to reply when a voice suddenly ricocheted down the corridor behind them, "Excuse me, are you meant to be in here? Yes, you two. I'm talking to you. And where are you taking this patient?"

Szymon froze in his tracks and stopped pushing the wheelchair. He slowly swivelled it around to face the two nurses, who were staring directly at them. Sallina, standing beside Szymon, was suddenly awash in anxiety.

"What do we do now?" Szymon whispered out of the corner of his mouth.

Sallina shook her head slightly as the portly female nurse took a few steps closer to them and examined their clothing and then their faces. She looked down and noticed they were both wearing trainers.

Nurse Priyanka had a youthful face and energetic demeanour that belied the fact that she was well into her forties already and the mother of three children of varying ages.

"What do you think you are doing with this patient?" the nurse enquired firmly upon realizing that what she had stumbled upon was two young teenagers dressed up in nurses' uniforms pushing a patient down the corridor. "Are you both up to something?"

Stuck for words, her mind racing, Sallina immediately reached for her necklace, which started to emit a faint glow. This caught Professor Tinzy's attention straightaway as he watched her from the corner of his eye. He tried not to show any further reaction.

"I'm very sorry, nurse," Professor Tinzy blurted in an attempt to deal with the situation. "These two are my grandchildren. We were just going to go out for a little stroll… it's marvellous weather outside and I feel perfectly fine. I promise we'll be back in no time at all."

Nurse Priyanka wasn't convinced. "If they're both your grandchildren, what are they doing dressed up in uniforms? We cannot allow children to be walking about in nurses' uniforms inside a hospital."

Princess Sallina smiled. "I'm so sorry, my mother works as a nurse here, and she wanted us to feel comfortable when we're in the hospital, so she let us borrow some clothes. She knows how scared I become when I enter a hospital. My friend is also terrified as well. He hates hospitals. We promise to return them straightaway when we're done."

This explanation took Nurse Priyanka by surprise. The suggestion that their mother was a nurse wasn't satisfactory either. Nurse Priyanka realized that she didn't want to get into an argument with these three oddballs, and she was moments away from notifying someone in security nearby, when suddenly the fire alarm went off.

Nurse Priyanka turned quickly to her colleague, then back towards the three of them. "You'd better stay right there; we have to check the ward."

The nurses shot off as Princess Sallina, Szymon, and Professor Tinzy watched them disappear.

Sallina turned to Szymon in surprise. "Looks like we've been saved by the bell! How fortunate."

Szymon took a small step away from the wall and revealed the fire alarm switch that he had activated whilst they were speaking to Nurse Priyanka.

"Luck had nothing to do with it. I couldn't think of anything else to do, so I flicked the switch. It looked important, and I was hoping it would cause a distraction. I'm sorry."

"Don't be! Let's go before they decide to come back and deal with us further," Professor Tinzy interjected. "They'll soon figure out what has happened, and you two will end up in a great deal of trouble. You'll probably be arrested." While he spoke, several other doctors and nurses dashed down the hallway and ran right past them.

Pulling themselves together, the trio slowly worked their way down the entire length of the corridor as they headed towards the nearest available exit.

As they arrived at the end, they approached a pair of lifts. They were on the first floor; they had to find a way to get downstairs to the ground level.

Princess Sallina pointed to the lifts. "It's our only way out of here with the Professor sitting in a wheelchair."

Szymon nodded and pressed the lift button. A few seconds later, the lift doors opened and a senior doctor, who had recently immigrated to the UK from Japan, stepped out. He had a strong Japanese accent, but he spoke exceptionally good English.

"Professor Tinkerman, I was just on my way to see you when the alarm was activated. Are you alright? You should be in your bed."

Professor Tinzy looked up at the kind doctor and smiled, believing now that the game was up. He decided it was time to confess.

"I'm sorry if we have caused any trouble or inconvenience, this was not what we intended. We—"

Szymon urgently jumped into the conversation. "We came across a fire in the ward down the end of the corridor. We were helping the Professor get out of harm's way."

The doctor looked down the corridor. There was quite a bit of commotion taking place further along as the nurses were helping the patients get out of the ward and into the corridor.

"Oh, no... you'd better stay here by the lift. If the fire spreads, do not use the lift, as there are emergency staircases further down the corridor. Someone will come to assist. I will go check out what's going on." The doctor made his way hurriedly down the corridor, seemingly unperturbed by the sight of two children in nurses' uniforms.

The lift doors were about to close on them when Szymon pressed the button again and they re-opened.

"Time to make ourselves scarce," Szymon said as he gestured toward the lift. He pushed Professor Tinzy's wheelchair into the lift, and Sallina followed them in.

Further down the corridor, the confused Japanese doctor turned to check on the trio by the lift, but all he saw were the lift doors closing. He had told them not to go anywhere, but they had ignored his good advice. And why had the nurses looked so young? The doctor shook his head dazedly. He really had no time to think about this matter at present, as he was already being surrounded by distressed patients, and the staff's priority was to vacate the floor where the alarm had been activated in case there was a genuine fire, and this wasn't a false alarm.

* * *

The lift soon reached the ground floor and the doors swished open breezily.

"Come on," said Szymon, as he maneuvered the wheelchair out. They headed straight for the main entrance. Sallina, head bowed, followed along, holding the Professor's hand.

But just as they successfully exited the hospital, Professor Tinzy grabbed the wheels of the wheelchair with both hands and abruptly stopped. Szymon didn't know how to react, but he didn't want to start a tug of war with the Professor, so he stopped pushing.

"What's the matter, Professor?" Sallina asked.

"I'm not really sure. I shouldn't be leaving—I'm a sick old man. I need help, medical attention. I should be in there. Shouldn't I?"

Sallina turned to Szymon, uncomfortable.

Szymon spoke hastily. "Professor Tinzy, you've been suffering from terrible amnesia and your memory is just beginning to recover. You are fine otherwise; your feelings of weakness are probably just a side effect of your terrible memory loss."

"What memory loss? Who are you two people? I've never seen the two of you before in my life. What are you doing to me? Why are we leaving? Where are we going?" The Professor sounded increasingly agitated as he spoke, his face registering a growing sense of alarm.

From inside the reception area of the hospital, the security guard, Trevor, began to pay more attention to what was going on just outside the main entrance of the hospital. He noticed how the two very short nurses weren't wearing properly fitting attire. Something didn't look right about them. He lifted his glasses and wiped them with a dirty hanky, and then put them back on. Things looked cloudier than they had a moment ago.

"Professor!" Szymon exclaimed in frustration. "We have to get out of here right now or we will be stopped again, and then we'll all be in a whole heap of trouble."

"Have you been in one of my classes before, young man? I don't recognize you, but there is something about you that rings a bell."

Sallina looked behind her at the entrance and noticed the security guard making his way towards the main doorway. She almost shrieked in fright as she turned back to the Professor.

"If we don't get out of here now, we will be in BIG trouble. Please, Professor Tinzy, we're your friends. You have to trust us."

Realizing she sounded sincere, the Professor lifted his hands from the wheels. Szymon hastily pushed the wheelchair forward as they quickly made their way down the path heading away from the hospital entrance.

"Thank you for trusting me without knowing why, Professor," Sallina remarked as she tried to keep up with them.

"You're so welcome, my Queen," the Professor replied. "Your Majesty."

This surprised Szymon, who muttered to her, "Well, he certainly has some wires crossed in that brain of his, doesn't he? Now you're the Queen, for goodness' sake. How much worse will this get?"

Suddenly, Professor Tinzy grabbed the wheels with his hands and stopped them in their tracks. "Oh, I just remembered...I need to go to the loo."

Sallina didn't react. She wanted to just keep moving along. The Professor, sensing that it was an inopportune moment, let go of the wheels.

Trevor had stopped at the entrance, and he watched them slowly disappear. In the distance he could still hear the fire alarm, and now there were patients and hospital staff milling about everywhere. He realized he had far more important things to do than chase after a confused-looking old man in a wheelchair and two rather short nurses who looked more than a little suspicious. There was a lot of commotion going on in the hospital, and those three seemed harmless enough.

Trevor was about to give his glasses another clean with his dirty hanky when his mobile phone suddenly rang, and he turned back inside as he answered it.

Chapter 14

The rest of the day proceeded without further issues. The trio was dropped off by minicab outside Professor Tinzy's house. Sallina and Szymon watched as the driver helped the Professor out of the cab and wheeled him to the front door. The Professor insisted that the two young unicorn-humans remain seated.

"I can manage perfectly well!" the Professor had declared emphatically, and Sallina and Szymon thought they'd better do as he requested rather than risk upsetting him again.

The minicab driver returned with a broad smile that ran end to end across his jovial face. He was a happy-looking middle-aged man who had originally come from Bangladesh and took great pride in his work and his car. It didn't take much for him to put a positive spin on his life.

Not only that, but he liked to do good deeds. He had insisted that he would help the Professor from the car to the house, which was another reason Sallina and Szymon stayed put.

"I've completed my first good deed for today, and I'm pleased," the driver said cheerily. "Now, where else can I take you two lovelies? I am yours to command, my princess."

Startled, Sallina looked at the driver with a puzzled expression and wondered for the briefest of moments if she had been found out. Then she shook her head. No, that wasn't possible. To humans, unicorns were nothing but a myth; they simply didn't exist in the real world. He had no idea who she really was.

After being returned to her home by the kind driver and paying him with the little bit of pocket money Margaret had given her for the day, Princess Sallina decided to go straight off to bed. She was completely exhausted, as it had proven to be a tricky day, and they had almost failed to help Professor Tinzy start remembering who he really was.

As it was, the police fortunately had not been called to the hospital to deal with what had amounted to a genuine patient kidnapping! Sallina knew enough about human culture to realize that pretending to be a nurse and then wilfully abducting a patient weren't actions she could easily get away with if the authorities became involved. Luckily, so much confusion had surrounded this incident that the matter was discreetly overlooked and viewed as a less-than-successful alarm test-evacuation that had plenty of room for improvement in the future.

She had seen how fearful Margaret had been when anyone official-looking called round, so she too quickly learned to be on her guard when people with official-looking clothing were involved, including nurses and doctors. After all, she was not legally Margaret's child. She could be taken away at any time. Fortunately, in the couple of months that Princess Sallina had been with Margaret, nothing bad had happened, and the few visits that had taken place by people who looked official were little to be concerned about.

As Sallina drifted off to sleep reflecting on how the day's events had unfolded in restoring the Professor's memories and rescuing him, she looked forward to the next day and seeing how the Professor was feeling and discovering what he remembered of himself and his true purpose in coming to this unusual place.

***

The following day, however, ended up being a total let-down, for neither Szymon nor the Professor were anywhere to be found. She had no idea whether either of them had even shown up at school. She was somewhat perplexed and started drifting into despair, as she thought there were a lot of things to discuss about the previous day's events and the effects of the spell. The troubling questions floating about in her mind needed answers.

Sallina was just about to walk away from the empty space on the bike rack where Szymon usually stored his bike when she suddenly caught sight of the Professor in the distance, standing behind a big tree. He seemed to be grinning and was quite mobile, free of his wheelchair. It looked like he had made a swift recovery from his incapacitation of the day before. He waved to her, indicating he wanted her to come over, and ducked back behind the tree to avoid the attention of other students.

As she neared the tree, the Professor again popped out from behind it, this time with arms raised to greet her excitedly.

"My dear, you'd better come along with me and be quick about it," Professor Tinzy spoke just a smidgen above a whisper, but it was charged with excitement and joy at seeing her before him.

"Are you feeling okay, Professor? I've been worried about you. I thought I may have not cast my spell properly yesterday and it was affecting you in some bad way. My worries kept me up for a good part of the night!"

"I'm feeling perfectly fine... your Highness! Thanks to you."

Sallina's eyes opened wide in surprise.

"You know what? I can remember almost everything now... well, maybe not everything, but I remember a lot of things," the Professor muttered rather quickly. "Come, come, we need to find some quiet place and have ourselves a little chat between two good friends." He headed off toward a side entrance to the school.

Sallina followed him into the school building and a small, quiet break room designated for the exclusive use of the teaching staff, with a few multi-coloured chairs and piles of books littering various shelves. And of course, the obligatory coffee- and tea-maker constituted a key part of the room's layout and purpose.

Once they were both inside, the Professor turned a key on the inside to lock the room. This surprised Sallina, and she wondered why the Professor was suddenly being so secretive.

"Sit, sit down, please. We need to talk, you and I, about important matters."

Sallina sat down, and the Professor quickly did, likewise, facing her with one eye on the door.

"I have so much I want to ask you, Princess. First things first, how did you find me here in this place? I mean, how did you get to Doberry, of all the places you could possibly be?"

"Ah," she said, "well, you did leave me with specific instructions in the event that you didn't return from your travels after several weeks' absence, and I opened the instructions and found out exactly where you were and how you got here. I found out about the secret room behind the great meeting room in the castle turret where you went to arrange your travel to this place. The room had been hidden away behind a large painting for many years, and not many knew about it. I found and pressed the secret lever to open it, which then led me to the room where the passage to this place can be found."

She went on to explain to Professor Tinzy how after going through a long and bendy corridor, she had gotten herself into this peculiar room filled with the magic that the Professor had occasionally used. The place was all dusty and littered with cobwebs, and clearly nobody had been inside for many years. It had been forgotten by almost all apart from the Professor, who had made the discovery of the powerful tunnel that had brought him to Doberry.

When she first arrived, the place was literally crawling with hundreds of spiders, but fortunately Starpoint spiders tend to be quite tame overall, and the majority are small, although some are as large as a hoof. Even larger ones were more often found in faraway lands. Rarely did one come across them at Starpoint, as they preferred to stay away from other creatures, especially those who were much larger than them.

She explained to the Professor how she had managed to activate the magic tunnel, which was like a rollercoaster ride, and how she landed on a heap on Earth in a pile of forest leaves, and how she had been found by accident by an elderly lady called Margaret who happened to be taking a walk in the forest on the day she arrived.

She told the Professor all about Margaret and how she had taken her in, and how she had only recently come back into the possession of her Starpoint necklace after believing it had been lost during her amazing journey. She was careful to avoid mentioning anything about Szymon and how she had come to know him by being nosy and following him to his house. She didn't want to admit that she had spied on her friend and what she had overheard, as it might have been too much information for the Professor, since he was still in the early stages of recovering his memories.

Professor Tinzy sat and listened to Princess Sallina's story, carefully digesting and reviewing all the information he was being given.

"Okay. Good. But you haven't told me how you came to be in possession of the remembrance scroll," the Professor said urgently.

Princess Sallina wasn't sure whether to tell the Professor in detail about Szymon and Unimage Konstanty. She feared that if she disclosed the involvement of Unimage Konstanty and explained that he had given her the scroll to help the Professor remember his true self, Szymon might be in a great deal of trouble and the Professor would not allow her to spend any time with Szymon in the future.

She understood that Szymon had planned to use her for his father's benefit and to serve him, but he had also helped her each step of the way. He might have been acting on his father's instructions, but the boy clearly had a steely will of his own. And to be honest, she quite liked him and felt that there was a strong bond forming between the two of them. The truth was, without his support and help, they would never have found a way to bring Professor Tinzy's memories back.

Sallina knew deep inside her heart that she would eventually have to disclose Szymon's actual identity and the role his father had played in rescuing the Professor and bringing back his absent memories, but she wasn't quite ready to reveal all these details to him. She had to first find out a bit more about Professor Tinzy and what he had been up to, and whether he was now back to his old self, before she revealed anything more sensitive that could stir up more trouble.

"I took it along with me for the trip," Sallina said, reluctantly telling a fib, which made her feel really bad. "I had a feeling it might come in handy, so I brought it along with me," she added to bolster her lie.

Professor Tinzy thought carefully about her response. Something in him wanted to question her actions further, but he didn't want to press her too much on the details now, as she had been through a difficult situation herself, and both she and the boy had put themselves at considerable risk when attempting to help him regain his memories. He was content to leave the matter for the time being and pick it up again at a later point in time.

"Coming here has put you in terrible danger, my dear. It's not something I'd ever have wished upon you. Since you are one of my all-time favourite students—and I truly mean this from my heart—I would have preferred to keep you out of harm's way altogether. But as you are here with me, there's very little I can do to get you back home, so here we both are, and we have an important task to fulfil for our kind.

"You ought to know that it won't be easy for either of us to return home, as it has taken me many years to figure out how to get here and then go back, and I'm not exactly sure I can remember most of this anyway. That's one of the problems of being an adult, and a rather old one at that."

The Professor sighed and Sallina smiled faintly in sympathy.

"One of my greatest concerns in coming back to this place is the risk of not being able to go back home again because of the memory loss it imposes on travellers—particularly those who are full-grown adults. It's a terrible thing that those who are more mature in age are forced to endure such a memory loss, and it's a difficult path back to remembrance."

"So what was the point of coming here to find the Pinny if we can't go back, Professor?" Sallina said, raising her voice in alarm. "Are you saying we may both be stuck on this crazy human world? And stuck here FOREVER?"

"Not at all, my dear. There's a way out of here for certain; I'm living proof of this, having come here and gone back several times before! I'm just saying that memory loss may well hinder things, especially the older one gets. You should know, the house I currently reside in here in Doberry… well, it's truly *mine*; I own it! I've owned the place for a very long time—for many years, in fact. Believe it or not, this land is in many ways a second home to me, and I'm quite fond of the place and the people who reside here. Well, some of them, at least. A few of them do get on my nerves."

Sallina relaxed a little then, feeling reassured by the Professor's enthusiasm and optimism about the future and returning home.

"You must remember that you're still so young and fleet of foot, my dear girl, and you're far less likely to suffer from memory loss in the same way I have. I remember myself now only because of the remembrance spell you fortunately cast, and I am truly glad you came along and helped me find myself again. So many lives in Starpoint are depending on us right now to find the Pinny to take back so we can protect our unicorn families and friends from this imminent threat we all face."

Sallina carefully considered what the Professor was saying. She wanted to understand more clearly. "I see… So, I'm lucky. That's why he was also spared and knows who he is; he's young like me. I wonder whether that's why his father sent him in the first place and avoided coming here himself."

"Who do you mean? Whose father?" the Professor asked, baffled.

"Oh, uh, no one. I was thinking about someone else. Guess I am a bit confused about most things right now!" Sallina chuckled. "I mean, I do remember who I am, but all this travelling about, and turning into a human, my goodness, it's still most confusing."

"Well, don't you worry. We are going to fix things, you and me. We are going to find a way to get hold of some Pinny and then we'll both go back together, and we'll be back home in Starpoint in no time at all! You can count on that."

"Okay, well, I'm so glad you have your memory back, Professor. So where do we start?"

"That, my dear, begins with someone important I'd like you to meet. I want to introduce you to a good friend of mine whom I've known for a significantly long time."

"Sure, of course. Ehm… who is it? Where is this person? Is it a person?"

"He's not far away. In fact, he's nearby. He's in my back garden!"

"Oh!" Sallina exclaimed in surprise.

"We can say hello now, if you're free, that is?" the Professor asked.

"Of course I am! There's no time like the present."

"Good. Then let's proceed."

How strange things had become, Sallina thought to herself as they left the building and discreetly exited the school grounds, heading for the Professor's home. Not only was she in a strange world, but she wasn't even herself in this odd shape and form. And here she was with her favourite Professor, whom she admired and respected greatly, and he had only just remembered who he really was.

For a moment, she wondered whether this was as strange as it was going to get in this bizarre adventure, or would it get even stranger in the days ahead. One thing was becoming clear to her: she had to keep an open mind, because everything here on this place called Earth was vastly different from Starpoint, and she needed to adjust and adapt to situations as required. She would need to stick closely to her task, and she knew that she could not do this alone; she would need the Professor beside her to make things happen.

Szymon had already proven to be a true friend. And even though she didn't entirely trust him, something in the back of her mind told her that he would remain on her side, and that he would end up playing an important role in the challenges that lay ahead of her.

As she walked along the street with the Professor, she thought about her life and where she was with the task that had been set before her: to rescue her people and help save her world.

What an odd place Doberry had proven to be, and what strange beings humans were when one got to know them a little—not that she knew many of them. In her heart, she yearned to be back in her true unicorn form, but she knew that this wasn't going to happen anytime soon. She needed to be patient because there were very important things waiting to be done, and so many people depended on her.

Chapter 15

Princess Sallina followed Professor Tinzy into his back garden. It was starting to drizzle, but neither of them minded the slight spattering of rain falling from the clouds that hovered above.

About fifty feet or so ahead in the lush garden, standing right at the end of the path, was a dull-looking, weather-beaten, little grey shed. Sallina followed the Professor as he walked toward the shed along a gravel-strewn patio path, the key to the shed already in his hand. He carefully inserted the key into the lock, turned it, and then firmly took hold of the door handle. The door creaked as it swung out toward him.

"Well, come in, dear girl. The rain might soon be getting heavier, and at least this shed is nice and dry."

Professor Tinzy entered, and Sallina followed him into the unknown.

It was quite dark within, as there was only a small square window that had been partially covered by some tatty black cardboard that barely allowed any light to enter. She could hardly see anything inside. However, she noticed piles of items scattered about, and they were stacked up to her shoulders almost everywhere she turned. This was clearly not an empty shed.

What disturbed her somewhat was that she could also make out the sound of someone breathing, and she knew it wasn't her or the Professor. Someone else was lurking about in this small shed, and they were making sure that they were hidden from plain sight.

"Is someone in here with us?" she asked the Professor. He didn't bother to respond; he was keeping himself very still.

The door to the shed slowly creaked shut on what seemed to be its own accord, and Sallina suddenly started to feel claustrophobic.

"Professor, I'm sure we're not alone here."

"Of course, we aren't," the Professor replied. "My friend also happens to live in here, and he's the one I'd like you to meet. Limpit, could you be so good as to show yourself? I've brought someone here specially to meet you."

The silence languished for a few moments longer, and Sallina could still hear breathing coupled with an odd gurgling sound, like someone was almost drowning trying to expunge the excess liquid from their lungs and thus avoid going under. It was in some ways a scary sound; although it was not loud or piercing, it carried with it a disturbing sense of danger.

"I can tell you are feeling uncomfortable," the Professor said. "My friend often sounds like he's a bit of a heavy smoker, which of course he is. You'll soon understand why."

From the far corner of the cluttered shed appeared a small, rotund red dragon. He was barely two feet in length, with the round, wide eyes of a baby, and droopy wings that radiated a reddish glow. Sallina could see his yellow, glowing eyes, and as he flapped his wings, it was as if they were catching the moonlight and somehow moving it about as it slowly helped to illuminate the little creature. She suddenly felt less threatened as she observed the tiny, pathetic creature who only resembled a great and mighty dragon. Even Yippy seemed more foreboding than this diminutive beast.

The creature coughed spasmodically and eyed the Professor with more than a mild degree of annoyance and frustration.

"Hey, Professor, where did you disappear to? Did you forget all about little old me?" Limpit said, then croaked something out of his smoky, fiery mouth. Sallina thought it was as if a frog had jumped out to save its poor, wretched life. "I've been so ridiculously hungry these past few days, and you didn't leave me any food... you didn't! You also forbade me from going anywhere, so I've been stuck inside waiting for you to show up. Do you know how tedious it has been, stuck inside here the whole time in this dark, smelly hovel?"

The Professor grinned. "Since when have you ever followed any of my instructions?"

"Well, what did you expect me to do? I wasn't going to burn down my tiny home, pathetic as it is, was I? Rubbish and these small wooden walls... well, it's all I've got." Limpit continued to gurgle and spit out wafts of smoke as he spoke.

He suddenly raised both his wings, rose into the air, and flapped them furiously as he headed over to a dark box close to the Princess. He sat.

"So, who do we have here?" he inquired. "I've never seen this one before."

Sallina felt compelled to take a tiny step back. It wasn't that she was afraid of it; after all, how could she be frightened of such a tiny dragon as this one? It was more the smell that repelled her, slightly foul and unpleasant. And it was evident that the smell was emanating from the occupant of the shed.

"You don't look like the type who's easily scared," Limpit quipped, following her retreat.

Sallina wasn't sure how to react to that. She gave it a moment's thought.

"I'm not. I just wanted to give you some extra space."

"Oh, that's kind of you," said Limpit. He turned his attention to the Professor. "At least she thinks of my comfort, unlike some."

Limpit flapped his wings again and rose into the air, hovering a few inches above the box.

"Well, first things first," he said to Professor Tinzy. "I think we need to set out some basic ground rules. You're not allowed to leave me here all by myself ever again. This kind of inconsiderate and autocratic behaviour must stop. If you ever decide to leave me unattended and unfed—and let's not forget, unloved—as I was, then don't you lock up the place and expect me to stay inside for some unknown duration. If you do this to me again… well, next time I'll choose to burn the place down."

"I'm perfectly fine with that suggestion," the Professor responded. He looked rather apologetically at Limpit. "I didn't mean to leave you, but unfortunately, I forgot so many things, and one of them was you."

"You *forgot*? How can you forget? Am I not important enough to be remembered…? I suppose not."

Professor Tinzy was not doing a good job in getting on with Limpit, and Sallina started to worry that these two were beginning to quarrel.

"How long has it been since you were last here? I can't even remember."

"I don't recall. I had a few problems to deal with since we last saw each other, and I'm sorry, Limpit, but I seem to have lost track of time," the Professor said apologetically.

"Well, it was several months ago. You brought me here from your house, and then you locked me up for what was meant to be a couple of days. You did leave a bit of food and drink, but it was clearly not enough. I ran out of that very quickly, and I've had nothing since. Then you simply vanished." Limpit was getting increasingly agitated.

"Oh, no," the Professor said remorsefully. "I'm so sorry, Limpit. Unfortunately, I had completely lost my mind. It was Princess Sallina who in fact helped me recover my precious memories, and she found the way to remind me of who I am. You have her to thank for my being here and rescuing you from your confinement."

Limpit processed the explanation for a few moments, not sure what to make of it.

"Oh, well, I suppose it's all right, as it wasn't your fault, not directly at least," he muttered, still rather peeved about having been trapped for so long. "At least it wasn't something you did to me intentionally. I wouldn't have liked it if you had done this to me on purpose. It would have been very mean. Fortunately, I'm a resourceful dragon and I managed to survive on frequent rainwater I captured from the leaks in the roof and a regular supply of minuscule insects and occasional rats."

"Well, as it happens, I do have a treat in store for you, and I hope in some small manner it can make up for the terrible discomfort I bestowed upon you."

The Professor took out a small chocolate bar and began to meticulously peel off the paper wrapping. He revealed it to Limpit, who immediately started to salivate with excitement, his pupils dilating.

"You horrible master. You know I can't resist a few mouthfuls of a delicious choccy, especially when I'm already so intensely famished," Limpit squealed with mounting excitement.

The chocolate bar was in Professor Tinzy's hand. He held it out to Limpit, waiting for him to react.

Instantly, Limpit's tongue lashed out like a frog's and snatched the entire bar out of the Professor's hand. Before Sallina could even blink, the chocolate and the wrapper had disappeared inside Limpit's mouth. Then came a sudden gulp, followed by a burp that ignited a small flame that must have cooked the chocolate in a flash as it slid down his gullet. Another belch was then emitted, along with an accompanying smaller-sized flame.

Instinctively, the Princess clasped her pendant tightly. She didn't know why she suddenly reacted, but there was something incredibly odd about Limpit that belied his miniature stature, though she couldn't quite place what it was.

"Do you know, lovely Princess," Limpit bellowed, "that before I came to this land, I measured a full 224 feet in length from my head to the end of my tail? And I had quite an imposing presence, to say the least. Unfortunately, and through no fault of my own, I found myself confronted by a couple of fearsome adversaries, and one of them was a great and powerful magician who turned me into this pathetic, diminished creature whom you see before you today."

This explanation took the Princess by complete surprise. "May I ask who these fearsome adversaries were?"

Limpit looked quickly toward the Professor, unsure.

"Don't worry. You are free to let her know what happened," the Professor said.

"There were these three Unimages, including the one you happen to see before you today, although these days he looks about as much a powerful Unimage as I do a fearsome dragon. It wasn't the Professor who was guilty of casting the spell—he wouldn't have had the heart. It was that irksome Unimage Paterline."

"To be fair to Unimage Paterline," Professor Tinzy qualified, "he had only just been informed on very good authority that you had burned down an entire village with your ferocious fiery breath, and that you had roasted almost half the villagers in the process."

"None of it was an intentional act of harm or wanton destruction, Professor. What was I to do? I had acquired this terrible toothache, and when I sought assistance from the resident dentist in the village, I accidentally got a little carried away each time my tooth ached, and he poked a spear into my mouth."

"That's not a good-enough excuse for almost burning down an entire village, is it, Limpit?" the Professor couldn't help but point out the blindingly obvious.

Limpit was, in fact, rather sorry, but he didn't say anything further about it. He knew he had done wrong, unintentionally or not.

Then he noticed the pendant on the chain draped around Sallina's neck. The pendant began to glow with a light-blue radiance, and he couldn't help but admire its magical beauty.

"Blue magic! Oh goodness, so rare," Limpit said. "I almost never get to see blue magic up close these days. Most magic is either green, or red, or yellow, or even, occasionally, black, but blue… that's an exceedingly rare sight to behold indeed!"

The Professor glanced at Sallina's pendant, raising his eyebrow involuntarily.

"She has the star necklace in her possession… oh, how lucky you are, young lady. Professor, does she know much about the star necklace and what magic it possesses?"

Professor Tinzy shot Limpit a somewhat annoyed look, but he said nothing. Sallina noticed the displeased expression as she clung onto her pendant, self-conscious about it being the subject of their discussion.

"Can you tell me what you know about my pendant, Limpit?" she asked the tiny dragon.

Limpit shook his head in dismay; he clearly was afraid to say anything more.

"It's… it's not for me to tell you about it, Princess. You will need to ask the Professor to find out more."

Princess Sallina turned her attention towards the Professor.

"Right now, it's not a good idea to get bogged down with unnecessary details, Princess," the Professor quickly responded in an attempt to dodge the question. "We have more important things to consider at this time."

"I get the feeling you both know something important that you're not disclosing to me," Sallina said. "You have to tell me what it is. It's not fair if you don't."

A quiet groan emanated from Professor Tinzy, and he shook his head in dismay. He glanced at the dragon. "You had to bring this business to her attention. Oh well, go on then, Limpit, tell her about the star pendant—at least some of it that's not so sensitive. I suppose she really ought to know the fundamentals, as she is its current chosen bearer."

Limpit started to get a bit excited.

"Oh, yes, I'd love to tell you some things about it! You know, it's not often that the Professor lets me share my special knowledge on magical artifacts—usually he tells me to keep my mouth well and truly sealed. Well then, Princess, I'll share a little bit about it, as I don't know that much, but my long—and at times illustrious—life has brought with it some useful knowledge and the occasional pearls of wisdom.

"The star necklace has a long and chequered history. It was passed down by generations of Unimages dating back many hundreds of years. There are so precious few magical objects in existence that can work without the enablement of Pinny, and the star necklace is one of these rare items. It finds its energy in another manner instead."

This intrigued Sallina. "Are you saying that it can do magic *without* the aid of Pinny? My gosh, that's a rare talent."

"Yes, I thought I just highlighted that particularly fine quality. Forgive me if I wasn't being clear earlier," Limpit snapped irritably and with more than a hint of sarcasm.

"Then from where does it derive its power? It must have to draw power from somewhere."

Limpit didn't respond to Sallina's question. Instead, he looked toward the Professor for a suitable explanation.

"That bit of information, I'm afraid, is a conversation for another time," Professor Tinzy replied to Sallina's question. "You've already learned something very valuable about it today. The reason you were able to effectively deploy the remembrance scroll on me was because you were in possession of the star pendant, which can work even in this magically deficient land, and without the aid of Pinny."

Sallina considered the Professor's response for a moment. She stopped fondling the pendant and tucked it back into her blouse. The light-blue glow quickly began to fade.

She always knew the star pendant was special in several ways but hadn't reckoned on this quality—that it could work its magic without the aid of Pinny, and it was its own magic enabler. But there were even more fascinating aspects to the pendant; she could sense it by the tone in the voices of both of them. It was obvious that Professor Tinzy and Limpit were purposely holding back on certain things they didn't yet want her to know. If only the necklace was powerful enough to stop the horrible meteor from reaching Starpoint, she wouldn't have to be here in Doberry, and neither would the Professor. Clearly, no single object was that powerful, or she'd know about it. Wouldn't she?

She wasn't yet ready to give up on exploring the topic, so she tried to dig a little more information out of them whilst she had a chance.

"So how powerful, exactly, *is* the star pendant? Do either of you know its true strength?"

Professor Tinzy shook his head. "I've heard it has some strange powers that managed to frighten a number of the great Unimages when they studied it closely, but everything does have its limitations, and sometimes it's best not to know what these limitations are."

"Well, I suppose it can't take us back to Starpoint or prevent a meteor from striking us and hurting everyone we know and care about there. It's obviously not that powerful."

Sallina grimaced as she tested both their patience and knowledge of the magical item in her possession.

"Nothing on its own can achieve such incredible greatness. The magic tunnel we use to travel between lands is eons old, and it too possesses a strange magic of its own whose origin nobody truly knows. However, even that cannot function properly without Pinny being enabled from at least one end to open up the passageway.

When all the Pinny is depleted, we won't be able to use the tunnel anymore, and the way here and back home will be lost. As for the meteor, we're not even sure whether all the alicorns, when enabled at their full power, can successfully deflect the object from impacting Starpoint in the near future. We can only hope that somehow the alicorns working at full power will be able to generate enough magical energy with the correct use of spells to divert the meteor away from our homes and send it off into space in a different direction," the Professor said.

A heavy silence filled the shed. Limpit was already only too well aware of the urgency of their desperate mission to secure a supply of Pinny.

He listened, waited a moment, and then announced proudly, with a touch of boastfulness, "So… it's lucky for you two that I'm one of the best Pinny sniffers in the business you'll ever come across."

"We'd be hard-pressed to find anyone who is better," the Professor added.

This helped take the edge off their awkward conversation, and Professor Tinzy and Princess Sallina relaxed a little.

"Why don't we go back inside the house and make ourselves more comfortable? It looks like the rain is soon going to worsen, and I cannot justify keeping you locked up in this shed any longer, Limpit."

Limpit flapped his wings with joy at the prospect of finally leaving behind this dark and miserable place where he had felt increasingly a captive, although if he had really wanted to get out, he could have destroyed the flimsy shed and fled.

"I'll fix us all a nice, scrumptious dinner," Professor Tinzy added. "I presume we are all hungry after a long day?"

"Oh yes, I for one am very hungry after a long slew of days. You both already know this to be a fact!" Limpit was quick to point out.

"I confess I could eat something too," Sallina said, equally buoyed by the thought of getting her hands on some nourishing and tasty food. "I've almost forgotten about food altogether, but our stomachs soon find a way to remind us of its importance."

Chapter 16

The first thing Professor Tinzy did after following Princess Sallina and Limpit into his house was to lock the front door. Then he shuffled over to the living room and looked out onto the quiet street.

"What or who are you looking for?" Sallina asked.

"Nothing—I'm just making sure nobody's out there watching us. Do make yourselves comfortable while I fix us all a delicious dinner to satiate our appetites."

As Professor Tinzy departed for the kitchen, Princess Sallina cast her eyes around the living room. It was a pleasant-enough place, although sparsely decorated, with just a few odd-looking trinkets scattered about and some photographs, along with a couple of paintings hanging on the wall.

The main sofa looked fairly worn, but it was comfortable. Sallina looked at Limpit, who was hovering in mid-air and studying her with boundless curiosity.

"Do you think there's enough Pinny in this land, Limpit? I do worry about this," the Princess asked the dragon.

Limpit grinned at her. "Oh, there's plenty of Pinny about, Princess; I'm pretty certain of that. This land happens to be known for its richness in Pinny, but it's not to be found anywhere nearby—you'll have to travel a heck of a long way to come across it."

Limpit shifted towards the set of shelves and pulled out a book with one of his claws.

"Take a look at this," Limpit said, tossing the tome over to Sallina, who just about managed to catch it.

"It's a learned book about Pinny in this land and tells you lots about where to find it and how hard it is to obtain. Don't be put off, though; there's still lots of it about, certainly more than we have back home. One just needs to know where to look and be smart about how they get one's claws on some of it."

Princess Sallina stared at the title on the front cover: *History of Painite*. Limpit floated across to where Sallina was sitting as she opened the book carefully to the first page, already riveted and intrigued.

"Pinny—or Painite, as they call it here—was discovered in the 1950s, by the human calendar," Limpit recited to her from memory. "At that time, only a handful of samples existed in this world. Fortunately, since then, humans have discovered lots more, although it remains quite rare when compared to other more common minerals that they have in abundance."

As he was speaking, Limpit found himself drawing nearer and nearer to the Princess. In fact, he was getting so close that it made her feel more than a little uncomfortable, and she edged away from his subtle advances. In turn, Limpit, realizing he was disturbing her, refrained from getting closer, and looked at her apologetically.

Sallina turned her attention once again to the book and a few black-and-white pictures that told her the story of how and where Painite had been first discovered.

"Looks like a very old book. How long have you had it on you?" she murmured.

"It's not that old—maybe fifteen to twenty years, which is nothing in real terms. Pinny was discovered by a British mineralogist and gem dealer named Arthur C.D. Pain and takes its name in this place after him... or should I say, after his name."

Limpit appeared to be a veritable font of knowledge when it came to all things Painite. He had clearly put great effort into studying it.

"Wow, it's not so different from what we call it, then. What a peculiar coincidence. So where can we get hold of some?" Sallina inquired.

"Ah, well, discoveries of Pinny are mostly made in a faraway place called Myanmar, which is more than five thousand miles away from where we presently happen to be," Limpit explained.

"Then what are we doing staying here in Doberry?" Sallina was suddenly flustered and impatient, and she wanted to get on with the mission. "Shouldn't we be heading off to this faraway place instead? There's no time to waste, is there? It could take days, weeks, or even longer to travel such a huge distance."

Limpit nodded. "Yes, you are right, of course. But we are very fortunate, Princess Sallina," he added.

"How so? Not another riddle from either of you! You talk to me like I'm just a child."

Limpit was about to answer when Professor Tinzy stepped hurriedly into the room, carrying a pot and making straight for the window again.

"I could have sworn I heard something out there. Why is it I have the feeling someone has been spying on us?" he muttered to himself. He looked down at the pot in his oven-mitted hands and took a few steps back towards Limpit and Princess Sallina.

"Umm, do either of you object to a smattering of spinach?"

Sallina gave him a quizzical look.

Limpit grinned. "Oh, I have a feeling she perhaps doesn't know what spinach is or even tastes like. How long has she been in this place? I mean, you would think she'd have come across it before. It's similar to kibblen, Princess, and it has a strong green colour that makes it look even more delicious and appealing. If you don't mind the taste of kibblen, you'll soon become fond of eating spinach."

Sallina smiled. "Sure, I like to eat kibblen. I always have, since I was tiny."

The Professor nodded, and he returned to the kitchen to continue with his cooking.

Limpit flapped his wings a little harder as he made his way to the front window to look out. What, he wondered, might have caught Professor Tinzy's attention?

He looked up and down the road outside the house, but there seemed nothing unusual that he could detect.

Little did they know, Szymon had earlier on followed Sallina and the Professor back to the house from the school, and he had hidden behind a large car. This time it was Szymon who was doing the spying, just like Sallina had previously done outside his house.

Limpit wasn't easy to spot, as there was a net curtain in the way that dramatically reduced the chances of anyone taking a good peek inside the house, but there was no mistaking what he could see through the window. It was a clear silhouette of a creature that Szymon was able to identify.

His father had warned him that Limpit was probably lurking about somewhere in this strange land he had been sent to and told his son to stay away from the dragon if he showed up. Konstanty had told him in no uncertain terms that Limpit was at the very least unpredictable and given to frequent mood swings, as well as spontaneously becoming dangerous. Although dragons, just like unicorns, traditionally found it difficult to cast magic without the aid of Pinny, many of their natural functions—such as breathing fire and flying about—were not restricted by the availability of this vital magical-enablement substance.

Back inside the Professor's house, Sallina had returned to quizzing Limpit.

"As I was saying, what exactly are we doing here in Doberry? Especially when the Pinny is to be found so far away."

Limpit shook his head in dismay, not knowing how to answer the question without taking the risk of leading her to even more confusion and getting himself into trouble with the Professor.

"I can't explain it to you, Princess. All I can say is I don't make the decisions here; I help out as and when I'm required, which isn't that often. Hence why I was kept locked up in a shed for an inordinate amount of time, neglected, and virtually forgotten until I was once again of use. I'm unimportant, really. A sideshow. Trivial, even. Talk to someone in authority instead of little old me. Talk to the great Professor, who stands before you."

"Clearly there's so much I still want to comprehend, but why did the Professor bring a notable sniffer dragon such as yourself here if you're so unimportant? I mean, there are quite a few dragons around back home, but they are already a dying species, and each year there seem to be fewer of them about."

Limpit shrugged, his wings uplifted but his mood sombre.

"I honestly don't know," he retorted. "But, you know, I can be somewhat useful in a few ways, so it is usually a good idea to have me hanging around. I may be small, I may be normally insignificant, but I'm also handy at times, that's for sure."

Sallina rose from her seat and decided to head to the window herself and take a look outside. She glanced up and down the street carefully. There appeared to be nothing unusual taking place. It seemed that the Professor's internal sensors were not functioning properly.

"Limpit, did the Unimages search for you because of your Pinny expertise for this mission? Or was there some other reason you were tracked down and probably forced to get involved? Did you come to help, or were you given no choice in the matter?" Sallina asked.

"My Pinny expertise was something they felt they needed, oh yes. You mean, when did the Unimages come and turn me into this sad, tiny apparition you see flapping his wings before you? Did they force me to come along? Is that what you're asking?"

"Yes, that's precisely what I'd like to know," responded Sallina. "I'm wondering whether they already had it in their minds to bring you over here, and that they didn't shrink you only as some kind of gross punishment for having lit up that village with your fiery breath—which of course was not a nice thing to do by any stretch of the imagination—but because they wanted you along on this Pinny quest.

The reason I ask is that all this talk about Pinny being relatively easy to obtain is surely not the case, especially if I am to believe what has been written in this book. Who better to bring along than an expert Pinny sniffer such as yourself? I believe they must have wanted you as a vital part of their mission, and you clearly are a crucial and valuable member in a whole host of ways, many of which I don't yet understand."

Limpit thought carefully about her question, and somehow her comments lifted his mood. "You know, I think you may be right there, Princess. I've never thought about it in the way you've just explained it. It's an enlightening way of looking at things. I do really like your way of thinking, and your logical mind is to be greatly admired. You're a bright little spark and not just an exalted royal… although to me you are quite big, given my current physical condition. I mean, I'm the small one here. Gosh, it still feels so unusual for me not to be the giant among lesser sized creatures."

This made Sallina giggle. "Yes, indeed. Look who's calling me a bright *little* spark: a tiny dragon that once was a large and formidable beast who terrified most who came across him. I don't mean to offend you, Limpit."

Professor Tinzy returned, wearing a big smile across his face. These days it was rare to see him in a better mood.

"Food shall be ready shortly, my dear friends. It's now doing its magic in the oven, and the spell will soon be cast to make sure it's delicious."

Limpit flew closer to the Professor. "Professor, you know many things that we don't. Sallina was asking me an important question, and I simply couldn't answer it. Perhaps you can enlighten us on something."

"Oh? What was her question?" the Professor asked.

"Well, if all the Pinny we're seeking is quite far away, what is it that we're doing hanging around here in this remote and strange place? I mean, why come to the sleepy little village of Doberry and mix with these irrelevant humans?"

The Professor let out a short belly laugh, which came as a bit of a surprise to Limpit and Sallina. He had obviously found the matter to be most amusing.

Belly laughs usually start at the belly and then work their way up through the lungs and then out into the open via the mouth, although sometimes when someone is in a heightened state of excitement, that may not be the only place they manage to exit from. They are usually deeper than the standard chortle, and some think they're more sincere. They also have a way of touching the core of a human being or other kind of creature and lightening the atmosphere. To most, they're seen as somewhat over-the-top and exaggerated, and in certain cases where a degree of formality is called for, they can even be misconstrued as being inadvertently rude.

"Well, for starters, this place we find ourselves in happens to be my humble home. I don't mean just this house, I mean Doberry, and the place that I happen to work in for a living. I count all of it as a second home. So, we're here because this is where I chose to reside when I initially came to this strange land. But, far more importantly, there happens to be an upcoming sale of Pinny that's taking place next week in central

London, which is not so far away from here. So, it's convenient for us to be in Doberry, do you see? Good things have a habit of coming to us."

Limpit jumped in. "What? Oh, that's wonderful. How far is this sale from here?"

"It's not far. In fact, it's just a few hours by car."

"A few hours by car. A car… oh, that's really exciting!" Limpit exclaimed. "But nobody here can even drive a car. How will we get to this place if we are required to travel in a motor car and none of us can drive?"

"We'll have to figure out some way to do it. It can't be all that difficult.

"Well, my good friends, I've been watching the news updates, and if the auction goes ahead on Monday next week, we'll all be heading down there to make an all-important purchase."

"An all-important purchase?" Limpit queried the Professor. "But I don't have any money to purchase anything, and neither, I suspect, do you. Who among us has any money? I doubt that school of yours pays its professors sufficiently to purchase Pinny."

"Oh, don't worry about trivial things such as getting hold of money, as I was given enough of it for my teaching work. I even have a bank account. I've been saving for a few years now, and I've enjoyed this thing they call 'interest', which helps grow one's savings. Interesting thing, interest. I can get my hands on as much money as we need. There's plenty of it out there if we require it."

"Oh, alright, then. This is great news for sure! We get the Pinny and find our way back to Starpoint as fast as possible, so we can help our citizens back home and protect them from the oncoming threat," Sallina exclaimed.

Professor Tinzy reacted enthusiastically to her response. "Spoken like a true and caring princess. I am immensely proud to hear of your dedication and concern for your subjects—I've never doubted it."

"Well, if you ask me, she still has a couple of things to learn before she can be described as a true and caring princess," Limpit muttered.

"And what would these be?" Professor Tinzy asked.

"Oh, nothing I can rattle off from the top of my head. Thinking of some useful suggestions for the young lady to take on board, well, there's a certain finesse required that surely seems to be lacking in my mannerisms, so I'll keep my mouth sealed and avoid making myself appear stupid in front of a great Unimage such as yourself," Limpit replied.

"Erhmm," the Princess interjected. "How about we focus on the task at hand and find a way to get a hold of some Pinny? You can advise me and judge my finer mannerisms at a later date, as I am always open-minded and willing to improve myself."

Limpit nodded. The Professor smiled, admiring Sallina's level-headedness.

"So… tell me, Professor, how are we going to get our hands on this motor car?" Sallina asked.

"Oh, my dear, that's really not a problem, as I happen to have one parked right outside which we can use when we're ready," he replied.

"You do?" Sallina said, taken by surprise. "That's great news!"

"I'll show you the contraption after dinner."

With that, he headed back to the kitchen to check up on the roast that was busily cooking in the oven.

Whilst they were engaged in their pre-dinner conversation, Szymon had being doing much more than just seeking to eavesdrop on them while he was concealed behind the big car. He had sneakily made his way over to the living-room window and removed his backpack, which he had carefully opened.

He pulled out a small black bag, untied the cord, and took out a small orb that looked very similar to the one from which his father had appeared in his house. He raised the orb in one hand and ignited a flame from a lighter in the other. Szymon lightly waved the flame above the orb, and out shot another flame from the sphere. This consolidated itself into a single eyeball, which focused its attention on the window.

Szymon put the lighter back in his pocket as he held the orb up to his head. Inside his mind, he could hear the echo of his father's voice.

"Take me closer to the window, my son. I want to see all there is," Konstanty said telepathically.

Now, it is worth noting that the power of the particular magic that allowed Konstanty to use the small orb for perception was so intense that some miles away, back at Szymon's house, Yippy began yapping away furiously again behind the living room door in the hallway as the large orb inside started glowing with a bright kaleidoscope of colours. The apparition needed to first manifest on the larger orb before it could be amplified to manifest on the smaller one, and the intensity of the glow in Szymon's house increased as Konstanty's head appeared and hovered above the globe there. Unimage Konstanty then projected his attention to the other side of town, onto the remote eye in the tiny orb resting in his son's hand.

This was a powerful spell that required a great deal of Pinny, and it was possible only because several things had been meticulously put into place to help make the magic happen.

Unimage Konstanty himself was, of course, back in Starpoint, focusing all his energies from there to create a distant link to Doberry. In this instance, because incredible power was needed to allow him to appear simultaneously in Szymon's and Professor Tinzy's homes, he had brought along a helping hand—or rather, hoof.

That's why Unimage Callindra was there, close to him. Sitting together, they both focused their powerful minds and channelled their magical energies onto an identical orb situated in the dark cellar of Unimage Callindra's home.

The combined strength and power of both Unimages had manifested a much stronger connection, allowing the signal to the orb in Szymon's house to be carried out even further. Magic was almost impossible to utilize in Doberry or anywhere else on Earth, so no one could anticipate the full effect of using Pinny so extensively there. In some ways, this was an experiment for the two Unimages back home. Konstanty had been confident it would work sufficiently well, as had been Unimage Callindra.

And so it was proving to be. The two Unimages even managed to chuckle softly to each other as they watched their unified power travelling the vast distance between worlds to faraway Earth.

Szymon, meanwhile, had removed the scroll from the black bag and was watching the blue light emanate from the scroll directly onto the orb, thus helping to power it. Szymon smiled too, awed by the fact that he here was in little old Doberry, acting as a conduit for his father many stars away… and it was working like a treat. It was utterly amazing.

He had not been as confident as his father when the plan to learn what was going on had been revealed to him on that very morning.

Szymon had been enjoying porridge at the breakfast table when the big orb lit up, and Yippy had started yapping his little heart out. Szymon duly jumped up and went to the living room with the bowl of porridge in his hand and became engaged in an intense conversation with his father.

Szymon had sighed heavily when Konstanty's intentions had been explained to him, believing he would be wasting his time. He really didn't want to spend hours after dark lurking outside Professor Tinzy's house and attempting something so unlikely to work. They all knew that magic in this land was barely workable at all, and without Pinny, it had little chance of even succeeding.

His father soon snapped him out of his contemplative state.

"I want to get something clear in your young head!" Unimage Konstanty had virtually bellowed as he hovered above the orb. "There is so much you don't yet know about so many things, and numerous lives and subsequent actions depend on what you do for us in that human world you're in. There is only one magic proven to work anywhere, including in this strange place in which you find yourself, and its blue magic, which can be found on Princess Sallina's powerful necklace. By activating the scroll and the orb we can borrow some of that magic, and we can use it with the scroll instead of using Pinny.

"Therefore, we have one chance to fix things, and we must use this opportunity wisely, before they realize we're using their own magic against them."

"What do you mean, 'fix things'?" Szymon asked.

"Well, you may not like to hear this, but there is something very important that you must do for me, because if you don't, we will have before us powerful enemies who will do their utmost at all times to thwart our actions and ruin our plans, and we must make sure this doesn't happen."

"I wouldn't call Professor Tinzy the enemy, and especially not Princess Sallina. That seems a harsh thing to say, Father," Szymon muttered in mild defiance.

"I don't mean them, stupid boy!" Konstanty raged. "I'm talking about a nasty, unpleasant, completely despicable, and totally hideous little creature who is also there with them in Doberry. You must neutralize that vile and insane little beast quickly before we can proceed any further with our important mission. The creature, who goes by the name of Limpit, is a tiny and incredibly bothersome dragon. It is our sworn enemy, and always has been. Do not underestimate this once-powerful dragon. It is a formidable beast despite looking so helpless and appearing so small."

"A tiny dragon, a formidable beast?" Szymon said, eyes lighting up. "Although I've always wanted to see a real dragon up clos—"

"Szymon! Concentrate! This is important! We're not on some sort of silly field trip for your school. This is all serious business, and so much here is at stake."

"Yes, Father, sorry, Father, I fully understand," Szymon spluttered, giving Konstanty his full and undivided attention.

"Don't for a second be fooled by that creature's diminutive size," Konstanty said, his eyes narrowing at the same time as they homed in on his son's. "This dragon is a truly formidable adversary, and not one sympathetic to our glorious causes and the mission we are here to accomplish for our kind. Are we clear?"

"Clear as falling raindrops landing on a pond," the boy muttered.

He was not willing to cross the will of his stern and overbearing father, one of the greatest Unimages who had ever existed across all the great and varied lands known and unknown to all living unicorns.

Not yet, at least.

Chapter 17

As Szymon crouched outside the living room window of Professor Tinzy's house, the tiny eye above the small orb was busy looking in. Konstanty was straining himself to look through the net curtain and soak in more magical energy from Princess Sallina's powerful necklace to make the covert surveillance possible between two distant worlds.

It could see a table across the other end of the living room, and sitting there was Professor Tinzy along with his student and guest, Princess Sallina. It also recognised the small dragon, Limpit, hovering above a chair.

Sallina was unconsciously adjusting her pendant. She was unaware that some of its power was being mysteriously tapped by a malevolent force just outside the building, but something subconscious was alerting her to danger, which made her uncomfortable.

Limpit stuck out his elongated tongue and scooped in another bite of the delicious meal on his plate. It was something that resembled meatloaf, potatoes, and a selection of garden salads, and it all looked and tasted unbelievably delicious.

Princess Sallina was using a knife and fork to tuck into her food. She chewed a small portion, her face expressionless.

"Do you like it?" the Professor asked.

"What's not to like? It's so delicious," she said half-heartedly.

"Tastes a lot like kibblen, if you ask me," Limpit said.

Sallina chewed some more, then swallowed. "It tastes okay to me."

"What do you mean, 'it tastes okay'?" the Professor quipped, somewhat surprised and disappointed by the lacklustre reaction. "I think it's a truly fine meal to be having in this land that is our temporary home."

"I completely agree with that notion," Limpit said in unwavering support. "It is a truly fine meal; I'm savouring each and every moment."

As if to prove his point, Limpit took hold of another slice of the meatloaf lookalike with his tongue and ingested it. His nostrils flared momentarily with flickering flames as he swallowed it down his miniscule gullet, and then he burped with contentment.

"Well, I really don't mind eating kibblen," said Sallina, "but it's not exactly my favourite dish, although it is appetizing enough and fills my belly."

"I call the dish 'Spinach Loaf,' as it contains spinach along with something humans call 'tofu.' Tofu is made from taking soy milk and then pressing the resulting curds into solid white blocks of varying degrees of softness, and it's designed to emulate the taste of meat."

"I see. Well, thank you for making sure I don't eat meat. I couldn't imagine that" Sallina said, trying to sound grateful and relieved at the same time.

"The problem with her is she's so used to eating at all those grand royal banquets, and for so long, that she's been completely spoilt for choice for years," Limpit blurted out with a huff. "You ought to try getting locked inside a small shed for weeks and even months—you'll soon learn to appreciate the little delicacies such as these beauties lying before us on this fine table."

"Oh, I'm sorry. I do appreciate it; I don't mean to offend anyone. I'm not behaving like a spoiled brat or anything, I hope. In fact, when I was little, I was the opposite entirely. In the first thirty years of my existence, I wasn't even allowed outside my own home, and I was conditioned to appear fairer and sweeter than anyone could be before my mother even dared to expose me to any of the good citizens of Starpoint. This rather made me keep my tastes and thoughts to myself, and I lacked the desire to express my feelings to others. I simply accepted everything that was given to me."

"Oh, why was that, then? Doesn't sound like a good way to treat a princess," Limpit said.

"It's not polite to ask someone questions of a personal nature," Professor Tinzy interjected.

"No, it's okay, thank you, Professor. I don't mind explaining myself," Sallina said, turning her gaze on the dragon. "You see,

Limpit, I'm not really an expert on royal protocol, but I know a little—enough to get by. And as I get older, I get better at it, but I don't enjoy it much, and I find so much of it to be rather tedious and a waste of time."

"Oh, really?" said Limpit, dismissively. "So what do you know about our current predicament?"

The Princess chose to ignore the dragon's flippancy. "It is said that in Starpoint, all races of unicorns are born equal and will be treated as equal no matter who they are or where they come from, royal stock or not. But unfortunately, when one has royal stock, you're often judged harshly by your fellow citizens, who set much higher expectations.

"Consequently, there were several concerns my mother had about the way I looked and behaved. I took more after my father, who himself had come from ordinary peasant stock out in the far farmlands where there exist only tiny villages. Although he rose to prominence as the companion to the Queen, he could never be seen or accepted as a future king. He knew that, and I suppose while he was with us, he accepted it.

"It became worse after I turned thirty, for then my father suddenly disappeared. There were many different rumours that he had done something terrible and had been secretly punished for his transgressions by being banished from the lands, but none of these theories were true. Or, should I say, nothing was proven.

"The truth turned out to be a lot more banal. Father was in fact taken away from the public spotlight because he was seriously ill, and his personal desire was not to be seen by others and for our family not to be subjected to the public gaze. So, Mother decided to abdicate him from the royal limelight until I had attained the mature age of seventy and could be recognised as a future heir to the throne.

"Whilst I was still young, she didn't want the line of succession to be challenged. Even when I turned fifty, she felt it would be easier for me to handle the outside world and for the citizens of Starpoint to accept me as their future Queen once I had attained a certain amount of maturity, thus diverting attention from my rather ordinary and not-too-well father."

"Oh, how terrible for you, my dear," Limpit said with genuine sympathy. "I didn't know about that and your poor father. I'm truly sorry. I meant no offense in asking you questions."

"None taken, Limpit. You didn't know, and you deserve to hear the truth," Sallina replied. "It's wrong of me to keep on insisting I'm told things honestly and openly, and then to hide my past and avoid answering anything in return."

"Well, that's all now in the past, and it was some years ago. It turns out that our Princess Sallina is incredibly bright and possesses a kind nature, and I would struggle to find anyone in Starpoint who even has a bad word to say about her," Professor Tinzy said reassuringly.

Outside the house, Konstanty's eye continued to observe and listen to the discussion going on, trying to pick up as much of the muffled conversation as possible—mainly through the assistance of lip reading. It could hear, but that function was limited as its main purpose was to see, and it was too far away to hear properly.

Unimage Konstanty had both the benefit of the eyes and, later on, the ears of his son in eavesdropping on the conversation, but Szymon's ears were not the most reliable, as he rarely kept them clean and finely tuned enough to absorb the more nuanced elements of conversations taking place at a fair distance.

"Well, from what I've previously made of royal protocol, most of it is filled with blatant lies and carefully masked deceit," Unimage Konstanty muttered to himself as he hovered over the orb in Szymon's house.

Yippy kept barking relentlessly at the door.

"Oh, do shut up, you frivolous, silly pooch. Have you not improved one bit?" Konstanty blurted at the over-excited canine, faintly remembering his previous existence as an impertinent apprentice.

The eye then returned to concentrating on what was happening beyond the window as Konstanty remained transfixed by the task at hand.

Eavesdropping became tiresome after a while, and Szymon found himself unable to concentrate much, nor could he continue to hold up the small orb without his arm and hand shaking from fatigue. A couple of passers-by looked over to see what was going on, which forced Szymon to quickly put the orb away and disappear into the shadows, crouching behind some bushes. Whilst hiding a second and then a third time, he suddenly yawned and closed his eyes. Before he knew it, he was drifting off to sleep.

The eye was still in Szymon's hand, even though he was asleep. Not sure what was going on, it turned to look up at the snoozing boy. There wasn't much the wielder of the eye could do about it, apart from trying to rouse him with a loud, *"WAKE UP!"* inside his head.

But it was no good, since Szymon was sound asleep. His father did all he could, and then both he and Unimage Callindra tried to coax Szymon awake with a succession of shouts of, "Szymon! Wake up!"

But zip, nothing. He was too tired to be disturbed from his slumber.

"Blooming boy! Foolhardy foal!" his father ranted, his magical eye shaking.

Some minutes later, the front door opened, and out stepped Professor Tinzy, followed by Princess Sallina. Professor Tinzy held something in his hand, which he depressed. Suddenly, a car light lit up and the car doors unlocked themselves. The Professor and Sallina walked towards it. Limpit watched them from the living room window whilst Szymon still snoozed away in the bushes.

Professor Tinzy and Sallina climbed into the car. The Professor chose the passenger side, while Sallina got in next to him in the driver's seat. It was a blue Ford Fiesta—quite an old one.

"So, who is going to drive this strange-looking machine?" the Princess enquired.

"Well, I was hoping you would do the honours, Princess," the Professor responded.

"Me? I don't know how to drive it. I've never driven a car in my life! How does it even work?"

The Professor tried to reassure her with, "It's supposed to be relatively easy." He handed her the car key. "You'll figure it out in no time."

Sallina took the key and held it in front of her eyes. "Tell me, what do I do with this? Perhaps it's for the door."

"I already unlocked the door. I think you need to put it into something inside that's found by the steering wheel, and then you turn it around to start up the car. I think that's all there is to it," the Professor said as he pointed towards the vehicle. "Then you let it drive."

Sallina stared at the Professor in bafflement. "This car is yours. How come you have never driven it before?"

"Oh, I have a human that sometimes comes by and takes me around in it. He usually makes sure that it runs alright. He seems to find it easy. Hence, I've left these kinds of trivial matters to him to deal with," the Professor replied.

Sallina looked around the dashboard, trying to figure out what to do, as Professor Tinzy pointed to a hole to the side of the steering wheel.

"I think the key goes in there," the Professor said helpfully.

Sallina inserted the key and wiggled it about. Suddenly, the car started up. This got her quite excited.

As she looked towards the Professor, her face suddenly turned sour.

"Won't it be dangerous for me to try and commandeer this machine? I might have an accident. I need to practice a bit so I can make sure I'm able to handle it."

"Oh, I suppose that would be a sensible way to go about it. The human who usually drives me about makes it look a doddle, so I just assumed anyone could quite quickly pick up how to drive! Not that I'm suggesting you're just anyone, I didn't mean that. But I suppose you're right; it will be better to practice in the morning, too, and not at night when it's dark, especially as you don't know how to use it properly."

Something caught the Professor's eye, and he looked hurriedly over toward his house. There was Limpit at the window, flapping his wings about and making a heck of a ruckus.

"Hmmm. Something's not right inside… Limpit is going bonkers!"

Sallina turned her attention towards the house. "We'd better go and check out what's happening with him."

She switched off the engine and passed the key back to the Professor.

"You should hang onto it. You'll need it again tomorrow when you start it up for our test drive," he said.

Sallina pocketed the key and they both climbed quickly out of the car and raced back to the house. Meanwhile, in the bushes, Szymon had been startled awake by Limpit's raucous dragon-cries and wing-flapping, and he awoke to find Limpit staring straight at him through the window.

"Uh-uh!" Szymon muttered to himself. "This is bad."

By the time that Professor Tinzy and Sallina had entered the house and moved swiftly to the living room window, Szymon was no longer visible.

The eye in Szymon's hand looked up at Szymon quizzically and shook itself left to right in disdainful disapproval. In Szymon's mind, he could now hear his father scolding him and trying to rouse him from his slumber.

"You mustn't drop off to sleep on me like this, son, not at such a crucial moment when we are investigating something important. We almost lost the element of surprise because you were not being careful!" Konstanty's voice boomed in Szymon's ears.

Szymon bowed his head. "I'm sorry, Father, I don't know what came over me. I haven't slept properly for a few days."

"Just don't let it happen again, ever. Now, son, when Tinzy and the girl are no longer staring at you from the window, and you can still detect the presence of that vile little creature inside the house, I want you to take me closer to the window so I can have a much better perspective on what's going on inside," Konstanty remarked inside Szymon's head.

Szymon wanted to remonstrate with him, but having already incurred his father's wrath, he decided the better of it and kept silent, leaving his thoughts to himself.

"I've something very special in store for that pesky dragon," Konstanty continued with a slight chuckle. "He will be in for a heck of a surprise."

Inside, Sallina and the Professor moved away from the window, satisfied that no one was outside and believing Limpit was simply having one of his eccentric moments, which even Sallina was getting used to.

"I did see something, I tell you!" Limpit continued to rant. "Someone was outside, and they were snooping on us."

Sallina sat herself back on the sofa and took the key out of her pocket, fiddling with it absent-mindedly while contemplating the thought of driving a car, which both scared and excited her in equal measure. The Professor, meanwhile, collected the dishes from the table and went back to the kitchen. Limpit continued to wait by the window on look-out—he was adamant that someone was out there.

Sure enough, he discovered he was right! For striding from behind the bushes was Szymon, and he was heading straight for the window. Then Limpit saw the small black orb Szymon was pointing directly at him. Most alarming of all, on it was a single ugly eyeball, staring at him in a most freakish way.

"Uh-uh, this doesn't look good. I have a bad feeling about our spy," Limpit muttered, mainly to himself. He once again began flapping his wings frantically. "I see it, I see it, there's someone here... There's someone right outside the house looking directly at me, a nasty snooper for sure! Come take a look for yourself. I swear it!"

Professor Tinzy couldn't hear Limpit hollering as he was busy in the kitchen, and Sallina was deeply absorbed in her car-driving fantasy as she twiddled the key in her hand and imagined what it would be like.

Everything that happened next happened incredibly fast.

As Limpit flapped his wings, a ball of fiery red light suddenly appeared out of nowhere and hovered in front of the eyeball. This light was being generated by Konstanty, back on Starpoint, from the bigger orb in Szymon's living room, as well as with the magic that was being transferred onto the scroll from Princess Sallina's necklace.

The fireball quickly expanded to a foot in diameter, and then it shot forward toward Limpit at lightning speed. It shattered the glass window and made a circular hole whilst also burning through the net curtain as it propelled itself toward the tiny dragon like a lightning bolt.

Such was the ferocity and remarkably raw power of this fireball that no ordinary person could have withstood its force, but Limpit was of course no ordinary person or creature. He was a great dragon, despite his unfortunately reduced size.

Limpit, in fact, heralded from the great mountains not more than a few days' march from Starpoint, and it was in his very nature to live with and breathe fire, both in and out. Fire was certainly not any kind of foe to him. In fact, if anything, it was a close and familiar friend. One could even go as far as to say that fire was the fabric of his very existence.

Even though Limpit had no fear of the flame, and it didn't pose a direct threat to him, he didn't like being smacked in the chest by an intense fireball, and its impact managed to take the wind out of him. So much so that he had to flap his wings twice and even three times as hard as usual to stay aloft and not get pushed back or down toward the ground. Mighty as he was, even with his extremely diminutive stature, he found himself struggling to manifest the energy he needed to expend to stay in the air, but expend it he did, and Limpit managed to hold the exact same position he had been in a few seconds earlier.

Konstanty was immediately infuriated when he saw that Limpit was more than able to absorb the impact of the fiery ball without suffering too much harm, which had been his intention to inflict.

"So, you don't have a problem dealing with my powerful fireball spell… well, I've got something even more special lined up for you that you might not like so much, you malformed, shrunken, detestable, hideous creature!" Konstanty bellowed as he hovered over the orb in Szymon's living room, getting more and more worked up. The sound of a highly agitated Konstanty set Yippy off with another ferocious round of barking as the mutt remained locked away beyond the living room door.

Whilst Konstanty was preparing to disburse his second powerful spell, Limpit was also becoming more agitated, which now had made Sallina jump up from the sofa and brought the Professor in hurriedly from the kitchen.

"What on earth was that commotion?"

The gaping hole in the window proved somewhat distressing. Princess Sallina swapped puzzled looks with the Professor before moving forward to attend to Limpit. But before she could step one foot forward, Professor Tinzy pulled her by the shoulder.

"Don't try it. This may be too dangerous. Don't worry about Limpit—he is more than able to handle himself when under attack."

But Sallina wanted to help the amicable beast she had recently befriended. She clasped her powerful, magical pendant, thinking hard about what kind of spell she could conjure up to protect the small dragon. It gave her some comfort to know that she did have access to some powerful magic she could call on when needed—even though she didn't know how best to use the object properly.

Limpit proudly spoke out. "Don't worry about me, Princess. I'm not easily beaten by any man or beast. There's a rather foolhardy Unimage at the other end of the evil eye staring at us from outside, and I have a pretty good idea who the nasty culprit could be."

"Evil eye?" the Professor said, looking more concerned, his grip on Sallina's shoulder tightening.

"Please, Professor, I want to help Limpit. Let me at least try to do something," Sallina pleaded.

"No, you can't assist him right now. It took powerful magic to do what was done through that window, and I fear greatly for your wellbeing. You're not a seasoned Unimage who can face the opponent Limpit's pitted against—you're merely a young lady unicorn, and I have an important responsibility to look after you and ensure you aren't put in harm's way."

Professor Tinzy was right to be cautious and hold Sallina back, because worsen the situation did a few seconds later. As Konstanty incanted his new spell, a deep-blue ball began circling above the mini orb. It looked like it was comprised of hundreds of tiny icicles, swirling furiously in the shape of a sphere. Like the fireball before, this new ball expanded quickly in diameter, and when it was about five feet wide from side to side, it began to spin around faster and faster as more small icicles took shape… and then they suddenly began shooting toward Limpit at high speed.

"You may have dodged my fiery fireball spell, you troublesome beast, but let's see if you can evade this far-more-powerful icy death spell I've just cast upon you," Konstanty sniped as he gazed through the eye at his intended victim.

The unusual thing about Konstanty's threats was that only Szymon could hear them, as the eye hovering above the orb had no mouth to speak from and no breath, and the magic wasn't the right type to add a separate voice. But somehow the threat connected with Limpit, echoing in his mind as if he had heard the words directly himself. Whether this was because the dragon possessed his own magical abilities and could tune into the words formed by the Unimage in Szymon's mind, or because he could detect the deeper nature of the magic present before him and connect with it in some strange and inexplicable way, remained unclear to the dragon, nor was it likely to be explained so easily by anyone else.

Back in the basement in Starpoint, even Unimage Callindra had to glance over at Konstanty as she realized that his personal vendetta toward Limpit was perhaps going too far and could backfire on them.

"This might not be the ideal moment to strike down that pathetic dragon," she remarked as Konstanty continued to build on the deep and dark spell that was manifesting in Szymon's living room and being transposed to the mini eye outside the Professor's house. "We have to be incredibly careful, as the magic captured from the pendant will soon run out, and then what can we do to sustain the magic in this strange land? Our magic doesn't work on its own, not without the aid of Pinny… and even then, we don't know how effective it will be. The last thing we want is for Princess Sallina to figure out that we are tapping into her magic powers from the pendant and then cut us off. We may need access to it in the future without her knowing about it."

But Konstanty wasn't bothering to listen to her; he was far too preoccupied with building his spell and preparing for his contemptible attempt to strike down this small dragon that had previously presented itself as a formidable opponent to many who attempted to defeat him. Eliminating Limpit had become deeply personal to him and was now part of his deepest desires, as he had disliked the dragon for so many decades. This was his grandest opportunity to strike at the vile beast and get him out of the way, and he relished the opportunity to make this diminished dragon suffer at his hands.

As if he could read Konstanty's mind, Limpit suddenly blurted out to anyone who could hear him, "You may judge me to be just a small and trivial opponent, you miserable Unimage of a unicorn, but I assure you, Unimage Konstanty, that I have all my best faculties about me as before, and I am able to defeat anyone who wishes to inflict harm on me or my friends at any time of day or night!"

It wasn't just Limpit who heard Konstanty. The Professor and Sallina could as well, since once again the magic from the pendant provided a very real voice for the Unimage even though there was only an eye, and just as Konstanty's voice had entered Szymon's mind, it entered theirs.

"Oh no, how terrible! This sounds like the voice of Szymon's father. It must be he who is behind this unprovoked attack!" Sallina said.

"What?" the Professor exclaimed in dismay. "You mean the boy who helped me, the one you were with when you found me in the hospital, that boy is Konstanty's son?"

Sallina nodded sheepishly, feeling a little ashamed for not having shared this important piece of information with Professor Tinzy before.

"Why didn't you tell me about this in the first place?" the Professor asked, but it was too late for the truth to help him. "Didn't you think it was important enough for me to know whilst we are engaged in our critical mission?"

"I'm so sorry, Professor. I didn't think it was something I needed to tell you about straightaway, and I was going to wait for the right time to go into the details," she lied in an attempt to protect herself and avoid being lambasted by her professor.

She knew only too well that she had been wrong in keeping this crucial information from him, even if she tried to justify it by saying she'd intended to tell him later on, but she had come to like Szymon a lot. It was only now that she realized Szymon might never be able to become a real friend, mainly because of who he was and the excessive control his father was always exerting on him.

Sallina was terribly apologetic as she spoke, "I didn't realize how stupidly determined his father would be to prevent us from saving our fellow citizens. I knew he was after the Pinny as well. I mean, I had some sense that was what he sought. It was, after all, the reason he sent Szymon over here, but I didn't think he'd want to hurt anyone to try to get hold of it."

"You're still so naïve and young, my dear Princess," Professor Tinzy replied, frustrated but sympathetic to her deepening emotional anguish. "If you had told me about it sooner, we wouldn't now be facing this extremely treacherous situation, and Limpit's life wouldn't be in such terrible danger."

Distraught and full of sorrow, Sallina was ready to burst into tears. She tore herself away from the Professor to get closer to Limpit and find some way to help him out. She was more determined than ever to protect the small dragon, especially as this situation was mostly her fault for not paying close enough attention to what was going on and not being completely honest with the Professor. And much to her surprise, she had grown to really like the irksome creature, despite his rather annoying mannerisms and often-peculiar ways. She wanted no harm to befall him.

But she didn't get very far, because just as she stepped forward, the frozen icicle ball came hurtling at Limpit and struck him before he could even blink. Within a split second, the magical weapon had surrounded the creature. Unlike the fireball, which had hit the dragon like a spear but bounced off with minimal impact, the cold-fireball spell grew larger and more powerful almost instantly when it was upon him, and within seconds it had engulfed him entirely.

Inside the frozen fireball, the centre began melting and turned to liquid, and Limpit felt like he was drowning inside an icy tomb. But Limpit was still a powerful dragon, and he immediately discharged his fireball breath, which evaporated some of the water and melted even more of the ice inside the ball. Seeing that his action was having some positive effect, Limpit let out the rest of the air in his lungs as a fiery flame, which caused more of the ice to melt and the water to turn to gas. He hoped to melt the icy fireball into water and then swim through the trap.

But this was not just some ordinary frozen-ball incantation: this enormously powerful spell was much more potent than any ordinary fireball spell Limpit had ever encountered, for it was able to regenerate, expand, and produce a lot more water and ice at an alarming rate.

Out of breath now, Limpit tried to acquire fresh oxygen, but all he could inhale was ice-cold water. Within seconds, he started choking. Fortunately, the hot centre of his lungs burned at such a high temperature that the water turned into steam almost immediately as he spasmodically coughed it out.

But Limpit knew he was going to be in big trouble soon enough. Like unicorns and even humans, he required air to breathe and exist, and even though dragons can go without taking in fresh air for some time, he had just expended most of his oxygen in trying to break through the powerful spell. He couldn't sustain an oxygen deficiency for very long. Limpit knew that if the frozen-ball spell could maintain a grip on him, he was just moments away from breathing his very last breath and slipping into a state of unconsciousness.

Sallina and the Professor watched, horrified, as Limpit made one final, desperate attempt to rid himself of the suffocating spell that was about to incapacitate and possibly kill him. Putting all his remaining energy into flapping his wings, he stretched them out as wide as they could possibly go and shot himself like a bullet toward the broken window. He went through the window so quickly that he shattered most of the remaining glass before rising vertically toward the roof like a rocket.

The problem was, the icy ball went with him, so even though he was able to swiftly move away from where he had been hovering, he was still trapped inside it, no matter how fast he was traveling. The frozen ball of water simply kept up with him.

Still, he was moving so fast that he managed to reach the edge of the icy wall that was encasing him and turning itself into his coffin. Limpit had no intention of giving up, knowing he was moments away from slipping into unconsciousness. With the upward momentum gained from flapping his wings and the speed with which he was moving, Limpit managed to break completely through the icy shell and set himself free as he thrust himself further upwards, rising high into the sky.

Taking in a last lungful of water mixed with air, Limpit coughed the remaining water out and started to breathe in fresh air. The air managed to enter his lungs and give him the vital oxygen supply he needed to keep on going and regain his composure.

The shell finally burst apart as Konstanty's concentration on it was finally broken. The ice fell to the ground, along with the water that had been inside it. The remnants of the icy cage hit the roof and came sliding down the sides as it began melting away.

The opportunistic eye had quickly left Szymon's outstretched hand and followed Limpit on his vertical trajectory, only to disappoint its master on seeing the frozen ball was no more. The icicles were lying bare on the roof as they melted into water, which cascaded down the front of the house. Higher the eye shot, but Limpit seemed to have disappeared, and Konstanty could not make out where he was now.

Chapter 18

Princess Sallina wanted nothing more than to help Limpit in his moment of greatest need and she bolted for the front door.

"Where are you going? Are you crazy?" the Professor cried.

"Limpit's up there, and he's still in trouble. I'm going to help," Sallina called back, twisting the door latch. Professor Tinzy was right behind her now.

"This has all gone way too far," Tinzy said, mainly as an observation to himself. "Something really has to be done about the situation. Unimage Konstanty has well and truly crossed the line, and things need to be set right."

As Sallina disappeared through the open door, the Professor shouted, "Wait here, Princess! I'm going to attend to this matter personally."

Sallina stopped in her tracks. She turned and looked Tinzy in the eye, and she could see he was ready and willing to get into this fight.

Limpit, meanwhile, was descending to the roof as the eye of Konstanty watched and brooded, knowing full well the special magic powering the eye would soon be petering out, Konstanty began spinning another frozen-ball spell, while Szymon, in the Professor's yard, incanted the spell fast and furiously to aid his father.

A new frozen ball manifested, but Konstanty didn't want to stop there. He made a second, then another; he was determined this time to finish the job no matter what it took.

Down on the ground, the remaining magic that infused the scroll began leaving the parchment and heading up towards the roof. Szymon watched the scroll become blank, the magic vaporising as Konstanty drew from it to make not just one but several powerful ice balls designed to destroy Limpit.

Then came the fresh attack, the first frozen ball suddenly shooting up directly at Limpit. It succeeded in only partly enveloping him, but the second and third balls merging with the first were enough to secure Limpit completely inside a new prison of ice.

This time, however, Limpit was ready. He took a huge breath and held it as the ice-and-liquid ball formed around him and tried to encase him.

The ball expanded until the last bit of magic on the scroll had been consumed. The eye of Konstanty watched gleefully as the large, icicle-covered ball above the house whirled, hovering ominously. The wielder of the eye knew that this time it had perfectly trapped Limpit.

Szymon swiftly picked up the scroll just as Professor Tinzy and Sallina ran up to him at the front of the house.

"What have you done, you fool?" the Professor blasted at the boy.

"I—I don't know, sir, but there's no more magic left on this scroll... it's all used up."

"If my friend is harmed by your irresponsible behaviour, I'll make sure you and your father both pay for it and are punished accordingly, you hear me?" The Professor's glare was severe and serious; he was literally shaking with fury.

Sallina, standing right beside him, was no less angry at her friend. "Szymon, you've betrayed us, and Limpit is in big trouble because of you. Why would you do such a horrible thing to us?"

Szymon said nothing, bowing his head in shame.

Sallina turned to the side of the house. There, she spotted a drainpipe running up to the roof. Without hesitation, Sallina grabbed hold of the pipe and began to climb.

"Don't, you'll fall and hurt yourself, Princess!" Tinzy pleaded. "It's too dangerous for you!"

But Sallina didn't pay any heed to his warning. She continued to climb, one pull and one step at a time, clinging tightly to the pipe as she did. She was about halfway up when the first bolt gave way and the pipe started to come loose from the wall.

"Princess!" the Professor cried, looking up with great concern.

Anxious now, Sallina tried to climb faster, but with every move she made, the pipe pulled further from the wall until, with nothing left to hold it up, it came crashing toward the ground— Sallina with it!

Sallina let go of the pipe and clasped her pendant. "Flip flop float, stop me at once!" The words came out so fast it was as if they were all racing toward the same finish line, and it seemed almost like she had managed to utter them all at the same time.

Luckily, the spell worked. A sudden release of blue light from the pendant; and there, what appeared to be a cushion of blue light, hovering beneath her as she fell to the ground. So instead of dropping fast, the Princess slowly floated down, and her feet lightly touched the ground.

Professor Tinzy stepped aside as Sallina, clasping her pendant, slowly connected with the ground and the blue light dissolved.

She looked up to see both the Professor and Szymon staring down at her.

Sallina was regaining her composure when a voice inside her head cried, "Help me, Princess! I'm caught inside a bigger ball, and if I try to fight it, I won't be able to breathe, so I'm holding my breath as long as I possibly can. I have only a few minutes of air remaining before I run out and I'll be trapped in it until I perish. I don't know what I can do to break free from this tomb. However, before I surrender, I will try one last time to break out of this icy prison I'm stuck in. It's that horrendous eye—it's controlling this deadly weapon, and it must be stopped somehow. Please help me!"

Sallina let go of the pendant and looked at Szymon, who still appeared both ashamed and confused.

"Your father has encased Limpit in a frozen ball with powerful magic. Limpit will surely run out of oxygen and drown in it if we don't somehow stop Unimage Konstanty. Your father aims to destroy Limpit, and I cannot allow it."

"I'm so sorry," Szymon said apologetically. "He sometimes gets more than a bit carried away, and I fear his reckless temper often gets the best of him."

"I don't care about his reckless temper or his ability to control himself. He really needs to be prevented from harming my friend right now. Will you at least help me to stop him before Limpit is killed?"

Szymon turned toward Professor Tinzy, who wasn't hiding his dissatisfaction with the boy either.

"If you let harm befall Limpit, I'll make sure you're personally punished, and your father is locked up for the rest of his life. Both of you will pay for committing murder and inflicting harm on such a notable dragon, who has been helping us on our crucial mission."

"I'm so sorry, sir," Szymon pleaded. "I honestly didn't know he was going to hurt the little creature. We only came to see what was going on, and I thought we wanted to help you with the mission."

"Lies, they're all nothing but deceptive lies. I don't believe a single word that comes out of Unimage Konstanty's mouth. He has always been the most grandiose of liars with a forked tongue, ever since he was little, and he hasn't changed one bit," Professor Tinzy rebutted defiantly.

This verbal fencing match seemed a huge waste of time to Sallina, who could still hear the faint pleas for help coming from Limpit as he tried to keep himself alive in the large frozen ball and conserve his remaining breath while the menacing eye kept watch.

Inside Szymon's house, a smug Unimage Konstanty was already feeling quite pleased with himself that he was finally going to win out against that troublesome creature and put it out of his misery forever.

"I know something we can do," Szymon suddenly blurted. "I know how we can stop him before it's too late."

"Tell me quickly!" the Princess said hurriedly. "There's no time to waste."

"We can turn off the orb at my house, which will stop the spell from working as the eye cannot cast the spell without the orb communicating back home," Szymon explained.

"You mean your father is casting his spell all the way from Starpoint, and that the orb in your house is his primary connection to this land? How did he find the magic here to cast it without Pinny?" the Professor asked.

Szymon didn't answer. It was too much for him to reveal such an important secret, and he still greatly feared his father's wrath.

"Tell me if you know. How can you expect me to trust you if you don't tell me the truth when I need you to?" Sallina asked him.

"I'm so sorry, Sallina. I haven't told you because if I tell you, Father will be very angry at me. But I want you to trust me, so I will.

"When you cast the remembrance spell, Father managed to capture some of the magic directly from your necklace. He told me that it was for everyone's good, but now I understand he bears a grudge against your minuscule dragon friend, and this has encouraged him to get carried away and do things I won't stand by and allow to happen. I'm so sorry about that. If I had known what he intended to do, I wouldn't have helped him. You must believe me," Szymon said sorrowfully.

This confession took Sallina by surprise. Her friend had betrayed her openly and put Limpit's life in great danger. She didn't know how she could ever forgive him for doing such a horrid thing, but now wasn't the time for her to be angry. Limpit was still in danger, and Szymon appeared to be genuinely concerned and willing to help.

"Very well, let's give your idea a go," Sallina replied. "Let's stop the orb before it's too late and Limpit perishes inside that dreadful icicle ball."

Professor Tinzy spoke up, "Don't trust him for a moment."

After having heard of the betrayal, he didn't want to go along with Szymon.

"I don't think we have any choice, Professor. You must do what you can here to help Limpit, and I'm going to go with Szymon to do my best to put a stop to it," Sallina said.

Outside, Szymon showed her where he had left his bicycle before hiding it in the bushes.

"Oh no! Not this two-wheeled contraption again!"

"It's okay, you can ride it. Use your magic. I'll run alongside you."

"People will see us…"

"Does it matter right now? Your friend's life is in great danger, and what others think of you shouldn't really matter under the circumstances. You can even try to pretend to be riding it by holding onto the handlebars if you're so concerned."

She knew he was right, of course. What did it matter what anyone else saw or thought when Limpit's life was in mortal danger? She nodded, and he stood the bike upright. Sallina clutched her pendant and cast a small spell. The bike now stood upright of its own accord.

She sat herself on the bike, then spoke a few more words. It started to lurch forward. She quickly grabbed the handlebars to steady herself.

Szymon started running alongside her.

"You'd better get in front of me so I can follow you to your house."

Szymon nodded and darted in front of her on the pavement.

"Hurry up!" she said. "Time's running out. Run as fast as you possibly can!"

As Sallina took off on the bike with Szymon running ahead of her, Professor Tinzy gazed up at Limpit.

"Poor Limpit," he muttered. But without the aid of magic, what use was he to anyone? Then an idea struck. The Professor ran back into the house and up the three flights of stairs until he reached the small square entrance leading to the loft. He pulled out a stick from a nearby cupboard, opened the loft latch, and brought down the small metallic ladder.

Hovering a few feet above the roof, the cocooned Limpit was having the life sucked out of him within the rapidly rotating, frozen ice ball under the watchful gaze of the killer eye.

From inside the ball, Limpit stared out with a deep sense of sadness. He knew he didn't have long before he ran out of air completely, and whatever little energy he had remaining was likely to be insufficient to release him from its vise-like grip.

Slowly, the cold water around him started to seep into his orifices. Despite the furnace heat of his interior, he doubted that the resulting steam from the water entering his lungs would do much when it was exhaled out into the ball, as this ball was far larger than the last one and the steam would gradually convert itself back into water and prove to be useless in helping him to escape.

Was this really the end for him? It certainly felt like it, but while he had some breath left in him, he still had hope.

With renewed concentration, Limpit made another desperate attempt to reach out to Princess Sallina with his thoughts, but she didn't seem to be there anymore. Had the eye done something to her as well? Was she also in trouble? He began to worry about not just his own wellbeing but also the safety of his close friends who had put themselves at peril to try and rescue him. Despite some harsh words exchanged, he and the Professor were old and good friends, and he already owed his life to Professor Tinzy.

When the Unimages had shown up to capture him, it was Professor Tinzy who had let Limpit know that he would not serve as a prisoner on their mission for Pinny in this faraway land, but more as a companion and fellow adventurer. He advised the dragon that he would be free to come and go as he pleased. This turned out to be a bit of an exaggeration, from Limpit's perspective, as he was always being told where to go and what to do! But if he wanted to return to his former self, he was required to see this mission through and help protect Starpoint from destruction.

Limpit was already an old dragon, and he remembered when Professor Tinzy was a lot younger and how they had encountered each other a couple of times previously over the decades. He recalled that the first time he'd met Professor Tinzy was when the new city of Starpoint was taking shape, after the Circle wars had ended. The Starpointers had overcome the Unimages of the old Circle order, and the world was able to return to a new state of peaceful co-existence and tranquillity among the unicorns and other living creatures.

But so much destruction had ravaged the land during the Circle wars that most unicorns decided to leave their farming lives behind and instead relocate to the relative safety of a brand-new city, where they would pull together and forge a bright new future for themselves free of the oppression and war that had recently blighted their lives. Within a few short years, almost ninety percent of all unicorns had made Starpoint their new home, and only a handful of small unicorn communities continued to exist outside its perimeter, the main ones on remote farms miles away.

It had been a long, eventful life, and he'd seen so many changes. Even so, he was reluctant to give up the time he naturally would have had left. Slowly, Limpit felt his life-force beginning to ebb away, and he knew his demise was coming ever closer. He had begun to close his eyes when he suddenly sensed some sort of activity beyond the outer wall of the frozen ball. Glancing slowly sideways, Limpit was amazed at a strange sight: a faint outline of the top half of Professor Tinzy poking out of the open loft window!

Professor Tinzy, whose lower half was perched on the seat of a folding chair, which in turn was perched upon an old trunk, turned his attention towards the small eye, then looked back at the large frozen ball levitating in the air not far from him. He felt lost, knowing that there was precious little he could do to help free his old friend, but he did realize that he was now in range of the dragon and could possibly be receptive to Limpit's telepathic powers.

He was right.

"Professor," he heard Limpit say inside his head. "You must be very careful. You cannot help me here... I am unable to break free from this powerful magic trap I find myself in, and I fear that soon I will be done for. Don't let them get to you, too."

This really riled up the Professor, as there was one thing he hated most: giving up on a friend. Putting himself first above others was another thing he abhorred.

"Konstanty," said the Professor, "I know you can hear me. Stop this insanity at once. You are at risk of murdering my friend, and if any harm befalls him as a result of your ill-guided actions, I will inform the Council and you will be fittingly punished for your transgressions."

Unfortunately, there was no response.

Meanwhile, Princess Sallina and Szymon were not more than a block away from Szymon's home, as Doberry wasn't such a big place for anyone to get around. They had made swift progress, although Szymon spent most of it puffing and wheezing while Sallina enjoyed the relative comfort of magic pedalling behind him. However, Szymon was made of resilient stuff, and more than once he picked up the pace despite his shortness of breath.

"We're almost back home," Szymon wheezed.

Moments later, Sallina and Szymon arrived at the house, and the bike landed by the side of the entrance path as Sallina jumped off and hurried towards the door.

Szymon quickly opened the door and ran inside, to be met instantly by the yapping Yippy, who was jumping up on his hind legs and looking rather excited and keen to be of use. Szymon ran into the living room, followed closely by Princess Sallina. Yippy, who had been waiting to get back inside all day, followed them in.

In the centre of the room stood the larger orb, and above the orb, the holographic image of Unimage Konstanty, reciting the spell that was keeping the large frozen ice ball in continued motion and draining the life from poor Limpit bit by bit.

"Stop it, Father, you're destroying him!" Szymon yelled.

But Konstanty wasn't there, nor was he paying attention to anything taking place in Szymon's living room. All his attention was focused on ensuring the spell was successful and that Limpit would soon perish, and his focus was on the weapon he had created to complete this task.

Back in the frozen-ball cocoon, Limpit was struggling to hold onto his last breath. He would soon have no choice but to exhale, and subsequently, against his wishes, he'd be left to suck in icy-cold water, which would invade his lungs and no doubt paralyze him to the point where he would most likely suffocate. And not long after, he would no longer be alive.

"Professor, if you can hear me, I'm so sorry to have been a nuisance to you," Limpit whimpered. "I only wanted to help. You know I willingly surrendered to the Unimages that time because I knew I would be safe in your trustworthy care, and I felt I could make a difference. You mustn't blame yourself for failing to help me on this unfortunate occasion. I understand that you have tried your best, but some things are just not possible.

"Not everything works out," Limpit added, more directing it to himself.

The Professor could only hear Limpit's sad thoughts echoing in his mind, but he had had enough of the dragon's whimpering and willingness to sacrifice himself. He pushed himself up onto the roof.

He was now off the chair and hanging on for dear life to the roof itself. He had the daring idea that if he could find a way to walk along it, he might be able to grab hold of the eye and cover it up with his hand, which could potentially stop it from being able to see and fuel the icy trap that was engulfing his friend. If the eye couldn't see the frozen ball, the ball might stop working altogether, and Limpit could in this way be saved.

"Please, Professor, you mustn't risk your life for mine. You are far too valuable to all Starpointers to put yourself in such terrible danger at my expense. I can't allow it."

The Professor huffed dismissively. He wasn't going to listen to Limpit's vain attempts to dissuade him from helping, and he ignored Limpit's pleas as he crawled gingerly on hand and foot atop the roof of his house.

The eye was but a few feet away. If only he could reach it and cover it so that it couldn't see...

Limpit was nearly at the point of giving up.

"Professor, I'm going... I'm so sorry to have been of bother. Don't strain yourself on my account. I only have seconds remaining. I will miss you... greatly."

"No, wait... don't you dare give up now, you cowardly rascal!" the Professor shouted.

This caught the attention of the eye, which quickly turned toward the Professor. Of course, Professor Tinzy didn't mean what he had said, and he knew that Limpit was only sacrificing himself to help protect the Professor and Sallina. But Professor Tinzy was getting awfully angry at the situation, and he was determined to make a difference. In fact, he was furious at what was going on and wasn't going to idly stand by and let terrible things happen without intervening and doing his very best to rectify what was going on.

The Professor slowly stood up, which was both awkward and hard on his ankles, as the roof was tiled and slippery as well as slanted. He was an old man who at any moment could easily slip and slide back down the roof and plummet to the ground below. Who knew what would break in his body, or whether he could even survive such a terrible fall?

In the basement of her house, Callindra could see the image of the Professor on the roof of his house as it appeared in front of Unimage Konstanty. She wasn't sure what to make of it, but she could tell straightaway that it was real, and it was probably happening right that very second.

Unimage Konstanty was deep in a trance, enacting his spell, as Callindra tapped him gently on the shoulder.

"Konstanty, you may consider being more careful with what you do next, for if we lose the Professor, there may be no other way to find the whereabouts of our precious Pinny. That wouldn't be good for either of us."

Konstanty heard her, but he kept his focus on his prize. "Oh, don't you worry. He's a wily old unicorn, that Professor, and no matter what he does, he always lands on his feet—and usually in very good health. I expect he shall succeed at this once again. Now leave me alone, as I'm nearly done with ridding myself of that arrogant little nuisance of a dragon for good."

Unimage Callindra didn't like being ignored even by one of her close allies, and as she watched the Professor trying so hard to maintain some kind of balance on his roof, she wasn't at all pleased by Unimage Konstanty's attitude toward her concerns. She had a bad feeling about losing the Professor at this stage of the—mission. She knew that a lot depended on him, and it wasn't his failure that she ultimately sought, but more his inability to successfully retain things whose absence she knew would provide a tremendous opportunity for the Circle and their most important mission.

Looking down at the end of the roof and the ground below as he steadied his feet, the Professor felt his balance start to fail him. He reached out to the eye, which was just inches away. But because Konstanty's eye was hovering, it was always moving, and it was just out of his grasp. The Professor cursed and slowly lowered himself to all fours, as at his age and state of fragility, the risk of tumbling over the edge looked far too great.

In Szymon's living room, Princess Sallina was becoming increasingly worried about what was likely to happen next. She could sense she was going to be too late to save her diminutive dragon friend.

"How do we stop him from hurting Limpit?" she asked Szymon.

Szymon hesitated, and Sallina thought, *He most likely doesn't know.*

"Goodbye, Professor…" Limpit whimpered. Professor Tinzy moaned to himself. He knew that his friend was about to perish at any moment.

Suddenly, Szymon had a spark of an idea. He instinctively leapt at the orb to topple it sideways from its base. Realizing what he was doing, Sallina started helping him. Together, with a great deal of effort, they managed to push the orb onto its side. As it toppled over, Konstanty's image began to flicker.

Above the roof of Professor Tinzy's house, the eye suddenly began to flicker and fade.

The frozen ball's rotation slowed.

Inside, Limpit's eyes closed, and he could hang on no longer. He gasped and found himself sucking in the cold, icy water… just as the frozen ball expanded outward in all directions.

As Limpit inhaled the water, he was shocked to feel oxygen filling his lungs once again! He opened his eyes and looked around to see with delight that he was hovering in the air, free from the icy trap, as the frozen ball dissipated around him.

Beneath him, not far away, a frail Professor Tinzy was desperately struggling to move on all fours across the roof, inching along bit by bit, nervous about his ability to remain on the roof and not slip and fall to the ground. But the Professor was also focusing his energy on the frozen ball, and a flame shot out from one hand as he chanted a spell that was helping to melt the ball away. Even the Professor had no idea how he was managing to make the magic work without Pinny, but he was, and that was all that mattered.

Little did he realise that Princess Sallina's medallion was now glowing brightly and he had found the way to draw enough energy from it. Although she wasn't with him, she wasn't all that far away, and the Professor had managed to connect with the self-generating energy reserves of the medallion for a brief moment in time.

The next movement of his knee, making contact with a tile, promptly cracked the tile... and the Professor went sliding with it.

The jolt took the Professor's breath away. His heart sank and he knew he was going to tumble off the roof and to the ground.

Just in time, Limpit swooped down and placed himself directly next to the Professor to help stop him from sliding off the edge of the roof. The Professor looked up at his dragon friend with grateful eyes as they both listened to the sound of tile smashing into pieces on the hard ground below.

Professor Tinzy was incredibly pleased to see his friend Limpit was out of harm's way and there beside him.

"Oh goodness me! You're safe and sound, and you're here with me now, saving my backside just after I tried to save yours," he said, quite excited.

"I am, and it's all thanks to you and the others... but for now, steady on, Professor. Let's get you back to that window so you can get off this slippery roof of yours, which is especially unsafe for an old person like you."

"Who are you calling an old person? I'm a never-aging unicorn, and in perfect health and with full mental capacity," the Professor quipped.

"Well... you rather are a person right now. If you had your four hoofs, I'd see no problem in managing your way back on your own, but on those ancient two legs of yours, and with the arthritis settling in, I would say you'd best be careful, at least as long as you inhabit a human's body and all the frailty that goes along with it."

"Thank you, dear Limpit. It's so good to see you back to your usual annoying, assured, prophetic self!" the Professor exclaimed, now with a wry grin spreading across his face.

In the living room of Szymon's house, Sallina and Szymon had fallen close to each other on the carpet and were surrounded by a gooey blue liquid that had seeped from the large orb.

"What is this awful-smelling stuff all around me?" the Princess said with a grimace.

"You don't want to know what it is," Szymon replied. "I had to create it myself, and it's not very nice, so best not to ask questions you don't want to know the answers to."

"Do you think Limpit's okay? I do hope he is."

"So do I. But right now, I can only tell you one thing for certain," Szymon said gloomily.

"What's that?"

"My father is going to be awfully mad at me for what we just did together, and I doubt he'll ever trust me like he did before."

They stared at each other, and then Sallina started to giggle. Szymon couldn't help himself. He began to laugh with her.

In the basement of Unimage Callindra's house, Unimage Konstanty's face had turned red all over in a fit of uncontrolled rage that was only going to get worse.

"That little rascal of a dragon managed to slip away from me once again… I almost had him this time! How in the world did he manage to do that?"

Unimage Callindra was disappointed as well, but deep down she knew it wasn't the right time to get rid of either Limpit or the Professor, as so far these two do-gooders had not come across any Pinny that could be brought back home to Starpoint, and that was their priority right now. Without any Pinny having been obtained, there was little point in disposing of the very unicorns who had been sent over there to track it down.

"You'll be able to finish him off another time, Unimage," Callindra assured him. "There's always another time for such inessential matters."

"I won't fail next time, that's for sure—I was so very close. You don't know how much I wanted him to just go and be done with. It would have made me happy."

"Failure should be treated like a stepping stone toward achieving even greater success, my dear Unimage," Callindra offered gently. "You didn't fail, you just learned some valuable lessons and fine-tuned your fighting skills for a much bigger fight that is yet to come. Ultimately, victory will soon be ours. Only the purest will rule these lands. It shall be sworn and abided by each unicorn alike, and the proper order of things will be restored. The fairest and purest are naturally meant to be in charge of everything; this is the way it is and always has been meant to be."

"That is true, wise one," Konstanty remarked. "But it doesn't make me wish to accept this outcome as being satisfactory, not one tiny bit. But I shall choose to abide by the greater purpose we serve and strive for."

"The future of Starpoint remains at stake, and all our lives, hopes, and dreams are intertwined, so we really have to set aside our personal vendettas for now and focus on the bigger picture," Callindra pointed out to him.

"Of course you are right, as always," Konstanty said deferentially. "I have the utmost faith in the noblest intentions of the chosen Circle, and I have no desire but to obey their wishes."

"The chosen Circle remains the only truth that exists, young Unimage. The rest of them are foolish unicorns who wish to make the impossible appear possible by fabricating countless lies. They seek to create a world that cannot be ruled and administered correctly, for those who are weak in mind and too good of spirit often will not do what is needed. It takes strength and the establishment of fear to effectively rule the land, as power comes when you can wield it and your subjects dare not to disobey you or the rule of law you've created for fear of what will happen to them."

"Fortunately for us all, we are the ones who will ensure all Starpointers are taught how to tread the righteous path towards a much greater glory and obey the noble wishes of the esteemed and pure Circle. And this will come to pass very soon—I see victory closing in. By hoof and by horn, we will do what's right for our kind, as the Circle are the chosen ones to rule our lands and far beyond."

"By hoof and by horn," Callindra chimed in adamantly. "Indeed, our time will soon come. Only the purest will rule in these fair lands. It shall be sworn and abided by each unicorn alike."

Chapter 19

The rest of the evening proved to be largely uneventful. Professor Tinzy offered Szymon the use of a spare room for the night, seeing as he was so clearly terrified of facing the anticipated wrath that was likely to come from his father. Szymon also didn't want to face the prospect of being connected again to Konstanty via the orb. Of course, Professor Tinzy was not at all pleased to have Szymon staying in his house, but what else could he do after hearing how Sallina and Szymon had raced back to Szymon's home and helped save Limpit from what appeared to be certain death?

By evening's end, Limpit was far too tired to do anything, and he lay fast asleep in the corner of the living room, snoring away. The diminutive dragon was no longer hovering but resting in his comfy dog-bed, like a worn-out mongrel who had retired for the day. Only a slight amount of grey smoke rose from his nostrils as he exhaled the air that he took in through his partially open mouth. Even when the room was full of talk for what seemed like hours about what had transpired, Limpit lay there in the corner, ears drooping, and eyelids half shut.

"So," said the Professor. "We know your father, Unimage Konstanty, is determined to get his hands on the Pinny, as are we. Only we don't know what he really wants it for, do we?"

Szymon just shook his head. He was aware that the Pinny was important, but he simply didn't know anything about his father's personal motivations for possessing it.

"Your father's reckless interference has already put our mission in grave danger, and I for one am not comfortable about involving you any further because of your unreliable allegiance to him. If it was up to me, I'd send you off, but Princess Sallina insists that you chose to act directly against your father's wishes when you realized Limpit was in serious danger. You played a crucial role in saving the poor creature's life. For that, I am eternally grateful."

Szymon listened silently, knowing it was better not to say anything at this juncture.

"But know this, youngster. I don't trust you, and I worry greatly that you well may in the future find some way to betray us, as you're ultimately your father's son."

Szymon wanted to speak out, but he remained quiet.

"Professor Tinzy," said Sallina, "I don't believe Szymon is capable of betraying us, and hasn't he proven his loyalty beyond any shadow of a doubt? I firmly believe his contribution will be crucial in helping us successfully complete our mission. This weekend, we will all travel to London together. Tell me, how can we possibly do this? I cannot drive, and neither can you, nor can Limpit. We need his help to get us there."

Professor Tinzy stared into Szymon's eyes.

"Can you drive a car?" he asked.

Gazing down at the floor, Szymon shook his head. Then he looked up and said, "I've never attempted it, sir, but how difficult can it be? I'm certainly willing to give it a go."

"That's not good enough," Tinzy retorted. "You're clearly of little help to us. Can't you see, Princess? He's just a foolish boy who on one occasion may have helped us, but what if some time in the future, he decides for whatever reason to act against us? I believe that he will ultimately follow in his father's footsteps, just like all the sons and daughters of Unimages eventually do."

"No! I will not follow him if it hurts any of those who I care for," Szymon blurted. "I will never do anything to harm Princess Sallina or Limpit—you have my word on that."

"Why should I believe you?" Professor Tinzy asked.

"Because…. because Sallina is my good friend… my only friend. And so is Limpit… or he is becoming my friend, I hope."

The Professor and Szymon locked eyes for a few moments. Szymon held the Professor's gaze. He did not feel afraid or meek in the Professor's presence, at least not for now.

The Professor heaved a great sigh. "Very well then, youngster. In this moment I won't stop you from helping us but take careful note of this! I will be watching you closely. One misstep, and I'll be there to catch you out."

***

The next day after breakfast, they found themselves sitting inside Professor Tinzy's Ford Fiesta with Szymon behind the wheel. Szymon had the car key in his hand, and Professor Tinzy sat next to him. In the rear passenger seats were Princess Sallina and the hovering Limpit.

A couple of cars whistled by down the road as they all looked at each other. Szymon glanced through the rear-view mirror, and Princess Sallina could immediately see that he looked genuinely frightened as he prepared himself mentally to drive the car.

"What—what do I do now?" Szymon asked the Professor. "I'm not really sure."

"From what I have previously observed, you insert the key into that hole there, and then you turn it. This should start up the engine."

"Oh, that sounds easy enough," Szymon replied, turning the key in the designated hole.

The car purred to life, and the sound of the petrol engine took them all by complete surprise apart from Professor Tinzy, who obviously had been inside his car before. Pulling himself together, Szymon attempted to look a little more serene and in control, as if there was nothing unusual in what he was attempting to do.

"Somebody know what will happen next?" he queried anyone who cared to answer back.

Professor Tinzy shook his head in dismay, thinking that this was going to prove to be a difficult test drive.

"This clearly is no good, youngster. I feel it's far too dangerous for you to be learning to drive in a place where there are many other cars zipping past us. We need to find ourselves a quiet and remote place to practice, like a car park or somewhere deserted, such as a closed-off warehouse in an industrial park. Let me think…"

"I know just the place, but at the moment I can't drive us there because I don't know how," Szymon mumbled.

"Oh! Where is it?" queried the Professor.

"It's by an old warehouse at the edge of Doberry. The car park is hardly ever in use. Occasionally a few children from school wander down there and play with their skateboards, but other than that, it's usually deserted."

"That's exactly where we shall go. It sounds perfectly suitable for our present needs," the Professor said cheerily.

Limpit looked toward Princess Sallina, baffled. She shrugged, puzzled as well, as she gazed back at the tiny dragon.

"Next question, if I may ask... how do we get there? Isn't that what we still need to work out? Or am I being thick-headed?" Limpit murmured.

"How about we utilise some of your magic, Princess," Szymon suggested, not having any better ideas.

"That might not be so easy... I don't know any car-driving spells," Sallina replied.

"Actually, you might," said the Professor. "The boy has a point."

"Really? How?"

"Szymon could be onto something. You see, if you can take us to that warehouse in this car by using your magic, then we can work out who can quickly learn to drive it in order to take us to London."

"If I am able to drive you over to the warehouse, then we won't need to learn to drive the car because I'll already be driving it," Sallina, confused, said in an attempt to exercise her logic.

"Well, that's where you're wrong entirely, Sallina. Your necklace can activate a spell that should be able to help us move the car to the warehouse but taking us far would be really difficult. You wouldn't be able to concentrate on the spell all the way to London, but a short distance is entirely possible," said the Professor.

"What spell do you mean? I'm not familiar with any such spell. Until recently, I had no idea what a car even was."

Szymon was listening attentively to Professor Tinzy's suggestion and taking it all in.

"I think I know what the Professor intends," he said.

"You do? Then how about filling me in?"

"If you use a standard levitation spell and rotate the wheels around for effect, it will look like the car is driving, although it's not. It's just flying in the air and taking us to the warehouse.

The reality is it's just a fraction of an inch off the ground, and the rotating wheels will help to avoid drawing any unnecessary attention."

"How far off the ground do you think I can levitate this heavy car with us all sitting inside?" she asked.

"I don't know—as little as possible so that it looks like it's on the road. It will need to appear as if it's driving normally to anyone who notices us passing by. However, what you're doing is transporting us through the magic of levitation," the Professor explained, almost sounding scientific.

"That's plain crazy. I've never levitated something as heavy as this car before and then made it fly. This car is super heavy, and to move it… it's impossible for me."

"It's not so different from when you rode your bike," Szymon said. "The principle is exactly the same."

"That was just a bike; this is different. We're in a motor car. And a very heavy one at that."

"You forget, you're in the possession of an immensely powerful magical pendant. I would not be surprised if the pendant can give you the means to do this. We simply need to get over to the warehouse, as I think it's the only way any of us can work out how to get there so I or someone can learn how to drive," said Szymon.

"No… I won't do it; it's going to be far too hard for me," Sallina said, shaking her head.

"Why don't you try at least? What's the harm in having a go?" Limpit proposed to her.

Sallina thought about this for a moment. She felt like saying no, but she realized she was at fault for not even being willing to give it a go, and, given the predicament they were in along with how important it was for them to make their way to London to obtain the Pinny, trying was the very least she could do. So what if she failed? At least she would have attempted to solve the problem.

"Okay, I'll have a go just the once. But I implore you, please don't expect me to perform miracles. I'm no wizard."

She clasped the pendant tightly in her hand as she started to visualize levitating the car a tiny bit off the ground. She began incanting something that sounded incomprehensible and was barely audible to the others present.

"I have no idea what words are gushing out of your mouth, so how's this spell going to work?" Limpit said, concerned. "Let's hope the magic can hear it calling, because I sure can't."

She ignored him and continued chanting. Her muttering became a little more coherent. "Spin and turn, now whizz along. Two-four wheels will do simply fine for me and my friends, now come along. Now lift us off the ground."

The wheels of the car slowly started turning of their own volition, but the car didn't seem to be going anywhere from its parking space.

She repeated the incantation, holding even more tightly onto the necklace, which suddenly lit up in bright blue. Her focus grew stronger, her chanting more determined, and her mind became even more focused.

The car suddenly lifted a little off the road, then up to around two inches from the tarmac. Limpit rolled down the electric window with his paw and looked down toward the ground. "You're doing it… you're doing it."

"Focus on where you want us to go, and the car will take us there," Professor Tinzy said softly, trying not to divert her attention from the incantation.

Sallina concentrated even harder and looked ahead onto the road. The Fiesta slowly made its way out of the parking space, moving sideways at first in an odd manner that looked unnatural, but fortunately nobody was around to take notice.

Then the car began moving forward very slowly.

"I think you need to get a bit closer to the ground; I'm looking through the side mirror and you're too high off the ground. People are bound to notice," Professor Tinzy advised her.

"Yes, I agree…far too high," Limpit chimed in.

"Oh, I really don't know where I'm going! Someone needs to give me directions. Where do I go from here?"

"Down to the end of the road, and then we turn left," Szymon replied. "I'll guide you; I know where it is."

The car progressed slowly down the road. The tires spun, but to any passers-by, the car still would seem to look a bit peculiar.

For one thing, the tires were spinning the wrong way around: whilst the car was going forward, the tires were spinning in reverse. Fortunately, it had also begun to rain, and this was helping to conceal the incorrect motion of the wheels.

It took them a good twelve minutes to arrive at the deserted car park in the warehouse. This was a little over a mile away, and when they got there, Princess Sallina immediately let go of her pendant and the blue light faded at once. Instantly, the Fiesta collapsed back onto the ground, but there was only a little bump as they were so close to the road's surface to begin with. The engine was still idling along, as it had not shifted into gear throughout the short journey.

"Well, we've managed to get to our destination without having a major incident," Szymon remarked, and he felt strangely reassured that their objective to drive Professor Tinzy's car wasn't necessarily going to end up a complete disaster.

Professor Tinzy was surprised as well that nothing had gone wrong. "We are all happily in one piece! This is good news indeed," he remarked.

He stuck his head outside the car. Rain was now pelting down, and his face was quickly covered by raindrops. He looked up at the cloudy sky for a moment.

"I think this is not a good time for anyone to be learning how to drive, as the weather has become quite challenging," Limpit stated, still glancing out the side window from the back seat. Limpit was quite enjoying the rain.

"Nonsense. There's never been a better time to attempt this, and driving in the rain is something one better get used to, as it rains so very often here," Professor Tinzy quipped.

"I don't think I can drive in the rain," Szymon said. "I can almost steer the wheel, but that's about it. The rain bothers me because the ground will be all wet and we'll end up slipping and sliding about. I worry I might lose control."

"Then how about I help you out with the accelerating and braking side of driving so you focus all your energies on the steering. Will that help?" Limpit asked. No immediate response came back, so Limpit took that as a subdued yes.

Limpit lifted upward and flapped his wings, and before anyone could say anything or react in any way to his proposal, he had managed to squeeze his way past Szymon's legs, stopping by the accelerator and brake pedals.

"Why don't you move your seat back a bit?" Limpit asked politely. "I could use a little more legroom down here if that's alright—this looks like hard work."

Szymon fidgeted about with the seat control in the car and slid the car seat back a few notches.

"Phew. That's a heap better. There's not much space down here, and I'm feeling somewhat cramped."

Professor Tinzy pointed out the obvious. "The problem with your being down there, Limpit, is that you can't see where this vehicle is going."

"That's no problem at all, Professor, as Szymon can tell me to go faster or slower, which will inform me whether to brake or accelerate as needed, and he can put his mind to the steering wheel."

"Oh, okay," Szymon acknowledged. "I'm willing to have a go. Can you accelerate this thing slowly?"

The Professor suddenly spoke up. "You do know that there's a clutch on this machine? It was shown to me. You have to depress it and then the driver is able to change gears with the stick by the side."

Szymon moved the stick to the first position as Limpit depressed the clutch, and then he let go. Then Limpit quickly pushed down on the accelerator.

Szymon noticed that the car was immediately picking up speed as Limpit forced his claw down harder onto the accelerator.

"That's very good, but we don't want to go any faster than this," Szymon said. "Until I get used to travelling at this speed, I'd like to take things easy—this is my first attempt."

"Right, then let's keep her steady as she rolls," Limpit replied.

Professor Tinzy began to look more concerned, and he appeared to be turning a little pale from their combined efforts.

"This is all well and good, but I'm not as confident we can do this once we're on a motorway, as cars will be buzzing all around us. There will be so many cars weaving in and out, and coordinating Szymon's steering with the speeding and slowing down by Limpit will prove to be a lot trickier to manage. Then there's the constant stick change as well, and Limpit moving about from one pedal to another, hoping he can do this in synchronisation."

"Don't you worry, Professor. I think we just need to practice this driving business some more; I don't think it's so hard. I feel like I'm already getting used to moving us about," Szymon said, pretending to be reassuring.

Whilst he was talking, a tree appeared. It began growing bigger and bigger just ahead of them as they headed towards the end of the car park.

"Watch out for the tree directly in front of us!" Professor Tinzy blasted. "Watch out, you two fools!"

"Yes, it's a very nice tree," Szymon said hastily.

"You need to slow down, boy, or you'll take us right into that tree!"

"Oh, yes," Szymon said. "Slow down, Limpit, there's a tree ahead. Hit the brake. NOW, Limpit! QUICK!"

Limpit looked about, confused.

"Do you want me to go slower now, or in a few seconds?"

"Now! Now means now! Slow down—we need to stop very soon!"

"Okay," he said. "I'm slowing us down, don't worry. I have this under control."

Limpit switched from the accelerator to the brake and pressed his claw down against it with a great deal of force. The Fiesta began to slow as the brake was applied. But unbeknownst to him, he managed to put his other claw on the accelerator, and the car also began to speed up. It jolted forward after slowing down, then slowed down again, and then jolted forward. The motion was making everyone inside feel queasy.

"Slow down now, Limpit!" Szymon hollered as the tree started to come even closer.

"Stop now!" Sallina yelled, realizing they were about to drive right into it.

Limpit placed both his front claws on the brakes. The car suddenly braked very hard and came to an abrupt stop, jolting all those inside and making them lurch forward. Fortunately, they were all wearing seat belts, and nobody got hurt.

The rain continued pouring down from above, but it didn't appear as ferocious as it had been a few minutes earlier.

Professor Tinzy stared in shock at the large trunk that stood directly in front of them, which belonged to a very large tree they had almost driven directly into.

"Well, we managed to stop ourselves in the nick of time—that's good news." He grimaced. "And fortunately, there was no accident. So far."

"Fantastic work, guys. We handled it correctly the first time round, and the driving lesson has proven to be an astounding success," Limpit reassured the others, looking up. He thrust himself into the air and headed back to the rear seat of the vehicle. "Szymon and I, we make a terrific driving team, don't we?"

"Hmm. I'm not sure it's going to be that safe for us to travel in this experimental manner all the way to London, if I'm to be totally honest with you all," the Professor mused.

As they sat there talking, they all noticed a man in the distance to one side with a plastic bag partially draped over his head and wearing an old, tattered-looking raincoat. The man approached them, and after a few moments stopped close by Szymon's window.

Szymon rolled down the window.

"Yes, can I help you? What is it you seek?" Szymon asked, not sure what to say or do.

"What do I seek? What do I seek? Are you blind? You almost drove into the tree in front of you," the man grumbled at them. "I came over to check everyone's okay. I was getting worried you'd hit it, rebounded, and hurt yourselves."

Szymon decided to study the man a little more carefully. He had a craggy beard that jutted from his chin and a pencil-thin moustache. His face looked more than a little weather-beaten, clearly the product of years of neglecting his appearance. The man looked like he hadn't slept in a proper bed for days if not weeks, maybe even a whole lot longer.

"I was watching you from my home, and I was starting to get worried your car was moving out of control," the man explained.

"Your home? Well, no need to worry. We are perfectly fine," Limpit said. The man turned and looked at the small dragon in the back. He wiped his eyes.

"What an unusual-looking dog you have—not one I've cast my eyes on before," he said. "I suggest you ought to be a little more careful when you attempt to pilot this vehicle. We wouldn't want anyone to suffer any injuries by getting into an unfortunate accident."

Szymon glanced towards Professor Tinzy, at a loss for words on how to react to the strange-looking man standing before them. The Professor's face remained expressionless. Szymon returned his gaze to the man.

"Thank you for your concern about our personal safety. But what do you know about driving a vehicle, if I may ask?"

"Well, I spent quite a few years as a driving instructor when I was a lot younger. I had a terrible accident at one point in time, so I know about these things. What to do, what not to. Then I worked in an office for a minicab company for more than fifteen years after I recovered. I couldn't bring myself to teach anyone anymore as I would worry about safety when people drove their vehicles. For various reasons that I'd much rather not get into, I then lost my job a year ago, and thereafter things rapidly went downhill. Here I am."

"You used to be a driving instructor," Szymon muttered in sheer disbelief as the others gawped, hardly believing their luck. "Then surely you can teach us how to drive. We'll... pay you for your work."

The man looked back at Szymon oddly.

"I no longer teach anyone how to drive—I'm now retired due to various circumstances beyond my control."

Professor Tinzy started to shake his head. This conversation was going nowhere, and they were wasting their time.

"Look, I don't know exactly who you are, sir, but we are all fine and unhurt. Thank you for your great concern for our safety, Mr....?"

"My name is Benjamin—call me Ben," the man said.

"Ben, look. You say you used to drive one of these things. You also mentioned you live around here, and it looks like you could use a little money if you're willing to help us learn how to operate this here contraption. Surely you can use the extra money."

"That is true enough. I can always use a little money, as it's been hard to get my hands on much of it for quite some time. Personally, I don't like to ask people for their money, so I manage as best I can with what little I can find or is given to me by the kindness of others, and often I find myself not having enough to pay for things."

"Well, I have a short proposal for you. You don't teach us because you have said it is something you are unable or unwilling to do. How about you drive us to London instead? If you are willing and able to do so yourself, we'll give you some money. All we ask for you to do is take us there and back this weekend," Professor Tinzy said.

"Oh, I see. Tell me, how much do you intend to pay me?" the man asked.

"How much would you consider a fair remuneration?" the Professor replied.

"I—I really don't know. A hundred would be quite nice… No, let's say a hundred and fifty quid, for taking you there and back, which is both ways. If you give me a hundred and fifty quid, I think I can do it. And you pay for your own petrol."

Professor Tinzy thought about the man's proposition. It didn't sound bad.

"Very well then, but first I will want to see whether you can competently drive this motor car in your present state. How about you get inside this vehicle and demonstrate to us all your driving skills, Ben."

"I can drive just about anything you'd like me to, my friend," Ben said proudly.

"Szymon, pop into the back and let's see what Ben here can do when he is comfortably sat behind the wheel," the Professor proposed.

Szymon looked toward the Professor, nodded, and got out of the car. He walked around to the rear, opened the door, and climbed into the back seat, squeezing himself next to Limpit, who ended up stuck in the middle.

Ben cautiously climbed into the car, which sat idling with the engine still running.

"Good, this is a manual car," he chirruped in his gravelly voice. "I don't like them automatics… designed for novices, they are."

Professor Tinzy started sniffing at the slightly stale odour that began to permeate the car. He looked at Ben. Ben's distinctive smell was also noticeable to the others. They also sniffed in a disapproving way.

"Not sure I'll be able to put up with *that smell* the entire way to London," Limpit muttered under his fiery breath. "Does he ever brush his teeth?"

"Now, let's not allow ourselves to get distracted," the Professor said, then more audibly to Ben, "Let's see what you can do then, ex-driving instructor and now our driver Ben." The Professor eyed the stranger with both suspicion and curiosity.

Ben ran his hand across his head to push some of the overgrown hair away from his eyes. He had a thick brown mop that fell over his forehead, and some of it was obscuring his vision. He put his hand on the gear stick and put it into first gear. He then put his foot down on the accelerator, and the Fiesta lurched forward.

"Watchhhhhh outttttt! The tree is still directly ahead of us," Professor Tinzy shouted, but it was too late. The car lurched straight into the trunk and came to an abrupt stop with a sudden jolt.

"Oops," Ben moaned under his breath. "Didn't see that one coming."

"'Oops' is right… what have you done, you complete idiot!" an irate Professor Tinzy yelled, scolding the stranger whilst trying to regain his composure. "I thought you knew how to drive this vehicle."

Limpit had gone flying from the middle of the back seats to the front and banged his head on the front dashboard.

"Ouch, that hurt as well." Limpit pivoted sideways and looked at Ben. "You obviously don't know how to drive anymore, you silly fool. How dare you call yourself a qualified driving instructor?"

Ben looked apologetically at the dragon; still not sure he was really seeing what he thought he was seeing. "I'm sorry, it has been quite some time since I last drove a car… or been sober. I thought I could do it, but maybe I was a little too enthusiastic."

"How long has it been since you last drove?" the Professor asked.

"I don't know. A good few years—maybe more. Time moves slowly for me, but before you know it, the years start to slip by. I was younger in those days when I drove wherever my heart desired. I've been on the streets for some time now. Occasionally they do let me stay in their fine house over there—well, it's more like a shed in the garden—but mostly I'm used to wandering the streets and have no proper home left to go."

Limpit suddenly perked up. "Ah, well, Ben, at least we seem to have one thing in common. Maybe you're not that bad after all. Just need to spread your wings and give them a little workout before you can rise up into the sky and fly.

"On the other hand, you managed to impact that tree with the bonnet of the Professor's car," he added curtly as he flapped his wings and rose into the air.

Ben was suddenly terrified as he realized that this dog had wings and could fly.

"You can't be a dog! What in the Devil's name are you?"

"What in the Devil's name am I?" Limpit repeated. "What do I look like, you insolent fool? I'm a pure-bred dragon of the finest stock. And a most disagreeable one when I'm facing a bumbling twit! I'm a master of great dragons, a leader of all the great beasts in all the lands."

Ben had had enough of taking criticism from this group of misfits. He opened the car door and bolted out into the rain without saying another word.

The others all sat down for a lingering moment, not sure what to say or do.

"Any other suggestions are welcome. Anyone?" asked Princess Sallina with a sigh.

"Seemed a lot like me on the brakes and Szymon at the wheel was turning out to be a safer option than him," Limpit muttered dully. "Sometimes it takes more than one to make things work properly."

"I don't think this vehicle is likely to be going anywhere soon, after our little accident," said Szymon. "It has been damaged now. I fear we've lost our ride to London."

"Then there must be another method that we can use to get to London safely," said Limpit. "If I was at my full size, you all could sit on me and I would fly us all, but alas, that is not to be. In my current state, I can't take any passengers."

Professor Tinzy gave their predicament some careful thought. He put his hand into one of his pockets and pulled out a small mobile phone. He pressed a few buttons slowly and with the utmost care, trying to recall the correct sequence, and then held the phone up to his ear and waited.

It rang a few times, and then someone answered.

"Is that Barchester?" asked the Professor. "Look, dear friend, I think we may need your assistance on an urgent matter of the greatest importance."

There was a moment's silence before he received a response. The voice of Barchester spoke back to him, "Yes, go on."

"We need to travel to London urgently. There are four of us who have to go. Would you be able to spare us a lift from my home, you know, to this special place in central London we need to get to?"

There was then another silence for a few moments.

"Tomorrow morning will be fine," said the voice from the phone. "He will be there for you bright and early. Shall we say around nine?"

"That's wonderful, Thomas," the Professor said heartily, then clicked the phone off and sat there. "He's saved us."

Sallina spoke up. "What do we do now?"

"Let's go home. I'm afraid we'll have to walk back as I don't think my car will be going anywhere."

"What will you do with your car then?" Szymon asked.

"Abandon it for the time being—it's of no further use to us," Professor Tinzy said, as a sense of sadness overcame him. "It's in no fit state to be driven."

"Oh, no. Will it be okay here, sitting alone?" Szymon asked the Professor.

"It should be perfectly fine. This doesn't appear to be a bustling place," the Professor replied. "I think I can arrange for a tow truck to come pick it up and bring it back to where it was parked before. I'll need to get it repaired at some point, but now's probably not a good time. We have things to do."

With that, Professor Tinzy climbed out of the car and stood motionless in the rain. He didn't seem to the others be too bothered by the tiny raindrops falling from the sky, and a few moments later, they were all standing outside the car looking up at the clouds above.

Szymon handed the Professor the car keys, and the Professor pressed a button on the fob to lock the doors to the vehicle, which they did all by themselves. Princess Sallina lifted an eyebrow and even Szymon looked impressed. Limpit wasn't interested in the car anymore, so he showed no reaction.

As they headed back to the Professor's house, Professor Tinzy took off his jacket and placed it over Limpit, trying to conceal him from any prying eyes that might be watching.

Then he noticed a half-broken supermarket shopping cart lying ditched by the side road and went towards it.

"Limpit, you ought to rest inside this thing, and I'll push it along."

"I'm fine—I'm not feeling tired. I can manage as I am."

"Limpit, it's not about being tired. We are outside in the open. Others can see us, and we need to be careful. Let's be discreet."

Limpit nodded. "I can do discreet." He flapped his wings under the jacket and landed in the trolley, folding his wings as he did so that he could fit in it. Professor Tinzy started to push the trolley down the remainder of the car park towards the nearby public road.

"We can't afford to be stopped by someone, especially the police, so this is a good way to hide our friend from the unwanted gazes of any passersby. Humans simply don't understand anything about dragons in this land, and we don't have time to be questioned by the authorities or have someone get in touch with the police."

The others nodded as they continued to head towards the house.

Chapter 20

After returning home safely without any further unwanted attention from strangers along the way, the party spent the rest of the day and evening in quiet personal reflection— although Princess Sallina spent most of that time pondering what it was going to be like travelling to London with the Professor's 'friend', and what might happen to the damaged Fiesta they had been forced to abandon in the car park.

Her mind raced through so many questions over and over again. How did the Professor manage to get hold of a car in the first place? Did he purchase it directly himself, or was it given to him by someone else? If another person had given the car to him, then who would it have been, and why? She had heard in passing conversations about places called "showrooms" that one visited to purchase such a mechanical contraption, but it seemed like an odd idea to own a tin box and have to take care of it like it was your valued possession, simply so one could move around in it. It was almost as if it was a treasured pet.

In Starpoint, all unicorns were able to move about freely of their own volition and nobody had to sit in a box of any kind to get somewhere, the only exception being when a unicorn passed away and the deceased needed to be taken by cart. In such an event, they were placed inside a wooden carriage that was then decked out with ribbons and plumes. The decorations made the carriage look truly beautiful, as it should for one's final journey after what had hopefully been a long and fruitful life... but no living creature would want to be trapped in a box like that or pushed by others.

As for physical items, those were usually transported on wooden pallets that unicorns deployed a magic spell to move, or if the items were smaller, they were carried without much trouble on a unicorn's back, using a special saddle that allowed for their safe and hassle-free transport from one point to another.

Finally, after everyone else had retired for the night, and having exhausted her mind over these trivial issues, Sallina dropped off to sleep right where she was, on the sofa.

***

She woke the next morning to the sounds of lively chatter and the smell of food being cooked in the kitchen. Everyone was feeling greatly refreshed, and they enjoyed a hearty breakfast that had been carefully prepared by Professor Tinzy: a delightful mixture of scrambled eggs, fried tomatoes, and mushrooms, along with freshly toasted bread.

Meat, of course, was not on the menu, because Starpointers didn't believe in eating something that had previously existed as a living being with its own eyes and feet and a will to survive. This was a terrible thing to consume, and the very thought of eating someone who had been leading a full and zestful life was no less than revolting. The very thought of it sent shivers down the spines of most unicorns, and it was also a little off-putting when it came to consuming eggs. Sure, the eggs weren't actually alive and kicking, but they could have been if left alone!

It became clearer to both Szymon and Sallina that Professor Tinzy and Limpit had already adapted themselves to this foreign landscape. Remorsefully, they both went along with it and pretended not to be aware of the significance of the eggs as potential forms of life.

Over breakfast, Professor Tinzy brought everyone up to speed on the journey to London that awaited them. He finished by instructing them to get dressed and be ready to travel within a few minutes.

He gave Sallina and Szymon each a small travel bag to carry some belongings on their journey. Szymon had considered returning home but was still scared of having to face his father if he did. So, for the third day in a row, he was dressed in the same clothes, which were now starting to look a little grubby, and—if one was entirely honest—were becoming smelly as well. Professor Tinzy noticed the boy's dishevelled look, which was also accompanied by an odour.

"Listen to me, young man," Professor Tinzy said rather gruffly, although he was attempting to be polite. "When we get

185

to London, we're going to take you out shopping and buy you a set of new clothes to wear. You can't keep on wearing the exact same thing each day—you'll start to stink like a farthog, or worse."

Farthogs were familiar animals back in the land of unicorns. They looked a bit like pigs, but they had some unusual differences that made them unique. They were famous in Starpoint for passing a great deal of wind whenever it suited them, which was more or less all the time. They were about three to four times the size of a normal Earth-type hog and were known to be quite fierce fighters if provoked.

In olden times, they had been a favourite food of dragons. Most of the only remaining dragons were tame and had become vegetarians out of consideration for other living beings, so farthogs now freely roamed the lands and multiplied profusely.

It didn't help that they would also smell incredibly foul when threatened, and that in itself was enough to put off the taste of farthog meat for most. They rarely made their way to Starpoint itself, but they sometimes posed a nuisance to some of the nearby farms and smaller villages, where they were often caught eating the precious crops that were being grown by the local farmers in the fields. At least farthogs were not hard to control, as Starpointers had a simple spell that could enchant a field and put farthogs off from venturing into it and sampling the crop.

"Who says *starting* to stink?" Limpit butted in with a little chortle, finding it most amusing and refreshing not to be on the receiving end of criticism for a change.

Sallina said nothing, though she also found it amusing, especially when she saw the slightly guilty look on Szymon's face.

"He must be truly afraid of his father," Sallina said to the Professor in passing.

"Clearly he is nothing short of terrified of him," said the Professor dismissively, but then he spoke no more about it.

The Princess didn't really expect anything else from the Professor; she knew that deep down he still didn't approve of Szymon becoming part of their company. She knew he didn't fully believe in Szymon, and that he trusted him far less. The very fact that Szymon was Unimage Konstanty's son was more than enough reason to continue to distrust him and maintain a safe distance. In fact, it was only because of her fond attachment to Szymon that the Professor somehow tolerated his presence and participation in their mission.

Once they were ready and packed, the human-unicorns and their miniature dragon piled out, with Professor Tinzy carrying Limpit wrapped in an oversized jacket. They looked up and down the street, wondering what their next mode of travel was going to be.

A few moments later, a blue Jaguar Saloon pulled over, with a properly attired driver wearing a silver-coloured cap. The driver—a tall man in glasses with a thin moustache—got out and introduced himself as Derek. In his late forties, he appeared to be somewhat overweight, with the tightly fitting jacket not doing much to conceal his paunch. Derek opened the rear door and glanced towards the Professor.

"Welcome back, Professor. Welcome to you all. I'm looking forward to taking you all down to central London."

The Professor made his way round to the front of the car and sat himself in the front passenger seat. Just before he got in, he glanced at Szymon and Sallina.

"Well, are you two getting inside with us or not?"

Obediently, they both climbed in, followed by Limpit, who had been hovering a short distance above the ground nearby. As Limpit floated in, his oversized jacket got stuck on the car door and almost slid off. Sallina managed to grab hold of it and ensure that it also made its way safely into the car. With everyone settled in, Derek closed the rear doors, returned to the driver's seat, and started up the engine.

The car cruised down the highway as it made its way safely to London. Silence had filled the vehicle for some time after the journey began, so Derek turned on the radio, which started to play classical music. The volume was intentionally low.

Professor Tinzy glanced across at Derek, but Derek ignored him and focused exclusively on his driving. In the back, Princess Sallina was looking at Szymon, and Limpit kept his eyes on both of them, glancing from left and right as if he was watching a game of tennis, waiting for someone to speak up.

Limpit eventually spoke up himself, tired of waiting for some sort of conversation to start. "Well, this is a nice way for us to travel. Here we are, riding in the lap of luxury. What a comfortable machine to be in."

"It's just a car," Sallina remarked. "A car's a car. What's luxurious about this one?"

"This happens to be a nicer kind of car, better than the other one we were in before," Szymon piped up.

"'Better' is usually a matter of perspective," the Professor replied. "Better on comfort, perhaps. Not better on the price one has to pay for it."

"How did you get hold of this car, Professor?" Sallina asked.

"This one... it's not mine. It belongs to a friend. We're just borrowing it."

Derek didn't say anything. He just kept on driving silently.

"I didn't know you even had a friend here," Sallina said, surprised. "Oh, I didn't mean it that way—I just didn't think you had any friends in this land."

"I have a few scattered about here and there. Not as many as I used to or would like to, but then I haven't been here for quite a while, and one does tend to lose touch if one isn't careful about keeping in touch on a regular basis. But I do have a few scattered about here and there even to this day, and dare I say they will remember me in a most positive way."

Derek remained quiet as the car ambled its way down the motorway.

The party fell silent for the remainder of the journey, which continued until they were getting very close to where they were going.

Sallina looked out of the window with a sense of marvel as she took in London's bustling skyline. "Wow, this really is a huge and magnificent city. I've never seen anything quite this big before in my entire life."

"There are many big cities in this land," said the Professor. "This is one of the biggest I've been to as well. You will find many humans living in all these big cities. They seem to like to live close together."

"I was wondering," Limpit interrupted a little sheepishly, "when we might be arriving at our intended destination… because I may, uh, need to have a little wee in a discreet way."

Sallina blushed as she realized why Limpit had been looking a bit fretful.

"Oh, Limpit, you could have said something about it earlier," she piped up, before letting an involuntary smile slip.

"I honestly didn't want to bother us on this smooth and trouble-free journey, but I'm starting to feel a little more… desperate about getting on with it," Limpit mumbled and then involuntarily coughed. "I'd hate to accidentally make a mess in this here… car."

"We'll be arriving at our destination quite soon," Derek said reassuringly. "Another few minutes, Mister Limpit. If you can hold it in for a few more minutes, we'll find you a place to go."

Limpit nodded. "Oh, sure, I can wait a little bit longer—I have a good sense of self control and do not want to cause any inconvenience."

Szymon looked at Sallina and whispered to her, "He doesn't appear to be too bothered by having a dragon in his car. Something tells me that he has seen one before and perhaps knows who and what Limpit is. Don't you get that feeling?"

She nodded. "Yes, it makes you wonder who this friend of the Professor really is, and where he's originally from. I'm starting to have some suspicions."

The car eventually arrived outside a grand-looking hotel in central London and pulled up at the main entrance. Sallina rolled down the car window as she looked out at the large building standing before her. The name of the hotel was Claridge's. Something told Sallina that this was a popular hotel, as it had a certain air of self-importance.

"We've made it here safe and sound," Professor Tinzy said. "Let's go check into our rooms."

As they climbed out of the car, a doorman stepped up with a trolley. "May I assist you with your baggage?" he asked Professor Tinzy.

"Oh, that's very kind of you, young man," replied the Professor.

Once the bags were stacked up on the trolley, the party made their way to reception to check themselves in.

Princess Sallina looked about in awe when she entered the grand lobby of this famous hotel. She didn't know anything about its history, but she could tell that this place was very special.

"How do you like it here?" Tinzy asked her.

"It's very nice—in fact, it's lovely. It's even better than my palace back home! And that's saying something. I mean, it's not a palace, but it's nice."

"Oh, it's one of my favourite places in this entire world," the Professor said. "I used to come here regularly, so some of the staff may still recognize me."

"May I say, it's most unusual for an ordinary school professor to be a guest in such a luxurious place," Szymon chimed into the conversation. "I didn't know you were a person of such importance, or that you could afford to stay here."

"Oh, heavens, yes—it is most unusual. It's far beyond what I can possibly afford to pay, but my friend is fairly well off, and he likes to lavish these luxuries on me from time to time. You could say I'm being spoiled rotten by his overly generous nature, which I'm also extending to the three of you."

"Must be a very good friend of yours indeed," said Szymon.

"Oh, I suppose you could say that. To him, this is nothing special. In fact, I would say it's quite ordinary for his lavish tastes. He's quite an indulgent fellow."

They checked in, and it turned out the rooms had been paid for in advance by the Professor's generous benefactor, whoever he was. The Professor was given his own personal room, and so were Szymon and Sallina.

Sallina was asked to fill in her full name and address, so she used her mother's surname to complete the form. Szymon quickly became Szymon Konstanty, which was the only thing he could come up with on such short notice, as Szymon had no other surname he could think of using.

In fact, it was most unusual for unicorns to have surnames, although it has been rumoured that they once had several names given to each at birth—though others would find it challenging to remember them all and in the right order, having forgotten these names over several generations. Apparently, after the great battle that had taken place four centuries ago, such formalities were dispensed with as nothing more than a frivolous distraction designed to separate unicorns into divisive groupings, and it was deemed counterproductive to leading a peaceful and happy co-existence.

"I think Father would be fond of this place," Szymon said to Sallina as they made their way up in the lift to their designated floor.

Sallina and Szymon's rooms were right next to each other. Professor Tinzy's larger room was just a few doors down. Limpit, covered again with the jacket, joined them. He was going to stay with the Professor.

"Well," said the Professor, "why don't we all take a productive little nap—we've certainly all earned it—and later on we'll get to enjoy a spot of tea downstairs. This hotel is world famous for its tea, and it's a lovely place to enjoy it."

"That sounds wonderful," Sallina replied, quite enjoying the comforts and opulence of her lush new surroundings.

Afternoon tea proved to be a somewhat ceremonial affair, and unsurprisingly, the brew was also delicious. The party enjoyed the delightful Claridge's blend of tea and tucked into the gorgeously rich pastries that were customarily consumed alongside the tea.

Limpit was told to stay behind in the Professor's suite. Even though he was partially disguised with the aid of the raincoat, he would be an odd shape, and there was the very real possibility that his pointy tail could protrude accidentally and cause a major disturbance. No, a busy Claridge's tearoom was no place for a dragon to be sipping tea!

"Professor, where is it we're going to go to obtain our Pinny?" Sallina asked as she tucked into another delicious Claridge's pastry and allowed it to tingle her taste buds.

"We'll be going to an auction house near here called Sotheby's. They'll be holding a private auction on Monday morning, and that's when we will have an opportunity to bid for the Pinny we require. Well, some Pinny, at least. I don't think there's much to be obtained on this occasion, but it's a start."

"Bid for the Pinny?" Szymon blurted. "You mean we have to pay for it?"

"Of course someone will have to pay to get hold of it in this land," the Professor replied impatiently. "In all my time in this strange land, one thing has proven to be consistent no matter where one is: everything carries a price, and Pinny is no exception to this most important rule. You could go as far as to say that what Pinny is to our land, money is to theirs.

"It's their magical essence, and it makes everything work. Nothing works properly without it. On Monday, they are going to auction off the rare object which we call Pinny, and it will be quite expensive in Earth terms, although it is far more unmeasurably valuable to us for reasons we all know. After the bid, this item becomes the rightful property of the highest bidder, who pays for it and then takes possession of the auctioned item. The bidding determines its final price, and who the owner is."

"How will we be able to afford it if it's so expensive, Professor?" Sallina gasped, a little shocked by this sudden revelation concerning payments and bidding.

"I wouldn't worry about the money side of things, my dear, as my friend shall pay for this. He has plenty of this money to meet whatever our requirements are, no matter what the final bid price may be. Let's just say we'll pay the highest and the Pinny will be ours."

"Oh, that's reassuring to know," Szymon muttered. "I wouldn't have any idea how to afford anything that's so valuable in this land. In fact, I've hardly any money at all on me. Money is not something either I or my—never mind."

"You'd be surprised, youngster, at how much money you could get your hoofs on if you know the proper ways to go about it," the Professor said. "You're the son of a great Unimage from Starpoint, and your father possesses many items of nearly unimaginable value that come from our land. This would make you extremely wealthy in a purely materialistic environment such as this with little effort."

"*Extremely wealthy...* I don't want it—that sounds perverse," Szymon said, a little baffled. "What is the meaning of being 'extremely wealthy'? I don't understand what it signifies, and it doesn't sound appealing or in any way dignifying to me. For us unicorns, wealth lies in being able to use our magic and share our knowledge and wisdom openly. It's in our ability to be free to do and be whatever we want to be, wherever we want to be, and in the safety of those we care about most. So I cannot imagine a wealth that is measured purely in the possession of material things that are devoid of purpose or of life with a beating heart. It is too strange a concept for me to properly grasp."

"Then you are perhaps a little bit wiser than I had previously thought," the Professor said with surprise.

This concession from the Professor made Sallina smile for a moment. It gave her a little newfound hope that perhaps the Professor was starting to change his feelings about her peculiar and strangely likable friend Szymon.

At least the Professor was able to look past material things, but the bigger question for her was whether the Professor would be willing to see Szymon for who he truly was, or would Szymon's lineage, rather than his individual actions, ultimately determine how the Professor judged Szymon's actions in the future? To her, even the Professor was to some extent a victim of illusory, predetermined thinking, something that unicorns have tried hard over the last few centuries to eradicate.

Judge no one by their personal ancestry, or by their breed, as neither is determined by those who bear it, but judge one and all by who they are and what they choose to stand for. This is how we can all co-exist peacefully, and it reduces and may even eradicate most if not all our conflicts.

This was an important concept held near and dear to the hearts of most unicorns, and one that she truly believed in herself. This was the reason she could see Szymon for who he really was, and not what others expected him to be.

Chapter 21

The weekend passed uneventfully for the travelling party, who had spent most of the time taking in the famous London tourist sites such as Piccadilly Circus and Leicester Square. They also made their way down the Mall to look at the Queen's magnificent residence. They marvelled when they saw Buckingham Palace. Sallina's jaw virtually dropped to the floor as she gazed in wonder at the regal building directly in front of her.

"It sure is something to behold," she muttered as Szymon and Professor Tinzy grinned. "How'd I love to have a home like this if I were to spend more time in this land! I would feel like a true Queen."

"Well, this one's been made for humans, but you're right, it's quite something," the Professor said as he pondered. "Yours on Starpoint isn't too shabby, though. I think you are a fortunate young lady to live in a palace."

"It's truly a place fit for a Queen… I mean, this palace here," Szymon contributed with unintended irony as his eyes took in the imposing sight.

Szymon was holding onto a small, box-like object. In the box was a small opening that looked like part of a cage. A rather unhappy Limpit stared out of it, his eyes also taking in the spectacle as Szymon lifted up the box.

"What an incredible, big house. Even at my original size, I reckon there'd be enough room for me to move in and make myself comfortable," Limpit muttered, mostly to himself.

***

On Sunday night, the party gathered together in Professor Tinzy's elegant suite, which was clearly far more lavish than their own more regularly sized rooms. Professor Tinzy sat plumped on the sofa as Limpit hovered nearby. Princess Sallina and Szymon rested in individual sofa chairs.

"Are you sure we can do this?" Professor Tinzy asked Sallina. Sallina nodded in acknowledgement. "Then we ought to try it now and make sure it works for tomorrow."

"And if it doesn't work when I try it, what then?" Sallina asked.

"If it doesn't, I'd better go to the auction alone. The most important thing is that we obtain the Pinny and we don't all need to go to the auction if there's a problem."

"I do so want to come along with you," Sallina pleaded. "I've never been to any kind of auction before, and I want to know how it works and help you out."

Szymon grinned. "I'd also like to come along. But I'm not sure your magic is going to work, if I'm being honest."

Sallina ignored his sudden negativity. "Did you get hold of that item I asked for, Professor?" she asked.

"Oh, yes, I've got it right here with me."

He stood up and headed towards the cabinet with the flat-screen television. Professor Tinzy picked up a packet of raw carrots and placed them on the coffee table close by the sofa.

Szymon studied them, horrified.

"Oh, no! Not these again!"

Sallina opened the packet and handed a carrot to her young friend.

"No thanks. I hate carrots," Szymon moaned.

"I know. But you told me you needed them for my magic to work, and I'm sure you can chew on a few more for the greater good."

"There always seems to be a good reason to eat those horrible-tasting things," Szymon argued sulkily. He reluctantly took the raw carrot and held it in his hand. Princess Sallina also took one and eyed it with a smile.

"Well then, what are we waiting for? Let's get chewing and incant the spell!" said Professor Tinzy.

Limpit was excited, as he knew that some magic was about to be called upon. "You know, with so little magic visible in this land, I do deeply miss seeing some in action again," he moaned, reminding himself that he was in a very strange and not-so-friendly place that in no way resembled his home world.

Princess Sallina tightly clasped the pendant that hung loose around her neck, and she closed her eyes to concentrate.

"I'm not sure whether I can make this magic work," she said as she joined in the chorus of doubt that was building around her. "I've never attempted this level of spell before, and without a nearby supply of Pinny."

A hushed silence followed, and hardly a breath could be heard.

Sallina began to hum for a few seconds, and then she broke into her chant.

"I shall travel from here to there, and from there to here. I go from young to old, from old to young, as I please. Now I add extra years for both Szymon and myself and make us look as if time has passed us by."

The pendant began to emit its familiar pale-blue hue. The incandescence became stronger, and a bright light burst through Sallina's fingers as she continued to cling tightly to the pendant.

The light shot outwards and completely bathed both her and Szymon in its magical glow.

Limpit watched, and he marvelled at what he saw before him. Both Sallina and Szymon starting to age beyond their years, until they looked like adults in their mid- to late-twenties. The pendant then stopped glowing and returned to its normal, lifeless state.

"Maybe she could also make me my full size again!" Limpit exclaimed, his wings flapping in excitement, "especially as I hate being so very tiny and mostly useless. I wish to be a fearsome beast once more, rather than giving off the appearance of an unwanted pest. It would be splendid if this was somehow possible."

"It would be wonderful, Limpit," Sallina commented, overhearing him. "But it's best we wait until we return home before we attempt something that could lead to unintended consequences. Don't forget that this appearance of age is only temporary—the magic doesn't last for long. Can you imagine how humans would react if they saw a fully grown dragon enter the auction house?"

"Why, what's the problem? I'd be perfectly normal," Limpit whimpered, but he knew that it was not to be.

Szymon glanced towards Sallina, and Sallina looked back at him. They could barely recognise each other.

"You look so very strange," she said.

"As do you. Suits you, though, in a peculiar sort of way."

Professor Tinzy grinned. He was delighted by the visible success of her spell.

"That's incredibly well done, Sallina! Simply outstanding crafting of what is quite a complex and intricate spell!"

Sallina and Szymon both rose to their feet and eyed each other curiously.

"How long will this silly illusion hold?" Szymon asked.

"It should carry on for a while. Honestly, I'm not entirely certain. It should maintain our new look for a while, with any luck. Professor, do you know how long it will last?"

Professor Tinzy gave her a blank look, and then he shook his head.

"Then it's settled. We will do this same trick again tomorrow. We're set to go to Sobberbees." Szymon was quite pleased with himself.

"Sotheby's," Professor Tinzy corrected him.

"Yes, an auction house," Sallina piped up. "I can't wait. I'm getting excited."

* * *

Monday morning, the Professor, Sallina, and Szymon made their way to Sotheby's, leaving Limpit behind once again.

The auction room wasn't too busy, with around fifteen or so bidders present and occupying nearby seats. The Professor, Sallina, and Szymon sat a few rows in front of the auction podium so that they could get a good view of the lots being presented without drawing too much attention to themselves.

Sallina was a bit surprised at the lack of numbers present, and the price of recent items that had fallen under the hammer whilst they waited seemed low. It became apparent that something as precious as Pinny wasn't of such great interest to inhabitants of this land. Otherwise, the place would have been packed with eager buyers, and it would have been offered at auction amongst a far more expensive collection of items.

You wouldn't have been able to get in if this auction had been taking place back home in Starpoint, thought Sallina.

There would have literally been thousands of unicorns swarming about just to get a good look at the most important substance in all of existence for conducting magic. Although of course Pinny wasn't bought and sold in Starpoint, as it was far too precious for that. It was mined and then kept safely under lock and key for official use in order to power the great alicorns and provide access to magic for all citizens.

Szymon and Sallina both had trouble adjusting to their older selves as they sat there patiently waiting for the auction to start, and both felt more than a little awkward in their further-developed adult bodies. They tried their best to conceal their awkwardness as much as they could, since they didn't want to attract any undue attention.

A few minutes later, a large projection screen was electronically lowered, and the lights were dimmed. After a few seconds of silence, an image suddenly popped up on the screen, giving them their first glimpse of the precious Pinny that was to be sold off at this auction.

A finely attired man in a business suit arrived with a small silver platter and placed this on the table next to the podium. He carefully lifted the cover to reveal the precious Pinny in all its glory. A camera mounted on a wall steadily zoomed in and transmitted the Pinny's image onto the large TV screen. Sallina immediately felt her throat dry up; she was about to gasp as she sat there, and even Szymon was staring at it in awe.

The auctioneer rather brusquely attempted to clear his throat. Then he apologized for his rather raspy voice, which reverberated awkwardly around the room via the microphone and was emitted through a series of speakers positioned in different places.

"Ladies and gentlemen, we now move on to our next item. This is a deep red, glassy painite crystal surrounded by several elegant rubies. It was discovered between the years 2000 and 2003. The item measures a mere 2.2 centimetres in length and is now available to bid for exclusively at Sotheby's. I start the bidding at one hundred thousand pounds. Who shall bid one hundred thousand pounds?"

Szymon turned to Professor Tinzy and whispered, "That's not much Pinny, is it?" The Professor silently nodded. A hand was raised in the front, belonging to a young woman in her late twenties as she glanced momentarily behind her. As Sallina and Szymon were sitting further back, they couldn't make out her face, only the back of her head.

"It's only a small amount of Pinny. Surely, we'll need more than this for our mission to be a success," Sallina, sitting close to the Professor, said.

"Please remain calm and stay quiet, my dear," the Professor whispered. "I must focus my attention. This is just an initial purchase. There will be further Pinny to follow." As he spoke, the bid doubled to two hundred thousand and then increased to three hundred thousand. It was at six hundred and fifty thousand when the Professor raised his hand and increased it to seven hundred thousand. There were a couple of attempts to raise it higher, and finally the young woman who had made the opening bid offered a staggering eight hundred thousand.

A small bidding war between the Professor and the mysterious young woman followed. The price went up even higher, from the eight hundred thousand, to nine hundred, to nine hundred and fifty thousand… and then it kept going on and on until it reached nearly two million pounds.

Only the young woman and the Professor appeared to be interested in paying such a vast sum of money for the Pinny. Finally, the Professor raised his hand and shouted, "Three million!"

The young woman turned towards the Professor but didn't reply. Moments later, the hammer fell, and it was sold to the Professor for three million pounds. That was it. The bidding was over, and the Professor had won.

"We've got it," Sallina said excitedly. "It's ours, we have the Pinny!"

"Yes, my dear, it's a splendid start for Starpoint," remarked the Professor. "We should leave now, as we have what we came here for."

The Professor rose to his feet and headed towards the exit situated at the back of the room. Szymon and Sallina followed him closely. They didn't take any notice of the young woman, who had slipped away in silence… not until they had made their way partially down the hallway. It was at that point that she shouted at them, "Hey, you guys, stop!"

They turned and eyed her with suspicion. She approached them, looking upset. She talked with a strong American accent and fired her words out at them like bullets. "You sure must want that stuff bad—you paid an absolute fortune for it. Hope it was worth the ridiculous price you offered.”

The Professor looked her over carefully. She was an attractive woman, with bright round eyes and long auburn hair that stretched down to her slender shoulders. She was well dressed and looked like someone who came from a well-to-do background.

“I’m deeply sorry, but I have no idea who you are. Who is it I’m addressing?” he asked.

“I’m a private collector from New York. I purchase these items on behalf of my undisclosed clients, and one of my important clients is going to be really disappointed.”

“Oh, I see. Then the item wasn’t intended for your own use?”

“No, it’s definitely not for me. I was intending to purchase it for my discreet VIP client. He had set a limit, and your bid exceeded it, so… there it is, and now you have it instead of him.”

“Well, I’m sorry if this has troubled you. We also happen to be keen on obtaining it for our client’s collection,” the Professor explained. “You of course have our deepest condolences for your loss; other auctions do happen from time to time, and no doubt there will be other such opportunities.”

“No need to be sad about a thing, Professor,” the young woman quickly retorted. “As you say, there will be other auctions, and the fact is that you paid far too much for this one. All things have a defined value and there’s no point in paying in excess of what they’re ultimately worth.”

“I sincerely doubt that to be the case—I think I received very good value for my money,” the Professor confidently remarked, though he appeared a little perturbed that this young woman seemed to know about his profession.

“Although you have me at a small disadvantage. I know you are a professor of esteem, but I don’t know what for… or your name?”

Guarded now, the Professor calmly replied, “Oh, I’m nobody important to be concerned with. In fact, I am a bit like you. Since I have also purchased it for my client, it’s not intended for my personal use. Good heavens, no. After all, it's a lot of money, isn't it?"

"I suppose you won't disclose to me who your client happens to be. I wouldn't blame you at all if you didn't."

"No, sadly I can't share that information with you—it's a confidential matter," he replied. He turned away from her, as he assumed the conversation was over.

"Wouldn't it be something if both our clients already knew each other? I would find that to be more than amusing, wouldn't you? You do look somehow familiar to me. There's something about you; I can't put my finger on it. You sure we haven't crossed paths before?"

The Professor had already started walking away from her, when suddenly he stopped. He turned around to look at her, troubled. "I sincerely doubt it to be the case, as our different lives are worlds apart."

He turned away again and continued to head off with Sallina and Szymon, who both closely accompanied him by his side.

The young woman watched the three of them leave. She wasn't too pleased that she had lost this valuable item to them and that she had been outbid by an odd-looking trio who were clearly out of place at Sotheby's. But she knew there would be other auctions for her to partake in, which was why she hadn't been willing to overpay for one particular rare Painite crystal, and a small one at that. In the back of her mind, she had the strangest feeling that it wasn't going to be the last time she would encounter them.

***

Later that evening, the party gathered in Professor Tinzy's luxurious hotel suite. They had returned to their former selves. Limpit kept his eyes firmly glued on the Pinny, which sat on the coffee table. Professor Tinzy was quite pleased with himself, as was Princess Sallina and Szymon, though they were also feeling disappointed.

"This limited amount of Pinny won't help us stop the huge meteorite from heading our way." Sallina raised the obvious issue as they all eyed their precious prize.

"No, I suppose it won't be enough to do the job. But at least it's a reasonable start, and we can prove that we are able to

201

provide Pinny and raise everyone's hopes that the solution will be found," the Professor replied, embarking on a more positive direction.

A buzz at the door made everyone suddenly turn their attention toward it. The Professor rose to his feet to answer.

"Who could that be?" Sallina pondered with a sense of alarm. Her question was soon answered as Professor Tinzy opened the door and Derek the driver entered in his uniform.

Derek noticed the Pinny immediately as it sat on the coffee table. He went straight for it.

"What's going on, Professor?" Szymon asked. He quickly positioned himself to block Derek from getting close to the Pinny. But Derek was too fast and too strong; he just manoeuvred his way around Szymon.

Professor Tinzy remained quiet as Derek picked up the Pinny and carefully placed it in a small rucksack. Szymon was about to grab hold of him when the Professor spoke.

"It's okay, Szymon, let him have it."

"Why's he taking away our Pinny?" Sallina blurted out, looking more alarmed than even Szymon.

"Because" said Derek, "I've been instructed to do so by the owner of this item."

Sallina looked confused. "What? Instructed! By whom?"

"By the man who paid for it—your client," Derek replied matter-of-factly.

Limpit jumped into the air, flapped his wings, and demanded answers. "Who paid for it? I want to know. We all want to know."

Professor Tinzy had already shut the door as he approached the coffee table.

"We need to depart. We will head back home with Derek in his car at once. Tonight, we'll be returning to Doberry."

"We're going home?" Szymon was shocked as he considered how little he wanted to go back to his home, where his father undoubtedly would be expecting and eagerly awaiting his return. Without question, the Unimage would have a barrage of questions to throw at him.

"Not to our homes in the other land. First, we're going somewhere else," Professor Tinzy remarked, still looking rather casual about the whole thing.

"Where is 'somewhere else'?" Sallina asked.

"You'll soon find out. Now you'd better go and pack your things. We're leaving shortly and I'm not in the mood for a long discussion," the Professor advised them, looking more than a little tired of all the bustling about.

Szymon and Sallina looked at each other blankly. Then they nodded and returned to their rooms to pack.

Limpit watched them leave before giving Professor Tinzy a curious glance that more than hinted at a degree of dissatisfaction with the manner in which the Professor had been conducting himself. In Limpit's mind, there were always far too many secrets being kept, and he for one wasn't so keen on always having to keep secrets from those he'd learned to trust and care for.

Derek soon left without saying another word, leaving Limpit and Professor Tinzy alone together inside the suite.

"You mind explaining to me what is going on?" Limpit remarked, breaking the unusual silence.

"There's nothing going on here, my friend. We simply need to get back, and then we shall figure out how to get that Pinny back to Starpoint."

"But it's too little to take back—it's not going to be enough," Limpit complained.

"At least it is something, and something is far better than nothing. Unless we can take this modest amount of Pinny back safely to Starpoint, there's little point in us searching for more, is there?"

Limpit mulled over the pragmatic response. He wasn't sure what to say in reply, so he kept his mouth shut.

In a way, the Professor had been right. They had no idea how they were going to get this Pinny back safely to Starpoint; it was meant to be their next mission. A bridge had to be available so that this and further amounts of Pinny could be brought home for powering the alicorns and to help save their world.

But, Limpet wondered, where was the Pinny going, and how would they be able to get it back if they didn't even have it? There was something very strange going on, and Limpit was feeling increasingly baffled.

Limpit remembered how Professor Tinzy had disappeared some years before to return to Starpoint, but Limpit himself hadn't yet been able to go back home, and he had been forced into exile on Earth. He knew there was great uncertainty as to how exactly they could travel to Starpoint safely and take the Pinny back to their own world.

The sad truth of the matter was that both Limpit and Professor Tinzy were pushing into old age. Neither was an ideal candidate for travelling between worlds, as both were likely to suffer from severe memory loss and be unable to remember who they were. The last time Professor Tinzy travelled back, he'd found himself spending weeks attempting to remember who he was.

When he recently returned to Earth, he had completely forgotten who he was. He had left poor Limpit locked up in that shed all by himself for so many weeks, and he had forced the dragon to promise not to break out. This was an experience that Limpit had no desire to repeat. Even as a dragon, Limpit found his memories were slipping, but somehow, he was able to regain them far faster than unicorns. But what if one day he couldn't recall them? What would happen then? He didn't want to think about it, so he emptied out his mind and tried to calm his thoughts until he was at peace.

* * *

Later that night, the party found themselves seated in the Jaguar, heading northwards and back to Doberry. They mostly remained silent as it was already late, everyone was tired, and nobody felt much like talking.

Despite all the things that had recently transpired, there was something comforting and soothing about sitting inside a strange device that rolled on four wheels; it had prompted both Szymon and Sallina to fall fast asleep. They were getting used to being driven around, and they didn't mind it that much anymore. Even Limpit managed to keep his thoughts down to a bare minimum, and he could almost drift off to enjoy a restful snooze.

Chapter 22

Derek carefully steered the Jaguar, with the Professor, Sallina, and Szymon all fast asleep and Limpit crouched and relatively still in the back. Limpit had woken up, but he managed to look peaceful and relaxed.

They were no more than fifty-two miles away from Doberry when everything went dangerously awry.

Derek had been playing a little soothing classical music and was humming the tune softly to himself when suddenly he had trouble breathing. It made him lose full control of the car, which began to swerve about precariously. Sweating profusely and gasping for breath, Derek struggled to properly steer the vehicle, zigzagging into the traffic coming the other way… and right into the path of an oncoming car. The other tenacious driver was forced to swerve to avoid colliding with the Jaguar.

BEEEEEEE-PPP!

The sudden side-to-side jolting of the Jaguar and the loud honking of nearby cars stirred Sallina from her slumber. She quickly gathered her senses and glanced round toward the driver's seat, peering at Derek. His arms appeared to be trembling and he was moaning to himself. She caught sight of his face through the rear-view mirror. He was sweating profusely, and his eyes were all misty, with red blotches appearing on his cheeks.

Professor Tinzy was the next to wake, and he glanced across at Derek and then back at Sallina.

"What's wrong with him? He doesn't look too well."

"I don't know, Professor!"

Startled by the sudden commotion, Limpit began to rustle about and his wings started to flap, but he had become somewhat wedged in by Sallina on one side as she leaned forward to check more closely on Derek.

Limpit's sudden agitation riled Szymon, who muttered grumpily, "Oi, careful, will you! Stop hitting me."

"Oh, I'm very sorry," Limpit replied. "Please accept my humblest apologies."

"What's wrong with our driver?" Szymon asked urgently, realising that the driver was having obvious difficulties up front.

"I—I may be having a sudden attack!" Derek wheezed. "I need to get some of my… my medicine. Quickly!"

"Hell's bells…" the Professor said, instinctively reaching across with his right hand to grab the steering wheel as best he could and hopefully provide a little more stability to the direction in which their car was traveling.

A car behind them honked loudly and flashed its warning lights.

"We'd better pull over, or we're going to get into a horrible accident!" the Professor bleated anxiously. "I think I'd better help you steer this thing, and we need to find someone who can help you medically, young man."

Derek, whose grip on the wheel was stronger than the Professor's, yanked hard to the right involuntarily… and then floored the accelerator. The car shot forward, almost ramming the vehicle directly in front of them.

"Let me help you to pull over! Go left! Not right. Let me help steer it!" Tinzy cried out. Derek, however, was so absorbed by whatever was happening to him that he didn't even listen to a word that the Professor had said.

Sallina had already clasped the pendant, and now it was turning blue.

"What are you doing?" Limpit asked her. "This isn't the time to mess about with your magic experiments."

Szymon tried to answer for her, not having a clue about what she was up to. "I think she must be… calling out to her mother?"

"Lift it up, take control, drive the car, hold the wheel, we don't go far, we don't slow down, we don't collide, we make it an easier ride," Sallina muttered briskly to herself.

The pendant lit up even more brightly, and a blue beam of light covered the entire wheel. As it did, Derek suddenly let go of the steering as if the wheel was on fire, and he shielded his face from the bright light.

"What are you doing with the car?" the Professor asked.

"I'm taking control of it. You know, like the way we practiced."

"You'd better be careful, or you'll get us all killed. Don't let anyone see you using magic, either."

Sallina focused her full attention on the task at hand, and in her mind's eye, she *was* the car. She could see all the cars in front of them as well as those behind her as she carefully steered the car and drove it towards the left from the fast lane to the slower lane. With all her concentration, she sought to slow it down, but she found the task difficult. What others around her didn't realize was that the car's wheels were no longer touching the ground; the car was now hovering by the tiniest distance above the road.

"I must slow it down carefully," she mumbled. "Limpit, I need your help, please."

Limpit didn't wait for a second invitation. He shot to the front and squeezed down by Derek's legs. Derek spotted Limpit's backside and tail sticking directly up towards his face. This didn't help Derek, who was continuing to have trouble breathing. As the seconds passed, his face was turning more and more red.

Limpit looked quickly at the foot pedals. "I think this stops it."

He pushed down hard with a claw, and the car's brakes screeched as Sallina lowered the wheels to the ground. The car started to slow down as it made contact with the road.

Professor Tinzy, his hand still on the wheel, gave it a heave to the left and drove the car onto the emergency shoulder. Before they knew it, the car had come to an abrupt stop.

Once the car had stopped, Sallina let go of the pendant and the blue light receded quickly and faded away. Derek was trying to regain his breath, and this time he managed to open the door and climb out of the car, almost being hit by a truck that passed him. He moved towards the edge of the motorway and then leant over a small fence to throw up.

Szymon stared gloomily out the window. "At least we're still alive, thankfully," he said.

Sallina nodded in acknowledgement, knowing they had had a narrow escape, as the traffic had been heavy around them.

"Well done, Sallina. You did a good job of rescuing us," Professor Tinzy said, turning to look at her.

"What about me? I had something to do with it as well," Limpit mumbled as he managed to turn himself upright this time and bring his claws up on the steering wheel. "It was I who successfully stopped it. How about showing some gratitude?"

"Yes, you too, Limpit. You both did a terrific job—credit to both of you."

"Well, it was a team effort," Limpit retorted. He grinned, chuffed with himself. "Sallina and I, we saved the day together. We do make an excellent team, if I may say so, don't you think?"

Szymon had the urge to get out of the car, so he opened the door. He stood up and made his way over to Derek. Derek seemed to be returning to his former self, and whatever had troubled him appeared to be clearing. Professor Tinzy watched as Szymon sought to comfort the driver.

"Your friend does keep on surprising me, Princess. I find it hard to fathom that this boy is truly the son of Unimage Konstanty. His entire composition appears to be rather different from his father's, to say the least."

Sallina didn't reply to the backhanded compliment; she just stared blankly out the window.

Twenty minutes later, Derek returned to the car and declared that he was well enough to drive again. The others decided he looked okay and agreed that he should continue, especially since he was the only one capable of properly driving the vehicle.

***

It was close to midnight by the time the Jaguar pulled up at its mysterious destination after heading down a long, narrow driveway and snaking along the road through a forest as it made its way towards a large, imposing building.

When the car pulled up into the gravel drive, Derek turned the engine off and climbed out. He shook his legs and took in a few deep breaths of air to further help him regain his composure. He then went around to the front of the car and opened the door for the Professor to climb out as well. Sallina nudged Szymon, who had fallen asleep. Szymon opened his eyes.

"We're here wherever 'here' happens to be," she remarked.

Limpit had also opened one eye as he emerged from his blissful snooze.

"I kind-of remember this place—pretty well, actually. It's as if I know it like the back of my paw, but I can't quite recall from when or how; it's there in my brain cells, somewhere," he muttered, mostly to himself.

"So, you've been here before?" Sallina asked him.

"I think so… I've probably been inside that house several times. I believe it's where Thomas Barchester resides."

"Who's Thomas Barchester?" Szymon asked.

"A good friend of the Professor's. Derek is his not-too-well driver. I thought you already knew."

Limpit, seeing an opening after Sallina got out of the car, wasted no time in leaving the vehicle. As soon as he was clear of the car, he shot up into the air in sheer delight.

"Oh, it's so splendid to have room for flapping about again!" he yelled. "I'm free, I'm free, and I feel more like myself now that I'm airborne."

"Stop making such an awful ruckus," the Professor rebuked the dragon. "People are most likely asleep at this late hour."

Limpit slowly descended back to the ground and hovered a few feet in the air.

"Oh, yes, sorry about that. I forgot how late it is. I apologize for being somewhat rude and inconsiderate at times. I hope I didn't wake up the old man. He's a light sleeper, as I remember."

When they entered the front hallway of the house, Sallina was immediately stricken by how vast the place was, and she quickly took notice of the lavish portraits hanging on all the walls.

"Lots of people have lived here before, I bet," she remarked. Her attempt at casualness was a front, as she was in awe of the place already.

Professor Tinzy grinned. "I suppose a lot have—it's an old house."

"Who is this… Thomas Barchester?" Sallina asked the Professor as Derek showed up with a couple of their cases and parked them in the hallway.

"I am this," a dry, more aged voice replied, and out of the shadows a grey-haired man appeared in an electric wheelchair that made a low whirring sound.

"Thomas!" the Professor exclaimed with great delight.

"You made it back safe and sound, I see," Thomas replied, also looking pleased to see his old friend.

"Well, we're just about in one piece," the Professor quipped. "We did encounter a little mishap along the way. Poor Derek got taken ill at a most inopportune time. Fortunately, we did manage to get here safely in the end."

"Oh, sorry to hear about that," Thomas replied. "Have you not been taking all your pills, Derek? You know you must."

Derek suddenly looked sullen as he stepped back out through the front door to lock up the car in the garage.

"He gets a bit ill sometimes. I've been telling him to keep taking his pills, but he prefers not to because he suspects they've been giving him awful stomach cramps. The poor man really must be checked out properly, but it's not so easy convincing him to go see the doctor. He's generally averse to all things medical."

Thomas then seemed to quickly forget about Derek's health issues. "Did you manage to get hold of that Pinny?" Thomas asked the Professor, sounding almost too casual.

"Oh yes, we found some. It's a tiny amount, but at least it's a start. Derek has it."

"That's brilliant," Thomas replied. "Good news indeed."

"Excuse me," Sallina interjected. "But I don't really know who you are…?"

"Of course not, my dear. As you probably already know, I'm Thomas Barchester, and I've been staying over here for a very long time. It's hard to believe that I too was once just like you, as it all seems so long ago. I've almost completely forgotten, and when it comes back to me from time to time, it's often like it was just a dream."

"Just like us?" Szymon enquired, looking at him quizzically.

"Yes, you know, a full-blooded unicorn," Thomas replied. "These days, I feel like my unicorn past never happened. But it did, didn't it?"

"Princess Sallina, Szymon," Professor Tinzy announced just as Limpit flew in through the open front door with a small *whoosh*. "You are speaking to none other than Unimage Barchester."

Limpit swept straight up to Thomas in his wheelchair and hovered a few feet away from him. He winked.

"How are you then, old man? I haven't seen you for quite a long while."

"Limpit, my dear friend. I've been missing you greatly. Yes, it has been a long while. Far too long a while."

"*You* are the Unimage Barchester," Sallina murmured in disbelief. "That's why your name was familiar to me. But Unimage Barchester vanished over a hundred years ago. Many feared he had died in some remote place, and nobody knew what had happened to his body. It's been a mystery, and some say his ghost was trapped in a faraway place, and that he was desperate to return to Starpoint but was unable to do so."

"Yes, I certainly have been in a faraway place, but I am no ghost, as you can see. Has it really been that long?" Thomas pondered. "I suppose it has. With time here passing around three times as quickly as it does back home… well, it makes me think it's an even longer time than that."

"You mean you've been here for *three hundred human years*?" Szymon suddenly blurted out, looking astonished.

"Well, yes. Almost as long as the Professor has, in fact. Although I've spent all my time here, unlike your good Professor."

"What? I don't understand! Now I'm getting really confused," said Sallina. "Have you also been coming here for so long, Professor?"

"Let's leave these difficult questions until the morning, shall we, as we're all quite tired and I think we could all do with a good night's sleep," Professor Tinzy said calmly, trying to draw the flurry of questions to a close.

Professor Tinzy, Sallina, and Szymon were then shown to their guest rooms upstairs. Derek led the party through the house, which Sallina found incredibly spacious and more than a little flamboyant in all sorts of ways. There were so many guest rooms scattered around, and everywhere there were paintings and strange-looking artifacts, and there were several statues that were dressed in full medieval body armour. Sallina counted at least twenty bedrooms, but there were definitely more.

She had to make a note to remember how to make her way back downstairs, which she did by counting the number of doors she had to pass and the turns she had to make from her room to the main staircase. There were several other staircases along the way, but she had no idea where those led and she wanted to make sure she wouldn't get lost, especially if she was wandering about on her own.

***

Later on that night, Sallina found herself tucked up in bed, wearing pyjamas that she had brought along. Her small sidelight was on, and she sat cross-legged in bed, clutching her pendant while she meditated. The pendant was glowing with its familiar blue colour, emitting a faint light that seemed to reach every corner and crevice of the room.

There was suddenly a short, sharp knock on the door. She didn't react for a few moments, as she was so deep in her trance-like state, and then the knock repeated itself. This time it caught her full attention.

"Come on in, whoever that is," she said. "The room's unlocked."

As soon as she said it, she regretted it, as she had no idea who was on the other side of the door.

The door slowly opened and Thomas Barchester entered in his electric wheelchair. He approached her bed.

"Forgive me for disturbing you at this late hour," he said. "I just wanted to check that you were feeling alright and that we've been looking after you properly."

Sallina had taken her hand off the pendant as soon as the door had opened, but it remained visible to Thomas as it rested on the outside of her pyjamas. His eyes lit up when he saw the pendant, but he tried to hide his emotions, as he didn't want Sallina to realise how highly he regarded the object.

"I had heard you were in possession of the Starpoint pendant, but I didn't believe this to be the case until now. I was so excited when Derek confirmed for me that you did in fact

213

have it in your possession and we would soon be able to see it in front of our eyes.”

“Why? Do you know things about it?” she asked him, and there was a defensive aspect to her tone.

“Oh yes. As a matter of fact, at one point I briefly had it in my personal possession, as I recall, although my memory of the time remains poor at best. I don’t remember a lot about the object’s properties. I struggle to remember things from long ago. I do know it’s special, and truly magical.”

“I cannot believe you’re that old, Unimage Barchester.”

“Oh, please, just call me Thomas. You know, it’s not easy being such an old person,” he said, thinking about his grand old age and the difficulties that he was having as he tried to get about in his wheelchair. “But I’m fortunate enough to have lived for so long, and I cannot complain.”

“Doesn’t it make you the oldest living unicorn on record, given you’re another three hundred years here in this land?”

Thomas thought about this remark for a few moments.

“I guess it would. But you should know something, as the Professor may not have shared this information with you before. At the time when there was a big war, several Unimages fled Starpoint, and they chose to come to live on Earth to escape those seeking to harm them. It’s entirely possible that I’m not the oldest living unicorn in exile in this land, because there may be a few others even older than me. These wizened souls have been lost to us and probably forgotten over the ages. And not all of them were bad. Good unicorns, as well as those who were allied with the other side, fled to different corners in the land, and they made sure they could not be found. Ever.”

Sallina considered Thomas’s revelation for a moment. “Are you suggesting that there are other Unimages besides yourself living in this land and passing as humans?”

“Not close by, of course, but they could in fact be anywhere in this very extensive land. And not just in this country; perhaps they live somewhere else entirely. The problem us older folk have is we cannot take a chance on travelling back home because we risk losing our memories. As the Professor has no doubt explained to you, it is disastrous for a Unimage to not be able to recall who he or she once was. I should know, since I have suffered from such a fate myself, and I know how painful it is not to be able to recall things."

"Tell me how you can remember who you are, Unimage Barchester, if your memory is so poor?" Sallina asked.

"Ah, that is a good question. Suffice it to say, I haven't travelled in a long time, so some things are slowly returning to me." Thomas suddenly fell silent, and he smiled. "Now I will have to leave you. I'm sure we will chat further about these things in the freshness of morning."

Sallina nodded and smiled back. *Perhaps Thomas Barchester is alright,* she thought. *He seems friendly enough, and as he's a good friend of Professor Tinzy. He must be an ally to our cause.*

"You'd better take care of that well, my dear," Thomas said, half-turning as he steered his wheelchair to the door. "It's a most precious item."

Thomas departed the room and vanished down the corridor, leaving the door slightly ajar.

Sallina jumped off her bed to close the door. First, she tentatively peered out into the corridor to see to where their host had vanished to, but there was nobody about.

There was something odd about Thomas that bothered her, but she just couldn't place what it was. There was clearly a lot more to Unimage Barchester than he let on. She shut the door and returned to the comfort of her bed. She switched off the sidelight, closed her eyes, and soon dropped off to sleep.

However, not long after she fell asleep, the door to the bedroom opened up again and Limpit floated in, virtually noiselessly. He silently hovered over the Princess, looking down at her.

"Princess," he whispered, but his mouth didn't move. "You shall remember what I tell you, although you won't know that it was me who told you it. I want you to be extremely careful with Thomas Barchester, as he is not the unicorn you believe him to be. He is not to be trusted, not for one second. Beware of him, as he is not a friend of ours. He can be very dangerous. In fact, I'm not entirely sure which side he finds himself on, that is if he recalls who he is. Sometimes, he forgets himself entirely."

The faint flutter of Sallina's eyes behind her closed eyelids confirmed for Limpit that his words had subconsciously registered in her brain. He swept silently to the door and closed it behind him with his claw. Sallina turned about in her bed, but she did not wake.

Chapter 23

The next morning found Sallina, Szymon, Professor Tinzy, and Limpit seated in the great dining room with Thomas. Breakfast was being served diligently by a tall, bald man in his sixties dressed up in a butler's uniform.

"This is good old Roger," Thomas said. "He does an incredible job taking good care of me. He'll also take good care of you whilst you stay in my humble house. He is the primary house servant, and he belongs not to me or to anyone, but to this house."

Roger did not react to the comments and continued to serve a full English breakfast from his serving trolley.

"Is this what I think it is?" Szymon asked.

"Oh, yes, please forgive me, I forget that unicorns are not fond of eating meat. The problem is I've lived here for so long, I've developed a peculiar kind of taste and liking for it. Roger, please remove the offending bacon from the dining table for the benefit of my good friends."

Roger proceeded to remove the bacon from the plates on the table, although it appeared to be quite a laborious process.

"I should disclose to you that I've only being eating meat for a few decades. I was, of course, the strictest vegetarian back home. I do appreciate that it's a shameful thing to be doing, but when you stay somewhere long enough, you tend to get accustomed to their manner of doing things."

"Not to worry, Thomas. It's totally understandable. On to more pressing matters—have you put our Pinny away in a safe place?" Professor Tinzy asked.

"Oh yes, there is none safer I can think of. It's carefully tucked away in my… safe, which is situated in the study. It's very secure there."

"Now that we have the Pinny, what do we do with it?" Sallina had to ask the obvious question.

"We need to get it home."

"But it's not going to be enough to stop that meteor! We will need a lot more if we are to not get blasted from outer space," Szymon butted in, a trifle agitated.

"You are absolutely right, of course, my dear boy. But unless we're somehow assured we can get it back home undamaged and in a fit state, there's little point in acquiring more of it. Is there?"

"Exactly right," agreed Professor Tinzy.

"Then, how do we plan to get back intact?" inquired Szymon. "My father had little idea how to get us back home."

"There is always a way, isn't there? Otherwise, how else did I make it back after my last visit?" Professor Tinzy remarked confidently. "Getting back is not the main problem... it's *who* gets to go back that is the important issue."

"You mean, who gets to make the journey back *first*?" Szymon asked.

"You see, neither Thomas nor I can go back at this point, young Szymon, as we both risk losing our remaining memories. And if that happens, we can never return here to obtain more Pinny. We needed the Princess to continue with the task, as she is young and able and can withstand the passage that robs those who are much older of their precious memories. It's also probably why you were picked for your part in it by your father. This therefore means that the only unicorns returning for the present are yourself and Sallina."

"What about Limpit? Does he also get to go back with us?" Sallina asked.

"Oh, Limpit isn't actually permitted to go. It wouldn't be possible," the Professor retorted, not happy to have to point it out, but nevertheless resolute in his views.

"Whyever not? He deserves to go home just like the rest of us. Is it his age?" Sallina asked.

"No, not that. It's something else... It's because, my dear, it's Limpit who makes the journey back and forth possible at all. We will need him on this end of the passageway to help keep the path open for the return trip."

Sallina thought about this for a moment, more confused than ever.

"Are you saying that Limpit is the one who sends us back? I don't understand what you mean."

"It's easy, really. I'm the one who helps make everything work in terms of travelling back and forth," Limpit said, but Sallina thought he didn't sound pleased about his importance. "It is I who hold the power, the magic that enables all those from Starpoint to return. If I were to go back, I'd be the last to go, because once I go back, nobody else can open the pathway from this end until I return."

"That's why you've been here for so long too," Sallina spoke without thinking, realizing Limpit's true significance in all this. "That means you've been here as long as Thomas Barchester."

"Yes. I came here to help unicorns travel back home. I've being doing this job for a very long time. I have snuck back on a few occasions, but each time I did, I too began to forget things, so the Professor and I have agreed that I need to stay here and avoid being tempted to go back myself. I helped Thomas Barchester arrive here the first time he came, before they figured out a way to do it directly from Starpoint, and I had hoped one day to return home and change back to my normal self. Many times, I've sworn that I wouldn't stay and do this again. But the simple fact of the matter is that there is nobody else, especially for the return journey, so they make sure I am always here to be of service."

Sallina was immediately saddened to hear how greatly Limpit had been a necessary and much-used tool for the Unimages in travelling between the two worlds. "I'm so sorry, Limpit, for your misfortune. Nobody should be so callously used like that, no matter how important this task may seem."

Limpit nodded silently. He looked at her and realised that he truly had a friend in Princess Sallina, and she really cared for his happiness and welfare. "Thank you, Princess. This means a lot to me."

"The upside of all this, though, is that we finally know how to go back: Limpit provides us with the means. So, we're ready to go back with our first Pinny find, and in the future, we can return and bring back more!" Szymon exclaimed.

"Not so fast, youngster," the Professor remarked. "There are still a few things to iron out before the two of you travel. I will have to re-learn some of the magic required for the path to open up and allow you to go back to Starpoint."

"Re-learn?" Sallina thought out loud, suddenly concerned. "Why is it that everything is always so difficult? As soon as we learn of one problem, another comes along right behind, and then another."

"Ah, that is always the way of things, isn't it? Not all my memory has been recovered, Princess. I'm still in the process of remembering some pretty important things."

"It would be beneficial if you could remember these things soon," Sallina said with more than a hint of frustration. "Personally, I'm keen to get back and let my mother know we have found some success with locating Pinny. I'm sure she must be very worried about the mission and myself. Will I remember everything when I go back?"

"Oh, yes, of course you will. You needn't worry about losing your memories. If that were to happen, we have additional help in that department," Thomas said.

"What kind of help do you mean?"

"Well, if you need to know anything about anything, there's a very useful place we can go that helps us out enormously," Thomas said with a knowing smile.

"Would you like to find out some more about this special place?" Roger asked as he passed by Sallina with his trolley.

"I think that's a good idea," the Professor replied heartily, wiping his mouth with a napkin while pushing his empty plate aside to indicate that he had eaten enough for now.

"Let's all go! I want to go too. What are we waiting for?" Limpit exclaimed, flapping his wings excitedly.

A short while later, after they had left the dining room, they arrived at another section of the house. A large, heavy door opened into a long, rectangular room. This was one of the largest in the house. In stepped Princess Sallina, Szymon, and the Professor, followed close behind by Thomas Barchester in his wheelchair, and a hovering Limpit.

Unable to contain himself in his excitement, Limpit flew ahead of the others, shouting, "This is my favourite place in the entire building!"

With his claws, he drew back the curtains. First one, then another, until all the curtains were drawn, and bright sunlight flooded in. Sallina and Szymon stared at the splendour of the room in awe.

"This here is the library!" Professor Tinzy exclaimed as he pointed to the long rows of books that lay stacked neatly on shelves all the way up to the ceiling.

The shelves ran down the entire length of the room, and there were rows upon rows to be seen. The library was a truly tremendous sight. There must have been at least ten thousand books, if not more.

Sallina and Szymon started browsing through the many shelves, reaching out and gently touching the spines of just a handful of old and majestic tomes.

Professor Tinzy stood next to Thomas as they watched the youngsters wander about in amazement and glee.

"Unfortunately, you won't find any books about Starpoint in here," the Professor cautioned, as he could see they were looking for something familiar.

Sallina turned around and headed back, eyeing him with curiosity.

"We keep the Starpoint books safely in the other library. That's where we can go to remember things that are important," he said.

"The other library? There's also another room like this?" Sallina was dumbstruck.

Thomas was already whirring straight through the library in his wheelchair, and he came to a halt at another closed door at the far end. He took out an electronic device from his pocket and pressed a small red button on it. The door mechanically opened inwards.

The second library room was curiously much smaller, and it had only a handful of books piled a lot less tidily on the various shelves. Sallina carefully stepped up close to one of the shelves and picked up a book at random.

"It's a Starpoint cooking companion for living your life in the fields," she muttered, opening it up delicately and leafing through the pages. "All these recipes involve the use of various forms of magic and Pinny," she said, pleased with her find. "This one's from home, that's for sure."

"Of course, it is. This here's a proper Starpoint collection," Thomas said wistfully. "The only one of its kind in this very strange land, in which we find ourselves caught up in the very important task at hand. A land which has for a long time been my home."

"What about going back? Is there a book on how we can deal with that?" Szymon asked urgently.

"Ah yes, there are some guidance notes on that in one of the books," Thomas replied. "That particular information, however, I keep under lock and key." He pointed to a large safe that was situated in the corner of the room.

Szymon walked up to the safe and studied it intently. "It looks pretty secure and sound. How about I take a little peek inside?"

Thomas quickly glanced at Professor Tinzy. "I think this is one to leave to the Unimages if you don't mind, youngster. When you're a little older and wiser, you'll come to realise the reasons why things must be done in a certain way. It may seem a little cruel and uncaring at times, but often knowledge has to be carefully rationed to those more in the know, so that the clever elders with wiser heads can work out how to serve the greater good and protect the herd."

"Am I at least allowed to borrow one or two of these other books?" Sallina asked Thomas, gazing at some of their curious titles.

"Sure, take as many as you like of the books—they are here for you to enjoy whilst you are my guest. But please don't empty my entire collection… I'd like to keep that intact as much as I can, as sometimes I so miss being home and these books remind me of the place I used to know," Thomas said with a sigh and what looked like a tear forming in the corner of his eye.

Szymon also decided to select a book. He grinned wickedly.

"Which one did you choose?" Sallina asked.

Szymon showed it to her: *How to Become a Unimage in 48 Hours, or at Least Pretend to be Wise when Casting your Magic.*

Sallina chuckled. "Well, it's not really that easy to become a Unimage!" she exclaimed as she looked for more books of interest. "The shortest study time to become a Unimage with any degree of wisdom I've ever heard of was over thirty years, and that's fast!"

Szymon leafed through a few of the book's pages. "There're a few useful pointers, but that's all it has. Nobody expects to become an expert in anything within a couple of days, do they? True knowledge and wisdom come through practice, and lots of it."

"Is it your personal ambition to become a Unimage, similar to your father?" Professor Tinzy asked him.

"I dunno. Maybe, but I don't want to be like him. And I can't really say what I want because there's still so much I don't know about everything."

"Well, then maybe this book can help you to understand a little more about what being a Unimage is all about. It will put you on the right path if it is the right one."

"I suppose it could, but I doubt it," he said, placing the book back on the shelf. "You're right, nobody can be expected to learn how to become a proper Unimage in a few days; that sort of thing takes a full lifetime to master. Even my father isn't that fantastic a Unimage, after all. I think sometimes he thinks a bit too highly of himself and often gets carried away."

Thomas had wheeled up to them. He spoke softly. "Your father was, and is, a remarkable Unimage by any account. Don't for a second underestimate him, for I believe he's destined for true greatness one fine day. You wait and see. He is a leader, and often those who are truly farsighted can be misunderstood by those who can't see beyond their own nostrils."

This surprised Sallina, who started to wonder why Thomas was holding Unimage Konstanty in such high regard. The comment perplexed even Professor Tinzy, who had come within earshot and was surprised to hear his friend speak so well of someone who was little more than a swindler and a trickster and was causing them a whole heap of trouble. This made Professor Tinzy feel even more suspicious of Thomas's allegiances, and increasingly concerned about his true intentions.

The rest of the day turned out to be uneventful, so Sallina went back to her room to do a little reading by herself. But she had not settled down long on the bed before she started to feel a sudden sense of loneliness coupled with a sense of desperation. After all, she was there in a strange land, staying in a strange house that belonged to an even stranger person, and she wasn't even in her natural form, having taken on the form of a human.

She was half-hoping that someone would suddenly come knocking on her door, but nobody did. Gradually, she managed to lose herself whilst reading, and she eventually drifted off into a deep sleep as passages in the books filled her mind with happy reminders of familiar places and unicorns back home.

Meanwhile, downstairs, a different set of events happened to be taking place.

Thomas Barchester had locked himself away in the Starpoint library, and on the desk was an orb. The orb was already lit from within, and Thomas found himself looking directly at Unimage Konstanty. Unimage Callindra was also there, next to Konstanty. As before, the pair were communicating from Callindra's cellar, and they were engaged in a confidential conversation with Thomas Barchester.

Thomas felt certain that this secret meeting would remain hidden from his guests or any other prying eyes. However, he didn't reckon on Limpit, who had been keeping a watchful eye and a sensitive ear on him ever since the Professor's party had arrived at the house. Curiosity and the compulsive desire to snoop about were the primary reasons Limpit was on the other side of the door, trying his very best to eavesdrop.

Limpit had to strain a lot to pick up any of the conversation going on inside, as the door was incredibly thick and largely muffled any sound. The best he could do was to hear and make sense of the occasional word here and there. What he did managed to pick up sounded a lot like:

"We need to get... back home... as we can. Starpoint is down to... alicorn. ... bring the Pinny back quickly... incredible advantage... by the Circle."

Limpit couldn't quite make out the last words exactly…was it 'yerkel' or 'percle'? Or could it have been 'sickle' or 'pickle'? It was rather hard to hear what was being said.

Inside the room, the mood was somewhat sombre. Thomas's gaze unflinchingly bored into Konstanty's mesmerizing eyes.

"Do you know how much I've sacrificed to be here? How many years I've spent in this odd land so I can find a way to bring Pinny back to you to help the cause? I've given up far too much already, and now you want me to hurry it up suddenly. Important work takes time and demands lots of it."

Limpit couldn't make most of this out, but he caught the gist of '*being in this land*', a mention of Pinny, and '*hurry up*'.

"Hurry it up you must," Unimage Callindra spoke blusteringly, backing up Unimage Konstanty. She was much older than Konstanty, and in Starpoint years not so far off from Thomas Barchester.

"We need you to do your utmost. It sounds like you have that beast under your control. You have the Princess staying in your house. You have the small initial amount of Pinny there with you; now find a way to send it back to us," she instructed tersely. "Get the job done, by hoof or by horn. Find a way to bring it back."

Thomas Barchester was furious, but he knew better than to let his temper loose while talking to two incredibly powerful Unimages, especially as he was talking to none other than Unimage Callindra, the second-highest ranking Unimage in all the Circle, and currently the serving leader to all those who followed the Circle's will.

"I intend do my utmost, you can count on that," he retorted in a raspy voice that, when he was put under pressure, came out sounding harsher and somewhat meaner than normal. "You know I will do my best, but it's so hard for me to do anything in this forsaken land. I scarcely remember anything of myself these days, and I have to keep on reading those infernal papers again and again just to remind myself of who it is I am and what I must do as my duty. I keep losing my mind, and it's a miracle I've somehow managed to hold it together."

"If it's so difficult, then get that idiotic Professor Tinzy to help you in the task. The stupid oaf has managed to recall a good number of his dreadful memories, and he should be able to help cast some kind of return spell. By all means, use a little Pinny as well, if it can help to open the path," Callindra brayed. "So little can be done using magic without the aid of Pinny, we all know that."

"What I simply don't understand, though, is why Unimage Konstanty tried to destroy Limpit. If Limpit had been destroyed, the chances of bringing the Pinny back would have shrunk considerably, as we require the aid of that troublesome miniature dragon to help open up the path with his powerful dragon fire. So far, I have come across nothing better than dragon fire to help forge a path through the void between the lands." Thomas explained.

Callindra's face abruptly disappeared, to be replaced by that of Unimage Konstanty, as if he had briskly cast her aside. He looked bitter and angry. "You do not question anything I do, not ever, are we clear?" he rasped angrily. "You…bumbling…absent-minded…aging fool, your perpetual state of ignorance remains inexcusable to us here, and you'd better face up to the reality that you are now purely useful as a minor accessory to our higher purpose—and to continue to be of any worth to us at all, you will do exactly as we say without question or comment."

Thomas was quite taken aback by this egregious insult. "I was only asking you both a harmless question. Forgive me if I've offended you in any way."

"One day you may fully remember who you are, and only then will I give you an appropriate answer befitting a Unimage of stature as you once were. Until then, you will trust my judgement implicitly without question and obey all my commands. In the darkness that you find yourself in, I am the only beacon of light to bring you back to us. Do we understand each other?"

Thomas felt compelled to say nothing after these curt remarks had been thrown at him so inconsiderately.

"I repeat myself. Am I making myself clear to you, Unimage Barchester?" Unimage Konstanty demanded.

"Yes, like a crystal-clear pond absent of ripples and an abundance of green vegetation and rot."

"Ah...good, then. I'm glad we both understand at least something when it comes to who is in charge."

With that, Unimage Konstanty quickly dissolved and was replaced by Unimage Callindra.

"We want the Pinny here within a day of our time. This doesn't give you long, Thomas Barchester, to get your act together. Figure it out—remember what you did before and do it again."

"No, it doesn't give me much time." He paused, then added, "Leave this matter to me. I'll find a way to get it done, by hoof or by horn. It will be just as you wish."

Upon hearing that, Unimage Callindra nodded, and her image faded into the ether. The orb's light dimmed down to nothing.

From the other side of the door, Limpit had managed to pick up some of the heated back-and-forth conversation that had ended up being a dressing down of former Unimage Thomas Barchester. The most pressing concern to the small dragon was who Thomas Barchester was working for. Clearly, he was in cahoots with what sounded like Unimage Konstanty, a voice he recognized, and Unimage Callindra, whose voice almost anyone could readily identify across the length and breadth of all Starpoint.

Unimage Callindra was one of the most famous unicorns in all Starpoint, and she was regarded as one of the most capable users of magic to have ever existed. Even Professor Tinzy was no match for her in terms of her deep knowledge of the high art and craft of devising and casting powerful magical spells, and the idea that she was personally determined to acquire Pinny through former Unimage Thomas Barchester was of immediate concern to Limpit. He suspected it would also be of the gravest concern to the Professor and the Princess. Something clearly wasn't right.

Callindra had always had a close affinity with the ancient unicorn cult known as the Circle, and her allegiance didn't come as a surprise; there were many such rumours flying about when it came to discussions on Unimages and their personal agendas. Ties with the Circle were considered fanciful and misguided, but due to the demise of the Circle so many years ago, they hardly posed a threat.

The Circle was thought of as nothing more than a spent force across the many lands, having faded over the centuries to little more than a dim and distant memory after the members surrendered their rule following a mighty battle. Literally nobody these days took any of their backward, outdated views seriously, or at least that was what Limpit thought.

If anything, they were known as the unwitting targets of tasteless humour, and they were in some quarters laughed at openly for their stupendous ignorance across many subjects of enlightenment. But as in thinking about many such fringe groups, one needed to be cautious.

Ideas and beliefs that at one time were seen as extreme and radical can at another time furrow themselves back into the mainstream and win over the hearts and minds of the greater masses, who can hardly see the implications. And when they finally do, it's usually far too late to change society's course as the once-radical views enter the mainstream.

The Circle may have existed right at the fringes of civilized society, but gradually over a few millennia their views had somehow worked their way back into the mainstream and were now being discussed and considered across all corners of Starpoint more openly, and without any sense of guilt or shame. With Unimage Callindra and Konstanty potentially serving to strengthen the Circle, this could lead to threatening the lives and wellbeing of all those who lived in the land, especially if their influence interfered with such an important mission such as preventing a meteor from destroying Starpoint.

The Circle, at its core, stood for the deepest desires of those who sought the greatest amount of privilege, and it represented a form of wicked self-serving elitism that discriminated against those that were defined as being less worthy. The Circle had flourished through the unquestioned rule by a small group of self-appointed elite unicorns as they presided over the many without any compunction to serve justice or fairness.

Justice for the Circle was what the Circle deemed it to be in any way that suited those in charge. There was no right and no wrong about it, there was certainly no fair and proper way for anyone to behave; there was only what those who led the Circle wanted from those below them, and top on their list of priorities was the need for unicorns to be of pure and noble stock.

For those precious few in charge, one was appointed to lead the Circle from the day he or she was born, having been pre-selected based on their heredity, with the solid, light colour and silky texture of their hide and their genetic lineage giving them the right to rule from the onset. This was termed as the ultimate in 'purity', and anyone with a darker or spotted hide wouldn't be eligible to become an exalted member of the Circle, having been brought into the world via the passing of mixed blood.

Those few who were in the know were fully aware that there were quite a few "imperfect pures" who sat on the Circle. This elite group of privileged higher ups had no qualms about imposing their harsh and unfair discrimination upon many of those far less fortunate subjects and excusing themselves from such judgement.

The modern reality of unicorns was that the vast majority were already of mixed stock, leaving those who were truly pure a decreasing minority that the Circle wanted to exalt and make the ruling class. Detecting small traces of impurity was always difficult to implement, but this didn't get in the way of the Circle deciding who stood where in the order of things, as the Circle had a way of picking its own leaders and denigrating the rest.

Limpit wondered how powerful the Circle might have become in the time he had been away from his land, because a weak Starpoint was likely to have become susceptible to all the lies and twisted half-truths that the Circle's devoted followers believed without question. As far as he knew, Unimage Callindra had thus far not dared to step forth and announce to the world that she was one of the Circle's chosen leaders. But if what he had heard was in any way correct, there clearly was something sinister in the works designed to move the Circle towards achieving far greater prominence over the coming days and months.

Limpit realized he needed to warn Professor Tinzy immediately about what he had just overheard, because he was confident that the good Professor had scarcely any idea about

Thomas Barchester's uncomfortably close affiliation with the Circle. It was likely to be tricky for him to warn the Professor, given that Unimage Konstanty's son was probably among them. This cunning and devious boy could prove an unseen danger because he was already so close to the Princess. But warn the Professor Limpit had to do, so Limpit flapped his wings lightly in the air and flew as slowly and as silently as he could down the long room of library books.

* * *

After concluding the conversation with Unimage Konstanty and Unimage Callindra, Thomas Barchester found himself once again in a position where he had little else to do than comply with all their commands. Some days, he so much wished that he could finally be rid of anything and everything to do with the numerous problems and ambitions of those he knew from Starpoint, especially as he remembered so little from his past that was good.

Fortunately, on several occasions he had been aided by the detailed notes and scribbles from his former self as well as those of Professor Tinzy, and it was these notes he had mostly relied upon to retain some connection with his past.

Professor Tinzy had managed to weather the storms much better than poor old Thomas Barchester. Perhaps it was because the Professor had been quite a bit younger when he began his travels to this distant land, and perhaps he was aided by the fact that he had achieved a higher level in his training in the various crafts of magic… although this was a feat that most Unimages weren't aware of, because the Professor didn't want them to know. Thomas knew that the Professor was in a much better position to remember than he was, and he often relied on him to maintain his knowledge of his past, either via direct communication or through detailed written notes.

It was whilst Thomas was pondering these things that he heard an unusual sound coming from the adjacent library room, and he immediately spun his wheelchair into motion and opened the door. He wheeled himself out into the long library room and strained his eyes to see whether something unusual had transpired while he had been preoccupied with his call, but the place appeared to be completely quiet, and all he could hear was the sound of his very own breath, so Thomas Barchester once again engaged his wheelchair and made his way down the full length of this vast room.

Once he arrived at the other end, he turned his wheelchair around and looked back toward the spot where he had been. He had the strangest feeling he wasn't alone. However, right now as he looked around the room, nothing appeared to be out of the ordinary, nor could he detect anyone's presence nearby.

After a few moments, he turned off the lights and departed, dismissing the notion that someone might have overheard or seen him speaking to his two conspirers of the Circle. It was more important to him that Konstanty and Callindra might have arrived at the conclusion that they were clearly in charge of pretty much everything Barchester did and who he had eventually become. It wasn't true, though, and he knew it. He was his own unicorn, and deep down he wasn't anybody's servant.

Chapter 24

Limpit wasted no time after he took flight from the library. He flew up the staircase to the first floor and zoomed down the hallway until he got to Professor Tinzy's door. He urgently rapped with his claw and began casting his eye down both lengths of the corridor while he waited for the Professor to let him in. It was a long wait, but eventually the door opened and Limpit burst into the room, spinning around a few times with uncontrolled excitement.

"Professor, Professor, I have something to tell you!" the diminutive dragon blurted, unable to hold back on such vitally important information that he needed to share with his esteemed and often forgetful Unimage. "I've come across something really significant. I've got to tell you what I just overheard! This is hugely important, Professor, it's enormous!"

The Professor eyed Limpit calmly with little more than a sense of idle curiosity, because this kind of erratic behaviour from his small friend was hardly anything unusual. Limpit was always suspecting this or that, working himself up into a state about the most obscure and trivial matters that concerned him and coming to wild conclusions that were often farfetched and untenable.

"What's wrong with things in the world now? Having trouble sleeping again? Is your snoring keeping you awake?"

"No, no. This is not about my snoring, Professor!" Limpit exclaimed, already out of breath from all the excitement and having made his hasty escape.

But before Limpit could utter anything further, there was a sharp knock on the door. Both the dragon and the Professor fell silent and cast their eyes in the direction of the sound.

The Professor calmly made his way towards the door and cautiously pressed his ear against it.

"Who is it? It's late to be calling."

On the other side of the door, Princess Sallina and Szymon were pacing up and down the hallway, and Sallina was about to knock again when she heard the Professor's faint voice from within.

"Professor," she whispered. "It's just us. Szymon and me. We need to speak to you—it's very urgent. It's about something important."

The Professor opened the door. Sallina and Szymon hurried in. Limpit was surprised by their unexpected visit.

"Well, what is this all about? What can be so urgent that we all need to meet like this, cloak-and-dagger like?" Tinzy asked.

"It's something I was thinking about, and I couldn't sleep as it kept on bothering me and keeping me awake. I think I've figured something out."

"Figured out what?" the Professor asked.

"It's about Limpit's fiery breath and size. I think that was the only reason you needed him to come here with you, and why he was always by your side on your previous travels. From what I can tell, he has no keener talent at finding Pinny than anyone else, and I honestly don't think a dragon has much in terms of special Pinny-sniffing skills from what I can see. If anyone has that kind of ability, it would be a unicorn, as we are renowned for sensing Pinny when it's close by—although over the years this skill has been in decline, and only a few can do it now with any degree of accuracy.

"You see, when you find yourself in a strange and peculiar land, you can—if you know how—incant a magic spell that opens the portal up to provide travel back to Starpoint. Therefore, that's not really the problem, is it? The magic involved is hardly revolutionary, to say the least; and to be honest, any half-witted Unimage can attempt this feat and most likely pull this off.

"First, one needs to recognize that the spell cannot be incanted and work from this side of the connection, as magic doesn't work so well from out here. But if you have someone on this side who is helping you make the connection, they can then cast the enchantment and help open a passage back from our land.

"However, the real challenge is that one does require something more powerful to cross the divide and establish some sort of steady pathway between these two worlds that is

233

sufficiently large enough for living creatures like us to travel through without a blockage along the way. It may be one thing to cast a spell that allows voice and thoughts to travel from one place to another, which should be relatively easy, for even a novice Unimage to arrange. But for moving something that's living and breathing over such a vast and almost unquantifiable distance, a much stronger and sturdier connection needs to be established—one that can be maintained without any interruption.

"I've thought about this matter a great deal for the past couple of days, and that's when I realized what this connection could potentially be. I think it's Limpit's breath that connects both ends and provides safe and sturdy passage between the two, and his size is crucial to him also travelling through the tunnel his breath opens."

Syzmon was starting to look confused, and he needed to understand what Princess Sallina was saying.

"What do you mean, Limpit's breath and physical size help with unicorns being able to travel?" he asked. "I already knew he has some kind of connection to this world, but I don't understand why his breath is so essential."

Sallina thought carefully about how she could explain this better. "When you open the gap by casting a magical incantation, it's Limpit's fiery breath that helps to keep this world connected with ours, as you need its raw magical power to provide a stronger link between the two lands so someone can cross back and forth. Limpit's breath fires up the tunnel and clears any blockages along the way.

"It also means that he needs to travel through the tunnel, which is of limited size. The reason Limpit has been shrunk to his size is expressly to serve in providing a passage through the tunnel for those who accompany him. A large Limpit wouldn't have been able to travel through the tunnel to come here. It is also far easier to control the passage from this end as well, as we have found out after several attempts early on. This is why Limpit has been stuck here for so long, and not had the opportunity to travel back."

The Professor unconsciously rubbed his chin as he carefully thought about Sallina's insightful speculation.

"That's quite an illuminating concept," he whispered to himself, baffled by how Limpit wasn't just a good cleaner of the tunnel before one set off on their travels, but was also the one who had served to guide the travellers through.

Except for Princess Sallina, of course. She managed to travel on her own. The reason for this is now starting to become clear: the powerful pendant also has the ability to provide a bridge between both worlds. This is something that I need to keep to myself for now, as this will potentially put Sallina in much greater danger.

"What I was unable to figure out, though, is why Limpit didn't realize how his breath and size worked when he released his breath into the tunnel, as he should have been able to remind you from his previous occasions. If he had told you how this worked, well, we wouldn't be wondering how to make a connection this time, would we?" she thought out loud. "More importantly, what if being close to Limpit when travelling through could help to prevent memory loss, which could make a big difference for you Professor and for other Unimages? You were so keen to leave him behind that perhaps you never considered this possibility."

Limpit was now the one who looked rather confused.

"Hell-o? I'm standing right here. You're all talking about me like I'm not present," he moaned, feeling a bit insulted as the others turned to look his way. "Of course, you are right, Princess, that I was asked to cast my fiery breath into the portal when it was opened, which I have done many a time, but I didn't know that the portal's actual proper function required my also travelling through it to protect those travelling back and forth. I thought it was just to help clear out any unwanted debris that might have been caught up along the way."

"You are truly and perhaps even uniquely magical, Limpit," Sallina said, "as dragons contain the essence of magic in their very being and exist with or without Pinny. In a land where magic is scarce and virtually non-existent, we have limited magical tools at our disposal. One of them is you and your fiery breath, and—" she hesitated, then clutched her pendant tightly for a moment, "—and the other is my pendant."

"This is all highly unusual and utterly fascinating, Sallina," the Professor exclaimed, looking, Sallina thought, more excited than he usually did. "I don't recall reading any of this in my notes. I think your suggestions provide a real breakthrough in our understanding of how the magic works between these lands. It may also help to protect memory loss so that I don't end up being some forgetful human Professor for the rest of my days. Bravo! You are so very perceptive."

"What notes are you talking about?" Sallina asked, having not heard the Professor mention these notes before.

"Oh… I'm referring to the notes Thomas Barchester keeps locked away in his safe. They are detailed records of my time spent in this land and everything he and I have experienced. Years ago, I took the liberty of writing down as much I could recall of my knowledge from home—just in case I forgot any of it or Barchester did.

"Remarkably, I've never come across anything dealing with Limpit's fiery breath before, or his diminutive size protecting memory loss, although it does clearly state that his breath needs to be used to provide safe passage. I have read my handwritten notes on many occasions, and they go through, in detail, the power of the incantation that helps to bring the two worlds close together, and how this must be properly prepared for it to work optimally. When we attempted the connection to travel between lands on several previous occasions, for unknown reasons at the time we failed. We have, however, been successful in communicating with each other without travelling, and this has provided some consolation. With Limpit's aid, and his breath, we were always successful, so his participation remains a must. The only exception ever was when you travelled through without anyone knowing. This still remains a mystery to me." Professor Tinzy then looked reassuringly at Limpit as he concluded his assessment of Limpit's essential role in travel between the two lands.

"To be on the safe side, we must head back to the library and check out the spells in the notes before we attempt this again," Szymon suggested.

"Yes. That's a very good idea," the Professor replied. "We'd better double check anything else I might have missed in my notes."

"No! That's a terrible idea," Limpit said, suddenly alarmed.

Limpit's immediate reaction took the Professor by complete surprise.

"Why would that be?" he asked.

But before Limpit could answer, they heard another sharp rap on the door.

"Oh, no," Limpit muttered. "He's found us; he knows I know."

The Professor didn't fully understand what Limpit was referring to, and he calmly made his way to the door. Once again, he cautiously placed his ear against the door, and then there was another sharp rap, which forced him to push his head away from the door.

"Who stands outside at this time?" he asked, attempting to remain composed.

"It's Thomas, Professor. I was checking up on you to make sure you are alright and there are no problems."

"Oh, I'm perfectly fine, thank you, Thomas—I'm close to drifting off to sleep. Let's talk tomorrow, shall we? It's already very late," the Professor answered, looking at the others as he spoke.

There was a moment of hushed silence on the other side of the door. They dared not even breathe as they waited for Barchester's response, and Limpit looked the most terrified.

"Very well then, Professor—I don't want to disturb you," came the belated reply. "Let's have a little chat in the morning over our breakfast. You are sure everything is okay in there?"

"Oh yes, I'm fine, and tired. Goodnight, Thomas."

"Goodnight, Professor. Sleep well."

They heard the floor creak as the wheelchair headed off along the hallway, and then they all turned their attention to Limpit, whose face had turned bright red in his attempt to suspend his breath.

He finally exhaled sharply. Some of the flames shot out of his mouth, and he gasped as he sucked in a large amount of air to refill his lungs.

"I didn't have a chance to warn you, Professor. It's about Thomas Barchester. There's something you should know."

"What is it? Out with it."

"He's—" Limpit started, and then he looked toward Szymon. "I don't know how to say this delicately. Well, he's been collaborating with Unimage Callindra and… and they're planning something dreadfully bad; it's definitely not good in any way."

"How do you know they have other bad intentions?" the Professor asked Limpit. "Maybe he was just having an occasional catch-up. Unimage Callindra may just be an old friend he speaks with from time to time. She may be concerned about his well-being and made a point of keeping in touch."

"No! They're planning to take all the Pinny for themselves and give it all to the Circle," Limpit blurted. "Can't you see? Unimage Konstanty and Unimage Callindra are both Circle."

This stunned the Professor, who wasn't expecting to hear something so dramatic.

"The Circle," he muttered. "What are you going on about? I don't believe there's an actual Circle; that's just a fantastical story they tell little unicorns so that they behave themselves. Half of what some claim to have happened was probably made up anyway. I mean, there are those who would like the Circle to return, but they are just trying, and it is up to us to make sure that they do not succeed."

"None of it is fantastic and it's not a children's story. The Circle is very much alive, and once again it thrives. Right now, as we speak, they are busy plotting our downfall. I've known about this danger for some time, but I didn't want to bring it up as I didn't think they were actively subverting our task," Limpit argued.

"Why would the Circle choose a moment such as this, when we're merely here on a rescue mission, to be active and plot against Starpoint?" the Professor asked. "Even if they are semi-active, we are not an obstruction to them and their fanciful goals. We are here merely to make sure that things continue as near to normal as possible in the future. They would surely wait until Starpoint is safe from the threat of the meteor before trying to do something rash."

"Because my Professor, this is the ideal time for them to rise once again. Starpoint is currently severely weakened, with the supply of Pinny almost depleted, and those who control the limited supply of Pinny shall no doubt gain control of the entire land. They see this particular moment as their golden opportunity to bring back their selfish causes and once again attempt to take over and rule all the land for themselves and subjugate the rest under their will!" Limpit exclaimed. "Evil strikes when there is confusion and chaos, as it knows this is the ideal time to gain the upper hand."

The others were silent as they thought about the accusations Limpit was making, and then the danger started to sink in.

"Nonsense… that's utterly preposterous. There is no more Circle, it's long gone. That rabble of fools was badly defeated several centuries ago, and their leaders banished to the outer edges of the lands, never to return and mix with ordinary unicorns again. We live in enlightened times, and this archaic Circle poses no credible threat to any of us. It's probably just a small handful of Unimages with their fancy ideas who think of themselves as the rebirth of an old-fangled movement, and they're copying a few foolish things they've taken out of their history books."

"You might believe that, Professor," Limpit said, "but the Circle is around and it's very active now, and therefore it poses a real threat. Even right now, it is present in this room."

"How can this even be possible?" the Professor asked.

"Just look around you, and then tell me… who do you see in this room?" Limpit gestured with his open claw.

"Now you're being silly. I see you, me, and Princess Sallina…and her friend Szymon."

"Yes, and who, then, is Szymon's father? Tell me."

The Professor started to look concerned. A frown started to develop on his face.

"I know you've been thinking it. Well, Unimage Callindra wasn't alone on the other side of Barchester's conversation. She was joined by Unimage Konstanty. He is also an active part of the reformed Circle. And who did Unimage Konstanty send here to do his bidding—tell me, Professor?"

Szymon suddenly started to feel alarmed. He knew his father had been politically involved in a number of discreet matters, but this was the first time that he had heard about the Circle and his father's potential direct involvement with them.

Sallina turned toward Szymon, at a loss for words. She of course knew about Szymon's father, and she certainly didn't trust him, not after what he had attempted to do to poor Limpit. She had, however, learned to like and trust Szymon, and once again she was feeling unsure as to whether her trust was misplaced.

"Szymon, did you know anything about your father's close involvement in the Circle?" she asked, trying to sound collected and calm.

Szymon looked at her and shook his head. "I'll be honest, I don't know much about what he gets up to, that's the truth. He's my father, and most of the time I have no idea what he does when he's not around. As you know, I'm already in a heap of trouble for having helped you out, so how can I be involved in anything that can potentially harm any of us? I know you don't trust me much, none of you do, but I'm trying to accept the present reality and deal with it as best I can while I prove to you that I am here to support you and will not in a million years let any of you down."

With that, Szymon turned away and headed for the door. He unlocked the latch, opened the door, and walked out.

Sallina was about to follow him outside when the Professor put his hand on her shoulder.

"I think it's best you let him go for now," the Professor said. "We haven't accused him of anything; we were just asking, and he's grown up enough to figure that out, even if it takes a little time and privacy for it to fall into place. He'll work things out. Give him some time. It's not easy to follow in your father's footsteps, especially when those very footsteps appear to be increasingly crooked and heading off in the wrong direction, taking you away from all that you once believed in. I think he's a strong and good-natured boy, and he has a strong will of his own, which will guide him in the direction his heart wishes to go. This isn't to say we shouldn't be careful and keep a watchful eye on him, but he has earned our trust for now, and I see no reason to not continue trusting him.”

Sallina stood still. She didn’t attempt to follow Szymon. Instead, she turned around and faced the Professor, looking him directly in the eyes.

“If Limpit is correct about this threat by the Circle, then we are all in a great deal of danger, and so is all of Starpoint,” she said.

“You are absolutely right, my dear. I fear that I have been far too naïve for far too long. I have let my good nature get in the way of seeing what is going on around us, and I have underestimated the dangerous threat we all face. And the worst possible time to deal with a dark and sinister force such as the Circle is in a time of great and terrible crisis. Because whilst we are busy trying to avert an oncoming disaster, they’re looking closely at us and waiting for us to slip up and make one tiny mistake. It looks like the meteor is not our only threat right now.”

“If Limpit is our only means of travel back to our world, then when Unimage Konstanty sought to destroy Limpit, he also risked losing his ability to obtain Pinny and bring it back to Starpoint safely,” Sallina said thoughtfully. “Do you think he knew what he was risking? He even risked the safe return of his son.”

“I suspect the Unimage was unaware of Limpit’s vital importance in our ability to travel between these lands, and by not letting him destroy Limpit, we have created opportunity as well as a greater danger to us all. Despite this threat being all too real, they are not yet as organised as we fear them to be, and we still have the time to prevent these interfering fools from bringing great harm upon everyone.”

“How so?” she asked.

“Well, we now know how to get back to Starpoint safely, but if the Unimages were to find out, then Limpit would be in even greater danger, and they will attempt to capture him for their own ends and take him away from us. But something else troubles me more.”

“What is that?”

"When Szymon came over, I suspect Unimage Konstanty may have known about the connection that Limpit helped forge and snuck him in without us knowing. But how did you get in? You managed to cross the lands without Limpit's aid, which now baffles me."

Limpit flapped his wings and came closer to them.

"I think I know how she did it. You've perhaps underestimated our side as well."

"How?" the Professor asked.

"She has the only other powerful magic in this land… she's wearing it. That is how she must have travelled across."

The Professor looked at the pendant hanging around Sallina's neck. It looked like the others were now also coming to terms with how powerful and dangerous this pendant really was.

"Of course. And when Unimage Konstanty figures that out, then both Limpit and Sallina will be in even greater danger than before. Maybe he already realises this and has started to make his bold plans to get a hold of it."

"How can they threaten us?" Sallina asked.

"That's easy. Our friend Szymon may inadvertently be helping them without him even knowing it," he replied.

Sallina stood there for a moment.

"Does that mean we cannot risk trusting Szymon anymore, as he can be manipulated to serve them even without his knowing?" she said, regretting the words she was saying, but knowing that it was an inescapable conclusion if what they had figured out was correct.

"No. We all believe that Szymon's intentions are good, but whether we like it or not, we need to keep a close eye on him," the Professor said. "He cares for you; I can see that. We'll watch him closely as well, and we ought to treat him kindly, because his support may yet create one of our greatest opportunities in overcoming them when the time comes."

She remained still for a bit, then nodded.

Sallina left the room, leaving Limpit and the Professor alone together.

"You've placed an awful lot of responsibility on such young shoulders, Professor," Limpit whispered after the door had closed. "In fact, you may have put the fate of our entire world in her hands and on her friendship with that young one."

"Not just in *her* hands, but in all our hands, including yours. I do hope she's up to it. But like this or not, the future of our land may rest upon her tender young shoulders as much as it rests upon ours. We are all in this terrible ordeal together, for better or for worse."

Limpit suddenly went quiet. He turned around and found a corner of the room in which to land and curl himself up for some well-deserved rest. He had spoken and heard enough for today, and now he needed to get some sleep. Tomorrow was likely to be another challenging day for them all, and he wanted to be as alert as he possibly could when he awoke a few hours from now.

Chapter 25

Sallina was on her way to check on Szymon to make sure he was alright and perhaps question him to check where he really stood, when she suddenly changed her mind. She decided to heed the Professor's advice to continue to trust but exercise caution; therefore, she went back to her room instead, to try to get some much-needed rest.

She really didn't feel comfortable about confronting Szymon about anything to do with his father, as she knew how hard it was for him to talk openly about his strained relationship with the loathsome Unimage. Besides, Szymon had only recently risked all to stand up against the powerful Unimage in order to save Limpit's life, and deep down she wanted to trust him rather than put herself in a confrontational position where she was openly cross-examining his good intentions.

The next day, they were once again sitting together in the great dining room, being served a welcoming and hearty breakfast. Roger, attired in his serving uniform, was dutifully attentive towards them just as before. He served them a delicious range of fresh fruits, vegetables, bread with jam, porridge, and several other delightful savouries that exceeded their expectations and tantalised their taste buds.

There was naturally a complete absence of raw or cooked meat, but this was because Roger already knew that none of the present company would desire it. Those who were present all heralded from his master's strange and bizarre world, which was never openly discussed between them, but was something alien to the way of life he knew. Roger had heard a good many stories about this incredible place, and he had seen things that were too odd to even put into words, but somehow, he had become accustomed to the strangeness of Starpoint and eventually learned to accept it and say nothing. Besides, Starpoint was a long way away, and he doubted whether he would ever visit that place in his lifetime.

Roger had been drafted into Thomas Barchester's service at a very tender age. His continued silence had been amply rewarded with long-term, secure employment that came with his own small, cosy cottage which was conveniently situated on the estate not far from the main building. Roger was a solitary individual by nature, and this suited both him and his master.

As Roger served Thomas fresh orange juice out of a beaker, he whispered to his master. It was one of those rare occasions where his voice was slightly audible to the others, as he hardly ever spoke, and when he did, he couldn't be heard only a couple of feet away.

He raised his volume a little higher, indicating that he didn't mind whether the others heard him as he announced, "The chamber and your other guests are now ready for the conducting of your spell, my Lord. Your imminent presence is awaited."

Thomas politely nodded and smiled. He clinked his glass with a spoon and formally addressed his guests from his wheelchair.

"Your attention, my good friends. It seems we are ready to attempt the connection back to our land to determine whether we can successfully transport our small amount of Pinny to our home."

Princess Sallina and the Professor exchanged quick glances, and then both cast their gazes directly toward Szymon, who had avoided responding or acknowledging the notice in any way. Limpit hovered silently by the floor, where he too was tucking into some fine savouries, and he as well preferred not to react to this announcement Barchester had made.

* * *

Back in the library annex that contained the magical books and various Starpoint paraphernalia, the Professor, Sallina, Szymon, and Limpit soon stood in front of the orb, which emitted a red-and-orange flame directly above its mouth. Thomas Barchester sat in his wheelchair, clutching his handwritten notes, which he had just removed from the safe.

"Well, this is it. Here we are. We are ready to proceed with our incantation," muttered Thomas, breaking a momentary lapse into silence. "I have devised a spell and spoken the words as I'm required, and a connection will soon be established between the worlds."

As he spoke, a distant and faint voice spoke back to them from across the vast divide.

"Unimage Barchester, are you there? Do you hear me?"

This alarmed Szymon, as it was the familiar voice of his father. Szymon could feel the hairs rise on the back of his neck, and suddenly he stood quite rigid.

Princess Sallina stepped closer to Szymon and grasped his hand. She sensed the sudden state of panic that was running through his entire body and showed up clearly in his sombre expression.

"I'm not sure I can do this right now," Szymon whispered to her, hoping that nobody else could hear.

"You must; it's very important," she whispered back to him, trying to keep the conversation as inaudible as possible to the others around her.

Thomas Barchester picked up a small pouch resting on his lap and opened it. He removed the precious Pinny and held it in his open hand.

"Princess Sallina, you shall now take this item back to Starpoint," he instructed her solemnly, as she stared directly at him.

She hesitated and looked toward the Professor.

"That's fine—you've been chosen to take it, Sallina," the Professor encouraged her. "This is your burden, my dear, and it's also a gift to help protect all our fellow unicorns from the oncoming threat. Szymon must also accompany you, as it may be too dangerous to go back alone."

She took a small step forward and took hold of the small amount of precious Pinny as Thomas Barchester placed it firmly in her hands.

"Keep it safely on you, Princess. It's for the protection of all fine citizens of Starpoint—their very lives depend on it," Barchester said gravely.

The daunting responsibility they bore in taking the Pinny back bothered Szymon. "No, I won't go back," he murmured, this time more audibly so others were able to hear. "My father, he has a connection with me. I fear this may put others in danger."

Szymon wasn't the only one appearing troubled. Limpit was also looking more than a little agitated, the dragon's small face starting to turn red.

"Nonsense, my boy, you and the Princess both need to do this!" Barchester retorted. "Your father is expecting you on the other side. You are returning as glorious heroes who are bringing back this precious Pinny to help save us all. There really is nothing to be frightened about, as it is a wonderful thing you are doing, and you should be proud of yourselves."

"I just heard him in my mind," Szymon muttered.

"What? Can he hear us?" Professor Tinzy asked.

"No, only I can hear him. I can't even speak to him," Szymon continued to explain. "It was only for a moment, but now he's gone."

Sallina wasn't going to let the previous incident with Unimage Konstanty be overlooked, so it was her turn to chime in. "I can understand Szymon's frustrations, as it wasn't so long ago that our friend Limpit was put in serious danger and Szymon had to make sure that nobody was accidentally or intentionally hurt." She looked at Szymon to provide him with some reassurance.

"Today is not about addressing the little differences there may be between us. Let's all remember that today is about saving our entire world—this should be the only thing that concerns us," Thomas interjected, seeking to move the topic of conversation back to the task at hand.

"Wait!" Professor Tinzy blurted out. "Before anyone attempts to go anywhere, we had better enact Limpit's flame ritual, which is an essential part of such an occasion."

"What flame ritual?" Barchester questioned, somewhat baffled.

"The ritual of releasing the flame," the Professor replied. "This is one that Limpit carries out each time we travel back, which serves to help cleanse the path ahead, and then he travels along with the party."

Limpit responded willingly, his tension subsiding now that he had something useful to do, and he hovered forward and stared into the orange-and-red flame in the orb as he tried to focus his attention squarely on it.

"Yes, I will help with my flame if you want me to. I shall give it my best effort as I always do, despite what others may think of me and the actions that were previously carried out against me," Limpit said, and the Professor raised both his eyebrows at the remark.

"What nonsense is this?" Thomas asked sternly. "We really don't need to mess about with providing silly ceremonial flames in an attempt to keep this little creature content. We need to get on with the business at hand. Or have I forgotten something? I hate it when this happens."

"This isn't merely about keeping Limpit happy, Thomas," the Professor replied curtly. "This is an essential part of the entire process, and we need to stick to following the proper procedures. You'd best refer to your notes in your book. It is such a pity that you keep forgetting things and need to be reminded of them again and again."

"Oh, I see… Well, if we must do this silly thing, then let's get on with it," Thomas said, somewhat befuddled by the Professor's insistence. He just wanted it to be done with, and if the Professor wanted to indulge in some theatrics to help liven up the occasion, then so be it.

"I'd recommend that each of us takes a measured step back, Unimage Konstanty, as I believe Limpit is about to release the full and ferocious intensity of his fiery breath down that long passage that connects both these worlds," the Professor cautioned the Unimages and whoever else was on the other side.

Thomas Barchester looked up at Limpit. The focus and heated look building on Limpit's face prompted him to hastily pull his wheelchair back from the orb.

Although Unimages Callindra and Konstanty couldn't see the ball of flame taking shape on the other side, both also took several careful steps back from the orb, having been warned and knowing full well that even at his diminutive size, Limpit remained a formidable beast.

Of course, it didn't take much of a warning for Unimage Konstanty to look concerned that there might be an unpleasant edge to Limpit's fireball exhalation, especially as he was expecting some form of retribution from his recent attack on the creature. If anything, Konstanty was half expecting Limpit to give it an extra amount of fiery burst to serve as a timely reminder to the Unimages at the other end of the path that he could adequately handle himself when required.

Limpit took in a deep breath of air that filled his lungs to capacity, seeming to expand in size as he did. And then, with all the energy that he could muster, he launched his hot, fiery, fireball breath from his mouth. It travelled straight towards the orb. The dragon's fire was instantly absorbed by the flame above the orb. Limpit's exhalation vanished inside the orange-and-red passageway as it travelled between the two connected worlds.

On the other side, where Unimage Callindra and Konstanty were both standing well back, Limpit's flame soon burst out of their orb and into the chamber, momentarily illuminating the room brightly and garnering a terrified reaction from those present.

In Barchester's library, the orange-and-yellow window of the orb widened past the top of the orb until it shrouded the entire orb itself and created what looked like a sort of passageway. A few seconds transpired and then the passageway started to manifest from its orange and red incandescence into a gaseous sea blue, appearing like a pool of water that was bubbling away, although this appeared before them vertically rather than horizontally.

"I believe we've got it working again. This is incredible!" Barchester proclaimed the success of the connection with an expression of excitement previously unseen on his otherwise quite weary and stern face. "A great path back now lies open for travel between our worlds."

Professor Tinzy spoke as he stood there utterly transfixed. "Yes, this is wonderful." He turned toward Sallina, leant in closely, and spoke into her ear, "You'd better leave now with Szymon back to Starpoint. Do be extra careful—you must trust no one, and most certainly not the first unicorns whom you meet, as they may have strange intentions that we are not certain about. Seek out your mother and ensure that she is brought up to date on recent events; she is in charge and can help ensure things are handled fairly and properly upon your arrival."

Sallina glanced back at the Professor. She was about to question him further, but he silently shook his head, indicating this wasn't the time to have a more involved conversation.

"When shall I come back here?" she asked, determined to at least have some idea of what would happen following their return to Starpoint. The idea of resuming her old life now seemed depressing, and she also knew that the Pinny they were taking back with them wasn't going to be enough to overcome the threat all citizens of Starpoint would face when the meteor came crashing into their world.

"Return as soon as you can once you've given them this Pinny. I think you should bring Szymon back as well if they allow him to return with you. He will not want to stay there with his father, and I have a feeling he would prefer to be close by your side. He has been a tremendous help so far. I don't know how I am able to sense it, but I think he is destined to help us complete our task. My trust in him has greatly improved as I have gotten to know him better."

Szymon wasn't sure what to say or do at that precise moment, but then Sallina resolved this uncertainty by tightly taking hold of his arm and pulling him along with her as they both stepped into the blue gaseous passageway in front of them.

One last time, she briefly turned to glance back at the Professor as they stepped through the portal, whilst she tightly held onto Szymon with one hand and clung onto the Pinny with the other. The gaseous substance quickly engulfed them both to the point where the Professor and Limpit were no longer visible to them.

They had gone.

Chapter 26

Sallina and Szymon stepped further into the thick blue gas until… WHOOOSHHHHH! They began plummeting. Sallina and Szymon both yelped as they fell through what felt like a huge, never-ending blue cloud. Sallina soon started to scream, and Szymon clung onto her tightly as she looked towards him. He didn't seem to be quite as frightened as she was. Remembering she had to hang onto the Pinny, Sallina tightly closed her hand and brought the Pinny closer to her chest.

Together, they hurtled down at some speed until their descent came to a gradual halt and they were virtually floating whilst descending in slow motion, as if they were being brought down gently with the aid of a couple of large parachutes. The journey could have been mere seconds or could even have lasted for days—Sallina couldn't quite tell, as time seemed to have lost all significance. As they looked towards each other to check that they were both okay, they realized their bodies were also transforming themselves into something else. Sallina and Szymon were no longer looking at each other in their human form but were returning to their original unicorn shapes.

Then they completely stopped falling and stood upright on their four hooves, bunched closely together on what looked and felt once again like solid ground. The blue gas began to evaporate, and Sallina realized they were now back in the room inside the castle where she had first begun her journey: Professor Tinzy's private research chamber.

Behind them, Sallina noticed the strange passageway, which was still radiating a bubbling blue vertical sea. At the other end of the room, they started to discern Unimages Konstanty and Callindra standing further away from them, as well as a large orb that was taking shape close to the Unimages. Before Sallina and Szymon could turn or move and step away, a large net fell right on top of them, and they were quickly surrounded by other unicorns whom they had never seen before.

"What's happening? What's going on here?" Sallina clamoured as she looked towards the Unimages, who were staring calmly at her and Szymon.

"Welcome back, my Princess," Callindra tried to say in her best welcoming voice but failing at it miserably.

"Welcome back, son," Unimage Konstanty chimed in. "You've made it back home safely, thank the stars. We've got you, and you're safely back where you belong."

"Have you brought the Pinny with you?" Callindra asked, having dispensed with her brief attempt at formalities.

Instinctively worried, Sallina lifted her front hoof and it unfurled to reveal her unicorn fingers. She found that resting in her hoof-hand was a small amount of Pinny, now seeming even smaller from her unicorn viewpoint. She sighed with relief, as for a moment she thought it might have gotten lost somewhere along the way.

Despite she and Szymon being trapped beneath a net, the net hadn't fallen directly upon them. Instead, it was floating just a few feet above their bodies. Still, it prevented them from escaping and taking off in any direction. The net was using a magic spell of some ilk, but they could tell the magic was relatively weak, and at times the net looked as if it could drop directly on top of them or even just evaporate and disappear altogether.

Callindra took a few small steps forward and produced a floating metallic plate, which she guided through the air until it hovered near Sallina.

"Pass me that lovely Pinny, Sallina, as we need to make immediate use of it," she demanded, dispensing with any pleasantries.

Sallina didn't respond. She looked at the Pinny in her hoof-hand and considered that she and Szymon were trapped and had little alternative but to comply. They were now back home, but this wasn't the welcome she had been hoping to receive. In fact, this was the most unwelcoming experience she had ever encountered in her own homeland. It most certainly was not the heroes' welcome that Thomas Barchester had predicted and assured them was how they'd be welcomed back!

Sallina let the Pinny drop onto the plate through the lining of the net.

"That's marvellous," Callindra said with a glint in her eye. "We will be sure to put this important substance to good use. Your timing is truly exquisite."

As Sallina looked around the familiar chamber, she quickly began to realize the other unicorns were not attired in a manner that she recognized, as none of them bore Queen Noony's Royal crest.

"Who are these guards surrounding us? They're not ones I've seen before. I do not recognise any of them."

"They're just friends of ours," Callindra replied matter-of-factly. "There's no need to concern yourself about them and where they come from. They will take you someplace safe to rest and recover from your arduous ordeal, Princess."

Unimage Konstanty stepped forward. "There is something else I wish to have as well."

Sallina didn't make any attempt to respond to the Unimage.

"I want that beautiful necklace of yours—so do take it off and pass it to me, will you?" he said, more forcefully this time.

Szymon stepped forward in front of Sallina and shook his head.

"That's not yours to take from her, Father—the necklace belongs to Sallina. You have no right to ask her for it."

"Oh, my dear son. You'd better stay out of this secondary matter. Move away from her. I will now have possession of the necklace, or else she's in a great deal of trouble."

Sallina shook her head and took a step back into the net. She was not about to forfeit her necklace, which she had grown accustomed to helping her work her way out of dangerous situations.

Unimage Callindra raised her front hoof into the air. "You will pass it to the Unimage Konstanty right now. Don't make him ask you again, or you won't like what comes next."

"No," Sallina replied, sharply defiant. "It's mine and it doesn't belong to him or anyone else." Sallina was starting to get very worked up about it.

"You cannot keep it with you at present—it's not safe for you to do so, my dear," Callindra said, attempting to calm the

Princess down. "It's for your own good. Things have changed a lot here, and you must do what is being asked, for the common good of all."

Then Callindra began chanting something incoherent and the necklace started to light up. It left Sallina's neck and hovered above her in the air. A moment later it glided away from her and was quickly caught in Unimage Konstanty's hoof-hand as he grabbed hold of it.

Sallina had no time to grab it, and when she tried to move, she couldn't. She seemed completely frozen where she stood, unable in any way to react.

"Thank you for giving it to me," he said, tucking it discreetly into his robe pocket.

"You've stolen it from me. I did not wish to give it to you. How dare you do this in my own home? You will be punished by the Royal guards, I swear it!" Sallina cried out.

"Shut up, little brat, and behave yourself for once in your life… you foolish princess!" Unimage Callindra snapped. "Now take them both away," she instructed the guards. "I want them out of my sight."

Sallina and Szymon were quickly ushered out of the room and along several long hallways that they had never been down before. Soon they appeared to be in a disused part of the castle. They were still trapped under the net that hovered directly above them as they were led to some unknown destination. When they passed by some windows, Sallina and Szymon managed to catch a brief glimpse of their city from up high. What they witnessed in that moment greatly concerned them… greatly concerned them and would haunt them for the rest of their lives.

Outside, the sky had turned an unusual dark grey, despite it being daytime; it was as if a veil had been placed like a blanket over the entire city. The sun seemed to be permanently masked by a myriad of dark, foreboding clouds that did nothing more than hover above and restrict the daylight coming through.

Then there were those familiar buildings that they immediately recognised, only now they were dark and drab. The whole city appeared to be purposely run down and battered, as if something terrible had occurred, like a war that had raged on for several years had left their wonderful home in tatters and a shell of what it once was.

"Why does everything look so horrible and different? What has happened to Starpoint?" Sallina muttered in disbelief to the guards, but none would respond or even look her in the face. It was not their position to do so, and they had been told not to respond to anything she asked them or said.

"Szymon," Sallina said, "something's gone horribly wrong here. It's like we've woken up in a living nightmare. This isn't the home we left."

Szymon was too stunned to respond. He too was shocked by what they had just witnessed and couldn't quite believe his eyes.

The two young unicorns were finally directed to a large, dark chamber. They stepped inside and a heavy wooden door shut behind them. They turned around in the chamber to find that they were locked up as prisoners.

"Are we now convicts being held captive in our own home?" Sallina asked with a heavy heart. She looked at Szymon, scared and unsure of what exactly was transpiring.

"I don't know—this is all very odd to me," Szymon muttered, still mystified by all that was happening around him.

The chamber that had suddenly become their prison was completely bare apart from some soft hay in one corner. Sallina and Szymon sat down on it and did their best to make themselves feel a little comfortable. They were forced to sit there like barbaric animals rather than civilized unicorns with the grace and dignity that modern life bestowed upon them.

"Wait until my mother finds out about this terrible mistreatment by those two impertinent Unimages," Sallina said. "Being mistreated in our own home like we're a bunch of wild animals."

"I doubt she even knows you're back here," Szymon said, even more puzzled than before.

"We need to do something about this. I'm not going to sit inside here and wait to be ordered about by two corrupt Unimages and some strange-looking guards who have shown up from who knows where!" Sallina exclaimed, deeply frustrated by the unwelcome circumstances that they'd found themselves in.

"Yes, but what can we do about it? We have no powers; we are weak." Szymon gazed forlornly at Sallina, then lowered his head. Sallina turned slightly to face the wall of their cell to fight back a tear.

While Sallina and Szymon saw that Starpoint had changed more than a little bit since the last time they were present in the land, they didn't yet realize why. With the last remaining Pinny almost depleted and the power of magic having been cut back to just part of one of the five alicorns, Starpoint had rapidly begun to deteriorate. The enablement of magic use in the city began to weaken it considerably, and its glory and beauty quickly started to fade away.

Without urgent replenishment of Pinny, it seemed that the entire city would soon crumble into a gigantic heap of rubble. Who even needed a meteor to come and destroy the unicorn city, since the absence of Pinny could do a good enough job all by itself?

Although unicorns were able to survive without the aid of much magic in their lives, it was widely regarded that they wouldn't be able to properly function without its powerful and pervasive support.

Some unicorns had previously speculated that without the aid of such magic, which required a regular supply of Pinny, unicorns would regress back into lower-state animals, and within a few short years they might lose all their superior magical powers and their speech along with their powerful intellect. This was, of course, a questionable assumption for anyone to make, since nobody could recall living in Starpoint without the ample support of magic all around them, and all five alicorns running at full capacity. Even all the written records that existed had been created with the power and aid of the pervasive unicorn magic that interwove the fabric of their lives. Without the aid of magic, who would be left to read any of these records, or even comprehend them?

It looked like Starpoint was facing an existential threat, and what Sallina and Szymon were witnessing was the consequence of magical properties and abilities swiftly fading away. What little remained was powering the last partly functioning alicorn in the city, and it was not going to last much longer without a ready supply of Pinny. And if anyone bothered to look at how much Pinny was left, they wouldn't even be able to see it with the naked eye if it were put right in front of their faces. What remained were merely the tiniest specks of what had formerly been a solid cluster of powerful Pinny crystals. In effect, Starpoint had been running on Pinny dust, which would inevitably expire completely in just a few days' time.

So grave was the city's precarious situation and the overall plight of the unicorns that the populace had been informed that Queen Noony, being largely responsible for having failed to address the threat, was being confined to her quarters.

She had not set hoof outside for days, whilst she silently pondered the end of meaningful life in Starpoint and the steady demise of unicorns across the many lands for who knew how many generations to come. Some of her citizens surmised that she had chosen to retreat from her civic duties because she realized she had failed to protect her citizens adequately and was now hiding in shame. But many of them understood that this was most likely idle gossip that was being perpetuated by sinister forces that had no shape or name, and nobody knew her real reasons for concealing herself. Either way, it wasn't good.

The truth was, she had been confined to her quarters by the collective will of the powerful Unimages, who together had decided to take over the running of the city and confine her to her stable quarters. They had unanimously decided that it was time to take all matters into their own hands and relieve the Queen of her control over affairs of the realm, which she was failing at so miserably and thereby letting all the citizens down.

Unimage Callindra had been appointed as the temporary leader of Starpoint based on her promise that within a matter of a few days, a couple of the alicorns would be restored to provide at least partial magic, and that an emergency booster of Pinny was already on its way by order of the Unimages and their emergency actions.

And now here it was, although it had been snatched away forcibly from those who had worked so hard to procure as much as they could secure so far, without the Unimages having to do any of the work. In order for the Unimages to maintain magical power and allow the city to function without the risk of descending into utter chaos, it was essential that nobody knew the actual truth of who had brought this Pinny back, as the will of the Unimages—which was presently being moulded by the desires of the Circle—was now fully at play. There was a lot of opportunity to be gained by exercising full control and controlling the dissemination of information to suit their needs.

It clearly suited the Unimages that Queen Noony was perceived as the one who had failed so dismally in protecting her own kind in their greatest hour of need, and that therefore the Council of Unimages was required to maintain order and restore the proper supply of magic across the city. It was Queen Noony, after all, who had sent off a foolish old Unimage, Tinzy, to some distant land beyond any known place that existed, on a farfetched mission to locate the much-needed Pinny in a land where magic supposedly didn't even exist.

How preposterous it was to entrust such an old fool with an important and, what no doubt had become, dubious mission! So, who could therefore trust a Queen who seemed to have lost all her marbles all at once, and had most likely become delusional as she approached her old age?

For many, it was as if their Queen was already senile, leading them all to catastrophe as the threat of the meteorite became ever greater and the sense of danger ever more real. She had fallen under the pressure of the external threat and lost her ability to act rationally and take charge.

Her solution? Send her only daughter off in pursuit of that old, crazy, foolhardy Professor, who had demonstrated a tendency to disappear and then return from who knew where several years later—far too late to be of any good, and not even knowing who in the world he was or where he had previously been. An old fool and a spoilt princess… how could either of them succeed when there was so much at stake? Clearly, more reliable leadership was urgently required, and, fortunately for the citizens of Starpoint, there was still the Circle of Unimages, who were able to run things so much better.

Fully and permanently taking power away from the Queen wasn't going to be easy for the Unimages, as she was still the

Queen of Starpoint and possessed an authority that had for generations been unquestioned. However, there was a clear set of rules written in the ancient laws of Starpoint that stipulated that if the powers of magic were ever threatened in the city and Starpoint was to ever lose its ability to function properly, then the Council of Unimages must be given extraordinary powers to re-establish law and order in the land, and they must be tasked with determining how to restore the magic during such uncertain and perilous times. These rules had been created in a time of war long ago, and until now they had been largely forgotten. However, in such grave times, these old rules needed to be resurrected and action had to be taken to resolve the problems that Starpoint was now facing, and the dangers that lay ahead for the unicorns who resided there and far beyond.

It was on this basis, the citizens were told, that the Council had conceded that the wise Unimages must take over the direct running of the city, and that Queen Noony was to be from this moment forward mostly confined to her quarters for quiet reflection. Not as some kind of prisoner, but as an honoured guest of the Council, to be protected and safeguarded at all costs for the day things might return to normal, although the arrival of this day could take several months or more.

The citizens of Starpoint were thankful that the wise and experienced Council of Unimages had taken it upon themselves to come up with more pragmatic and sensible solutions than the Queen's, and they placed their trust and faith in them. They also were relieved to hear that the poor, suffering Queen would be well looked after by the wise Council of Unimages, and she would be afforded every opportunity to embark immediately on a prolonged recovery.

There were, of course, some who didn't quite see it that way, as they were much more sceptical of what was potentially transpiring. There were rumours of a 'return of the old Circle' that had been circulating around for a while—that it was in fact this mysterious Circle that was largely to blame for the reduction of the Pinny supply in the first place, and that they had purposely engineered what amounted to a dire situation purely to secure power for their own ends.

There were even a few outliers who claimed that Unimage Callindra was in reality a senior member of the Circle and had purposely removed the Queen so that she could assume control and fulfil her own ambitions, and that over a period of time she herself would take the throne and appoint herself the new Queen of Starpoint.

Most Starpointers only wanted the bad times to pack up and go away, and things to return to some kind of normal, so those who had a stronger inkling of the truth were considered touched by a sudden madness and treated the same way as their ill and weakened Queen. Nobody would dare to openly challenge the Unimages anyway, since they had exercised the power to confine the Queen to her chambers. The same fate could befall any of them if they began to question the absolute right and authority of the council and their decision-making. And so, the limited number of prison cells in Starpoint soon began to fill, and as more were herded off and locked up, others soon began to fear saying anything at all that might upset those who were now in charge.

The only obstacles that appeared to be in the Council's way were these two relatively unimportant and impetuous young unicorns who were currently being held captive, supposedly for their own well-being, but who appeared to know a little more than the other citizens and were being kept out of the way in case they were to sow further confusion and discontent with their version of the 'truth'.

Therefore, they were under no circumstances to be released so that they could tell their particular side of the story, as there were already some rumours beginning to spread that it was they who had succeeded in bringing some Pinny back. The Unimages in charge hoped that at some point soon the young people would simply vanish back to this other land, never to be heard from again once the present problems were successfully overcome. They were likely to be nothing but trouble, and the last thing Unimages needed to invite into their already difficult lives was more trouble.

Wasn't it bad enough that not only was the Pinny supply running out, but there was also this nasty meteor heading directly towards them? Only wise old heads would know what to do under such adverse circumstances, and the citizens had no choice but to offer trust to the council in return for the faint hope that things would soon sort themselves out and their lives would return to normal.

Getting rid of the Princess and Szymon was all part of the plan that had been hatched by Unimage Callindra and other members of the secretive Circle not too long ago. They knew that these two youngsters were still useful to them in some ways, but they also ran the risk of the pair interfering with the return and restoration of the Circle into the proper order of things if this was not properly handled and kept under careful and measured control.

There had been some resistance by Unimage Konstanty on having to abandon his son in this faraway land, but he soon began to tell himself that it would be in his son's best interest, and that a reasonable spell of time spent on some distant world would do him good. Maybe in a few years' time, his son would come to his senses and recover, and he would be welcomed back into the new fold of the glorious Circle and be recognised as one of its most valued members.

Chapter 27

Princess Sallina lay fast asleep on a neat pile of hay at one end of the cold, stark room, while Szymon had done his utmost to make himself comfortable on another pile of hay in the far corner, when both were suddenly awakened by a strange noise from behind the door of their cell.

It was their second night as prisoners in the Princess's home. Both had found sharing a confined space difficult, and they had not long gotten off to sleep when a strange whisper disturbed them from their slumber.

"Princess, it's me." The voice spoke up again, and this time it was more clearly audible. "Don't be asleep… wake up if you are. I can't shout, I hope you can hear me."

Half asleep, Sallina made her way to the door and placed her ear against the wood to try and hear better.

"Are you able to hear me?" the voice continued.

"I am," she responded. "Who is it I'm speaking to?"

"It's me, Unimage Paterline," the voice replied reassuringly, but there was a nervous edge to it. Something in his tone told her that things were not right and that this was a frightened old Unimage.

"Unimage Paterline, what are you doing here? It's not safe for you to be here talking to us."

"I'm attempting to help you out of this predicament," the voice came back. "I have a very important message from your mother, the Queen. She is aware that you've returned to us, and she so much wants to see you. But you cannot go to her right at this moment. You youngsters are being held as prisoners, and there is no way that Unimage Callindra is going to let you talk to your mother directly. In fact, your mother is also being kept a prisoner by the Council."

"Why is she a prisoner?" asked Sallina.

"Because you are all in a lot of trouble. You've gotten yourselves into a fine old mess, and I'm not sure any of us can do much about it, as much as we'd like to."

"Can anyone help us? We have to get out of here," Sallina pleaded. "Can you not find some way to get us out of this ridiculous place? I feel like I'm being treated as an animal."

"No, you mustn't leave your room at present. You don't understand—you are not safe anywhere in this castle. In fact, you're not safe anywhere in Starpoint. As long as you are safely locked up, they will do nothing to harm you. But if you are let out, someone may take it upon themselves to hurt you."

"But we cannot stay locked up in here like a couple of wild, caged animals!" Sallina cried out.

"Shhhhhhh. Quieten down, please. The guards may hear us. I must leave in a moment. The Queen just wanted you to be aware that she knows you are here safely, and she is thinking about you. Do not be afraid of what is to come… something will soon be worked out, and she is confident she can find a way to help you escape."

"I'm not afraid of any of them. Tell my mother that… I miss her, and I'm not afraid of any of them!" Sallina cried out defiantly.

"Well, you really ought to be. They are a bunch of highly dangerous manipulators who have the whole city in their clutches. The Circle has taken control of our land, and they will no doubt turn all those who attempt to prevent them from pursuing their ambitions into their slaves and lock them away somewhere for the remainder of their lives."

"What do you mean, 'ambitions'? What are they planning?"

"It is the way of the Circle," Paterline continued. "All those of us who are not pure will eventually be forced to serve under them as slaves. They will restore their ancient vision from the ancient order of the Circle and remake Starpoint in their abhorrent image. They passionately believe that only the purest have the right to rule and use magic, and all those who are not pure will exist merely to serve them. All those who are mixed, which accounts for more than ninety percent of all citizens, will therefore become slaves to the ambitions of the pure. They will have no rights, no comforts; they will live out their lives only to serve."

"What complete and utter nonsense," Sallina said. "That kind of backward thinking disappeared centuries ago. It's all so barbaric. What happened to the Pinny we brought back? Starpoint appears to be in serious trouble, and they must have begun to restore the use of magic with it."

"The Pinny… it's not here anymore. It was taken away to serve their more urgent needs. We believe they have greater needs than serving the citizens of Starpoint. They are the Circle, and they do as they please."

"Taken away? What do you mean, serve *their* urgent needs? Where have they taken it? For what purpose? How can there be any greater need than helping the citizens of Starpoint and averting the threat of the meteor?"

Unimage Paterline remained quiet for a moment.

"I cannot talk here for so long. You will need to be patient; help will come at the right moment. We will find the opportunity to help you when we can. Your best course of action is to wait for the opportune moment and then escape. Either go somewhere remote, like a faraway village, or even go back to the land you came from, which lies mostly beyond their reach."

"This is quite ridiculous. How can they even consider locking me up like this in my own home, or expect me to flee like some condemned criminal?" Sallina moaned.

"You must remain quiet and be patient for now, Princess, as there are others around you who are also on our side, and we are not facing this threat alone. But nothing changes that quickly, and we have a lot of work to do to get back to what is right. Take good care."

With that, Unimage Paterline slipped away as discreetly as he had arrived.

"Unimage Paterline? Hello? Are you still there?"

There was no reply. Sallina and Szymon looked at each other blankly.

"I need to find a way to get my pendant back. Your father shouldn't have taken this away from me. It's so wrong. How dare he?"

"I'm sorry about that, and I will help you get it back if I can," Szymon said sorrowfully. "I tried to stop him from taking it, but he is strong, and he doesn't want to listen to me anymore."

"How can you possibly help me?" she asked. "You're so afraid of him."

"I don't know yet, but I'll figure out a way. I'm not letting him do this to you. We will fight back, I promise you."

The rest of the night passed by uninterrupted until the turning of the key in the door indicated the arrival of two guards bringing what was supposedly their breakfast but was in fact stale food that was probably a good five days old by then.

As they sat on the hay in their dishevelled states and did their best to eat, the door again opened and Unimage Konstanty entered the room by himself.

Szymon didn't even react as his father walked up to them and looked down at his son without even a smile or acknowledgement that this was his own and only child. Then he spoke as if he was conducting some official business.

"How are you keeping?"

Szymon didn't reply and instead looked toward Sallina.

"I wanted to check on you and make sure you're both comfortable," Konstanty said softly. All of a sudden, his mood changed, and he relaxed. "I've missed you, son, much more than you will ever understand."

He tried to break into a warm, tender smile this time, but both Szymon and Sallina could see how weak it really was. It wasn't hard for Szymon to figure out that buried beneath the shallow veneer was a cold and callous heart that had already sold itself out to the Circle.

Szymon looked directly at his father, this time registering his anger in the way he stared at him.

"Father, I am sorry for what I did when I was out there, and I know you are angry. But what you are doing is wrong. You must stop this at once."

"You are sorry? I am wrong? Do you know what you are saying? Have you lost your mind?"

"Yes. I'm sorry for everything that has happened… I didn't mean it that way. But there was a good reason I had to stop you from hurting Limpit. I didn't mean to stand up against you, but I had to stop you from hurting him for reasons you were unaware of at the time."

"What was your reason for interfering with my important work? I'd like to hear that," Konstanty said, his eyes darkening.

"I can't tell you about it in front of her—it's very sensitive. Can we speak somewhere in private?"

This suddenly inflamed Sallina's temper and she quickly shot an angry glance at Szymon. "Don't you say anything to him! You will put Limpit in even greater danger if you do. You cannot trust him; he doesn't care for you or me. He only cares for them."

Straight away she felt like she was being betrayed once more by Szymon, and she wondered whether she could ever trust him as her friend. She thought about him while she fumed.

"If you take me away from here, I promise I will tell you everything you need to know," Szymon said meekly, ignoring Sallina's flareup.

Konstanty turned to Sallina, who was clearly fuming even more now. He could tell that there was something Szymon must know that she didn't want Konstanty to find out. This immediately piqued his interest as he studied them both with greater curiosity.

"Very well then, come with me, my boy. Let's talk, father to son."

Konstanty turned and departed, announcing to the guards, "My son shall accompany me for a short while; I take full responsibility. I will keep a close eye on him at all times."

Szymon got to his four feet and followed his father out, staying close. Sallina was by now completely wound up, but she had to bite her lip as there was nothing she could do.

"Don't do this. You'll betray us all!" she screamed out desperately as she jumped up and stormed toward the door. The door shut sharply on her as Konstanty and Szymon headed away down the corridor.

Now she was there all alone. She began to cry.

"Szymon, how can you betray us? How can you betray me?" she cried out, this time wanting to be heard but suspecting that there was nobody around who cared enough to listen.

* * *

Szymon silently followed his father into another room in the castle, where there stood a table and some chairs. Konstanty sat down and began eating. He took a drink from a large golden chalice.

"Why don't you eat with me, son? I want you to have some proper food. I'm sure you must be hungry after the rubbish they served you in there. I don't want you to go hungry."

Szymon looked at the food and sat himself down opposite his father.

"Firstly, I have to tell you a secret that the Princess doesn't want me to reveal to you," Szymon said earnestly.

"What secret would that be?" said Konstanty, looking mildly bemused.

Szymon took a deep breath to prepare for his carefully considered response.

"It's to do with Limpit. You see, sir, Limpit isn't merely a tiny old dragon who has been accompanying the Professor on his journeys as a pet or a friend. He's a lot more than that."

"How so? Explain."

Szymon picked up some fruit and took a bite.

"The honest truth is… without Limpit, they wouldn't be able to come back from that distant place they travelled to. You see, it's Limpit's fiery breath that allows safe passage back to Starpoint. Professor Tinzy has always brought Limpit with him when he journeyed to the strange land, because Limpit is required to open the path back.

"If you had slaughtered Limpit as you attempted to, then the Pinny would never have been able to come back here, and all your efforts would now be in vain. Don't you see, Father? I was trying to help keep you from failing, and there was no time to explain this. I am still on your side. Do you think I care for Limpit one tiny bit, that stupid little oaf of a dragon?"

Unimage Konstanty continued to chew his food while pondering what Szymon had just revealed to him. He remained silent for a few moments, then drank some more from his golden chalice.

"That's interesting information, my son, but I already knew quite a bit about that," Konstanty finally said in a perfunctory manner. "Are you trying to tell me that you stopped me from… slaughtering that vile beast, Limpit… to protect us all from failing in accomplishing this important mission? Is that what you're saying to me? That your intentions were always to assist me in my work?"

"It's precisely why I did what I did, Father. I would otherwise never stand against you, especially for a stupid little beast that I have no personal attachment to. Do you think I care the slightest for this vile little creature, a horrible tiny dragon with a sordid history? What a pathetic creature Limpit is."

Despite Konstanty finding the proposition somewhat troubling, his son's words rang with a certain sense of truthfulness that he simply couldn't deny. Also, he so wanted to believe in his son, as he missed the boy already and the very thought that his own flesh and blood could turn against him had concerned him deeply.

To Szymon, it felt like the complete opposite. He was extremely fond of Limpit, and to talk about him in such a negative way bothered him greatly, but he kept reminding himself that he had no choice but to pretend. Somehow, he must convince his father that Limpit, Princess Sallina, and Professor Tinzy meant nothing at all to him.

Meanwhile, Konstanty was wondering, *Is the boy telling me the truth? Is he a lot smarter than I have given him credit for? Now that he is almost a grown-up, it appears he might have inherited my cunning and brains. He is, after all, my son—my flesh and blood.*

"You do realize that by passing me this important information, you're betraying your good friend Princess Sallina. I doubt she can ever forgive you for telling me this about Limpit, even though I knew most of it already."

Unimage Konstanty knew that Szymon's relationship with Sallina had previously been important to him, and this was a way of prodding him to make sure that his son wasn't trying to outwit him as well.

Szymon looked saddened for a moment, but quickly regained his composure and nodded. "I will always choose to stand by my father. I wish to one day become a great Unimage, just like you, and I shall do whatever I need to in order to accomplish my most noble goal. The Princess is just a spoiled brat, and she only had magical abilities because of that necklace. Without it, she's nothing."

Unimage Konstanty picked up the chalice and polished off the remaining liquid.

"That's very insightful, my son. For a while I genuinely thought I had lost you. I'm so glad I didn't, and that deep down you're the son I've been proud to bring up. You know, I remain proud of you, and it's wonderful for a father to be so proud of his son. Nothing in this world makes me happier." For a brief moment, Unimage Konstanty believed the poetic words he was speaking to his son, but it was only for a brief moment in time that he was able to fool himself.

Szymon smiled and started to eat more of the appetizing fare on the table. He was incredibly hungry after receiving nothing but horrible stale food since being cooped up with the Princess. Unimage Konstanty watched as his son consumed his meal. When Unimage Konstanty turned away, Szymon tucked some of the fruit into his pocket, as he was hoping to bring some back for Princess Sallina.

Szymon gulped down another bite of food, then said, "Father, if you want me to go back in there, I will. And if you want me to continue to spy on her and her kind, I'll do it just for you."

Unimage Konstanty laughed at the suggestion. "No, my son. You think I will leave you with that stupid girl after you've betrayed her? She'll have you for breakfast if she finds out. You'll wake up at night with her front hoofs at your throat. Don't underestimate her for one second! Under her soft and feeble exterior, she's not so different from her mother. She can be a formidable enemy if you allow her the chance."

Konstanty chuckled some more. "You'll come back with me; we're going home. Welcome back, my son. I have missed you greatly. I want you back where you belong."

* * *

Once he returned home, Szymon enjoyed the momentary luxury that went along with his father's high standing even though he secretly worried about Sallina and caught up on some sleep in his favourite spot in the sumptuous garden in the back of the house. His father, meanwhile, wasted no time in updating Unimage Callindra and informing her about Limpit and his role in all this.

"To think you almost eliminated that foul creature, and in doing so, this vital mission could have been put at such risk," Callindra said gravely, weighing the decisions they had previously taken.

"I guess I instinctively knew it was the right thing to send my son there. He is such a sly boy, and he's just like his father in so many ways," Konstanty said, quite pleased with himself.

"Indeed, it appears to be so, and he has already proven himself to be very useful to our cause. But we have a problem now that we need to deal with. We desperately require more Pinny, and I don't trust him, even though he has proven to be useful to us. Now that he and the Princess will surely fall out, how can we send them both back to bring us more Pinny? This thought troubles me," she pondered openly.

Unimage Konstanty gave this matter serious thought.

"The Pinny we have needs to be shared with Starpoint, or things will completely fall apart here, and therefore it will at best last us only a couple of weeks. We must go back and obtain more as soon as we can," he reminded Callindra.

"Of course. That's precisely what I've been thinking about. Then I see only one course of action that's available to us," Callindra retorted. "But we must limit what we give them, because the sooner they feel things are getting back to normal, the more open minded they will become, and you cannot tame the horde without them experiencing a sense of uncertainty and fear in their day to day lives. It's when they eventually get used to this uncertainty and fear that you really have them, and they are yours to command. It is this fear that allows us to properly administer control and maintain strict order. It's then time for us to move on to the next step of reorganising everything the way that we want it."

"What course of action may that be, wise Unimage?" he asked, his eyes alight with morbid fascination.

He knew that of all the Unimages, Callindra was the sharpest and the most cunning. It was no coincidence that she virtually led the Circle, and she was probably the main reason they were now regaining their power over the land.

Callindra's eyes lit up. "We have to send the Princess back with Szymon to get us some more Pinny. They will both be told that if they don't return within a week with additional Pinny so we can protect our land, then we will have no choice but to take even more drastic action. And to make sure there is no misunderstanding on how important this task is, the first action will be to execute the Queen in public."

Now Konstanty's eyes lit up too. He'd never imagined Callindra would even think such a terrible thing, let alone say it. But then he sobered.

"Such drastic action has never been attempted before in Starpoint. After all, she is still the Queen," Konstanty said, his mind racing at the thought of such action being carried out in public. "I'm not sure that all creatures of Starpoint shall stand by obediently if we even attempt to do such a thing as beheading the most senior member of the royal family. There are many who will remain loyal to their Queen no matter what we tell them. Even though the Council has temporarily taken over and is running things due to the emergencies we face, it will no doubt be seen as sacrilege if we choose to harm her in any way."

"My dear young Unimage. We do not intend to harm her; we just need Princess Sallina to *think* that we will. That will be enough for her to focus her attention more fully on her mission," said Callindra. "She wants to save her beloved homeland, and now she will also have another great reason, which is to save her mother's life. The more pressing problem is that Szymon will not be quite as popular with the Professor and the Princess when he is sent back with her. I'm not sure how to handle that side of it. They will clearly not trust him anymore if they suspect him to be a traitor."

"You're right, he won't be trusted," replied Konstanty. "But he doesn't need to be trusted or popular. Szymon will need to explain to Tinzy and the Princess that we only seek to obtain the Pinny, and once it's safely in our grasp, we can restore order and fend off the imminent threat of the meteor striking Starpoint and destroying us all. That should be enough to keep the peace between them and to focus our energies on the mission at hand.

"Besides, if they do decide to confront him, he can tell them that I already knew about Limpit's importance, so in fact he had never betrayed a thing. Once things get better, we can deal with the Queen and her daughter as we so choose, and nobody shall dare question our authority once we restore Starpoint to its full and magnificent glory. When we are the undisputed leaders who heroically rescued Starpoint, who will dare to question our wisdom and how we choose to govern around here?

"You know, Callindra, it's one of the oldest tricks in the book. The problems that one creates and then solves are far better and easier to implement than those that are foisted upon us, and then we have to work about dealing with them in the dark, without any pre-planning involved. Look at the trouble we've had with the meteor. If we had created this in the first place, it would have been so much easier."

Callindra nodded.

"Yes, you are probably right about how things are best done. It was always the grand vision of the Circle to depose the throne, and for the Unimages to fully take over to rule the land. By our succeeding in this aim, only the pure shall be allowed to exert control, and the traditional order will once again be restored. You are always right, my dear Unimage. How wonderful to see you embracing our grand vision so positively. I have certainly chosen well to have you stand by my side," she said, demonstrating a degree of excitement Konstanty had rarely witnessed in her before.

"My role is to serve the Circle in any way that I can, as there is no greater honour than in giving it my fullest and most heartful support. Only the purest are destined to rule these lands. Isn't that so?"

Callindra knew, of course, that underneath his smooth exterior, Unimage Konstanty was a rather sly unicorn, and she knew that in the years to come he might eventually pose a threat to her very rule. She could see his ambitions as clear as the light of day, and she knew that he already saw himself as a future leader of all the unicorns, more than likely to one day challenge her in being the rightful leader of the Circle.

In his mind, he saw himself as the noblest of the pure, and he would stop at nothing to get to the top. Ultimately, all his actions were designed to be self-serving, despite his enthusiastic willingness to claim that he was operating for a much greater cause. But greed and desire were powerful forces that could be harnessed and used effectively. And, more importantly, they could be leveraged if one had the means to control the one below you.

His ascent to real power would still be some years away—even he knew that—and she would in good time find some crafty and subtle way to get rid of him as a potential threat to her ongoing rule. She had plenty of time to take care of that matter. Sly as he could be, he was unlikely to prove any real match for her, and she would soon gain all the power she required to lead Starpoint's tribe and, in turn, become the one great ruler above all the unicorns in Starpoint and beyond. She was to be the purest of the pure, as she had made herself to be that way, and there was nobody out there who would be able to stand against her.

Of course, Callindra knew that the whole façade of purity was all an elaborately crafted illusion, based on a dazzling assortment of deceptions that allowed one group of exalted unicorns to feel vastly superior to the rest, and to create a sense of pre-ordained hierarchy that was necessary for all things to function smoothly in a society. Without the masses who were at the bottom serving the wishes of the privileged, who were ordained to run things, how could society function?

What is the meaning of being pure, after all? she pondered to herself.

Was it really the colour of her hide that determined who she was, or the brightness of her eyes? Or was it the deep chasms of her innermost desires, along with the exalted status of her official title as a Unimage leader, which she had fought so hard over many years to attain?

She knew that without the aid of powerful magic, even she wouldn't exactly qualify as being pure, as she had shaped herself in this way and had over time accepted her acquired status as a natural evolution, even though it wasn't. She didn't need to think long about these trivial concerns, as she already knew where she stood and had long ago accepted her deceit as her right due to her superior intellect.

It didn't really matter where you came from, it was who you eventually became that counted the most. Being seen as 'pure' was a route that suited her needs and gave her things in a way that other paths couldn't. Pure powered her like Pinny powered magic. Pure was not just an abstract idea; it was a useful tool to help control those around her.

More importantly, she also knew how to seize control with these useful tools that she had at her disposal.

Chapter 28

All alone, Princess Sallina cried herself to sleep as she lay on the hay that third night. There seemed little hope, now that Szymon had deserted her, and she remained locked up in her own castle. But just as she was drifting off to sleep, she heard a distinctive voice emanating from behind the door.

She rose quickly to her feet and made her way over.

"Who speaks there?" she whispered. No reply was forthcoming.

"I know someone's out there. Is it you, Unimage Paterline? Have you returned?"

Slowly, the door creaked open, and a cloaked figure took a few short footsteps into the cell.

In one swift motion, the cloaked figure removed its cover, and Princess Sallina saw that it was none other than Szymon who stood before her.

"You! How *dare* you show your face to me? You—you betrayed us all!" she squealed as her emotions flared up.

"Shh, Princess, you have to calm yourself," Szymon said, glancing round at the door. "I've come to get you away from this place and help you escape from this prison. Your mother, she is desperate to see you. She's waiting right this minute—it's best not to delay."

Sallina suddenly felt relieved when she heard her mother, the Queen, was waiting to see her. It had been far too long since she had even spoken to her mother, and she felt reassured that maybe things were not quite as bad as they seemed.

"Why are you helping me?" she asked Szymon cautiously. "You know I won't trust you ever again after that stunt you pulled with your father."

"What I did, I had to do. How else could I gain my father's trust unless he was somehow convinced that I had betrayed you? Believe me, making it seem like I was on his side all along was the only way I could help us in this awful situation," Szymon said calmly, trying to assure her of his genuine intent. "You said so yourself that we shouldn't stay here. We must get away. There are some other things that you need to know, but this is not the time, Princess, for us to play catch-up. First, I must take you to your mother. After that, we both need to safely get away from this castle, as they will soon come to look for both you and me. Now come along, there's a lot to be done."

Szymon motioned for the Princess to follow him as he turned toward the door. But Sallina wasn't yet convinced that Szymon was genuinely acting in her best interest. She stood her ground.

"I honestly do not feel I can trust you even one bit, Szymon," she explained. "How do I know my mother awaits me? How do I know that anything you are telling me is the truth?"

Szymon halted in his tracks, turned, and took a couple of steps back to the Princess. A small pouch hung by his side. Using the limited powers of the son of a Unimage, he concentrated, and the pouch opened as if by its own volition. Out of the pouch, Sallina's pendant rose into the air, hovered, and then made its way over to Sallina and descended over her mane. As if it knew the exact width of Sallina's neck, it expanded to fit her perfectly.

"I reclaimed this from my father. We both know that it belongs to you and nobody else, and I want you to have it back. You know he desires it greatly. He will not be so happy when he discovers that I've taken it. In fact, he's going to be awfully mad at me," Szymon explained.

This succeeded in placating the Princess, who was now only too pleased to have reclaimed her necklace. If Szymon had any intention of betraying her further, he wouldn't have given her back this pendant—she was certain of that.

Satisfied, they both headed down the hallway, where a couple of guards appeared fast asleep on their feet, having been drugged in some strange manner that she couldn't work out. As they made their way around the next corner, she spotted Unimage Paterline, who was keeping a close watch to ensure that no other guards suddenly turned up.

As soon as she saw Unimage Paterline, she relaxed even more. The wise and old Unimage was one of the few magic creators in all Starpoint who she felt she could trust without suspicion, aside from Professor Tinzy, of course.

She followed Unimage Paterline and Szymon along various corridors, some that she was quite familiar with already. There were quite a few sections of the castle that were disused and had provided a wonderful opportunity for her to undertake exciting adventures when she was little, especially when the weather outside was poor and all playing had been restricted to indoor activities. There were other times when going out wasn't safe, and she had been told to contain herself to the confines of the great castle. But it had been years since she had traversed these corridors, and now only the faintest memories of them remained in her mind. However, there was the occasional window that she would pass that showed her certain parts of the castle she was more familiar with, and this helped to bring her some further comfort.

Occasionally as they wandered down the long, winding corridors, they had to evade a guard on duty who was walking around, but guards were few and scattered about at this late hour in such a secluded section of the castle, so it wasn't that hard to avoid them.

The guards appeared unfamiliar to her; they were not adorned with the usual Royal trappings she had been cocooned in throughout her life, and she concluded they had somehow been appointed by the Council of Unimages directly. They were probably loyal to a select few closely tied to the mysterious Circle, who had played an active part in this takeover.

It took a good twenty minutes for them to get through the vast secluded area of the castle and make their way to a section she knew more about. Then it was a couple more minutes until she found herself near the Royal chambers.

As they approached the Royal chambers, two official guards of the castle, who carried the Royal crest, immediately asked them to identify who they were. When Unimage Paterline showed himself in the light, closely followed by Princess Sallina—whom they already knew by sight—the guards quickly stepped back and let them pass through without any further incident. In fact, they looked embarrassed that they had even attempted to stop someone of the Royal family, even if that individual was still a youngster.

Many of the guards didn't even know that Queen Noony had been confined to her quarters against her own will; most of them simply assumed that she desired to be in a private space during such troubling times. Although there were rumours suggesting this may have really occurred, the Royal Guards who were still active had dismissed this as some kind of bizarre fantasy invented by a few warped minds who enjoyed causing mischief and creating confusion.

Often the problem with embracing the truth is that there are different versions of the truth out there existing simultaneously. Those who are adept at disseminating large-scale lies understand that a potent mixture of well-crafted falsehoods can be far more appealing when they are stacked up against the truth—especially in troubled times, when the truth can often be deeply unpleasant.

Several times in the long history of the Unimages, lies had been artfully presented as alternative truths and permitted to flourish, even by those who knew better than to mislead fellow citizens in this way. These enticing variations would swiftly enchant the herd. Poor old Truth was left ridiculed and scorned until it no longer mattered what was in fact true and what had now become the widely adopted lie. By that time, those who once had the means to challenge these lies could no longer oppose what the majority accepted as being right. Almost invariably, those few unfortunates who could still see the true light and were terrified of the enveloping darkness eventually decided to go along with such well-crafted falsehoods, as opposing them would only cause an intolerable degree of discomfort and pain in their societal interactions.

Princess Sallina was starting to grapple with the problems in embracing the truth. The Circle had long ago flourished by having the herd accept their lies, and now that the truth was once again unpleasant, their lies were proving popular. If Princess Sallina and her small group of travellers were to reveal the situation for what it really was, they would need to convince most—if not all—unicorns in Starpoint, especially the Unimages, that their way of life was in great peril.

Not only were they threatened by a meteor, but they were also dangerously close to losing the freedoms that unicorns so naturally cherish. Who would want to believe such a thing, and who would want to figure out how to keep the magic flowing with Pinny? All of this was beyond the ability of most unicorns to grapple with and be able to work out some kind of a solution.

Finally, the trio arrived safely at the main doorway of Queen Noony's chambers, and the two guards who were stationed outside quickly unlocked the door and let them through.

Princess Sallina burst into the room as she looked about for her mother, but the Queen wasn't to be found. They made their way through the grand living room, until they entered the doorway into another chamber.

There they found Queen Noony in her pyjamas, munching away in silence on a snack. She looked up instantly and recognized her missing daughter, which caught her by surprise. She jumped to her four feet and rushed up to Sallina in a state of intense excitement and gave her a big, warm hug. They touched their heads, and tears streamed from Queen Noony's eyes.

"My goodness. You're safe!" the Queen exclaimed. "I was so worried that something terrible had happened to you!" She studied her child carefully to make sure she was there in one piece. "Did you come back from the other place? Where did they keep you? They locked you up, I heard."

Princess Sallina nodded.

"How long have you been here?"

"It's quite a long story, Mother," Sallina replied. "But first, I want to know what's going on here in Starpoint. Why are you locked up inside your private rooms, and why did they lock me up as well in what was nothing more than a stable?"

"Locked you up inside some stable! I didn't know they locked you up like that. How dare they lock you in a stable? They've no right to do such a hideous thing to a lovely princess!" Queen Noony exclaimed angrily.

"Why are we being locked up?" Sallina asked. "What's going on?"

Queen Noony also had a question for her daughter. "Who is this fellow with you?"

"I—" Szymon started to speak, but Sallina quickly cut him off.

"He's with me. We travelled back here together. Look at yourself, Mother; you're virtually a prisoner in your own castle," Sallina blurted out, not afraid to confront the truth with her mother.

"Well, at least they haven't locked me up in such an undignified way as you, and I'm being confined in this place of my own free will," she explained. She then paused and considered her situation. "Well, I suppose that's not strictly true, is it? They have told me I mustn't leave my rooms for a while, as it's not safe out there, as there are some unicorns who wish to do me harm. I should let things first return to normal before I dare to venture out and wander around the castle once again. They say it's for my own personal safety and to help protect the future of our monarchy."

"Safe from whom, exactly? Did they manage to explain that?" said Sallina.

"That meteor has brought about a lot of fear, and there are irate citizens who don't wish me to be in charge, or so I am told. As long as it's still coming directly for us, I suppose I need to restrict my movements for my own safety. But I know there's more going on, and I sometime despair that whilst I wait here for this threat to pass, others are actively plotting against my rule. But I believe that one way or another, things will soon resolve themselves, as the meteor is not far away and it's coming ever closer. Patience is a good thing though, isn't it?"

Sallina couldn't take it anymore. "For goodness' sake, wake up mother! What do you mean, 'not far away'? I thought it was some distance away and would take weeks or even months to get here," Sallina said sharply, her voice rising even higher.

"Oh, my dear. You've not been around these past days. Two weeks ago—I think it was two weeks ago, time has been starting to play tricks on me—a couple of small meteors showered directly on us not far from our home. The whole ground trembled and shook, and a few of the houses in Starpoint almost collapsed. One did. It turned to rubble. Fortunately, this castle is terrifically strong; it is built of such heavy stone, and it has sat here for literally many hundreds of years. This place remains fully intact. But some items in some of the rooms, some chandeliers, some bookshelves, several statues… well, they did fall or slide or get shaken about, and things have been getting destroyed all around the place. This has of course sent shockwaves throughout all Starpoint and far beyond. Everyone knows now: none of us are safe until the meteor no longer threatens us.

"On top of this, the supply of Pinny has been running seriously low, and all the wonderful magic we're accustomed to hasn't been working like it should. Our fellow unicorns are struggling to go about their everyday business, and so many things are being affected.

"That's when the Council was forced to intervene. They advised us that they were getting close to finding a reliable new source of Pinny, and that within a few days they would bring back some fresh Pinny and put it to good use. I hear they have found a small initial batch, although I have no idea from where, and I did feel comforted that we were in the Council's safe and capable hands.

"Even if you couldn't do anything yourself, my dear, on your most noble quest, at least the Council was able to draw up their plans to help make sure we don't end up running completely out of our ability to do anything with magic. And part of me thinks that your earlier attempt also helped them in some way."

"I don't understand. What Pinny were they promising you?"

"They didn't go into many details, but they showed us someone which gave us all fresh hope again, someone who has brought comfort to us all in our desperate hour of need."

"What? Who are you talking about?" said Sallina, dumbfounded.

"My dear girl. We all saw him, just like he was there before us. He was looking quite a lot older, of course, more wrinkled because of the passage of time, with so many years having come and gone. I suppose he wasn't the way that some of us still remembered him, but it was unquestionable that he was still there and alive, and willing to do what was needed to serve the realm. More importantly, he was totally committed to helping us in our greatest hour of need."

"Who, Mother, are you talking about?" Sallina asked again.

"Unimage Barchester, of course. He is one of the greatest Unimages to have ever lived in Starpoint. And he's still very much alive! We are so wonderfully blessed to have him back and in charge of the search for Pinny."

"Thomas Barchester? What? No way!" Sallina cried out in frustration.

"Is that the name he goes by in that strange land you went off to? To us he is Unimage Barchester, and he informed us all that he had successfully managed to secure a small supply of Pinny and that they'd soon be bringing it back here to replenish the magic. And more was on its way. I believe the first batch has now arrived! And by some wonderful and comforting coincidence—so have you! This is good news indeed!" the Queen said. "I'm so pleased they took good care of you and made sure both you and the Pinny safely made it back to Starpoint. But why they put you in a stable, this I simply don't understand—it's a mystery."

"We—we were the ones who brought it back… Thomas Barchester is not to be trusted for one second. He is definitely not of sound mind—he is in fact very forgetful—and I swear he's not at all a likable or reliable person."

"Not a likable person… what are you saying? Are we talking about the same Unimage Barchester? We surely can't be. Have you taken leave of your senses?"

"No, I haven't. I know exactly what I'm on about. Thomas Barchester's been colluding with those Unimages—Unimage Callindra, and my friend Szymon's father, Konstanty. They've all been lying to you. Can't you see? You're being deceived! They want to be thought of as saviours so that they're trusted by all of us, and then they will proceed to take over everything and do what they like. I think they've almost gotten away with it. All this time, you've been locked up in here, afraid to see what's really going on. There are many guards now patrolling the castle, ones I've never ever seen before. My guess is they're probably working for them. Terrible things are happening in our home, right here in Starpoint. We need to do something fast."

Queen Noony pondered what her daughter was telling her and studied her carefully.

Szymon felt it was an opportune moment to chime in. 'It's true. She's—"

Sallina quickly cut him off. "It's okay, give my mother some time. She needs to think it through. It's a lot for her to take in. She's not used to being betrayed."

Queen Noony stepped back. "Have you got proof of any of this?"

This frustrated Sallina. "What proof do you need from me? Look at yourself. You're locked up inside here. We were locked up in a stable. They took away my pendant, but Szymon helped me to get it back. Professor Tinzy is now stuck in the other land and most likely unable to return for who knows how long. And Limpit was almost killed by Konstanty, but he luckily survived and has already helped us with bringing back the Pinny."

Suddenly Queen Noony looked alarmed. "Limpit, the dragon?"

Sallina nodded. The Queen reflected a moment longer.

"Oh no, if Limpit is involved, it cannot be good. Plus, he's not so keen on travelling—he hardly ever flies anywhere in his old age, at least not since they shrunk him down in size to punish him. They said they needed him that size for some mission they were on; they never told me much about it."

"Do you know Limpit, then?" Sallina asked.

"Do I know Limpit? When I was small, we used to be friends. We'd often spend time together, Limpit and I—we go way back. Limpit was also close to your father. It was a very long time ago. But he had to leave us many years back… he had things he needed to do. That's when he got into a whole lot of trouble. This was before you were born, dear. Didn't he tell you about us?"

Sallina shook her head. "He only tells us what he wants us to know. He's a bit secretive that way. Unimage Konstanty almost killed him, but thanks to Szymon, we helped save him. He's now with Professor Tinzy. They're waiting for us to go back to get some more Pinny. But the things we've seen going on here… it's bad."

Sallina and Szymon saw that Queen Noony was now looking all tearful, as if the truth was beginning to dawn on her and she was finally accepting that she had allowed herself to be misled.

"Oh my, I was so worried about so many things in my head that I lost my ability to rationally work things through without falling into well-laid traps. If Limpit is being threatened by sinister forces out there and he is defending you and Professor Tinzy, then it's worse than I thought possible, and there is indeed a takeover plot going on as we speak, and we're all in a heap of trouble."

"Mother, there is so much I would like to tell you right now. This is not the time for a lengthy conversation, but do know this: it was Szymon and I who brought the Pinny back to Starpoint by ourselves, and only because Professor Tinzy was also able to help in getting hold of it and returning it here. Thomas Barchester was indirectly involved, but he is not being entirely honest with you or anyone. In fact, if we had relied on his skills and charms, I doubt we'd have succeeded. The most important contributor to bringing the Pinny back was my little friend Limpit, who you already know much better than I do."

"Limpit!" her mother exclaimed. "How could I ever forget that adorable beast? Such an honourable dragon. It was horrid, what that bunch did to him. Shrinking him down for some important work he supposedly had to do. But who am I to judge what needs to be done in an hour of crisis? He had to pay off some debts for supposedly bad things he'd done before, and the Unimages would then no doubt look after him."

Queen Noony was saddened as she thought back on what had been happening all around her recently, and what she had been told to endure without putting up any resistance. Being locked up like a convict in her own chambers was not her idea of how to effectively rule the land, and having all her great powers stripped away by the Council was not something she had wanted to experience. She felt like she had had all her four legs amputated and that she was now left as a floating body, adrift without any purpose or the means to do anything about the circumstances the inhabitants of Starpoint found themselves in.

But as Sallina watched, she could see that her mother was returning to a state of self-delusion, as the truth that had been revealed to her was clearly too uncomfortable to accept.

"Well, I suppose it's all for a common good, isn't it? So long as they get things back to normal, that's all that matters," the Queen said positively. "And so long as you're back here with me, what else could a mother ask for? I'm sure the Council has these matters under control, and good will prevail. With Pinny starting to flow, things will eventually go back to normal, and I'll soon be able to walk around the castle and Starpoint with pride and a smile on my face. The difficult times will pass. Come here!" The Queen opened up her arms to tenderly embrace her daughter.

"No, this is not the time for us to resign ourselves to what others intend to do to us. We have got to leave this place right now," Sallina said with authority. "What is going on here is not right. It's also not safe for you to stay in this chamber, Mother."

"Where can we go? This is our home! My home!" Queen Noony exclaimed as she pondered the challenges that lay ahead. "There is no place for any of us to hide from that dreadful meteor. It's hurtling through space on its way to us, and it's coming to wipe us all out. Squash us all like we're tiny little insects. If the Council can't put a stop to this madness, then who can? Without Pinny, we are all surely lost."

Szymon touched Sallina's shoulder gently.

"I don't think we can help her right now," he said softly, trying to keep the conversation between just the two of them. "We must go before they find us here. The Queen is probably safer staying where she is for now. I can't help but wonder how much she's aware of what's happening around her. She appears to have lost touch with reality, and I fear she's suffering from high levels of stress and anxiety."

"What did he say?" Queen Noony asked. "Sweetness, I'm glad you've made a new friend, but we ought to stay separate from the others. It is a time to keep apart from the rest of the herd, don't you think? We are regal. Of royal ancestry."

"Why do you suggest such things, Mother? Szymon is my friend, and without his help, there would be no Pinny."

"It's what Unimage Callindra recommended I do. In times of peril, the ruling class must stay away from the others. We need to be protected so we can lead our fellow unicorns to the brighter and better future that waits ahead. Once the meteor threat is over and the Pinny gives us the means to restore the land, we'll still need our leaders. That's me, that's you… it's about preserving what is right and just."

"Unfortunately, we're wasting time here, Princess. We must leave or the guards will no doubt find us, and then we will both be back in the stables under lock and key," Szymon whispered to Sallina.

"Where do we go? What do we do?" Sallina queried sombrely. "I'm not sure what can be done."

Szymon took a few further steps away and motioned to Sallina to accompany him. Unimage Paterline watched them move off a distance. He hadn't wanted to be involved in their discussions and had stayed back throughout them so that they could have a private conversation. He was a lot more concerned about who could potentially burst through the doors at any moment and succeed in capturing them. He also knew that in being there with them, he'd be treated as an accomplice and would be locked up too.

"We ought to hurry up," Unimage Paterline insisted, as Sallina and Szymon looked each other in the eyes on their way to the doorway.

"We need to return to Doberry. We must find a way to obtain more Pinny. Without more Pinny, we won't be able to stop the meteor and protect Starpoint. What we've brought back isn't enough."

"What about Mother? I can't leave her here. She could be in danger," Sallina challenged Szymon.

"What can we do to help her now? We cannot take her along with us. She is safest staying right here. Nobody is likely to harm her in her own private quarters. They wouldn't dare upset all of Starpoint by doing anything stupid. She presents no threat to them."

Princess Sallina felt torn between helping her mother and following Szymon's latest advice.

Unimage Paterline cantered up closer to them.

"The longer you remain here, the greater the danger to all of us. By now the guards will have noticed you're both missing and will have raised the alarm. They'll be looking for you. Here will no doubt be one of the first places they'll come to look, suspecting you will seek out your mother."

"The safest place for us, Princess, is Doberry, where we came from," Szymon said. "We can work out there how we'll handle these problems once we have gained some leverage. Only Pinny will give us a chance to fix things and deal with this dangerous Circle."

Princess Sallina was becoming tearful. She had only just gotten back home and found her mother again. The last thing she felt like doing was going back to Doberry. She wanted to stay there and help her mother get a better grip on what was happening around her, and especially make sure that she was safe. But she knew that Szymon was right. They needed to go back to find some more Pinny.

Only with enough Pinny did Starpoint stand any chance of survival against the meteor. Everything right now was at stake, and they already had an important part to play in all of it. Even if the Circle managed to exploit the situation for their own benefit, at least the unicorns would be safe and no longer threatened with destruction.

"Okay, we'd better go," she muttered, not at all happy about her decision. "I want to say goodbye to my mother. I need a minute."

Szymon nodded.

Princess Sallina turned and approached her mother, who was now frightfully sad and feeling all alone.

"I know what you are going to tell me, Sallina," Queen Noony said dejectedly.

"I'm so sorry, Mother. I want to stay here with you, but I can't."

"You must try to help us. I am so proud of you, I really am."

Sallina rested her face against her mother's, and they hugged once again.

"Promise me you'll try to stay safe?" Sallina asked.

"Only if you promise me that you will as well. And don't be angry at the Council— they're doing the very best they can," Queen Noony responded.

There was a flood of tears on its way to drip out of their eyes as they clasped each other for a few more brief moments.

As they clung onto each other tightly, some sounds were emanating from behind the main door. Unimage Paterline had been keeping close watch, and he was immediately alarmed.

"They're coming now. It's too late!" he cried out softly, trying to keep his voice down. "They know you're here."

Sallina broke free of her mother. Szymon and Unimage Paterline both rushed toward the front door.

Queen Noony spoke hastily. "Not that direction—there's another way to get out of here without detection. Follow me, I'll show you the way."

Queen Noony quickly led them through a couple more rooms and into one of her bed chambers. There was a large fireplace in that bed chamber, and she moved one of the tongs lying in a basket, which appeared to act as some kind of physical lever. The fireplace opened outward, and a hidden path revealed itself directly behind it.

"Take this secret passage. It will guide you through a tunnel from where you can find your way back through the castle to wherever you want to go," she hurriedly whispered.

Unimage Paterline and Szymon rushed into the passage. It was narrow, so they had to enter it single file. Sallina looked back at her mother one last time, and then she turned and fled.

Queen Noony managed to restore the fireplace just in time as the main door to her chambers opened and guards poured in, accompanied by Unimage Konstanty. He had a determined look on his face.

The unfamiliar guards took a good look around, but nobody else was there but the Queen. The Queen's eyes were narrowed somewhat, and her brow was furrowed. Her unmistakable look of annoyance didn't help anyone feel happy about being there. She might not have known who these guards were, but they knew who she was, and they were uncomfortable about being inside her private quarters.

No words were spoken. Unimage Konstanty simply huffed to himself and then left the Queen to her own chambers. The place quieted, feeling again like a prison.

Queen Noony sighed to herself. What was it that had bothered her daughter so much about Unimage Konstanty and the Council? She was sure it was nothing of any great importance. Her daughter was most likely panicking about the meteor threat, and thankfully the Council had these matters under control. Pinny was already on its way, and there would be much more of it soon after, and the meteor would then be averted to somewhere else far away from Starpoint, and everyone would be safe once again. She would then be able wander about the castle like she had done so many times before since she was small, and she would be a proper Queen once again. She'd look forward to her daughter's safe return from the distant land where she was on her very important mission. All would be well soon enough.

Layer by layer, she wrapped herself in the comfort of her false beliefs, and they themselves were turning into convenient lies that she dared not question. If she did, things would start to look extremely unpleasant. Who wanted that?

Chapter 29

Princess Sallina, Szymon, and Unimage Paterline scurried down the twisting, turning corridors, ducking and darting undetected past the occasional royal guard and some guards that were unfamiliar—until they finally reached Professor Tinzy's secretive research chamber, which housed the magic-tunnel portal and orb. They were determined not to be noticed by anyone, as they knew that right now there were very few who they could trust in Starpoint.

The research chamber had belonged to Professor Tinzy ever since Sallina could remember. The somewhat unkempt room had several tables scattered about, which were strewn with odd-looking flasks and beakers filled with peculiar-looking substances. Wherever you looked, there were books stacked high on tables. There were more books on shelves against two of the walls; some of which were half-open with dust on the pages, and others which were still firmly sealed and unlikely to have been viewed for many years or even decades.

On one side of the chamber lay an object that looked like a giant cone, and around it was a few sparkly lights that became brighter or dimmer depending on what state the object was presently in. The lights never completely faded out, and they always seemed to possess a faint glow about them.

Sallina headed up to the object and turned around to make sure that Szymon and Unimage Paterline were close by her side. Paterline had managed to shut the door behind him, keeping a close ear out for the sound of approaching guards.

"I cannot promise you they won't find us in here," Paterline said to the two young unicorns. "I suspect it's only a matter of time until they'll come looking and figure out that you may have decided to return to the other land. Others already know about this room; it has not been much of a secret as of late. You can be certain that the Council will consider this one of the most likely places to search for you. You'd better do what you must before anyone attempts to interfere."

"Then nobody must come inside here in the future," Princess Sallina insisted. "Can you place a lock spell on the outside that can only be broken from someone on the inside? This way we'll be protected when we come back."

"I suppose I can try, but my power isn't so great anymore, with most of us Unimages having lost a lot of our abilities as access to magic has diminished in recent days. I will try, though. It's the least I can do. On the plus side, the power of all the Unimages has been waning, so I can at the very least buy you some time."

Sallina focused on her pendant, which lit up in a bright, incandescent blue and emitted a charge of light against the door.

"This ought to help with casting the spell, as you can draw on its power as if it was Pinny—and you only need to seal the room after you go out," Sallina explained to Paterline. "We don't want to find ourselves coming back here and being caught up in a nasty net again, so hopefully it will hold together as long as nobody knows it was you."

Unimage Paterline nodded. "Good luck to both of you. There are a few of us left who hope beyond hope that you can bring us some more Pinny and not fall under the evil spell of the Circle whilst attempting to do so."

Unimage Paterline opened the glowing door, and he stepped out.

Sallina moved towards a control. She pressed a few buttons and started to focus her full attention on what was in front of her. Next to the cone-shaped object was an orb. After Sallina concentrated with her utmost attention, the orb and the cone-shaped object began to light up. She clasped the pendant to give her the extra energy that she needed.

"We're lucky to have such potent magic aiding us," Szymon said. "There are more than a few Unimages who would no doubt like to have their hoofs on this power you possess, my father included."

The cone-shaped object slowly grew brighter and brighter, until after a minute or so, it was shining a brilliant incandescent white.

From the other side of the door, Sallina could hear the faint voice of Unimage Paterline, and she made out the words, "Bless you, children. Take care of yourselves." Then she could just about hear the spell being cast and felt the power of the pendant helping Paterline enact his spell. Then she knew it was time for her to go.

Princess Sallina was the first to step into the large, cone-shaped object, followed closely by Szymon, who wasn't going to let her get too far ahead of him. A few seconds later, they were both gone. They'd left Starpoint, and were on their way back to Professor Tinzy, Limpit, and Thomas Barchester.

Chapter 30

"Whooooooooooooooooooooooooaaaaa," Sallina cried out again. Only this time, she wasn't enjoying the thrill of this ride or the fear that came along with it.

It slowed down for a bit as it went up to some unknown high point, and then whoooooooooooooooosssshhhh, she was hurtling down the magic tunnel once more at full throttle, screaming her lungs out. She was followed closely by Szymon, who though less expressive, was having a similar experience.

Fortunately, the ride didn't feel as long as last time, and before she knew it, she had landed back in Thomas Barchester's magic chamber, from which she had departed, with Szymon close by her side.

They were now both in human form and felt exposed, as they were without anything on. There was something about unicorn clothing that didn't want to travel well between these distant lands, and she didn't like the fact that she was wearing literally nothing.

Fortunately, she wouldn't have to face the ignominy of trying to find something to hide her nakedness, for some garments landed at her feet straight away.

"Put them on, Princess," Limpit called out. "The room is dark, so we fortunately can't see much, but we don't want you to be embarrassed when the lights come on."

"How about me?" Szymon pleaded, as he too was feeling self-conscious. He had hardly uttered his request when he was slapped in the face with some clothes.

"This ought to do you, too," Limpit said, snorting.

As Sallina quickly got dressed, she looked toward Limpit, who kept averting his gaze as he too was feeling embarrassed.

"How did you know we were coming back at this precise time?"

"Oh, I didn't," Limpit replied. "I've been waiting here for you ever since you both left. I wasn't going to let you come back and find yourselves naked and all alone in a dark room; it didn't seem fair. So, I waited."

"Oh, that's so kind," said Sallina gratefully. "What would we do without you here by our side?"

Limpit blushed as much as a tiny dragon could and then looked back at Sallina, who was now properly attired. Szymon was still fiddling about with his trousers, which seemed a bit loose.

"It's been a couple of weeks since you left, and Professor Tinzy will want to know straight away that you are now safely back. Let's go wake him up."

"Wake him?" Sallina said. "You sure that's a good idea? It's the middle of the night, if I've got it right from my time calculation."

"Better not wake him up. We can update him when we enjoy breakfast in a few hours," said Szymon.

"As you wish," Limpit replied. "I am in no particular hurry, and I can tell him you told me to wait for morning, so he won't blame me for not going back to him sooner. And to be honest, I could use a little more sleep."

***

It wasn't until later that morning that Sallina saw Professor Tinzy, who was enjoying his heated porridge when she walked into the dining room. Thomas Barchester was also there, busily chomping on some fresh fruit with a fine set of teeth for someone his age.

Professor Tinzy looked up at Sallina and smiled, pleased to see that the young Princess had returned safe and sound. He got up and approached her, a warm smile on his face.

"Thank goodness you made it back in one piece! I hope everything is alright back home?" he said. "You don't know how pleased we are to see you again. There are so many things I ought to tell you, but first, we need to eat."

Princess Sallina went over and sat herself down next to Szymon. They were tucking into some food when the door opened, and another woman entered. She looked familiar to Sallina, but she couldn't quite make her out.

"We have new guests," Barchester announced.

"Or should you say old guests? How wonderful to see you," the woman said, sitting close to Thomas Barchester.

Barchester turned to Sallina. "You may remember each other. This is Mayla, my adopted child."

Sallina was surprised to hear about this; Barchester had not mentioned Mayla's name or anything about her before.

"You may recall seeing her at the auction at Sotheby's?"

Suddenly, it all came flooding back to her. Mayla was the woman they had bid against and beaten.

"I didn't know you were also with us?" Sallina managed to say.

"Oh, I wasn't. I was sent down to buy the Pinny, but then Father asked me to let you win it when he remembered I was there as well, so I stopped my bidding. He can be forgetful at times, as you well know."

"You mean you also didn't know we were both on the same side?"

Mayla pulled out her phone. "Of course not. I wouldn't have bid against you if I did. We're on the same team."

Princess Sallina was quite confused. She turned to Professor Tinzy. "Did you know anything about this?" she asked.

Professor Tinzy shook his head. "Gosh no, I had no inkling at all… but Thomas is ever so forgetful these days." He glanced at Barchester. "I suppose you were just making sure we were able to get hold of the Pinny no matter what, and I suppose it didn't matter whether we or Mayla had won the bid, so long as one of us obtained it so we could take it back."

The Professor smiled thinly towards Barchester and then at Sallina.

But this didn't come across as being a sufficiently good explanation to Princess Sallina, and she was not yet ready to let the matter go. She eyed Barchester with a deeper sense of disdain.

Was he indeed being forgetful? she thought to herself.

"If you had had your mental faculties working properly," said Sallina, "we could have worked closely together instead of pulling apart in different directions. I think a little more foresight would have been a lot smarter. Why is it that everything ends up being more complicated? It would have saved us the trip down there in the first place."

Thomas Barchester pretended to mull over her remarks for a few seconds, and then he tucked back into his fruit. "Of course, you are right, Princess. I am deeply sorry if this has caused you any inconvenience. Still, you have learned how Pinny can be acquired, and we are here together now and the smarter for it, and I say we ought to work as a team from now on.

"Tell me, Sallina, what news do you have on the current state of things back home?"

Sallina didn't know what to disclose to Thomas Barchester of the shift in power back in Starpoint and the dire situation that she had just witnessed first-hand. She already distrusted him. Perhaps he was being absent-minded again, but there was something about Thomas Barchester that deeply unsettled her. It's almost as if he wasn't as forgetful as he was making out at times, and somewhere inside that famously bright Unimage mind was the old, wily elder figure driven by a distinctly different purpose—one where he had foolhardily allied himself to the powers of oppression emerging from the Circle in their desire to take over the Council.

But then Sallina thought to herself, *What's the point of even trying to deceive an old fool? He probably knows already what's been going on in Starpoint, and he's just feigning ignorance.*

"It's not really that good," she blurted out. "The whole of Starpoint appears to have been turned upside down since a number of smaller meteors struck nearby. And with the Pinny almost gone, there's a lack of proper leadership. I'm afraid you wouldn't recognize it from what it was."

"What complete lack of leadership are you referring to?" Barchester asked.

"I mean with my mother being forcibly locked up inside her chamber. The Council looks like it has assumed control over pretty much everything, and quite frankly, they don't seem to have much of an idea of what they're doing. The place is quickly heading from bad to worse."

This last remark took Barchester by surprise, even though he was aware of how he had been serving the Circle and how repulsive that would be to his friends gathered around him.

"I've always had the highest opinion of the Council, so I'm a little surprised to hear the unpleasant things you're saying about them. Is there someone in particular who is troubling you?"

"I suppose… I'm not exactly sure. They're all as bad as each other. But the one I think I trust the least is Unimage Callindra; she's certainly up to no good, if you ask me. She and… Szymon's father… are at the root of the problem. My guess is that Callindra is at the heart of this Circle uprising."

"Now, Sallina," Professor Tinzy chimed in. "Let's not get ahead of ourselves and come across as being overly critical of someone so senior and respected as Unimage Callindra. You would need to possess substantial proof to back up such harsh criticism of someone who is held so highly in Starpoint."

Of course, Tinzy was already well aware of Unimage Callindra's questionable activities, but he wanted Sallina to learn that accusations without sufficient proof were not likely to get her very far.

"I'd say it's a lot more than just a hunch," Sallina quipped. "The ones they call the Circle, well, she's deeply involved with them for sure. They're up to no good, if you ask me, and I really don't like any of them and how they behave toward others. In fact, I think they're all a bunch of bullies."

The others noticed that this seemed to bother Barchester greatly, for his face was now turning bright red.

"One other thing I ought to mention," Sallina couldn't help but add, "is that I was informed that Unimage Barchester had been making regular appearances at the Council meetings, and that the unicorns of Starpoint have been 'greatly inspired by his continued reassurances that things here are under control, and with the hard work he has been undertaking in securing Pinny, it will soon return to normal.'

"I'd like to know how you are backing up these reassurances you've been giving the Council, because personally I don't see that much here under control. For starters, we desperately need to get our hands on a heap more Pinny if Starpoint is going to recover, and I'd like to know where we can find it."

Silence filled the room, and everyone there reflected on what Princess Sallina had just said.

It was Mayla who spoke next. "Well…I have purchased a shipment online from a reputed dealer in America a few days ago. This is due to arrive within the next forty-eight hours, and it is twice the amount that we had before."

Professor Tinzy suddenly spoke up, "I hope this will be sufficient to avert that nasty meteor from doing any damage to our homes. I fear we may soon be out of time."

"I think it will have to do," Barchester said. "The hour of even greater danger to Starpoint keeps on drawing nearer, and we don't have much time left to power up all the alicorns and use our greatest magic. We'll need to take swift action soon."

"And how do we know that we have enough? I mean, if we get hold of this Pinny, how do we even return it to Starpoint?" Szymon said, looking round at everyone. "We weren't exactly welcomed the last time we arrived, and I don't plan on being locked up again in some stable and treated like a common prisoner."

"Neither do I," Sallina chimed in.

Barchester put his knife and fork down and cast his fiercest gaze yet towards the Princess. "The same way we have handled it before. You will both need to take it back and hand it straight to the Unimages, who will know what to do. We cannot go there ourselves due to our advanced age, or we definitely would."

Szymon smiled coyly, trying in his way to alleviate the tension that had been simmering in the room. "I'm fine with doing as I'm told, I am. I'll be only too happy to help protect our land and our herd. I'm sure the Princess feels the same way as well. The threat right now is up there hurtling towards our world, and the rest is minor in comparison. There's no point in bickering over who runs things if there's nothing left to run, is there?"

"What?" Sallina responded, surprised. "Are you—" Then she shut up.

There was something in Szymon's expression that reached out to her and told her now wasn't the time to quibble. She knew, of course, that he was right. But at the same time, he was wrong, because if the Circle took credit for saving Starpoint, they would no doubt exploit it to their maximum advantage.

Sallina observed Szymon carefully, then nodded in acquiescence. She couldn't quite figure out why Szymon was coming across as being so supportive of Barchester, but she decided to give her intense desire to argue and question everything a bit of a rest and carry on with enjoying the remainder of her breakfast.

It wasn't until sometime following their breakfast, when they had all left the dining hall, that she decided to confront Szymon discreetly in the upstairs corridor on her way back to her room.

"What's wrong with you? What are you thinking? Why were you being so nice to that miserable old fool Barchester?"

"I wasn't being nice," Szymon responded. "Right now, picking a fight with that two-faced Unimage is not the best way to resolve any of our problems. We have this Pinny coming, and the least we can do is to help take what's desperately needed back to Starpoint and support everyone who remains in terrible danger from a gigantic meteor. Our home still remains in catastrophic danger; we have to do this!"

"I know... I know," Sallina replied, accepting the harsh realities of the situation. "But something is not right with that senile old man, and I intend to find out what is really going on here. Every fibre of my being is telling me that he's playing us, and I don't like being played."

"What do you mean, 'played'?" Szymon asked.

"I want to go and check Barchester's safe later on tonight. I would like to see what else he keeps locked up in there. There may be some secrets we are still unaware of."

Szymon was surprised by her forthright suggestion. "You sure you want to do that? We are likely to get into an awful lot of trouble if anyone were to catch us snooping about. There are a lot of eyes and ears in this place, and I doubt our being down there will go unnoticed."

"'Snooping about' is not how you ought to describe it. Nobody is snooping about. Or are they?" a voice bellowed directly behind them. Startled, they turned to see Limpit hovering a few feet away, looking somewhat bemused.

"Sorry, I wasn't intending to eavesdrop on your conversation. I was, in fact, on my way back to the Professor's room when I noticed the both of you a little ahead of me, and I didn't want to interrupt your conversation. So, I moseyed along close by, not wanting to ruin the flow."

"'Flow'? That's okay, Limpit. No harm in moseying along, either. In fact, you may be able to help us with something important," Sallina remarked.

"Oh, yes, I'd be delighted to be of service. How may I help? I owe you two my life, and I am honour-bound to be of assistance in any way I can."

"Well, we'd like you to come with us and examine what else that devious trickster Thomas Barchester has got hidden inside his safe that's sitting in his magic library room."

"Oh, that sounds like a lot of fun!" Limpit squealed with excitement. "You can count on me to come snooping along. I'm certainly game for a bit of sneaking hither and thither, and breaking into someone's safe to find out what's going on. But there is one condition I must insist on."

"What's that?" said Sallina, unsure of how to react.

"We need to inform the Professor of what we'll be getting up to. I don't want to keep him in the dark about our sneaking-along plans, especially if they are going behind the back of a highly regarded Unimage."

Sallina thought about this for a moment.

"Very well then, we will tell the Professor about our plans beforehand. I agree that we need to let him know… although, I do hope he won't try and stop us."

***

Unfortunately, the reaction they had expected from Professor Tinzy turned out to be quite anticlimactic, as he didn't want them snooping behind Thomas Barchester's back.

"Don't be so foolish, Sallina," Professor Tinzy scolded as he waved his finger at her. "You will risk undermining the Council by choosing to sneak along behind the back of a great Unimage and sticking your nose into many of his personal things, especially without having any actual proof. There are some important matters that don't concern you."

"How do they not concern me? What that devious trickster is up to will almost certainly concern all of us equally, and I for one intend to find out what's really going on."

"Well, let me spell this out for you then. We are talking about examining Barchester's personal possessions without his permission, and a fine young Princess such as yourself shouldn't be underhandedly checking up on someone as esteemed as Unimage Barchester. Not unless you can prove that he has bad intentions all along."

"Well, none of us trust him," Sallina blustered. "He has more than once been openly deceitful. He never even told us that he was communicating with the Unimages back home and discussing with them our plans to find Pinny here, and I don't think we can trust his daughter, either. I reckon he did remember we were there and at the last minute preferred to have her win the bid. When we won it instead, they then had to play along. I do not trust him for one second."

Professor Tinzy wasn't quite sure he could prevent this initiative that Sallina was intending to undertake from happening, so the best he could potentially hope for was to come along for the ride and try to make sure nothing bad happened.

"Very well, then. If you insist on doing this, I'll have to accompany you. I will not leave you to your own devices this time, as I do worry that something could go terribly wrong, and I wouldn't forgive myself if it did."

Sallina was ready to continue fighting the Professor about her justifiable intentions, but then she decided it wasn't worth the hassle, as he had given her permission. She conceded in, "You're welcome to come along with us if you must, Professor—neither Szymon nor I will try to stop you. But, either way, I intend to find out what else lies in that safe of his. I feel I must have a better idea of what he's up to."

Sallina was somewhat surprised to find it was Limpit who decided to speak up in her favour as the Professor reviewed his position.

"I want to say, I'm totally with the Princess on this one. Barchester is hiding something up his sleeves, and he cannot be trusted. We are all better off forewarned if we can get an idea of what he really is up to."

***

That night, the little gang of amateur snoopers managed to cautiously sneak their way into the magic room where Thomas Barchester kept his safe. Once they were there, they also found it easy to pick the lock on the safe. The picking of the safe was a skill that Limpit had developed over the years, and it didn't take him long to spring the safe open by using a couple of hairpins and a deft eye as well as a highly sensitive pair of dragon ears. This wasn't a skill that dragons typically possessed, but being such a petite dragon, Limpit had to develop some new skills that suited the diminished frame he was trapped in, and lock-picking had been one his obvious talents to finesse.

The fact is, Limpit had frequently practiced by picking the lock of the shed, and he had often enjoyed time outside whenever Professor Tinzy had taken his long absences, but he wasn't one to admit this openly to anyone. This was a secret he intended to keep to himself. Eating foul little insects was never his thing; just the thought of it turned his stomach. And his telling the Professor could open a whole new slew of questions. The Professor would want to learn more about where he went, what he was up to, and whether he had caused any trouble on these unsanctioned excursions.

No thanks, he thought. *I don't need this grief.*

Limpit had been more than a little careful in embarking on his solitary travels around Doberry, and he had astutely avoided contacting pesky humans at all costs. He had always had a penchant for sweet things, so it was hardly a surprise that sweets would go missing in some of the local stores. But those who ran the stores would put these small losses down to either inefficient inventory control or some foolhardy actions of children, who, after entering the premises, were occasionally prone to pilfering the odd treat. The merchants couldn't prove either case, nor did they care much as the sums were so small in terms of their losses, so they mostly turned a blind eye to these minor discrepancies.

"I got it!" Limpit exclaimed in uncontrolled excitement as the safe finally opened.

Once the safe stood fully ajar, they began to rummage through the selection of items that were kept therein.

Included in Thomas Barchester's collection were a few handwritten notebooks, most of which were composed of long, drawn-out scrawls that covered every single page and looked like they were his own personal diaries.

One of the books raised an eyebrow from Professor Tinzy when he leafed through the first few pages.

"My word. Goodness gracious, how bizarre this is."

"What's bizarre about it?" Szymon asked.

"These writings. Well, they're all in my handwriting. I must have written this diary myself some time ago and completely forgotten."

Professor Tinzy then opened another diary, and it was also inscribed in his handwriting.

A third book was also the same.

"Thomas Barchester has been keeping my personal writings tucked up in his safe and he didn't say a thing about it. I knew he had many notes, but he also appears to have all of mine with his. I wonder why he would do such a thing. I don't even remember writing all this stuff down, although clearly, I did. Oh, I still forget so many things. I must have kept them here as well. Silly me."

Szymon decided to place a closer watch by the door whilst this was going on, as he was beginning to get concerned that someone might soon discover them snooping in here.

Sallina picked up a diary and examined it closely. "I think you ought to take one of these back with you to study more closely. I doubt that miserable old fool even looks at them much anymore—they appear to be covered with dust, which indicates these notebooks haven't been disturbed for some time."

"Wouldn't this be like stealing?" Professor Tinzy asked, not sure if it was a good idea to be taking anything from the safe.

"How can it be stealing, Professor? They're *your* books; you wrote these in your own handwriting. You can't be accused of stealing your own notes. I think you ought to go through at least one of them closely and try to determine why Thomas Barchester has not informed you that he has these in his possession."

"Well, you might be right, in that case," the Professor reluctantly admitted. He tucked one up under his arm, and Sallina placed the others carefully back in the safe.

"We must be careful not to arouse any suspicions. Therefore, I am returning the others in the same way as they were kept before. Unless he goes through them each and counts all the notebooks, I doubt he will even notice that one of them is missing."

"What about the dust?" Limpit asked. "It has been disturbed by our hands and paws."

"Not much I can do about that, but I don't think Barchester will examine them so closely."

Sallina was about to close the safe when she placed her hand right into the back and pulled out an even dustier notebook that was small and crumpled and had been stashed separately from the others. Sallina hastily turned the pages.

"This one appears a lot more interesting," she said, her eyes widening. "I think I'm going to borrow this for a day or so. As it was stuffed right in the back, I doubt he'll notice it's missing as well."

The Professor wasn't comfortable about taking two notebooks at the same time, but he couldn't deny that something strange was going on, and he felt that he couldn't forcibly prevent her from removing them, especially as they had been written by him in the first place.

How could I not give her permission to read my writings? he thought.

"I think we should leave soon," Szymon said from his position at the door. "The longer we remain, the greater our risk of being found."

Limpit nodded in complete agreement. "I've an unpleasant feeling about being here, too. We ought to go. It's like we're being watched by someone. I can't tell how I know this, but I can feel a presence all the same."

Professor Tinzy closed the safe, and a few minutes later, they all sneaked out of the magic library room and into the larger, less-interesting library. Then they cautiously made their way to the exit door of the larger library chamber.

What they hadn't noticed was the CCTV camera tracking their every movement up and down the long room. This was sending a feed to a small room located in the back of the large building. In the small room sat a tired Roger, who had been awoken when the repetitive low beeping of an alarm had been triggered. With bleary eyes, he closely watched as the party made its way back through the long room and returned to their bedchambers.

Roger didn't mutter a thing; he simply watched them in silence as they passed the cameras that had picked on their trespassing. The next morning, he promptly informed Thomas Barchester in private of what he had witnessed the night before.

Chapter 31

The following morning, Roger served breakfast in the large dining room with his customary level of excellence as he presented his delicious offerings.

Thomas Barchester sat with his guests, taking only a few nibbles of the food on his plate. Professor Tinzy sat beside him. Szymon and Mayla were seated nearby, but neither Limpit nor Princess Sallina was present.

"Where is our dear Princess?" Barchester enquired.

"I don't know," the Professor said quickly, eyes fixed on his plate. He paused, then looked up to meet Barchester's curious gaze. "I presume she's asleep in her room. She must have been up late last night. She's probably struggling to get herself out of bed."

Barchester continued to eye the Professor and Szymon without indicating that he was suspicious of them, knowing full well what they had been up to the night before. Roger, too, showed virtually no reaction and continued to serve them in his diligent manner without uttering a single word.

"Yes, sometimes it can be awfully hard to fall sleep, especially when it's so warm inside the house," Barchester remarked emphatically. "I was feeling hot indoors last night—I had to open my windows. Roger, did you sleep at all well last night?"

Roger nodded silently in confirmation.

"How about you, Professor? Did you sleep well in this heat?"

"I slept like a log. When you're as old as me, sleep can come only too easily, but often it doesn't last for long. One awakens many times during the night."

"Oh, I wish I could—I'm the opposite. I'm a bit of an insomniac, have been one as far back as I can remember. You know, you can have these fancy air conditioners as well, which keep the rooms nice and cool, but very few houses in Doberry bother with such devices because most of the year it's not needed."

Barchester and the Professor exchanged a few more glances as they continued with their breakfast.

It was Mayla who broke the growing awkward silence that was pervading the room.

"I do have a little good news. The delivery is due at lunchtime today. I had a message on my phone about it this morning, and I'm expecting the Pinny to arrive within a few hours at our door by courier."

This was indeed welcome news for all of them at the table.

"That's wonderful, isn't it?" Barchester said. "With some luck, we can send the Pinny to Starpoint later today. They're truly desperate for some more, and your Princess and her friend can then be on their way."

The door opened and Princess Sallina entered with Limpit hovering behind her.

"Do you think it will be sufficient this time, Unimage Barchester?" she asked as she passed him, pretending she was still groggy from her limited amount of sleep.

"Enough for what?"

"Enough to stop the huge meteor that's out to crush us all, of course!" she replied as she took her seat at the table.

Roger approached and placed a serviette next to her plate and positioned her cutlery in preparation for serving her. Princess Sallina looked up at Roger, but he didn't look back at her. Instead, he focused on his duties, as if he was trying to perform them invisibly.

"My father—Thomas—told me we only need enough Pinny to divert the meteor from its present course," Mayla commented. "And based on his very careful calculations, he thinks this particular supply should be adequate for the job."

Princess Sallina smiled.

"Well, that's wonderful news then. I suppose Szymon and I will be off later today to bring the Pinny back to Starpoint as soon as we possibly can."

Barchester wasn't quite sure what to make of her comments, as there was both an earnestness and flippancy in them, and she managed to somehow convey both sentiments together.

"I get the distinct feeling that you're not so keen to be going back home this time, Princess," he said.

"What would make you think such a thing? There is no greater thought on my mind right now than to rescue all our friends and family, and each and every citizen of Starpoint, from that terrible meteor that could end all our lives. We are only here for this one reason. Otherwise, I assure you, I have no intention of staying here and having breakfast in this huge, unfriendly place and walking about on my two hind legs and looking like a spoilt chimpanzee."

"Well said, and quite right you are!" Professor Tinzy trumpeted. "Princess Sallina has been the most dedicated… person on this mission, and I applaud her for that."

This got Limpit chuckling. It proved to be infectious and spread around the table. Even Mayla found it to be quite amusing.

"Given that only Roger and I are humans, and have been for our entire lifetime to date, I take this as a positive remark, Princess," Mayla said. "I'd have no idea how to be a unicorn, and I doubt I will ever experience such a thing. It would for me at least be interesting to try it though… very interesting."

"I want to ask you something, Mayla, if I may," Sallina asked humbly.

"Do, please ask away."

"You are not one of us. You are clearly as human as Roger. What do you think of us unicorns being here in Doberry? You appear to know a lot about us and our behaviour, but you never say anything about what you really think about our mission and what we've come here to do."

Mayla was quiet for a moment.

"To be honest, all I know is what I've heard or read about, but Starpoint sounds like a fascinating place to live one's life. One day I would love to visit Starpoint to see where my father comes from and what the fuss is all about. It does sound quite splendid."

"One day you certainly will be presented the opportunity, my dear," Barchester assured her. "You will find it to be a wondrous place full of magic and beauty the likes of which you have never witnessed before in your entire life."

"Yes, I do look forward to that," Mayla said. "It is my dream to visit Starpoint when things are back to the way they were.

Who knows, I may be there and even be transformed into a unicorn… Perhaps it goes in reverse for humans if they visit your home. I do wonder how it would feel."

Princess Sallina appeared satisfied with the response, although the very notion of humans turning into unicorns suddenly disturbed her. Was it even possible? After all, she was able to transform from a unicorn into a human; what if the reverse was also true?

Suddenly, a frightening thought entered her mind. *What if humans were to visit Starpoint one day in the future and transform themselves into unicorns? Would they be welcome there? Would they be well-behaved and respect the proper unicorns and their customs? What would happen to our world if it were invaded by humans, and many thousands would come?*

There appear to be so many humans living in this world, and Starpoint feels very small and so insignificant in comparison. Could we be swamped by humans? And how would unicorns deal with this? Would we welcome them, or treat them as undesirable outsiders invading our homes? She herself was bothered. What would the Council, and what would the Circle, make of it?

These thoughts frightened her, but luckily, she had something far more important to take her mind off this.

"If the Pinny arrives later on today, will it just be me and Szymon travelling back to Starpoint?"

"Yes, of course," Barchester responded, taking her bait. "As you know, it is unwise for us older folk to travel to and fro between these lands."

"Yes," Sallina responded, "that would normally be the case, but I have uncovered something fascinating over the past few days that could allow the Professor to come back with us on this journey without losing any of his memory, and I would like to share it with you."

"How is that even possible?" Barchester asked her.

"Well, Limpit and I have been doing some research of our own. And we may have found a way that we can transport an older person back to Starpoint without it affecting their memory and allowing that to remain wholly intact."

Barchester reacted negatively. "I swear that's not possible. If it was the case, believe me, I would have discovered it and returned a long time ago. What I would have given to have gone back to my old and familiar ways! You really don't appreciate how much you miss something until you no longer have it."

"Well, I can say that it is possible to do this. Both Limpit and I have gone through the workings of the spell in detail, and such means do exist for the Professor to return safely and for him to be unharmed in terms of memory loss."

This suggestion surprised even Professor Tinzy. "How can it be possible?" he asked. "If I had known about this possibility earlier, I would have done so myself and saved myself a lot of bother over so many years."

"I cannot tell you how I know it's possible, but when we enact the passage back through the tunnel, anyone who stays close to Limpit is likely to be better protected by his magic and the continued production of his fiery breath when going through the passage of the long tunnel."

"That's simply ridiculous," Barchester remarked. "If anyone was surrounded by Limpit's fiery breath for such a duration, they'd be burnt to a crisp."

"Not so," Sallina replied. "I can safely enact a protection-from-fire spell that can protect the unicorn, and Limpit's fiery breath, I believe, has the power to protect an adult's memory from suffering."

There was a deliberate moment of silence in the dining room as everyone took in the remarkable findings that Sallina had disclosed. Sallina had struggled for hours last night about whether to share this powerful information, as it could easily encourage Unimages to more frequently visit this strange land, but she had decided her primary concern was to protect her homeland.

Quite honestly, she was getting sick of having to be the one who kept going back and forth with Szymon. In her opinion, that should be left to older, wiser unicorns. She had already decided that she would not return to Doberry, and she would stay in Starpoint forever more and put this experience behind her. She had had enough of coming to Doberry and hunting for elusive Pinny. If she was right, she wouldn't be needed any further, and others could come over here instead.

What she wasn't certain of was whether it meant that Limpit could either stay in Doberry or return home as he willed and use his breath with the spell from either end of the tunnel; that was not something she could figure out yet. Fortunately, it wasn't essential to know the answer at that precise moment in time.

"I must insist on asking you," Barchester demanded, "how you came across such useful information, so that we can check the theory and verify whether it's true."

It was at this point that Princess Sallina took something out from a small shoulder bag that she had brought into the room with her.

She placed the single item on the table.

Limpit looked a bit nervous when she revealed its source. He wasn't sure how Barchester would react to seeing one of his precious books in someone else's possession.

"What is that?" Barchester asked. "I think it looks familiar."

"Well… it's a book of spells. It's been hidden in here for some time, by the looks of it. It also appears that nobody has bothered to examine it for ages. Early this morning, we did precisely that. And that's when I learned some more about travel between the worlds and how certain harmful effects may be avoided."

That caused Barchester to raise an eyebrow. "And how did you come across this book, I'd like to know?" he enquired.

"I don't know… it's strange. Someone brought it to my room, and when I woke up early this morning, it was lying by the door."

This caught Barchester off-guard. He cast an uncertain glance toward Roger, who returned the expression with a similar look of doubt and surprise.

"Oh, yes, I do remember now. I had asked Roger to drop off some reading material for you the other day. He must have dropped it off for you first thing in the morning and forgotten to do so on the previous occasion. He too can be a little forgetful at times."

Roger looked toward his master and nodded, even though this was not true.

"That's truly remarkable," Professor Tinzy said. He got up, headed over to the notebook, and picked it up to examine it closely.

Sallina had placed a marker on the page where the protection spell was written. Wiping off some dust, the Professor returned to his chair, and he went through the spell.

"This is truly an incredible discovery. Sallina is right about what it may enable us to do. One of us can travel back to Starpoint without our memory being affected. Why did I not notice this before? Even this book looks so familiar to me. It's not in my handwriting, but the handwriting does look familiar as well. It looks as if one of us older folk could accompany you on this trip."

"That should be you, Professor," Sallina added.

"Yes, perhaps it should be. I think Unimage Barchester and I will need to have a private conversation on what to do about this important new discovery. We will inform you of our deliberations after we've made a more informed discussion in the next hour."

Sallina looked at Mayla, who glanced back at her.

"First things first, though!" Barchester commanded. "We need to make sure that the Pinny does arrive here safely before we can plan anything further. None of us is going back empty handed, that's for sure."

Mayla nodded in affirmation.

***

An hour later, Professor Tinzy and Thomas Barchester were heading down the private grounds outside the house to discuss this new finding. Roger was pushing Barchester's wheelchair alongside the Professor.

The two men were both locked deep inside their personal thoughts, when Barchester broke the silence, "I think I ought to be the one who goes back, not you."

"Why would that be?" Professor Tinzy asked.

"Because of my position on the Council. As a former leader of the Council, I can help unite the Unimages, and together we can stop the meteor from continuing its deadly journey and laying waste to our world. Later, I can send Limpit back with the Princess and she can collect you as well."

The Professor thought about this in silence before responding, "I think you may be right, Unimage Barchester. But I want your word that Princess Sallina and Szymon shall not be locked up or punished in any way for what they have done to help us in securing the Pinny. Both have been crucial to accomplishing this mission, and without their able assistance, we wouldn't be here having this discussion and soon on our way, to fix things. Plus, I want Limpit to be safe, because without him I could be stuck here for eternity. Much as I'd like to believe Princess Sallina's theories are correct, they remain untested and unproven."

"Of course, they will not be criticized or punished for any of their more-than-worthy actions. They are our heroes."

"I will insist on your word on this. It is the word of a Unimage, so be careful if you give it to me. Breaking it would obligate you to relinquish your seat on the Council for the rest of your life."

"And you shall have it without hesitation!" Barchester replied adamantly.

The two unicorns who appeared as men continued to traverse the grounds silently, Roger pushing Thomas Barchester's wheelchair as if deaf to all that had passed between them.

As they arrived at the end of the garden path, Unimage Barchester placed a hand on the Professor's arm.

"So, tell me, Professor, do you really want to go back to Starpoint? I get the sense that you yearn for home, and nothing would please you more than to go back to Starpoint."

"To be honest, I'm not sure I do anymore, Thomas. I'm truly tired of all the problems and conflicts we have had to endure back home, and to be perfectly honest, I've become more accustomed to my human form than I sometimes care to admit. I can still recall who I am as a unicorn, and I don't want to risk losing any more of myself than I already have. If it is indeed safe, then I will come and visit, but I am getting accustomed to being here, and someone needs to keep an eye on bringing back more Pinny from time to time. So why not me?"

"You are truly a fine Unimage, Professor, and a wise unicorn. You have helped me to keep myself together for all these years, and without those diaries and your detailed notes, I wouldn't even know who I am, as so much of me has been lost and sadly none of it looks like it will ever come back to me ever again. This house, everything I have… none of it is mine, as you know; it's all yours. If you do stay, you should know that it remains in a trust held in your name, and I am merely its custodian. I owe you everything."

"Thank you for protecting and looking after this for me. But to be honest, I now know a little about what it's like to be human, and I do not wish to have such obscene amounts of wealth on display and to live in self-imposed isolation like those who possess far too much for their own good—it's not something I seek. I have always preferred leading a simpler and ordinary life, which I currently enjoy with what I do… I so much like being a professor and teaching children in school and coming home to my nice cosy home at the end of the day."

"Very well then, Roger can look after it for you as long as you wish to keep it."

"There's one more thing, Thomas. You need to return Limpit to Doberry immediately when you are on the other side, and I will instruct Limpit to go back as soon as he can. The Pinny you take with you might be enough to divert the meteor, but there will soon be a need to find more Pinny, and Limpit ought to come back and help me find some more.

"Without him here by my side, I will feel truly lost, and he has proven to be a reliable and worthy companion to have by one's side. You can send another Unimage through instead of yourself if you prefer to stay there, and I think it's time to let Princess Sallina and Szymon grow up as proper unicorns and not exist as humans. Let them remain at Starpoint, where they should lead the lives that they are already accustomed to."

There was a sudden rustle in the bushes ahead of them, and both Unimages and Roger turned their attention towards it. Roger headed over briskly and poked around as the two Unimages silently watched.

Hidden deep in the undergrowth was Limpit, eavesdropping on them as usual. He had tucked himself in well enough that Roger didn't notice him as he probed and parted some branches and foliage. Roger returned to his master and shook his head.

Relaxing, Barchester continued his discussion with the Professor.

"Of course, I have to be honest, Professor. These days I have little desire to return home. In some ways, I would prefer to live out the rest of my days here in solitude rather than return to Starpoint. Just like you, I much prefer to keep to myself and not become involved in all the weary affairs of Unimage leaders that fill their waking thoughts. But I feel I must return for now, as there is some work to be done if we intend to fix things."

Professor Tinzy nodded, "Then we are not all that different, you and I. We share the same burden of duty to our people."

"We have been friends for a very long time," Barchester remarked. He turned to his manservant. "Roger… you shall take good care of Professor Tinzy and make sure that he is kept safe and properly looked after. Mayla, of course, will remain here and also continue to find new Pinny. One day they will send for her, and she will come to Starpoint and see what it's like being a unicorn in our land. But for the present, she has plenty of things to be getting on with right here."

Roger didn't say anything as the conversation between the two Unimages continued for a while longer. He only nodded silently and pushed the wheelchair as required.

The rest of the walk proved to be quieter, and with the clouds building up and a light drizzle starting to take shape, both Professor Tinzy and Thomas Barchester decided to make their way back to the large house and thus avoid the rain.

Limpit had managed to pass by undetected, and he too returned to the house.

***

Just as expected, a package arrived around 1:30 pm, and they all gathered around the dining room table as Mayla opened it with care. She removed the small wooden box that was inside, and when she opened it, she was dazzled by the small amount of Pinny she found therein. It was incredible!

Thomas Barchester grinned. "We have it now… we must have enough Pinny for us to divert that horrible meteor. You are an absolute darling, my sweet Mayla. This Pinny will save us all. Starpoint owes you all a great debt of gratitude."

315

"Don't thank me," Mayla replied. "Thank the internet. Without the internet, this wouldn't have been possible. We live in a wonderful age in this world, where you can go anywhere and do anything in an instant. It's a bit like our magic. In some ways, it's even more powerful."

"So, when do we go?" Szymon said, raising the obvious question.

"Within the hour," Barchester said. "I will be going with you."

This took Princess Sallina by surprise.

"What about you, Professor?" she asked Tinzy.

"I'd best stay for a little while longer," he replied. "We have discussed it at length, and we both feel it's the correct course of action."

"Why? You have to come with us. We need you to deal with the Council."

"I would do so, but this is Unimage Barchester's turn, and he's more than capable of handling the Council. I'll be next, don't you worry."

"No!" Sallina exclaimed. "I won't go without you."

"Sallina, why don't you come and have a quiet word with me in private?"

Princess Sallina was rather tearful as she made her way over to the Professor.

"Let's step outside… this is something meant for our ears only."

They left the room, Thomas Barchester watching keenly.

"She'll be fine," he assured the others. "They are close to each other. They need a private moment."

Szymon was about to follow Professor Tinzy and Sallina out when Limpit flew over to hover directly in front of him and flapped his wings towards him.

"Thomas Barchester is right. Give her space—I'm sure things will be just fine."

Szymon reluctantly nodded and went no further.

Sallina and the Professor walked to the far end of the hallway, where they would hopefully not be overheard.

"You know I don't want to go back without you," the Princess said.

"I know that, Princess. But there are reasons I'm allowing Unimage Barchester to return instead of me. Firstly, he is the only one on the Council more senior than Unimage Callindra, and once he sees first-hand the likely outcomes of the Circle returning to power, he'll be on our side when the time comes. His previous years of loyal duty to the Council affords him that opportunity to redeem himself in the eyes of the other Unimages, and deal with the growing popularity of the Circle in the way it should be dealt with."

"How can you be certain it will make any difference?" she asked him. "You know he's been talking to them the entire time, and I don't trust him even a smidgeon. For all we know, he's completely on their side."

"But I know Barchester," Professor Tinzy remarked. "For all his trickery and often-conniving ways, his heart deep down is good, and his purpose to protect our people is pure. I believe in that, and something tells me he'll do the right thing.

"There are other reasons to factor in as well. You see, I'm not sure how well this spell will work on us elders, and we can't risk it on both of us. Your theory makes sense, and discovering it is incredible, but it remains untested. I, for one, cannot afford to take such a grave risk. My fear is that it may not work on those already exposed, and if I go and lose my mind any further than I already have, this will put the future of any search for Pinny in great jeopardy. If this Pinny we send back today is sufficient for the meteor, it still won't last all that long, and we will soon need to obtain more to keep things going back home."

Princess Sallina thought about this for a few moments.

"But you'll be left here by yourself. You and those humans."

"I won't be alone for long. Limpit will return as soon as he can, and I'm sure he'll keep me safe and guarded while we wait for your return. I won't let Limpit go back there for his own good, therefore I've instructed him to make his way back as soon as he sees you've made it across safely and you're not in any immediate danger."

Princess Sallina wasn't too happy with what she was hearing, but she couldn't deny that what the Professor was saying made sense. She had been so terrified when he had lost his mind before, and the last thing she wanted was for him to completely forget who he was. That would leave her all alone… with nobody she could really trust, apart from a miniature dragon who was bearing a few grudges that could one day resurface. Heaven knew what would happen then.

"How much does Unimage Barchester recall of his past?" she asked.

"At best, just a little. You see, I'm pretty sure I was the one who wrote those diaries so I could help him remember who he had once been. I recognise my own writing. Even today, his memories of his former self remain weak and cloudy most of the time, and in my deepest thoughts I fear there may not be much left of the great Unimage of old. But I do hope there's just enough to do what needs to be done and, if he so chooses, to be accepted back into the home he once knew."

"I didn't know you wrote all the diaries for Barchester."

"Yes, I'm sure of it now. I had to help him remember, and I helped him to fill in some of the blanks. He was the one who found the path to this strange place long ago, and he asked me to help him when he embarked on his initial set of journeys here. But he had already done many more travels before I even began to come over, and on each occasion, he lost a little more of his memory, despite his great magical powers and years of experience and wisdom.

"There is one secret I now must pass on to you, but you must promise me you will never tell anyone about it. It must remain with just the two of us. Promise me."

"I promise. What is it?" she asked him earnestly. She was intensely curious about what the Professor was going to share with her in confidence.

"The pendant you've been wearing, the one that gives you magic when you are here and can do all kinds of wonderful things…"

"Yes?" she asked.

"It previously belonged to him."

This took Princess Sallina by complete surprise.

"You mean, this *is his*?"

"It *was* his a very long time ago," the Professor replied. "But he doesn't remember it, luckily, and I purposely took out any mention of it from those diaries that I helped to write for him.

When I decided to pass it on to you, I knew it would serve you much better than it could ever serve him. A Unimage who cannot remember who he once was shouldn't be wearing the most powerful magic of all in Starpoint around his neck."

"The most powerful magic of all—"

"Yes—that's why it can work even without the aid of Pinny. It is the only magic to do so and frees the wearer from needing Pinny to cast any spells. In fact, it also acts as an enabler of Pinny, but that is limited and only within close range of the wearer. It takes powerful magic to extend this range, but even that is limited in what it can do. Only the bearer of the pendant possesses its true powers."

The Princess couldn't believe what she was hearing.

"But with Pinny," the Professor continued, "its power is truly immense. Combine it with Pinny, and the magic of the pendant can be both dangerous and destructive beyond what you can ever imagine. This is why others will covet it and try to take it away from you, and why Unimage Konstanty has kept his eye on it from the moment he realised where it was.

"Do not let anyone else see that you possess it, and always keep it close to you. It cannot be taken away from you without your consent; it must be freely given. Therefore, do not give it away to anyone for any reason whatsoever, no matter what it may be. It shall always protect you, and without your consent it will not be of use to anyone else anyway. It will just be an ordinary pendant worth very little to the wearer. Just a pleasant to look at decoration."

"But," Sallina muttered, astonished, "Unimage Konstanty… he took it away from me."

"He appeared to, but it didn't take long for it to find its way back to you. Such is the magical will of the pendant, that no matter what anyone tries, it will not leave its master unless its master wills it to go. It knew you wanted it back, so it found a way to come back to you. And it gave nothing of itself to anyone else, as you still wished it to be yours."

"So how did I get this pendant from Barchester?"

"Ah, well… When you cannot even remember who you are, it's not much to give away freely something you don't know much about. Unimage Barchester gave it to me of his own free will, and then I passed it on to you."

"What did you offer him in return for such a gift?"

"Oh, that's easy. Everything you see around you was my gift to him for giving me the pendant, to be his to use as he wished. He enjoys the house, Roger, his car… all of it… it was my generous gift to him, and these things are his for as long as he desires to have them."

"You mean, this was once all yours? You owned it all?"

"Well, in a way it still is. Thomas Barchester gets to use it as he wants; he lives in it, but the ownership of all you see around you remains mine. But none of it means anything to me, Princess. The only things that matter are those I care about and protecting unicorns back home. Never value things above and beyond those who you care about and seek only the good in magic. Possessing things beyond one's basic needs is never a good thing, as it leads to endless greed and makes those around you jealous of what you have that they don't. Never forget this.

"It is the same principle with magic. There is magic out there that is very powerful, but it's not good. Covet it for the sake of gaining power, and you may rise in self-importance, but you will never be truly content or in control. Good magic always comes with its limitations, and it only does what is necessary for the common good, not just to satisfy you."

"Now I'm getting totally confused," Sallina said. "You choose to live in your little house in Doberry and work as a professor in some local human school, when you have all this wealth and can do with it what you please?"

"But, my dear, the wealth you wear around your neck is far superior to all these material possessions. It's not what you have around you that counts; it's what you decide to do with it that really counts. Wealth can so easily be misleading and take one down the wrong paths in life, for what you see and what is real and of true value are rarely the same in any land I've known, whether we're here or back home in Starpoint."

Sallina didn't quite know what to make of these insights that Professor Tinzy was sharing with her. "I have so much to learn about life, I guess—I am still quite young."

"Yes, you do, but we never stop learning, none of us do. You are still young; you will make new and wondrous discoveries that will enrich your heart and your mind. Life has a way of teaching us these lessons when we least expect them, and sometimes these lessons can also be painful. And no matter how hurtful they may seem, treat such precious knowledge and awareness as true gifts that will help you in your journey through life and enrich you beyond anything material that you may acquire and one day must let go."

"I will miss you greatly, Professor. I will come back as quickly as I can if you don't return soon. I will not leave you on your own here."

"I shall miss you, too. One final thing, my dear… I do not fully trust Thomas Barchester, either. We must be prepared for whatever may happen when you return to Starpoint. This Pinny mustn't fall into the hands of the Circle; it must be shared fairly by all the Unimages and be seen as a gift to all who live in Starpoint from their generous and caring Queen, your mother."

"We shall prepare ourselves for whatever lies in store for us."

"That's a smart girl. I am so very proud of you," the Professor muttered. Despite the adulation, he was getting weary of the conversation. "You'll one day make a fine Queen."

Sallina went quiet for a moment, her mind racing ahead to the new dilemma they faced. How could they properly prepare themselves for the potential tricks the Circle might attempt to pull on them when they returned to the Professor's research laboratory back home? How could she control Barchester if he betrayed them and sided with the Circle? What traps still lay ahead of her, and could she really trust Szymon despite all her heart wanting to? But she had to cut short all the concerns that were sprouting in her mind and focus on just one thing: Starpoint had to be saved.

She was leaving the mission to find Pinny behind her for now and replacing it with something even more important. Going back was quickly turning into a rescue mission where they had to overcome the threat of the meteor set on destroying everything she cared about in her homeland, and she had to do her part to help save the lives of all her fellow unicorns.

"Focus," Sallina said to herself again and again. "Focus now."

Chapter 32

Two hours later, the party had assembled in Thomas Barchester's magic library room. Princess Sallina and Szymon were dressed in their least-favourite clothes, as they knew these would be lost forever upon their arrival and transformation back into unicorns.

Although Limpit wasn't too pleased to be travelling to Starpoint in the company of Thomas Barchester, the dragon was looking forward to returning home at last after a lengthy absence, even if it was just for a few minutes. He took some comfort from the fact that Princess Sallina and Szymon would also be going with him.

In the magic library, the orb stood lit up, waiting with an already hot and fiery flame of orange and red. Sallina and Szymon both knew that on the other side, a similar event was taking place, and most likely this was being managed by Szymon's father and Unimage Callindra.

Princess Sallina clasped the pendant, which lit up a bright blue. As had by now become a frequent sight for the others to behold, Sallina mumbled a spell under her breath that nobody could quite make out, and then the blue light of the pendant began to expand in size. The light then shot over to Thomas Barchester and enveloped him completely… and then just as fast, it disappeared.

"The fiery protection spell will now be active on you, too," Sallina said. "It will not last long, so you need to make use of it as soon as you possibly can."

"Then we'd better commence with Limpit's ritual at once!" Professor Tinzy hollered emphatically. "Once he exhales his flame, he will hold some of it back to travel through the tunnel and protect Unimage Barchester from suffering further memory loss whilst travelling. Timing will be essential here, as the flame needs to protect the Unimage constantly from suffering memory degradation. This is one worry I have if Limpit doesn't accompany Thomas and stay close to him: how will Limpit know exactly where in the tunnel the party is travelling?"

Limpit then, as before, took in a deep breath of air that filled up his lungs, and then with all the might he could muster, started to exhale his hot, incandescent flame towards the orb. It shot out of his mouth and headed directly towards the already-glowing orb, with the dragon's flame being sucked inside the less intense orange-and-red flames.

On the other side, in Starpoint, Unimage Callindra and Konstanty watched as once again the bright dragon flame burst out of their orb and for a few moments lit up the entire chamber.

The flame of the orb grew quickly and created what looked like a visible doorway leading back to the magic library, as it spewed out a deep sea-blue gaseous shape that replaced what was previously a bright and burning flame.

"We're back in business!" Barchester proclaimed triumphantly "The path home is open, and we are ready!

"Give me the Pinny, for it is time to make our journey," he commanded.

The Pinny, now in a small case, was being held in Professor Tinzy's hands.

Professor Tinzy glanced at Princess Sallina. "I think it will be better to keep it in Princess Sallina's possession, as we still don't know what effect the journey may have on your memories, Unimage Barchester. Once you're across, she can pass it to you."

The Unimage wasn't happy with this, but time was now ticking, and he dared not risk Limpit using up too much of his breath before they made it through.

"Very well then, as you insist," he said. "You can pass it back to me when we get to the other side. We'd best hasten our departure, as the door is currently open, and we have little time."

With this, Sallina and Szymon took one last glance at Professor Tinzy and then stepped through the tunnel. They were quickly followed by a hovering Limpit, with Thomas Barchester right beside him. The journey thus began.

As they whizzed through the tunnel, Thomas Barchester clung to Limpit's rear claws with both hands, and Limpit's fiery breath surrounded the Unimage, who was also being kept safe from the flame with the fire-protection spell that stopped him from being incinerated.

More importantly, Thomas Barchester managed to keep all his wits about him this time round—at least those wits he had managed to retain—as his physical body had begun to transform back into his previous unicorn shape, which was a feeling he hadn't experienced for quite a long while.

As Sallina and Szymon looked back, both Limpit and Unimage Barchester appeared directly behind them. Limpit still remained airborne, but it was evident that he had expended his last breath, as he hungrily sucked in fresh air to refill his now-empty lungs. He gasped and his nostrils puffed as he took in several deep breaths of air, and as he did, he swung from one side to the other, almost losing his ability to hover safely in the air. But a few flaps of his wings and he soon regained his flight composure.

At the other end of the room, Sallina and Szymon both could make out the forms of Unimage Konstanty and Callindra standing close by the large orb. And as if in a moment of déjà vu, a large net descended onto them, immediately preventing them from moving about of their own free will. Once again, they were trapped.

Unimage Barchester looked firmly at Unimage Konstanty as the net descended.

"Is that necessary? You're getting exactly what you want."

"I'm afraid it is," Konstanty replied, razor-sharp and fully alert. "We will take all the necessary precautions. There's much at stake."

But Sallina had half expected this, as had Szymon. Sallina's pendant lit bright blue and then several large cutting shears manifested out of nothing and started to tear into the rope. She had enacted a powerful cutting spell she had prepared in advance, and it had been especially tailored for the type of net she expected on their arrival. It wasn't long before there were enough rips in the net to allow both Sallina and Szymon to escape their confines with relative ease, and Limpit wasted no time in following through one of these gaps as well. The three of them took off from the chamber and raced past the surprised guards as they dashed to an open doorway that led to a corridor.

Suddenly, Unimage Barchester blurted out, "She's got my Pinny! Go after her!"

The escapees were already galloping down the corridor. "Come on!" Sallina cried. "We have to be quick!"

"You still got the Pinny?" asked Szymon breathlessly, feeling both terrified and excited at the same time.

"It's safely in my pouch—I can feel its presence."

As they arrived at the end of the corridor, a lone guard wearing the Royal Crest appeared, shocked by the sight of Princess Sallina and Szymon hurtling down the hallway on all four hooves towards him.

"Step aside, guard!" Sallina bellowed. "We are in an awful hurry and don't wish to be detained!"

The guard didn't know how to react, but his instinct immediately kicked in and he moved aside to let them pass by. It wasn't just the way she instructed him to move; it was also the fact that he stood in their way, and it didn't look like either was going to slow down, let alone stop.

At the end of the corridor, Sallina turned to see several of the Circle's guards in hot pursuit not far behind.

"We have to get rid of them soon, or there will be many more of these strange guards and we'll soon be cornered!" she shouted out, panting and tired from their tunnel trip and incredible physical transformation. She spotted a painting of her mother, Queen Noony, at the end of a cul-de-sac corridor.

"Watch! Follow me closely! I know where we are."

Sallina leaped into the painting and Szymon followed her, wondering what she was doing but not daring to hesitate for a moment, whilst Limpit flew straight through what turned out to be a hollow image made of light. As they landed on the other side and felt solid ground under their hoofs, they found themselves in an even darker corridor that a moment ago hadn't even existed.

"Let's not hang about here," Sallina urged. "They'll soon work out where we've gone. We're fortunate the guards chasing us don't know these corridors as well as I do."

On the other side of the hologram painting, the Circle guards had come to an abrupt halt, trying to ascertain where their quarry had vanished. Galloping into the hallway, Unimage

Konstanty quickly assessed the confused situation, trotting up to the image of Queen Noony and making a closer examination. He poked his hoof at the painting and to his surprise, it went all the way through. He realized then that it was just an illusion.

"What are you waiting for? Go find them NOW!" Konstanty said fiercely.

The Circle guards immediately leapt into action and jumped through the large painting, but by the time they landed on the other side, Princess Sallina, Szymon, and Limpit were already long gone.

Unimage Callindra caught up with Unimage Konstanty, who was chuckling to himself as he looked at the painting of Queen Noony.

"What's so funny?" Callindra asked.

"Oh, I was just thinking about that painting. If I were Princess Sallina, where would I run if I found myself back in the castle? Do you think she may have given us a clue without realising it?"

Callindra looked at him quizzically, then at the holographic painting. Then she got the message. She let out a sharp chortle herself, which sent shivers down the spines of the remaining guards close by; it grated even on Konstanty as a most unpleasant sound, but he tried not to show her how annoying it was.

"Of course, she would. Why don't we go pay a visit to Mother Dear?" Unimage Callindra said sarcastically. "Been a while since I last dropped by."

"I think, Callindra, you'll find it's a lot faster to get there through this hidden corridor," Konstanty added, pointing at the painting.

"I'm not going through that dreadful thing," Callindra rasped. "You can go through it if you want, but there's no way I'm letting that silly Queen pass through my entire body! I would feel violated."

"Well, as you wish," Konstanty said, taking off and jumping through the painting without further thought.

"Foolhardy Unimage," Callindra muttered to herself. "He's still got a few things to learn about proper conduct and appearance. What would the guards think if I suddenly jumped into the Queen? My goodness, the thought of it is truly dreadful!"

Callindra knew that Konstanty would beat her to the chambers of Queen Noony, but that didn't bother her that much. She would soon capture this petulant young unicorn, and then she would retrieve the Pinny to serve her own needs.

***

Queen Noony was seated on a chair, knitting a unicorn jumper for her dear daughter, who she was looking forward to seeing some time soon, when the back door in the other room opened and she heard sudden movement. She rose on her hind legs and made her way to the room as she landed on all fours. To her surprise, she found her daughter and Szymon standing there looking for someone.

"My dearest girl, you've come back!" the Queen exclaimed with wild excitement. "Oh, my goodness. Is everything good, or are you in trouble?"

"No, I mean, yes," Sallina replied. "You must come with me right now—it's really not safe in here. There will be a horde of Circle guards arriving any second, and we cannot stand still even for one moment to explain anything to you."

"Why, you must be in a serious pickle!"

"Not right now, Mother—we have to leave at once. Why aren't you listening to what I'm telling you?"

"What about my knitting? I can't just leave all this behind."

"Yes, you can. You will! We can pick it up later, for goodness' sake. Mother, pull yourself together now. We have far more important things to do than knitting whatever it is. Something's wrong with you. How can you be so lacking in everything?"

"Very well then, let's go. I'm not lacking in anything, dear."

Queen Noony hastily followed her daughter as they left her chambers and made their way along various smaller corridors and across several secret routes that had been scarcely used over the years. After climbing numerous steps, they arrived inside a large meeting room in one of the smaller castle turrets, which was seldom used anymore.

There were no less than 384 steps up this turret, which left them all out of breath—except for Limpit, of course! He simply levitated his way upwards with hardly any effort.

"Why are we even in here?" the Queen asked, trying to catch hold of her breath.

"The time has come, Mother," Sallina calmly replied between taking deep breaths of air. "We must put a stop to that meteor and restore Starpoint to its former self, and we must do it properly without being fooled by those who seek to benefit from it."

"How can we do that?" Queen Noony asked her, surprised. "We don't yet have what we need, do we? We're waiting for the Council to sort this out."

"We do have what we need," Sallina replied. She allowed the small case with Pinny to lift out of her pouch and hover directly in front of her. The case opened to reveal the Pinny, which started to glow. "There's enough here to shake that rock and push it off somewhere else away from us."

"Oh, my goodness me!" Queen Noony exclaimed. "You brought us back more lovely Pinny!"

"Oh yes, and Professor Tinzy believes it to be enough to successfully divert that meteor and stop it from destroying all of Starpoint."

Queen Noony had always been fascinated with the mystical powers of Pinny, but then she caught sight of the pendant around Sallina's neck that was glowing a bright blue and became transfixed by that as well. Pinny was the enabler of all magic, and there was Pinny inside that pendant. What was incredible was that the Pinny inside this pendant never got used up; it had lasted for centuries. Think about it! *Never.*

"Is that what I think it to be? Behold, another wonder before me!"

"Yes, it is."

"You possess the Starpoint pendant. You are so full of surprises, my dear girl."

Szymon had had enough of all the polite chitter-chatter and wanted to move the conversation along at a much faster pace.

"It's all well and good for you two be catching up—with all due respect, your Majesty—but we have to right now call together a Council meeting and announce to all the Unimages that we are in a position to take on the meteor and stop it from bringing us any harm."

"Yes, we should do that at once," Queen Noony agreed, but she was still thinking about how she could even make such a thing possible. In her traditional role as Queen, she would have no trouble calling a Council meeting and having the Council members gather even on short notice, but she did not have the authority at present, given her enforced incarceration. She was virtually a prisoner in her own home, and she had temporarily forfeited her rights.

She was pondering this dilemma when someone appeared at the top of the stairs and entered the room. Queen Noony turned to see Unimage Paterline, accompanied by Unimage Barchester.

"Oh, goodness me. Now I'm seeing pale ghosts as well!" Queen Noony almost shrieked as she spoke.

"I'm afraid they've found us!" Szymon cried out in surprise. "There's nowhere left for us to run to."

"Calm yourself, my boy," Barchester said. "We are both here to help you. Despite what you may have thought of me, I was never overly fond of those dreaded Circle followers, and I'm certainly not intending to stand by and do absolutely nothing whilst these devious schemers take over and find a way to make a sordid mess of everything we know and hold dear."

"How do we stop them, then?" Szymon asked Barchester. "They have too many guards already in the royal castle, and they are pretty much controlling the entire city."

"Yes, but we don't need to stop them at this precise moment in time—that's not our current aim. We need to halt that meteor first, and if we can halt a great big nasty meteor, then the entire city will owe us a tremendous debt of gratitude, and the Circle will find it a lot more difficult to impose their sinister will upon the heroes who came to the rescue."

"How can we trust you?" Sallina asked the old Unimage openly. "I do not trust you even a tiny bit."

"Well, you are entitled not to trust me if you like; I can understand how you may feel about me. But do understand this. I knew of the things you took from my library of magic a few days ago, and I didn't attempt to prevent your pursuits. Since you stepped foot in the house, I have carefully observed your every movement. You see, my dear, I have always been unflinchingly loyal to Unimage Tinzy, or should I say, Professor Tinzy. He and I, we both go a long way back… in fact, I owe him my life. In fact, everything."

"Then why did you discuss things with the Circle if you are so loyal to the Professor?" Sallina asked, cross-examining him.

"Because, my dear, it is often wiser to know things about your enemy from within than try to work out what they're up to when you're sitting on the outside. By doing so, you can intently study what their true intentions are, and be able to anticipate their next movements. Thereby, one can take the necessary steps to challenge and eventually overcome them."

Szymon shook his head in dismay and stepped to the side to whisper to Sallina, "He's much better at this than me, and I convinced my father I was still on his side. To be perfectly honest, I wouldn't believe a single word he tells us. He has shown himself to be conniving and truly devious, and I don't, not for one second, believe he is on our side."

Limpit coughed unexpectedly and let out a small belch of flame that helped to re-focus everyone's attention. Limpit had eavesdropped on the conversation, and he joined them and began to whisper just out of Unimage Barchester's earshot.

"I believe Unimage Barchester," Limpit said. "I secretly tailed him a few days ago in the gardens when he was gabbing with the Professor, and I overheard their conversation. It is my considered opinion that Thomas Barchester may be absentminded at times, there's no question of that, but he has never—as far as I recall—made any moves against the wishes of the Professor, and he has always acted in the best interests of Starpoint's many inhabitants."

Princess Sallina thought about this frank and straightforward assessment for a lingering moment.

"If Limpit trusts this foolish old Unimage, I suppose it's good enough for me. Let's see if the old timer's is truly willing to help us." Then she turned to Barchester and addressed him with an unusual level of assertiveness, as if she was in charge. "What we need to know, Unimage Barchester, is how can we go about calling a Council meeting so we can take swift measures against that oncoming meteor."

"Ah, well, that's where I may be of some use. In my traditional role as a Council head, I am still permitted to call the meeting to order if I so desire—even it has been some years since I had served in that capacity. I'm an honorary member of the Council and was its legitimately appointed head for an awfully long time. Therefore, I shall call an emergency meeting within the next couple of hours, and since it will be an instruction initiated by me, they are duty-bound to come."

"Then let's hold this meeting!" Queen Noony declared triumphantly. "We need to make it happen."

Chapter 33

The call went out far and wide across the city and beyond to all able Council members to reconvene for a special emergency meeting. Those who couldn't for justifiable reasons, such as ill health or other pressing matters, were excused, as it was on very short notice. Eyebrows were swiftly raised when it was declared the call had been made by none other than Unimage Barchester and inscribed on the Royal stationery of Queen Noony. Who could dare question the urgent wishes of the Queen acting in unison with a previous head of the Council, especially one who was still highly revered and a true legend among unicorns?

Many unicorns wanted to see Unimage Barchester in the flesh and bone, as they could scarcely believe that he had returned after such a protracted absence from his public duties. Many wondered what had happened to him during all these years, but now wasn't the time to be questioning the past; now was the time to find a way to find a way to help fix the future.

Alongside the call for the emergency meeting came the welcome news that more Pinny had been brought over to Starpoint and was being carefully placed in the alicorns to start to return everyone's lives to normalcy. The citizens of Starpoint were immediately overjoyed to learn that by nightfall there would be no less than three fully functioning alicorns enabling the use of magic across the realm once again.

But nothing ever turns out to be that easy. Despite the recent good news, there were those who soon questioned the ability of Unimage Barchester and the Council to use the power of the three Alicorns to successfully deflect the impending threat of the meteor. "Will there be enough Pinny to do the job? How powerful is the old Council, and can they stop that huge meteor from striking with the limited supply they presently have?"

These worries were sitting heavily on many unicorns' minds, not the least of whom were Princess Sallina and Unimage Szymon, who had both been invited to the Council chamber meeting that was being held later that day. They found themselves seated in the back as they watched this great gathering of Unimages, who, on such short notice, had converged in the grand meeting room.

At the head of the table was Queen Noony. Unimage Callindra and Unimage Konstanty sat together to one side, both preoccupied with whispering secrets to each other, and Szymon was asking himself what it was they were so preoccupied with.

In the middle of the room, Unimage Barchester stood firmly, and he looked around the room at his fellow Unimages. Queen Noony had taken command of the proceedings as she thumped the table with a hammer to attract everyone's attention and stop them all from chattering to each other. The room quickly fell silent.

"The time has now come for us to use the powers we have at our disposal in order to successfully divert the meteor from striking Starpoint and thereby threatening our very existence," Queen Noony majestically stated.

"Who do we pick to lead our gently woven spellcasting, which will avert the historic threat we all face by the gigantic meteor?" Konstanty enquired, in what amounted to a rather casual manner. It was as if had just ordered his favourite tea with a precise description on what temperature it needed to be served at.

As he spoke, four Unicorn guards entered the room with a large orb that rested on a board and hovered a mere couple of feet in the air. The orb was carefully placed in the centre of the room. Limpit appeared on the other side, and Unimage Barchester gave him a nod. Limpit exhaled his fiery breath, and this lit the orb as the Unimages around the table looked upon him with utter astonishment and surprise.

"You dare to bring a dragon into our sacred room!" Unimage Konstanty bellowed in disgust. "It's a grievous insult to the entire Council."

Queen Noony raised her right front hoof. "Let's not get so ahead of ourselves, Unimage Konstanty. Limpit has been summoned at my personal request. You will understand why it matters in a moment. Be a little patient—it's a wise quality for one to possess in such delicate times, and one cannot have too much of a good thing."

A couple of minutes passed, and the fire revealed a face. It was a human face, and it was Unimage Tinzy, or Professor Tinzy, as he was now widely known.

There was a tsunami of confused whispers across the large room between the Unimages and this was coupled with several looks of astonishment.

"Who is this Tinzy, really?"

"Is that really *the* Professor Tinzy who addresses us?"

"What have they done to him? This one's an impostor."

"He looks so different, more shrivelled."

"He must be very ill. Poor soul, it truly looks like a painful condition."

And more.

Queen Noony raised her front right hoof again. "I want silence in the room!" The room quickly fell silent.

Unimage Konstanty and Unimage Callindra were still whispering to each other when the face of Professor Tinzy transformed itself back into his unicorn shape in the fire. Then Professor Tinzy addressed the Council with a level of concentration not seen from him in quite some time. This was the old Professor everyone had known, and the stories of endurance, heroism, and selflessness that they remembered upon hearing his authoritative and reassuring voice infused everyone with optimism and fresh hope.

"I am sorry I cannot be here with you in my original unicorn form. I remain in this faraway land that helped us to find Pinny because we intend to bring you even more, which is sorely needed. Today is a truly momentous day. Today, we hopefully can find the way to stop the meteor from posing a danger to us all. Today, we can create an incredibly powerful spell that will stop this meteor from raining its destruction onto all of us and destroying our homes. Today is the day we take back control of our own lives and our destiny. The power to improve our lives rests with all unicorns, and those who are chosen to lead us carry a burden of responsibility that no unicorn can afford to take lightly."

Some sporadic cheering followed in the room, as a few of the Unimages appeared quite pleased by what Professor Tinzy had just said.

"I on my own am unable to bring about such change," Professor Tinzy continued. "Therefore, I have asked my good friend Unimage Barchester to perform the spell for all of us. I ask you all to join in the spellcasting when we evocate this powerful spell, as united and together we will possess the means to avert a terrible disaster, whereas divided and fighting with each other we will only end up defeating ourselves. We need to act together; it's the only way we can outsmart this hideous monster."

The moment of silence that followed was eventually broken by Unimage Callindra. "There is no spell that can put a stop to that meteor," she blurted out, not afraid to challenge the almost universally revered Unimage Tinzy. "How do you expect us to believe you possess such a powerful spell? Why didn't you show it to us before if that is the case? Why'd it take so terribly long to tell us about this, and why do you choose to do it now, when it's so late in the day and the meteor is just around the corner?"

Professor Tinzy knew that Unimage Callindra was extremely clever and far more cutting than the sharpest blade, which is why he had carefully thought about the questions she'd likely be firing at him when he made his virtual appearance in the grand meeting room. The fact that he wasn't present could be considered a weakness in attempting to triumph against the powerful and relentless meteor, but he had confidence in the wisdom of the other Unimages and believed that they'd end up doing the right thing without him being there in the flesh, not just allow themselves to sheepishly follow another elder based on an agenda that hadn't been made clear. What troubled him the most was that he alone didn't possess the power to cast the spell to beat the meteor. It would require the united efforts of most, and most likely all, of the Unimages present to activate the powerful magic needed to effectively eliminate the threat.

Professor Tinzy cleared his throat before he spoke. "There was an old spell that I had almost forgotten and have recently revisited. It holds the power to make powerful magic traverse such vast distances, which is required to reach out to the meteor. I have the spell in my thoughts, and it is time. Hopefully, together we will successfully cast the spell to dispel this horrendous threat we all face and either crush the meteor out of existence or at least divert it from its present path… a path that is leading this enormous lump of matter directly to our homes.”

Unimage Callindra saw this as her opportunity to step in with some open criticism. “‘Hopefully’… why is everything ‘hopefully’ with you? If you fail now when you cast this spell, you’ll only end up diminishing our pitifully short supply of precious Pinny that we have found and put all of us in even greater danger. Nobody wants to go back to what we’ve just endured in past days, when our Pinny was so terribly low.”

“You mean the Pinny supply Princess Sallina found and succeeded in bringing back upon her recent return?” Professor Tinzy quipped wryly. “I want to be clear about who is doing what… We are all to be credited for casting this powerful spell here today and, if we are successful, each playing our part. But it was Princess Sallina who first set us on the path to finding the Pinny. Without her able assistance, none of us would even be here to try and prevent the meteor from continuing its path towards Starpoint.”

“Ah, you’re referring to the Pinny supply that my son also brought back with him,” Unimage Konstanty chimed in assertively. “You’ll find a lot of this was down to my expert direction and his good sense to follow my instructions as closely as he could. I am extremely proud of my son’s pivotal role in securing Pinny, which wouldn’t have been possible without his able assistance and the support of certain Unimages who are also present in this room. These are the few who are standing up in this time of utmost peril. I refer of course to the esteemed Circle and the Unimages who serve it with complete devotion, as well as total commitment to preserving and protecting our great land. We have kept things going during our time of distress and managed to make do with what little we had.”

There were a few sudden gasps in the room as Unimage Konstanty stood up on his back legs, and so did Unimage Callindra. But they were not alone. A few moments later, Unimage Snimminz stood up as well, and for the first time Professor Tinzy realized there were more than two members of the Circle operating in the Unimages' Council. Unimage Lommunar then slowly rose, struggling to his hind legs. As he was the oldest in the Council, nobody had any idea that he too had been a member of the Circle. This revelation was even more shocking to the Professor. It looked like the Circle had successfully infiltrated the Council and were already in charge. At its present rate, it wouldn't be long before the Circle and Council became indistinguishable from one another.

It was Unimage Lommunar this time who cleared his throat. "You see, Professor Tinzy, the Circle has been at the heart of all that has been recently done to protect our land, and it is the only true explanation as to how we have Pinny here. We have the chance to cast our curious spell and send that meteor packing. Tell me, Professor, precisely where did this spell come from in the first place? We'd like to know a little more about it."

Professor Tinzy was wary about responding to a direct question. He was averse to lying, especially when it came to addressing Queen Noony and the Council, where he felt a clear duty to be direct and always tell them the truth. "I came across this spell in a foreign land. A faraway foreign land that was hard to travel to, and hard to return from."

"Sounds like a load of mumbling about some nonsense. Tell me, Professor, where, precisely, is this land?" Unimage Lommunar continued with the line of questioning.

Professor Tinzy felt reluctant to answer the question, but he also believed he had little choice but to try, as it was his sworn duty to speak openly to the Council before him that had gathered at the specific request of Unimage Barchester.

"It's in a land called Earth. There's an island in the land called England, and on the island there's a much smaller place called Doberry. The spell was in the care of Unimage Barchester, and was discovered in his magic library, carefully tucked up in his safe."

This suddenly got several tongues wagging and the Unimages started to whisper amongst themselves as they pondered the latest news.

It was Unimage Barchester who then called for order, as he cleared his throat and stood up on his hind legs, looking as authoritative as he could.

"Yes, it has been securely kept in my safe," Barchester openly confessed. "But I had forgotten it was even there, which was such a terrible thing. Fortunately, I asked the Professor to carefully review my various notes and diaries that I was accustomed to keeping in detail, and he duly did. It was purely by chance that he came across the spell, but it is also extremely fortuitous for us that he did find it in this hour of need. We are all grateful that he is so diligent in his endeavours and pays such close attention to details."

Unimage Callindra sat back down, and the other Circle members did likewise.

"Ah," Callindra said. "You see, Professor? Unimage Barchester has been an appointed advisor to the Circle for some time, and he had been acting under our instructions all along. So, even with this spell you bring before us, it looks like it was the Circle who in fact provided the opportunity to protect us from the meteor."

Unimage Barchester nodded in acceptance, but he was not fooled by Unimage Callindra's striking remarks. She always had this way of turning things around and making herself the one who was always on form.

"Yes, I've been supporting the Circle—and all Starpoint, for that matter—as much as I could, as I wanted to ensure we were protected from the meteor. But, fellow unicorns, now is the time for us to come together as one and thwart the menace attacking us from space. We must act in unison, not behave as if we're all members of different orders doing things separately. Unity in this perilous hour remains our main strength, and this is surely not the time to be quibbling amongst ourselves. Divided we are weaker, and we may yet fail."

"Well spoken, Unimage Barchester," Professor Tinzy commended him. "Very well spoken. Are we ready to cast the spell? Unimage Barchester will now disseminate the spell instructions to the Council for us to proceed."

With this, Unimage Barchester produced a pouch of papers, and each paper flew out of the pouch and landed directly on the desk of every single Unimage present in the room.

As this took place, Princess Sallina and Szymon noticed something unusual was going on in the background. Whilst the

Unimages had been talking, many more guards had entered the room, but these guards were not wearing the Royal crest. In fact, they had a different crest that looked like they were serving the Circle, since this had a round circle with a single alicorn horn drawn on it. They had seen this crest several times before as they'd attempted to get away from the Circle. Both right away sensed that their presence in the chamber foreboded trouble.

Sallina nudged Szymon. "Something's not right here," she whispered to him. "Why are the Circle guards now outnumbering the Royal guards in the room? I'd best speak to the Queen right this minute."

"How can you?" Szymon whispered back. "We're about to enact a great spell—it'll cause too much commotion and it may ruin the enchantment. You heard what was just said. We must do this together or we stand to fail."

Princess Sallina looked towards the Unimages and the Queen and she knew that Szymon was right, though in her heart she also knew something very strange was going on, and that it could place all of them in much greater danger at any time.

Once all the Unimages had reviewed the spell, Unimage Barchester and Professor Tinzy began making the incantation, reciting several of the verses in a strange language no one present had ever heard before. This was an old spell from a very long time ago, and it was based on a unicorn language that hadn't been spoken out loud for hundreds of years.

Princess Sallina and Szymon watched from the back of the chamber as not far from the orb an image of the meteor hurtling through space and heading in their direction came into view. Unimage Barchester looked up in horror as he saw the meteor continuing to make its way toward Starpoint.

Barchester and Professor Tinzy continued with the complex incantation and were now joined by the other Unimages. As Sallina looked around the room, she noticed that Unimage Konstanty and Unimage Callindra were once again whispering to each other and not taking the incantation as seriously as the others. She looked towards Unimage Lommunar, who was also watching silently, along with Unimage Snimminz.

"The Circle members appear to be holding back for some reason," Szymon whispered. "They're all up to something. My father included."

Princess Sallina rose to her feet and made her way over to the Queen. The Queen was keeping an eye on the Unimages when she was distracted by four Circle guards who suddenly appeared close by her side.

As Princess Sallina took a few further steps towards her mother, she was stopped by two Circle guards who blocked her by standing in her way. Szymon quickly jumped to his feet and headed toward the Princess, but he too was prevented from coming closer by a Circle guard who got in his way.

This annoyed Limpit, who was starting to get worked up from observing what was going on, and his nostrils started flaring with fire. Princess Sallina shook her head as she eyed Limpit, indicating that this wasn't the right time to do anything rash that might prevent the spell from being successfully enacted.

Thomas Barchester looked up at the meteor while reciting the verses. The participating Unimages were putting all their efforts into supporting the incantation, and Barchester could see that the meteor was in fact slowing down, as it wasn't spinning as fast as it did before.

"The spell. Look! It's working," Barchester gasped. He glanced around the room and for the first time noticed that the Circle Unimages were not participating with the incantation.

Unimage Callindra had risen to her feet and taken a few short steps toward Queen Noony. Standing before the monarch, she gave her a disconcerting look.

"This is now officially Unimage business," Callindra said coldly to the Queen. "We do not need you present now. You will be escorted back to your chambers, where you will stay until we have need of you again."

Queen Noony was truly shocked. "How dare you speak to me in such a tone? I am the reigning Queen, and you all answer to me. Each of the Unimages answers to me. I am the one in charge."

Unimage Callindra smirked. "Actually, we don't anymore. Starpoint is now under the direct control of the Council, and the

Council is being led by the wisdom of the Circle, so it is I who am in charge, along with my mentor, Unimage Lommunar. Even this powerful ancient spell dates back to a period when the Circle was in charge. You see, we are back."

Queen Noony looked over toward Unimage Lommunar, who was studying her. Then he spoke up, softly but emphatically.

"The age of the Circle has now returned after a very long absence, and Starpoint will in the future be ruled directly by the Circle once again, not by yourself or this pathetically weak and unimaginative Council of fools who have no clue what they are doing."

"You must stop the meteor, or we shall all be destroyed," Queen Noony insisted, appeared to suddenly return to her former self. Not only were the Circle members not participating anymore, but they were also causing a distraction that was putting off the others who were trying hard to incant the spell.

Professor Tinzy had noticed something else was going on back in the chamber but dared not break the spell, so he was keeping his focus fully on the incantation. The other participating Unimages were doing likewise, but it was getting increasingly difficult to block out what was going on around them.

However, at the same time, the Professor was casting some of his thoughts directly to Sallina, who suddenly heard his voice echo inside her hand.

"Princess, it's me, it's the Professor. I am using what little reserve energy I have left to ask you to do something to help us get through this enchantment. If the other Unimages don't unite right at this moment, we will be unable stop the meteor and we will all be doomed. You must do something! Do not hesitate to take decisive action or all will be lost."

Princess Sallina looked at the Circle guards who stood around her, realizing it was almost impossible for her to manoeuvre around them. She could also see how helpless her mother was as she was being impertinently addressed by Unimage Callindra, who was now joined by Unimage Konstanty. They clearly had the upper hoof.

"You'd best depart from this chamber." Unimage Konstanty spoke sternly to her, and Queen Noony didn't know what to say in response. The only thing she could think of was that her being there wasn't helping anyone, so she decided. She turned her head away and left, escorted by the Circle guards. She didn't want to be the reason that the spell failed, so she decided to go and confront the impertinent Circle members later.

As she took a few strides away, she stopped and turned to address Unimage Callindra. "At the very least, support the Professor and Unimage Barchester at this crucial time, or there will be nothing left for anyone to rule. You cannot rule nothing, can you? No matter how important you think you are. Do not place yourself above all those you lead. At the end of it, you are merely their servant— you'd be wise to remember that."

She exited the grand meeting room without saying another word.

Princess Sallina watched helplessly as her mother departed. Szymon decided he had had enough of the underhand tactics being enacted by those who sought their own interests above those of the herd. He quickly skirted the guard who was blocking him and stepped up to the Princess.

"We've got to stop them from taking control of everything— they're not just being a nuisance, they're downright dangerous," Szymon whispered to her. But he was already too late; his father was standing by his side, looking down at him darkly.

"You've become a regular disappointment to me. There's still a lot that I need to instruct you about how to properly conduct your affairs."

"You have to help the Professor, or he won't have enough power to stop the meteor from destroying us," the Princess pleaded. Unimage Konstanty looked at her and nodded.

"Oh, we will, but first things first, my dear. The meteor isn't the only major issue we face in this chamber. There are other important things at stake."

Konstanty made his way to Unimage Barchester and faced him directly as Barchester continued with the recitation.

"Unimage Barchester. If you desire the support of the Circle, you will need to go back to that strange human place you like so much and promise us you will never ever come here again. You will allow yourself to be banished there forever."

Konstanty continued, "This had better be the last we ever see or hear of you, or you will have broken your Unimage oath we now insist you make. And you can take that pesky Princess and my ill-behaved son along with you, as far as I'm concerned. We will provide you with further instructions on bringing back more Pinny when we need it. In the future, I foresee a steady supply coming through that will more than replenish our stock of enablement magic, and for this you will have done something useful for a change."

Barchester struggled to comprehend what was going on while trying to retain focus on the incantation, but it was clear the Circle had chosen this moment to present their terms, knowing that by not helping, they would most likely render the spell to stop the meteorite obsolete.

"Nod now if you agree," Konstanty instructed. "Remember, you will be oath bound as a Unimage, and you will never be able to return. Careful what you decide. A lot is at stake."

As Konstanty spoke, Barchester peered over at Unimage Lommunar. He still couldn't believe that such a wise and respectable Unimage was part of this devious and wicked Circle of self-interested, power-hungry usurpers. It was such a terrible pity that someone so wise was willing to shortchange his principles for short-term gains in enhancing his power and influence over others. Barchester had always wanted to believe that unicorns, unlike humans, had mastered their greed and wicked desires to control others, but clearly, he had been wrong. His kind were just as bad—maybe even worse—than humans he had encountered.

How could anyone entertain the notion of allowing total annihilation to be secondary to one's personal ambitions and thirst for power and glory? No sane unicorn would entertain such a reckless notion and put the very survival of everyone after their own ambitions, but here they were. They obviously believed they were in the right and knew what was in the best interest of all others in the herd. Not only that, their shortsightedness was also a threat to the future survival of everyone in the land.

"Very well," Barchester mumbled before continuing quickly with the incantation. "I will agree under oath."

"One further small thing as well," Konstanty added. "You will take good care of my son as if he is your own—you must promise me this. I do not wish to see him back here again for an exceptionally long time. He is far too weak, and I have no time to correct such despicable weakness. I have important work to do, and I've concluded that I cannot trust him.

"It might be better if Princess Sallina stays with us for her own safety; therefore, she will not be allowed to go back. We will keep a close eye on her from now on and lock her up along with her mother. Those two together are no good together— they have a habit of getting in the way. I don't think they are needed here anymore, so they will be retired."

Barchester nodded without breaking his spell, but he was not happy.

"And the final thing is that you will inform all those here in Starpoint that it was the Circle who brought the Pinny back and it was the Circle who stopped the meteor on this day from destroying them. You will give us all the credit we so rightfully deserve and have worked hard to reclaim. Without the aid of the Circle, there is no Council and there is no Starpoint, is that clear? Credit should go where it deserves."

Barchester looked like he was in pain from agreeing to this last selfish demand, but his focus was still on the incantation being directed at the meteor. He knew the ramifications of what Konstanty was demanding were that Starpoint would fall completely into the hands of the dreaded Circle, and the Council would end up simply becoming a mouthpiece and instrument of the will of those who now sought to lead it.

This was truly a terrible situation, but it was still far better than everyone being destroyed by the meteor and the end of Starpoint and the existence of unicorns. One crisis demanded their immediate intervention and there was no other way out of it, whereas he and Professor Tinzy still had some time to fix the other rising threat to the herd no matter how terrible it now seemed.

Princess Sallina had diverted her attention to what was going on with Unimage Barchester, but there remained little she could do as she was surround by Circle guards. She tried to move herself towards Barchester, but a couple of the guards blocked her, and she had no choice but to remain still and observe what was taking place between Barchester and Konstanty. She watched as Unimage Barchester continued with his incantation, and Konstanty and Callindra, now satisfied with what they had wanted, casually returned to their table.

Limpit had seen quite enough of all the ruckus and now decided to take matters into his own hands, or rather, paws.

Limpit flew over the heads of the guards and went right above Unimage Barchester. He wanted to speak to Barchester, but the old Unimage was still far too caught up with his incantation.

Limpit was about to go charging towards Unimage Konstanty and Callindra when he saw them start to recite the incantation of the spell. He looked towards Princess Sallina, who was eying him and shaking her head as she realized that the dragon was angry and could potentially ruin everything.

"No Limpit, DON'T!" she cried out and Limpit heard and stopped as he hovered quietly in the air.

As all the Unimages of the Circle began to join in the incantation, they together grew louder, and the chorus of their voices became more distinct.

Professor Tinzy, Unimage Barchester, and all the members of the Circle increased the intensity of the incantation, and the whole room started to appear distorted. Nothing around Limpit was clearly visible anymore, such was the power of the incantation.

Above Unimage Barchester, the meteor continued hurtling toward Starpoint, but it seemed to spin more and more slowly as the spell grew in its magnificent intensity. Several more Circle guards now piled into the grand meeting room, taking their stations.

Moments later, it was as if all the papers with the words of the spell were set on fire, and the meteor above Unimage Barchester was facing a powerful gust of howling wind so intense that it turned the brown and red of the meteor into a gigantic space-ball of blue ice.

Outside in the city, the three pinny-powered alicorns were now brightly lit up and working at full intensity. The incantation grew even louder and more intense, and it seemed like everyone in the city of Starpoint could hear it. The castle was lit up in bright blue, and this powerful force of energy that began to emanate from the alicorns and the castle fired up into the evening sky. It was the brightest blue light anyone had ever seen. It was as wide as five buildings, and it shot high into the sky as it made its way toward the oncoming meteor out there in space.

And high above the sky, the meteor had now stopped spinning as it was surrounded by this bright blue light.

Now, even the Circle guards appeared to be perplexed as the grand meeting room lit up with bright, radiant blue. Such was the spectacle of light, that all those who were present and saw it were entranced and in awe.

Saying something under her, breath Princess Sallina tightly clasped her necklace, which emitted a separate, bright-white light.

She took a few careful steps forward whilst the others looked like they were caught up in their incantations and made her way over to Szymon. Facing Szymon, she reached out to him with her voice.

"Come, we must get away from here. It's not safe for us in Starpoint anymore; they are already too powerful, and once this spell is done, they'll banish you and imprison me with my mother. We have no choice but to stick together, as united we stand a chance to deal with this another time."

"But," Szymon responded, "I don't want to go back. I want to stay here and fight my father. He can't be allowed to get away with what he's doing."

"We must go back to the Professor," she replied. "When this is all over, they'll need us to get more Pinny, and Limpit must also return before he is trapped here, and the pathway is once again sealed. We are not meant to be here in Starpoint right now. We are both destined to be exiled, whether we like it or not. Don't you see? The Pinny is the secret to wielding power in Starpoint. The Circle has been exploiting us for it, and for now they have succeeded. However, if we can find a way to control the Pinny, we can one day reclaim the upper hoof. The only way to fight these fools is from the outside in, not from the inside out."

Szymon reluctantly nodded.

Sallina looked towards Limpit. "You need to go back as well, Limpit—the Professor is waiting for you. Return the way you came and wait for us by the forest where I first appeared. I will travel a little later in the tunnel, which will take Szymon and myself there, as there is still something we must do before I can join you. Do not keep the path open after you go. SHUT IT AT ONCE, or others may follow you."

Limpit, unsure but responsive, nodded and flapped his wings.

Sallina and Szymon made their way out of the grand meeting room. Limpit returned to the cauldron in the room and vanished back into the flame he had come from, returning to his point of origin.

Konstanty caught them leaving in the corner of his eye, but he was now so engrossed in the incantation of the spell they were conjuring that he dared not remove his focus. Any slight deviation could effectively ruin the spell, and this was perhaps the only time they would all be gathered to destroy or avert the meteor. It was the same with the other members of the Circle, including Unimage Callindra.

Once Sallina and Szymon were safely outside the room, the two of them fled away down the steps, almost slipping and falling a few times. They galloped through several corridors, including a few secret ones, as they tried to avoid detection by either the Royal or Circle guards.

As they dashed down one corridor, Sallina said hastily, "I still need to see my mother before we go. I cannot leave without seeing her one more time."

"Are you sure this is a good moment for a family reunion? We should have gone back with Limpit. We're not welcome here."

"I really don't know anything anymore. I fear if we do not leave this place soon, we may not be able to. We have to get away from Starpoint. But we have to make sure the Queen understands what we're going to do."

"Do you think they will succeed in stopping the meteor with the spell?"

"Yes, I certainly hope so, but this is only the beginning," she replied hurriedly. "The Circle will not give up its grip on power now that it has succeeded in reclaiming it, and we have another fight on our hands if we intend to stop them."

As they ran past a window, they could see the three powerful alicorns lighting up and sending the bright-blue energy skywards. One couldn't see the clouds in the sky anymore, so pure and bright was the magical light as it lit up the entire sky.

"Princess, look, the alicorns, they are exerting a great and powerful magic that I have never seen before. It's stunning. I think it's working."

Princess Sallina peered eagerly out the large window. "How much Pinny do you think it's using up?" she asked.

"I have no idea, but I bet it's a lot," said Szymon.

Sallina pondered. "I doubt there will be much left of it after this. They will soon be in desperate need of some more. This is both our greatest weakness as unicorns and may also give us a chance to fix things back to how they were."

"Do we want to give it to them?" Szymon asked her as he stood nearby.

"Of course we will, because Starpoint needs much more Pinny to survive. However, to protect my mother and to protect all the unicorns, we need to be in a good position, where we have both strength and leverage. Staying here in our natural forms will only diminish us… and they'll most likely lock me up, just as they've done with mother. They will exile you—it's what your father wants to have happen. We have little choice but to leave our homes and return to the Professor."

Szymon nodded. "I will go along with whatever you ask me to do. I know you speak the truth and seek the best for us all."

Outside, things were becoming a lot more intense as the alicorns began to rattle and shake because of the intense discharge of energy that was taking place.

The rattling and shaking were felt in the grand meeting room as the Unimages continued with their powerful incantation. To a casual onlooker, it looked like the very fabric of the city of Starpoint was being shaken right to its core, and one could ponder whether it was likely to tear the entire city apart as if it had been hit by a gigantic earthquake.

In the chamber above Unimage Barchester, something unusual was now taking place. The meteor had stopped moving forward. The blue energy that surrounded it was making it dissolve. It kept on dissolving and becoming smaller and smaller, until after a few minutes there was hardly anything there but vapor. It was as if the entire meteor had been erased. It simply vanished in the blue energy. Nobody really knew whether it had truly vanished or just been diverted to somewhere else, but it didn't matter. Either way, the task had been completed, and the threat was no more.

The meteor threat appeared to be over. Unimage Barchester couldn't help but marvel at the powerful spell that had worked so effectively and rapidly. How mighty the spell had been, that it had eliminated the meteor from existence!

After the meteor had disappeared, the Unimages all ceased their incantations, as if in unison. For a few seconds, it became completely silent and peaceful in the room, and the blue energy discharge outside began to dissipate. Within moments, it had even vanished from the room. There was nothing left but a bit of leftover gas.

Unimage Paterline was the first to speak as he caught his breath. "I think we've done it. We've beaten it. The meteor is no more."

The others looked at each other, baffled, and then looked over toward the seat where the Queen had been sitting until she had been told to leave. Their Queen was not there anymore; she had been sent off. Instead, it was Unimage Callindra who now sat on the throne as she eyed the other Unimages, a nasty smirk on her face.

"Yes, the good deed has been done to save us all. The vile rock is now gone," she announced royally. "All of Starpoint should acknowledge that the meteor is no longer a threat, and that we the Council and Circle have overcome this mighty foe."

Unimage Barchester and Professor Tinzy were both quiet as they watched her.

The Professor's unicorn shape began fading, as it was just an image, and his human face, which was still coming through above the orb, also started to fade in the last few seconds he could be seen.

"Unimage Barchester will now reveal to all of Starpoint what we have done here, and how the Circle has in fact saved us all," Callindra continued.

Unimage Lommunar was pleased. This had been a long-held dream of his: for the Circle to return to its former glory and once again rule the land. It now appeared that this vision was finally coming true.

"The time of the return of the Circle is now upon us," Lommunar chimed in. "We will continue to live our lives in a great time with new hopes and ambitions, where Starpoint shall become far more powerful and capable than ever before. We will make Starpoint greater than it ever was. There will be appointed a new Queen in Starpoint, one who befits the title and throne she sits on, and I will be the first to cast my vote that this Queen shall be Queen Callindra. Hail Queen Callindra! Our new ruler sits before us."

There were some surprised expressions across the room as these words were spoken. There was a moment of silence, but it was soon broken. Then, it was replaced by acceptance, as all those knew that this was going to be the only option available: comply or suffer the consequences, which were bound to be harsh.

"Hail Queen Callindra!" Unimage Konstanty exalted loudly.

Others followed, but not necessarily with as much conviction; they just felt it wise not to go against the current flow of events.

"I didn't hear it spoken from everyone. Why don't we try this again? Demonstrate your loyalty, speak, and join us. We are the re-birth of the Circle, and we have with us a new and powerful Queen who will protect us all from any kind of danger. We are all saved," Unimage Konstanty said. "There's been a change of reign."

As one, the entire contingent of Unimages vociferously gave Callindra their blessings as the new Queen as she eyed them all individually and at once, and she smiled. Her time had finally come.

Unimage Barchester looked on in sheer horror but also kept his silence, more out of fear than anything else. At least the meteor threat had been effectively dealt with, and finding a way to address this new problem was something he would need time to focus on in the future. He looked over at the orb. The image of the Professor had faded to nothing.

Would he see the Professor again soon, he wondered silently to himself? He felt all alone in the room, more alone than he had when he was lost in his other identity as Thomas Barchester in Doberry.

Here in Starpoint, he felt he really had no friends around him, only a sneaky and vicious enemy that constantly craved power and sought to take complete control over above everything else. They had already put in harm's way the lives of so many of the citizens of Starpoint to pursue their own personal gain and to serve their own ambitions. He now knew that he faced a desperate new struggle, which lay ahead of him, and that he had to become a lot smarter in how he would go about taking on the dreadful Circle.

"It is time to inform our fellow unicorns about this great and wonderful victory, Unimage Barchester," Konstanty said, gazing at him malevolently. "A victory that owes all its success to the unwavering and loyal support of the Circle and these here Unimages and the new Queen."

The only words that escaped Barchester's lips were the reluctant words of acknowledgement that every fibre of his intellectual being was attempting to resist but for now could not. "Of course, I will."

Chapter 34

Princess Sallina and Szymon cantered down the corridor. They had to return to Doberry, for there was no way they could remain here without being captured and manipulated to serve the wicked needs of the rising power of the Circle, which they had been unable to prevent from achieving prominence and taking over control of all Starpoint.

Despite this desperate situation, they had at least the comfort of knowing that Starpoint was, for now, able to function again, and wasn't being threatened by an outside force, and that the meteor threat had been overcome. The new threat was coming at them from within, and even though they were both very young, they knew that a threat from the inside would be a lot more dangerous and difficult to overcome than a threat attacking them from the outside.

As they passed by several of the windows, they saw the power of the alicorns slowly starting to wane, and they knew that the spell had most likely used up most, if not all, the power of the Pinny they had brought back home. At least this was a price worth paying, but it wouldn't be long before Starpoint slipped back into steady decay as the lack of enablement magic prevented things from working properly.

Princess Sallina had wanted to see her mother once more before departing, but she really had so little time left. Had she been wrong to not go back with Limpit? Perhaps they should have fled when they had the chance. Now it might be too late, and they could both be captured and locked up.

Out of breath, they returned to Unimage Tinzy's magic-research laboratory, and there they quickly went about activating the conical transporting device that was going to send them back to Doberry.

Sallina busily prepared the tunnel. She stepped toward the controls, and using her front right hoof-hand, pressed a few buttons, deep in concentration. She had thought of using the tunnel that Limpit had come through but had no idea if it could be used for them to go back and didn't want to take the chance.

Limpit had used the magic meant for communication to travel, but whether this connection could help them move through the two worlds remained unknown. He had hopefully made it back, but would there be enough for them both? She simply didn't know. But that was not the only reason she had not gone back earlier. She had to see her mother and warn her of the terrible dangers that lay ahead.

"Princess, I know you want to see you mother, but if we don't leave now, we may never get back. I fear that any further delay may mean our capture. Please, let's go now," Szymon pleaded.

Sallina didn't want to hear what Szymon was saying, she was so determined to see her mother one more time. She was making her way out to the door, when Szymon stepped in front of her and blocked the way.

"Please, Princess. We both have reasons to stay. Me for my father, who I will find a way to stop. You for your mother. I promise you we'll find a way to talk to her when we are back, and we will have the Professor there and Limpit to help us.

"Without Pinny, all will be lost anyway, and the threat of the meteor will be replaced by the utter destruction of Starpoint. How long do you think this place will last without enough Pinny?"

Sallina listened attentively. She didn't want to accept what Szymon was telling her, but he was speaking the truth. The truth can often be painful to hear, and it rarely is the most convenient option when one weighs up different paths one can take.

"The best way to protect the Queen is to leave right now," Szymon pleaded one last time. They could already hear hoofs in the corridor, and they knew that within a minute there would be Circle guards in the chamber. "We have witnessed the rebirth of Starpoint, and we can bring back good news to the Professor and Limpit. This by itself has made our delay in returning worthwhile. Right now, is not the time to help your mother. We need to think of ourselves first, or we won't be able to help anyone."

"Alright," she muttered, with heavy heart and a troubled mind. "You're probably right. It's best we go."

The cone-shaped object had started to light up, and it slowly became brighter and brighter until it turned a brilliant white. Knowing that it was only a matter of time before Circle guards would arrive, they stepped towards the giant cone and were engulfed by the blue gaseous substance that started forming around them.

Once again, Princess Sallina and Szymon found themselves travelling through the tunnel back to Doberry and experiencing the strange, dizzying effects as their bodies and minds went through their exhilarating transition before they came plummeting back down to the forest earth of Doberry.

Neither Sallina nor Szymon remembered anything significant after that, and the next sensation Sallina felt was a hot and moist breath on her face that made her suddenly recoil and cover her face with her arm for protection. She opened her eyes to see Limpit looking down at her, smiling as only a dragon can—with his fangs glistening and tongue wagging at the same time.

Szymon moaned as he sat up and looked around. He was suddenly alarmed to realize that neither he nor Sallina had any clothes on their bodies, and with embarrassment he tried to cover himself with nearby foliage. Fortunately, night had already arrived, and there was little light apart from the glow of the moon. Sallina looked toward Szymon and giggled.

Limpit suddenly shot off a few yards and returned with what looked like an old blanket. Sallina wrapped it around herself as she got onto her feet.

"What about me?" Szymon complained as he tried to put some more leaves around himself to cover himself.

"Oh, sorry," and Limpit took off again. Szymon sat there for a couple of minutes, gazing away from Sallina as she tried to regain her balance and look around.

Limpit returned, carrying a thick branch with leaves. "The blanket won't be enough for you both. Here Szymon, use this."

"You remembered when I told you where to find us… I'm glad you did," Sallina commented to Limpit.

"How do I put this on?" Szymon asked the dragon.

"I don't know. Perhaps just hold it carefully," Limpit replied. "I've been waiting for hours for you. I came straight here after I got back. For a while I thought I may never see you again. Thankfully, I was wrong, and here you both are safe and well."

Szymon didn't know what to say or do, but he got to his feet and covered himself as best he could.

"I'll try not to look your way," Sallina said, feeling a little guilty about being the one with a blanket.

"There's really not much to see," Limpit sniggered.

Sallina found another branch that had some leaves. She snapped it off and passed it to Szymon.

"That should serve to protect your back side," she said, giggling a bit more. She tried her best to control herself, but she couldn't help finding the situation funny.

It was the first light moment they had experienced in quite some time, and it was to be savoured and enjoyed as much as possible.

"Thanks," Szymon replied and placed the branch behind him.

The three of them headed off through the forest until they finally made their way to Sallina's home. It was sometime late in the morning, and the day looked slightly overcast.

"We'd better get inside—I think it may rain very soon," Szymon said with a grimace, still struggling with his branches.

"Luckily, Margaret always keeps a key hidden for this kind of situation," Sallina remarked. She moved a nearby flowerpot, and behind it was the front-door key. The flowerpot was now sitting a few inches away from where it had been. She opened the door, and they made their way inside.

Inside, Sallina found loose clothes. She passed some to Szymon, and after showers they were both fully dressed and ready for something to eat.

"What do you suggest we do?" Szymon asked Sallina as he dug into a bowl of cereal. "We need to come up with a better plan."

"I don't know."

There was a sound and the front door opened.

"Oh, no. It's Margaret. You'd better hide, Limpit," Sallina blurted.

Limpit looked about nervously, then shot out of the room and into the hallway and flew up the stairs. Luckily, Margaret was just shutting the front door and didn't realize that Limpit had literally just flashed past her. As she turned, Limpit had fortunately made it to the top of the stairs.

She glanced upstairs and she could have sworn she saw what looked like an animal's tail flapping in the air for a split second, but it all happened so fast that she just shook her head in disbelief and ignored the sight she had just witnessed, deciding it was a momentary hallucination.

"Are you home, my dear? I see someone has taken the key!" she shouted.

"I'm in the kitchen," Sallina replied.

Margaret entered the kitchen to find Sallina finishing off her breakfast and Szymon sitting there next to her. She was a little bit surprised to find a strange-looking boy in the house, but then she recalled that Sallina had on a couple of occasions before mentioned a boy called Szymon, and that this must be her new friend.

"Hello," she said feebly, trying not to look like she was overly curious or critical.

"Hello back... I hope you don't mind me dropping in on your home. Sallina offered me some breakfast, and we were both very hungry. We've come a long way."

"Course not—this here is Sallina's house too," Margaret replied. "I will make us all a fresh cup of tea if you'd like one." She headed towards the kettle and filled it with water.

"I don't think we have the time. We're about to take off to school, looking at the clock on the way," Sallina said.

"Oh, really? That's rather odd. It's Saturday—I don't think there will be anyone else there," Margaret said, confused.

"Oh, we wanted to check on whether a teacher is there—he did suggest we could come in on a Saturday. But you are right, of course. It can wait until Monday."

Szymon rose to his feet. "I should go; I have to get back to my place."

"Oh, so you're local, are you?" Margaret looked at Szymon quizzically. "Aren't those Sallina's clothes you're wearing?"

"Oh yes, they are. You see, Szymon fell into this stream. We went for a bit of a stroll in the forest earlier this morning, and as it was dark, he slipped and fell into the water. So, I lent him some of mine." Sallina hastily covered the question with a suitable answer, trying to mask an awkward situation with a convenient little lie.

She had learned that this was something that humans did a lot, and they seemed to be good at it. Not only that, but it also wasn't considered to be such a bad thing. In fact, there were important people who had fashioned extraordinary careers by telling elaborate liars.

"I'm sorry to hear of your misfortune," was the only thing Margaret could say. "I hope you are feeling alright. You didn't catch a cold or anything, did you?"

"No, I'm fine, I take to water like a fish" Szymon replied. He then made his way to the front door, unhappy that nobody had reacted to his joke.

"He's not from around here, is he?" Margaret whispered to Sallina.

"I'm going to walk back with Szymon to his house. I shouldn't be long," Sallina said, following him out into the hallway.

Szymon opened the front door and Limpit quickly flew down the stairs and straight out. Sallina followed quickly behind.

"See you later," Sallina shouted as she closed the door.

"Be careful out there," Margaret called, though Sallina was halfway down the garden path by then.

As they made their way down the road outside Sallina's house, Sallina and Szymon decided the best thing to do was to go straight to Professor Tinzy's house. They needed to get to the Professor as soon as they possibly could, as there was so much for them to discuss and understand in terms of recent events. They covered Limpit up in Sallina's jacket so as not attract undue attention, which became even less of a problem when the clouds broke above them, and rain started pouring down from the heavens.

It took them over half an hour to walk to the Professor's house in the rain, and when they stood sopping wet at the front door, Sallina rang the doorbell and knocked several times. There was no answer. Limpit broke cover from the jacket and flew up to the front window. He attempted to peep into the house, but the net curtains were still drawn, so he could not really see anything. He then flew up to the first floor and tried to investigate the house from the next floor up, but there was still nothing much to see. No life, no movement. Nobody was around.

Limpit returned to the front door. "I fear something's gone wrong. He ought to be inside," he said, worried. "Stand back—I can melt this lock and we'll check inside."

Sallina and Szymon stepped back. Sallina had a quick look around her, as she was concerned that others could see this unusual red dragon hovering by the Professor's front door and might decide to call the police or even the RSPCA. She had heard about the RSPCA from a friend in the school; they were humans who helped rescue and look after stray animals and took them to shelters.

Limpit took a deep breath and blew out a highly focused flame onto the front-door handle and lock.

"I hope this doesn't burn the Professor's house to the ground," Szymon muttered to Sallina as they watched the lock melting.

Moments later, Limpit nudged the door with his head, but it didn't move. Realising his error, he placed his claw where the melted metal was and pulled the door instead.

The door slowly began to swing outwards.

Szymon grabbed the side of the door above Limpit, and they pried it fully open.

"Ouch, that's really hot," Szymon moaned, as even the wood had heated up considerably on the door. "And your breath is something else. You're lucky the whole door hadn't caught fire, it's so hot."

"I was being very super careful," Limpit said, and a few seconds later they were in and the door was shut once again.

Inside, the first place they decided to check was the living room.

"Professor!" Sallina shouted, but she heard no response.

They looked around everywhere downstairs, then upstairs, but there was no sign of the Professor anywhere.

They were just coming down when the front door creaked open. Standing at the entrance was Professor Tinzy, holding a bag of groceries.

"I knew immediately something was not right," he said. "Someone had melted the front-door handle. For a moment, I considered who could even have done that. Then it occurred to me, there is one I know who could do this effortlessly."

"Sorry. It was me," Limpit said apologetically. "We didn't have a key and it was raining, so we had to get in. Besides, we were worried something had happened to you."

"Is everything alright?" the Professor asked.

"I doubt it. I mean, how can it be?" Sallina responded with another question. "They've taken over everything back home. My mother is a prisoner. They're forcing Thomas Barchester to side with them."

The four of them looked at each other, none of them wanting to be the first to discuss these abject failures that were preoccupying their collective consciences and filling them with so many gloomy thoughts.

"I know. Let's have a nice cup of tea!" the Professor exclaimed perkily in a bid to ease the disquiet. "I find a nice cup of tea can do so much in lifting one's spirit."

Ten minutes later, in the living room and fully refreshed, Sallina opened the discussion.

"We need to talk about what we do next, given there has been a sudden change in circumstances."

"I honestly don't know what to suggest. It's all so very baffling... how in the world did all this happen?" Professor Tinzy replied.

"The Queen is being held hostage in her own home," Szymon said. "And the Circle looks like it has won control of Starpoint—they now appear to be in charge of everything."

The Professor attempted to comfort them with a few calming words. "Oh, my dear boy, let's for a moment appreciate that together we've managed to stop that nasty meteor from destroying our existence on Starpoint. We saved everyone. Tomorrow will be another day, and we shall shift our attention onto the Circle next, and we will work out a way to stop them from inflicting the terrible things they are planning on our good folk back home."

"I fear the terrible things they plan. They have done so much harm already," Sallina said solemnly.

"Oh, my dear, you are right, and I fear that this is just the beginning. They have craved and sought power for their own selfish intent. The Circle has a quite different ideology from what we are used to. Unicorns for centuries have managed to live together in relative peace and harmony, and we have slowly but surely evolved and civilised ourselves to treat each other as equal beings.

"Whether you had more than one colour to your hide, or you had stripes or even dots, or you were a little too tall or short, perhaps too fat or thin… none of this really mattered. All that counted was that everyone was treated as being equal, and we all found a way to play our part in looking after each other and ensuring the wellbeing of our homes and our fellow citizens. With inequality comes discrimination, no matter how much you try to avoid it, and I find it truly incomprehensible that others cannot see this. Give some folk a lot more and others a lot less, and how can one avoid this?

"Discrimination is fuelled by the differences in wealth and power between us, you must always remember that. I am so proud that you as a Princess understand this now, and that you do not have a single part of you that makes you feel you need to be superior to anyone else in the herd. We must all strive to achieve a greater fairness for all or accept that we have fairness for none. Life is nothing if one cannot try to be fairer and kinder to others, wouldn't you agree?

"Unfortunately, that's not what the Circle is all about. The Circle believes there is a natural order to all living things, and that they have been designated to rule and all others exist to serve them. The Circle instils privilege in their own and restricts the power and magic in all Starpoint—and beyond—to a chosen few. Ultimately, this is what they are all about. Their justification is that without them in charge, the others cannot survive and prosper to attain the pureness they already possess."

"I don't understand why they choose to be so selfish," Sallina said dourly. "Isn't that unfair and horrible? How can they behave in such a self-entitled manner and do so many horrible things without proper consideration of the wellbeing of all those around them?"

"You may think it unfair, but they see it differently. They see it as their given right and the proper means for matters to be handled. You see, Princess, an ideology—any ideology—defines us. And what we consider important as our beliefs, such as equality and fairness and sharing with others, they're also just subjective beliefs and not necessarily the way things are handled in other places and at other times. It's usually those who are in charge who determine how we behave, as they set the rules. With the Circle, they intend to enforce their will and way upon us all."

"How do you know all this about them?" Szymon asked the Professor.

"Oh, I know because I was once young when the Circle was in power, and I was there when a great battle was fought, and we barely managed to beat them at the time, and I honestly believe we'll beat them again."

"You mean you were alive before the great battle against the darkness, also known as the Calling?" Sallina asked, amazed.

Limpit couldn't help himself; he started to chortle.

"What is so funny? This is no laughing matter."

"It's you who is funny—you don't know who you are talking to."

"What do you mean?" Szymon said.

"Professor Tinzy is a very old unicorn. I don't know how he's managed to stick around for so long. He was alive before Unimage Lommunar. He was there before either Unimage Callindra or Unimage Barchester. He is, in fact, the oldest unicorn you are ever likely to meet in your lifetime."

"How can this be?" Sallina asked.

"That's because Professor Tinzy is in fact Unimage Tinzin," Limpit informed them.

A hushed silence descended.

"But Unimage Tinzin perished in the great battle when the evil Circle was defeated, and the Calling was banished from

Starpoint during the great battle." Sallina spoke out, recounting her history lessons.

"Oh, well, he did die in a way, since he disappeared into the wilderness for many long years, not to be heard from again. And he found the way to come here to Doberry and visit this strange and sometimes wonderful place.

"After some time, he chose to become Professor Tinzy, and the legendary Unimage Tinzin faded into a ghost from the past. When he returned to Starpoint, he became known as Unimage Tinzy after he earned enough of a reputation in his ability to cast magic to join the Council and be trusted by the Queen."

Sallina and Szymon looked at the Professor in complete surprise.

"That's enough history, Limpit," said the Professor. "I am no longer that old Unimage you speak of who passed away long ago… I am just an aging Unimage who is also known as Professor Tinzy, and that's quite enough for me to be in these perilous times."

"It still doesn't answer the most important question we have before us: what do we do now?" Szymon asked, thoroughly confused.

"Oh, you'll find an answer soon enough. I wager that the Pinny in Starpoint will soon have run out, and that it won't be long before we hear from the Circle when they ask us once again to help them secure some more. You see, we will— whether we like it or not—continue to feed their power by finding and giving them the Pinny that Starpoint needs," Tinzy pointed out. "Evil has a way of clutching one by the throat and then choking you if you don't do what it asks, whilst it smiles and pretends to be your saviour."

"Are we going to help them out, then?" Szymon asked. "I don't ever want to talk to my father again. I'd be perfectly fine in denying them Pinny in future."

"Oh, I think we'll have to give them some," Tinzy continued to explain. "Because despite who they are and what they stand for, they cannot accomplish anything without us 'impures' whom they deeply despise, and we here care about all unicorns that live and breathe. No matter what, we will not let any of them down, no matter who is temporarily in charge."

"No, we won't," Sallina reiterated defiantly. "We have to help our fellow citizens in need. They still require our assistance, no matter what those Circle Unimages claim."

"Then how do we go about finding the Pinny?" Szymon asked.

"Just as we have done before," remarked the Professor. "Roger will take us back to the house and we will continue our essential work with the help of Unimage Barchester, or should I say, Thomas Barchester. Barchester won't be here with us, but that's probably a good thing. Back in Starpoint, we have at least one stout ally on our side, and the good Queen of course can be counted on when the time comes—I'm sure of that."

"Isn't it your house anyway?" Sallina clarified. "Because I cannot imagine that silly old man Thomas Barchester being able to own something as big as that; he strikes me as nothing short of a fool who constantly forgets who he is."

"Oh, it was once the house of an old Unimage, but he has long since vanished. This house is intended for all those who seek shelter in this foreign world. It's for us all, including Thomas Barchester, who many years ago earned the right to be looked after and cared for no matter how much his path may have led him astray. Besides, don't ever underestimate him; he has never left our side. Deep down, he is one of the good unicorns, and he loves Starpoint for what it is, and not for what the Circle wishes to change it into."

"Why should Barchester be the master of the house?" Sallina asked, indicating her annoyance.

"Although I have no idea when or how he will find a way to return here, he has lived in this place a long time and made it his home. If he does return, then he is welcome to look after it, as we will be far too busy running around looking for Pinny anyway. He is a good master of the house and will never turn away a fellow unicorn who seeks refuge there. Let's see how things work out," the Professor thought out loud.

* * *

Back on Starpoint, Thomas Barchester had very few options to do anything different from what he had been instructed to do, as he too was securely locked up in his chamber with guards stationed directly outside, preventing him from walking freely around the castle.

Thomas Barchester knew he had managed to fail his friends by not stopping the Circle from taking control, and he was deeply saddened by what had occurred. There was some relief that they had managed to stop the meteor threat, but now there was an even more formidable foe who stood before them, and he had no idea how to face this dangerous new challenge without support.

He was exhausted; he was tired from the life he had lived for so many decades now back in Doberry, and he wanted nothing more than to pass on this new burden to someone else. In a way, he had already done what he could, as he had helped Princess Sallina, Szymon, Limpit, and the Professor find the Pinny and help to save Starpoint from the threat of the oncoming meteor.

How was he going to be able to help them now, he asked himself? Being locked up in his chambers, there really was nothing much that he could do. Sitting by himself in his room, he contemplated a bleak future, fearing that the worst was yet to come as the Circle exerted its power and authority over all the inhabitants of Starpoint and beyond.

Queen Noony had also been confined to her chambers, and she too was greatly concerned about what was going to happen next to her fellow unicorns now that the Circle had put itself back in charge.

She had been asked to make an announcement on her birthday, which was only a day away, and she dreaded the prospect of having to lie to her citizens. Both she and Thomas Barchester were to give a public address and let all the unicorns know how tremendous a job the Circle had done for all of Starpoint's inhabitants, and how it was mainly thanks to their efforts that they were all safe now, although that situation at best was temporary, given the last remnants of Pinny powering the Alicorns.

She was also to tell them that it was her wish to make Unimage Callindra the new Queen of Starpoint, and that she was to retire herself from public life to live out her remaining days peacefully and in isolation. She so much wished she didn't have to do such an awful thing, but she knew inside she had little choice but to obey their instructions and thus help ensure the safety of all her fellow citizens as well as indirectly protect her daughter.

In her heart, she knew that none of this was over. No, this was just the beginning of sweeping changes yet to come, and she would need to be there when the time came to help protect her daughter and all her fellow unicorns, and for them she must stay strong and not surrender her fight. For the moment, it seemed that stepping aside was the only sensible decision she could make, and that way she could at least live to fight another day. She might have lost a battle, but the war with the Circle was about to be waged, and it wasn't over yet.

* * *

There was only a day to go till the Queen's birthday when the Council met up again to discuss their plans, sitting around pontificating about their future inside the grand meeting room. Queen Callindra was now fully in charge of the Council. She had been officially exalted to her elevated position without any formal ritual or procedure; it had just been declared to take immediate effect, and word had already spread around Starpoint that a new Queen ruled the land.

There were concerns about whether Queen Noony was likely to follow the script she had been given, and Unimage Konstanty had been appointed to keep a close and critical eye on her and ensure a powerful mindwash spell would be cast in case she chose to err even the slightest from her script. A mindwash spell wasn't that powerful of a spell, and it was one that Unimage Konstanty could perform relatively easily, but Queen Noony wasn't just any ordinary unicorn.

There was still some concern she might be able to resist the spell and find a way to defy their wishes. Therefore, the spell's intensity had to be set at a much higher level than usual and could inflict permanent damage on the subject if cast, so even Unimage Konstanty planned to use it only as a last resort.

On the plus side, Unimage Konstanty felt confident he could control the level of the spell and that it was a risk was worth taking if needed. Without the Queen openly consenting to Callindra taking her place, there would be a lingering suspicion that somehow the Circle had forced Noony to abdicate against

366

her will, and that they had seized power via unjust means. Only an open admission that it was Queen Noony's personal wishes for this handover to occur could alleviate some of those suspicions and help restore order whilst the future of Starpoint was being planned and implemented in the weeks and months ahead.

The Council soon moved on to discussing how to obtain more Pinny, and once again Unimage Konstanty was nominated to take charge of the quest in this foreign land that all members of the Council were now familiar with. Konstanty had been criticized for not being able to control his son Szymon in his previous attempts, but most felt that this was something he was able to address to ensure them that this time, things were going to be kept in much better control. A bit like Unimage Callindra, Konstanty had a remarkable way with words, and knew how to present something negative in a much more positive light.

"My son is still reporting directly to me every detail of what's going on over there," the Unimage said. "The truth is that he has been loyal to me throughout these challenging times. He was the one who worked tirelessly with Princess Sallina to search for the Pinny in the first place. He was the one who found Professor Tinzy and helped him regain his memory. He even ate these carrots he hated to further the cause and protect us all. He was also the one who brought the Pinny back when others were less keen, and some were attempting stop the Council from taking over.

"It was he who showed us how Thomas Barchester could be safely returned to Starpoint, and he was also instrumental in making the incantation spell work. The only time he every stood against me was when I fought a battle with that creature, Limpit, and he only did this because in his mind he knew that Limpit was still needed for our noble purpose. At least, for now. But one day I will find a way to get rid of him for good.

"My son Szymon was the one who found the old spell in the magic library, and it was he who convinced the others to pull together to make sure Starpoint could be saved from the meteor. Now he is back in that strange place with the Princess and the Professor, and he is doing a fine job on the whole. It will be he who finds the Pinny over there and saves us again. I have complete faith and trust in my son, for he has never let me down, not once."

The Unimages listened to what Konstanty told them and they marvelled at his craftiness and his son's. Like father, like son, they thought. They all accepted and finally understood why such a young Unimage as Konstanty was being held in such high regard. Without such craftiness at work, power could never have been seized, as it was only through stealth and cunning that such great changes often took place; deception and manipulation were immensely powerful tools for those who sought to shape the lives of others. The Council knew this only too well, and the Circle lived by it with absolute conviction.

How else could they have risen from the ashes and assumed such great control? It was lies, deception, threats, and manipulations—these are all useful tools when employed for a great cause. Especially when only the outcome mattered and not the means to get there. After all, history books often obscure the truth and focus their attention mainly on the outcomes. The truth is often too painful for anyone to digest.

The other members of the Council didn't, of course, have the opportunity to overhear the quiet whispers between Queen Callindra and Unimage Konstanty as they headed off down a corridor after the meeting, but those words were not meant for their ears.

"I'm not as sure about your son," Queen Callindra complained with more than a modicum of scorn. "How can we be certain that it's not the other way around, and he has been playing us rather than us who are playing him? In the hands of the enemy, he remains a weapon that can be used against us."

"You needn't worry about this, my Queen. I happen to have something up my sleeve to deal with any eventuality when it comes to handling my son," Konstanty reassured her.

"What would that be?" Queen Callindra asked as her curiosity got the better of her. "I'd love to hear about it."

"Ah, all in good time," he replied. "If I told you everything that I was up to, you might think you don't need me anymore." He grinned wryly. "I prefer to remain useful—in fact, essential—on an ongoing basis... it helps me to sleep much better at night."

"I would never think of getting rid of you, my ever-so-eager accomplice," Callindra replied. "You are far too valuable to me, as you are to the Circle. In fact, you have become indispensable."

Konstanty smiled demurely, but he was really thinking, *Of course I am indispensable. And one day I shall be anointed the rightful King, and even you will serve me and bow before me like all the rest. You think you are cunning and clever. You have no idea who stands before you and what I am truly capable of.*

But of course, he would never openly say this to her. His darker thoughts were something he kept remarkably close to his heart, and it touched on his deepest desires to rule and oversee every living unicorn in Starpoint and beyond. In his mind, he was meant to be the purest of the pure, the greatest unicorn of all time to walk the lands, which was why he should be the only one to rule every single unicorn in this magical kingdom of theirs, and they'd all bow down before him.

Chapter 35

The next day was a beautiful and bright sunny day in Starpoint, and by lunchtime hundreds of unicorns had gathered around on this most auspicious occasion and were looking up toward the castle's main balcony. Today was former Queen Noony's birthday, and a time for all those in Starpoint to rejoice and celebrate the passing of another year of the great Queen's enchanted and privileged life. But to Starpoint's inhabitants the privilege was theirs, as so adoring and lucky they were to have such a kind and gracious Queen to rule them wisely and keep things ticking along.

A giant cake almost two stories high lay perched in front of the balcony, and on this cake were numerous lit candles. There were so many that nobody bothered to count them anymore, as nobody wanted to know just how old Queen Noony was.

But all was not as it seemed, as the alicorns were now barely able to function, and even the candles were being blown out, one by one, as the passing wind extinguished their bright lights. The magic of the land was once again at risk of depletion. Once again, a miracle was needed to find and bring back more Pinny to keep things going as before.

Queen Noony had already made her truly short speech, which she had struggled to get through. She had told the unicorns about the incantation of the powerful spell and how it had disintegrated the meteor that was only a few days from crushing all life in Starpoint. Unknown to those who watched her, she was already entranced by Unimage Konstanty's powerful mind-wash spell, and she was struggling to remember anything from after the spell had been cast, as her brain felt like it was being cooked over an open fire and she was feeling more than a little barbequed. Despite Konstanty not wishing to use such a powerful spell with such unintended negative consequences, like all those who constantly crave for power and influence upon others, all their rules and principles are up for reassessment when required.

She was making her closing remarks as she looked upon her former subjects with more than a hint of passing concern and sadness. She knew that what she was saying was all wrong, but she had no choice, as she was being directed by a powerful spell. She was also wilfully lying to them to protect her daughter and all her citizens, and the mind-wash spell sat like a cloud over everything she thought and said. With its sinister force it was exerting undue influence on her ability to think and function. She couldn't resist the onslaught of thoughts that had been forced into her mind, and the script that she had been asked to present. It was as if she had become a puppet controlled by someone else and she had no mind of her own left.

"It is with a great deal of sadness that I have decided to now step down from my position as Queen, and that Unimage Callindra will be taking my place as your new chosen Queen. I choose her because—"

She stopped for a moment and took a deep breath. She looked over at Unimage Konstanty, who stood not far away from her, reassured that the mind-wash spell was doing what it should, and hoping perhaps that he might not have turned up the intensity a little bit more than he had needed to.

"—I so want to protect us all from harm, and from evil. In my heart, I want to ensure there will be no further threats, and that all the good citizens of Starpoint in the future are treated fairly and justly and protected from enemies known and unknown."

Queen Callindra cast her eye towards Unimage Konstanty, wondering whether the spell was doing its job.

"Now I have one final thing to tell you before I retire to my private life and Queen Callindra takes my place. Please, do not believe everything that everyone tells you, no matter who tells it or how much you want to believe it to be true. If you do, then you may regret it forever, as some lies cannot be so easily undone—"

Queen Noony tried to continue speaking, but the power of the mind-wash spell was invading her thoughts and leaving her simmering in confusion. The more she resisted it, the more aggressively the spell worked, and right now she felt like it was setting fire to her mind.

Then she couldn't quite remember what she wanted to say next.

"I thank you for being so kind to me over the years…"

Then she fainted.

There were sudden gasps in the crowd as two Royal guards rushed over to her rescue. She was taken away from the balcony and immediately returned to her chamber where she could rest in her bed. Few of the citizens even bothered to notice that the Royal Guards were closely accompanied by Circle Guards, who in fact outnumbered them greatly. They were also much better armed.

It was then Queen Callindra's turn to speak. She needed to calm down the crowd below her.

"It's such an enormous day for newly-appointed Citizen Noony. She will miss you all and we will miss her in her former public life. Let's all give her a big round of applause to show her our deepest appreciation for all she has done for Starpoint over the years and wish her the very best."

This brought about an enthusiastic response by the crowd, and everyone started to applaud and cheer and feel better.

But the Queen was unable to hear the support she still had in the crowd, as she was being carried to her chamber on a stretcher by some of the Royal guards and accompanied by those appointed by the Circle.

Queen Callindra took a few small steps toward Unimage Konstanty and whispered in his ear, "I don't ever want her to speak in public like this again. You should have given her the full treatment even if it killed her—she almost ruined the day."

Unimage Konstanty nodded silently. He had every intention of obeying his new Queen for now. He had shown just the slightest amount of kindness to Queen Noony and avoided giving her the full dose, and he was already starting to regret it. But nothing bad had happened, and the few seeds of doubt that might have been sown within the crowd would soon be undone and would disappear as the Circle took back full control of the lands.

The crowd was easily calmed when music piped up, performed by some of Starpoint's finest artists and musicians, and everyone present was given a taste of the delicious giant cake that had been lying there on proud display.

Still, not all unicorns felt like the day had gone well, and some still harboured more than a few personal suspicions about the rising influence of the Circle.

The Circle might have saved the day today, but history had previously taught them not to trust those who seek to discriminate, to divide, and to always be wary of those who claim to hold their best intentions but secretly harbour deep personal motives of their own, and to always beware those who seek to harness great power for their own individual ends.

Some unicorns felt Queen Noony had somehow tried to warn them in her last few words spoken in public at the time but didn't have quite enough energy to speak her mind, as she had been put through such intense strain and pressure over the preceding days.

Either way, not all unicorns were convinced that Queen Noony needed to be replaced by the new unproven Queen Callindra, and there were more than a few growing suspicions about the future intentions of the Council, which was now being openly led by the Circle. This new Queen, who nobody really knew much about, could make things worse rather than better.

They hoped and prayed to themselves that nothing terrible would come their way again, but many couldn't help but feel that something seemed wrong, and that darker times lay ahead of them. A Queen doesn't just walk away from her duties, especially not a good Queen like Queen Noony. They'd known her for a long time, and she had always stood her ground and fought for all the citizens.

Only time would tell what the Circle's true intentions would turn out to be, and how proper and decent a Queen Callindra would become. There were worries already surfacing that she wasn't, in fact, going to be much of a Queen, and that anointing her as such was more of an act taken by the Council. To make matters worse, the Council was being led by the Circle, and Callindra's promotion to Queen was there to quash any likely opposition.

For some unicorns, there was a heightened sense of foreboding mixed with a growing level of fear, for ever since the threat of the meteor, there had appeared this new sense of danger and how it could suddenly come out of nowhere and upend everyone's lives.

But for now, it was just a lingering fear, and those who were starting to feel it hoped and prayed it was only an unnecessary trouble that was playing on their darkest thoughts and not something that could prove itself to be founded and affect all their lives in the future.

As the Circle had discovered many hundreds of years previously, fear was something where if you steadily increased its dosage over a protracted period, it would eventually entrap all those who were subjected to it without their even knowing they were under someone's control. You only had to take care of the occasional dissidents, and your loyal subjects would often be the first to flush them out.

There were some forms of magic that proved to be far more potent and didn't require the enablement power of Pinny and unicorn magic to work. These spells possessed a unique magic of their very own, and their spell casters had little more power in casting them beyond knowing how to deceive those who were so easily led.

But far away in a land called Doberry in a place called England, which was part of a much larger land called Earth, there was a Unimage professor called Tinzy, a boy called Szymon, a girl called Sallina, and a tiny, harmless-looking dragon called Limpit who was hardly any larger than an ordinary dog. They had a few ideas of their own, and they were not about to let the Circle get away with their sinister plans. They were a few outcasts who would go on to herald a new age for the unicorns of Starpoint and far beyond. But for now, it was still ever so early to see what they could truly accomplish.

Even they had no idea.

Chapter 36

A couple of days had passed, and Szymon returned once again to his house, but this time he was accompanied by Princess Sallina, Limpit, and Professor Tinzy.

Szymon had quickly discovered that his father was already attempting to contact him, and it was in his living room a few minutes after a connection was made that the orb once again lit up and his father's familiar, brooding unicorn face stared at him across the great divide between Starpoint and Doberry.

Professor Tinzy stood across from the orb, deeply suspicious of what Szymon's father was going to ask his son, but he realized that to protect those at home, they needed to maintain some kind of connection with Starpoint. There had been no news yet from Unimage Barchester, and the Professor was certain that Barchester was being confined to his chambers and most likely unable to do anything that risked interfering with the Circle's wishes.

When Unimage Konstanty's image appeared in the room, he had a good look around, and soon he noticed that Professor Tinzy, Sallina, and Limpit were at one end watching him intently. This troubled him, as he wanted to have a private word with his son, but he also knew he had to play the game and at least appear as if he had everyone's best interests at heart.

"How are you, my dear son?" Unimage Konstanty asked.

"Fine, sir," came the curt reply.

"Professor Tinzy, it's good to see you well over there."

"Where's Unimage Barchester?" Professor Tinzy asked. "I'd like to know how he's doing. Is he alright?"

"Oh! He's just resting. He's not been that well—the incantation took a lot out of him," Konstanty answered.

"I wish to speak to him as soon as it's possible."

"I think you already know why we are contacting you," Konstanty said, changing the subject. "We once again require your urgent assistance. Pinny supplies are already dangerously low, and there's desperate need for some more."

"And why should we help you if you won't even let us talk to Unimage Barchester?" the Professor asked.

Queen Callindra appeared and joined Unimage Konstanty, hovering above the orb.

"Because, my dear Professor, if you don't help us, so many here in Starpoint will needlessly suffer, because life without Pinny shall become so unbearable, especially for those who function further down the social ladder. And since you tend to care so much for those unfortunates who are weaker or poorer, it is a constant weakness of yours. So, well, I suppose it's your duty to help us and to indirectly help them."

Professor Tinzy thought about this. He wasn't sure how to respond.

"We are here to help everyone," Szymon said. "We will help, of course."

"That's good, my boy. I knew I could count on you to see the bigger picture," Konstanty said with a smile.

"I want to speak to my mother, the Queen," Sallina demanded.

"Sadly, for her, she is no longer Queen, and not involved in official matters," Callindra interjected. "I am Queen now, and I'm in charge. You can speak to me."

Sallina didn't like to hear that, and she was about to say something when Professor Tinzy butted in, "It doesn't matter whether she is Queen or not. Before we offer to help you, Sallina will get the chance to speak to her mother and I will get the chance to speak to Unimage Barchester. Or you can come here yourself, Queen or not, and find the Pinny without our support. I would like to see how popular you very quickly become if you cannot produce any more Pinny to power the alicorns."

Unimage Konstanty and Queen Callindra stared at them silently for a moment.

"Very well then," Callindra replied calmly. "We will arrange a few short chats for you. We want us all to get along, don't we? After all, we're on the same side, aren't we?"

With this, the call was suddenly cut short and the faces of Queen Callindra and Unimage Konstanty vanished.

"That seemed a bit abrupt in the way it ended," Limpit said. "I get the distinct feeling they're not too pleased with our inconsequential demands."

"Oh, they don't need to be pleased," the Professor said. "Now the fight to rescue Starpoint from the Circle truly begins, and we're all that our dear citizens have to come to their rescue."

"We won't let them steal everything away from us," Sallina said defiantly. "We value our freedoms, our way of life, and our diversity. It's what makes us who we are."

Professor Tinzy thought for a moment about what Sallina had said.

"We'll have to give them something to keep our hoofs firmly in the game, but we will ensure that by doing so, we also get something back in return. I'm afraid we're going to be negotiating our position each step of the way. And, step by step, we will find a way to reclaim what is right and restore the proper order to our land."

Limpit listened attentively to their conversation, and then he decided to interject, "Oh, sure, but mark my words, that lot are not going to surrender anything without putting up a fight, and they certainly don't fight fairly. If we want to beat them, it won't be negotiating that will win the day. No, we will need a lot more than clever conversation. We'll need grit, we'll need plenty of muscle, and above all, I suspect we'll need a whole lot of crafty magic."

There was a fighting spirit there in Szymon's house in the hearts of the four on that day as they looked at each other and reminded themselves of what was truly important, and it was a determination that wasn't going to be easily quashed.

And although they didn't know it yet, there were many Starpoint citizens back home who also shared their views and felt the same way, who were just waiting for the right unicorns to show them the way, to marshal and lead them into a much better future than the dismal path that lay ahead. They all knew that once the Circle assumed power and control over Starpoint's citizens across their land, gone would be the days when they felt they were in control of their own destinies.